Awards for Cayla Kluver's debut book, *Legacy*

• Bronze medalist in the 2008 Moonbeam Children's Book Awards for Young Adult Fiction

• Finalist in two categories in the National Best Books Awards 2008 sponsored by USA Book News

• First-place winner (reviewer's choice) in the Reader Views Literary Awards 2008 for Young Adult Fiction

• Young Voices Foundation book of the month for January 2009

Praise for Cayla Kluver

"Anyone who says teens can't write should meet 16-year-old Cayla Kluver.... Kluver's writing is impressive, fluid and focuses heavily on social customs and deep, complex characters; the skill of the writing and the resulting story make *Legacy* one book that any fantasy fan should pick up at the earliest opportunity."
—*Cleveland Literature Examiner*

"If you're looking for a richly painted tapestry of words, a fantasy sort of book written as if Jane Austen were still alive and had decided to write fantasies involving princesses, then you're sure to love *Legacy*."
—*Curled Up With a Good Kid's Book,* five stars

"Well-paced and well-written, *Legacy* has passages of idyllic prose, tensions between lovers, and a powerful narrative in the description of a tournament battle.... But there are enough story threads left hanging to ensure that book two, *Allegiance,* will be a fitting sequel and to ensure Cayla Kluver's legacy as a stellar author and storyteller."
—*ForeWord Clarion Reviews,* five stars

"*Legacy* is a breathtakingly beautiful story about one girl's struggle to overcome the expectations of a kingdom and find her own happiness.... Full of political struggle, duty, legends, brilliant characters, and beautiful prose, *Legacy* will leave readers wanting more."
—*Chick Lit Teens* (www.chicklitteens.com)

"First let me just say wow. I am in love with this book and with Cayla's beautiful writing.... *Legacy* is a mix of *King Arthur* and *Romeo and Juliet* in a way...it's now on my top 5 favorite books with *Twilight* and *The Hunger Games*."
—*La Femme Readers* (lafemmereaders.blogspot.com)

Books by Cayla Kluver
from Harlequin TEEN

The Legacy Trilogy

Legacy
Allegiance

and coming in late 2012

Sacrifice

Cayla Kluver

Allegiance

HARLEQUIN® TEEN

ISBN-13: 978-0-373-21043-5

ALLEGIANCE

This edition published by arrangement with Harlequin Books S.A.

For questions and comments about the quality of this book please contact us at Customer_eCare@Harlequin.ca.

www.HarlequinTEEN.com

Printed in U.S.A.

MAPS

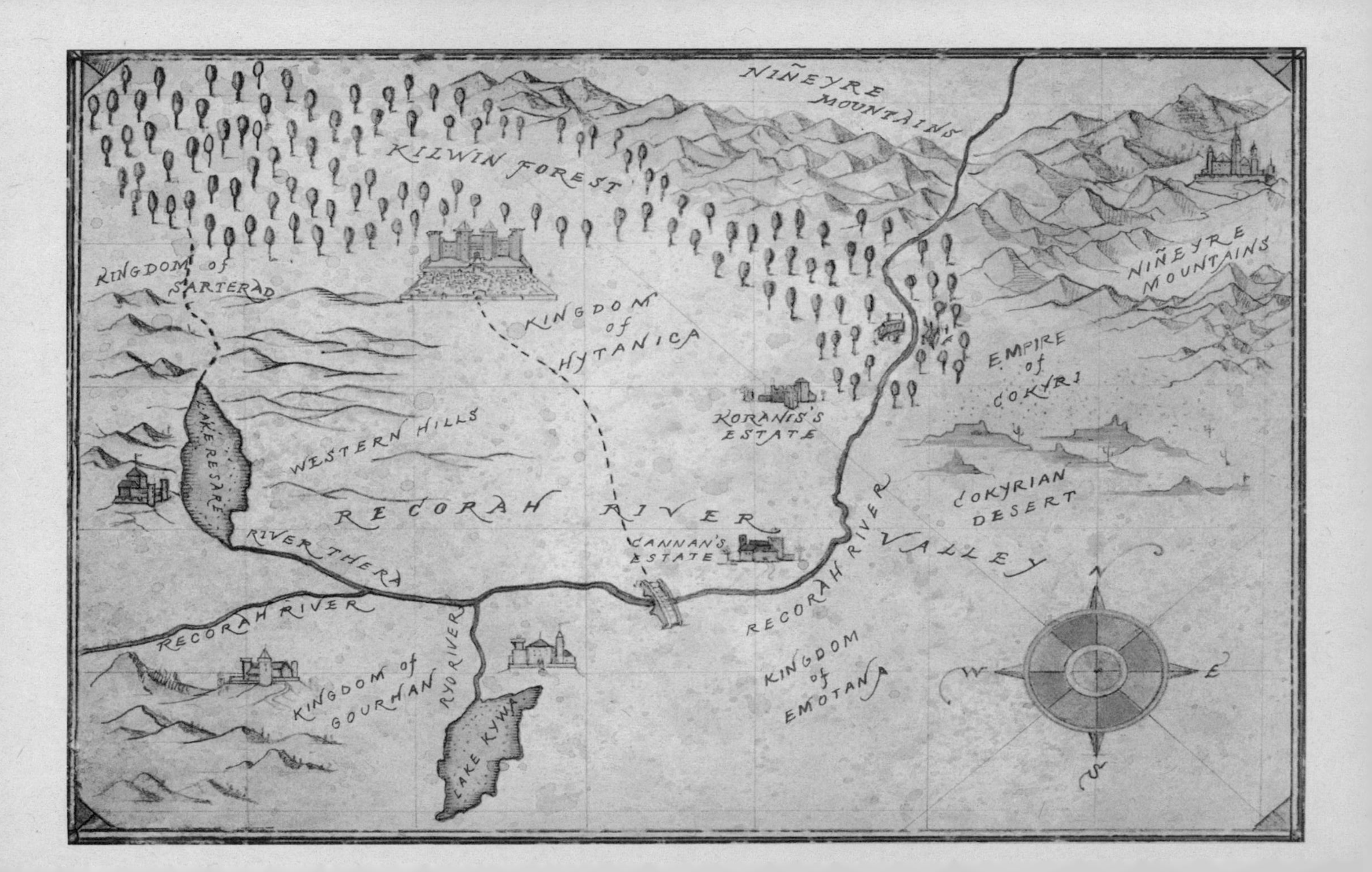
NIÑEYRE MOUNTAINS
KILWIN FOREST
NIÑEYRE MOUNTAINS
KINGDOM of SARTERAD
KINGDOM of HYTANICA
EMPIRE of COKYRI
LAKE RESARE
WESTERN HILLS
KORANIS'S ESTATE
COKYRIAN DESERT
RECORAH RIVER
CANNAN'S ESTATE
RIVER THERA
RECORAH RIVER VALLEY
RECORAH RIVER
RYO RIVER
RECORAH RIVER
KINGDOM of GOURMAN
KINGDOM of EMOTANA
LAKE KYWA
N
W
E
S

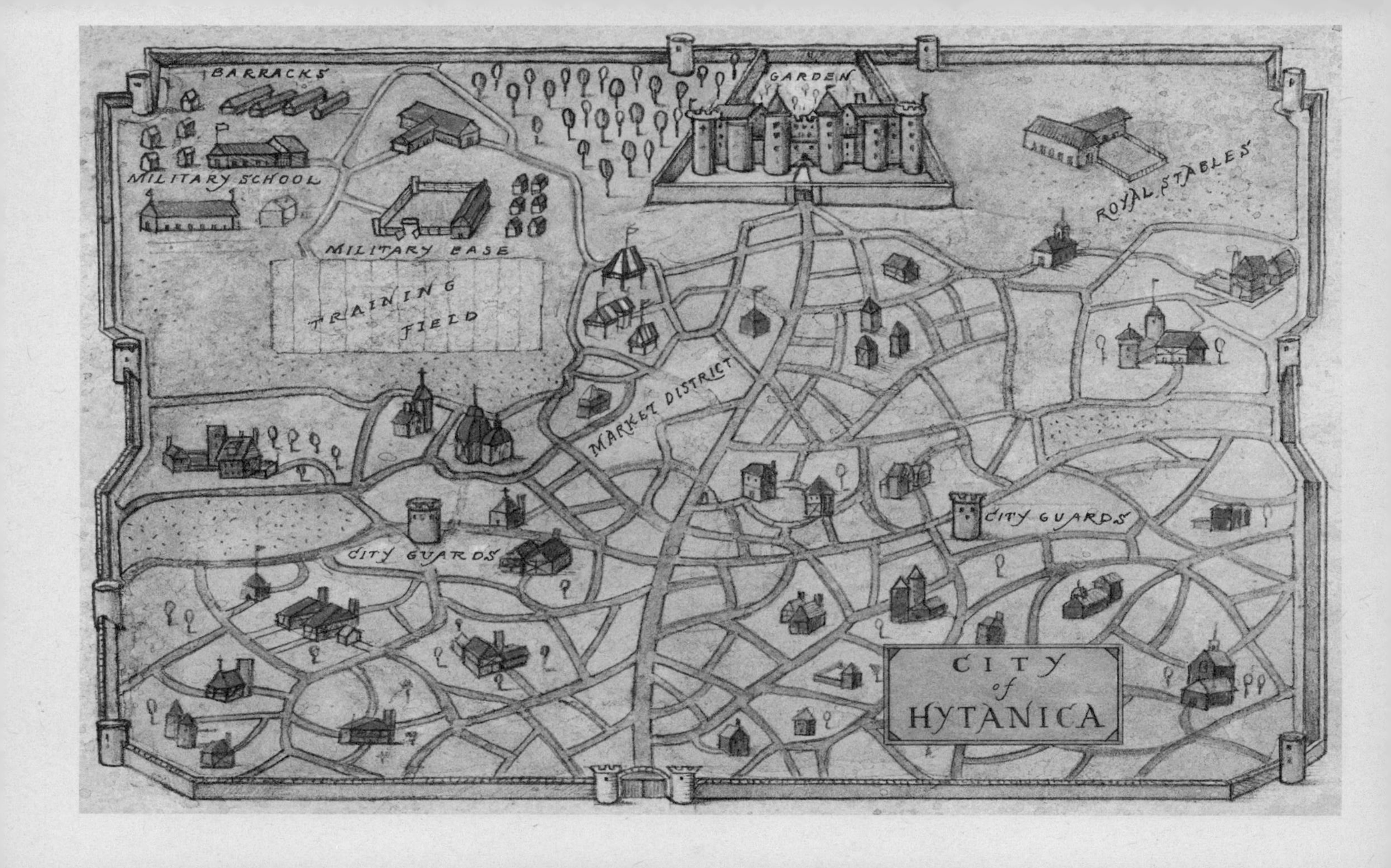
CITY of HYTANICA
BARRACKS
GARDEN
MILITARY SCHOOL
ROYAL STABLES
MILITARY BASE
TRAINING FIELD
MARKET DISTRICT
CITY GUARDS
CITY GUARDS

PROLOGUE

THE HALL WAS EMPTY EXCEPT FOR A CLOAKED figure who stood motionless upon a black marble dais. He waited, watching the doors at the far end with eyes as bright as emeralds and as threatening as livid clouds on the horizon. Hair red like the embers of a dying fire shrouded his features. The rest of his powerful form was rendered nearly invisible by the shadows, for even the light from the torches lining the walls seemed reluctant to approach him.

The doors opened, swinging inward to reveal the silhouettes of the young man he had summoned and the two guards who flanked him. The guards had been ordered to bring the youth to this place, for he could no longer be trusted.

Ignoring his escorts, the seventeen-year-old entered, walking tall and unafraid. He was completely defenseless, bearing no weapons, yet there was no hesitation in his stride. Without a sign of deference he stopped before the dais, glaring up at the formidable figure, but the man ignored this insolence and spoke instead to the guards.

"You are dismissed," he murmured. "Leave us."

The guards hurriedly obeyed, and he focused his attention on his troublesome charge.

"I trust you have rested well?" he inquired, feigning cordiality.

"Well enough."

The man gave a slight nod, irritation etching lines in his otherwise smooth face.

"Now that you have returned to us, Narian, and have been given time to recover your strength, your training must recommence. Your foolish action in running away has already driven us to wage war with Hytanica. I must prepare you for the time when you will join that effort. You will be the one to bring Hytanica to ruin."

"I will not lead troops against my homeland," Narian declared. "I've told you what I know. I won't help you destroy Hytanica."

Sighing, the man, who was the master of this hall, moved to his left and descended the stairs from the dais to the floor.

"I feared you might say that," he said, coming to stand before the young man, towering over him by several inches. "Have you forgotten to whom you owe your allegiance? The Hytanicans are enemies of Cokyri. They are *your* enemies."

"The *enemy* treated me well," Narian countered, clenching his jaw.

The man began to circle the boy he had helped raise, examining him, looking for a weakness. As he moved, he spoke, his voice chilling in its civility.

"A Cokyrian in need of punishment was brought before me today. He writhed in agony for hours under the torment of my hand, pleading for mercy, until I drew my sword and cut off his head. It rolled to the very spot where you stand. *He* was a thief, Narian. To show me disrespect is a far worse offense. Can you imagine what *your* punishment will be?"

"I am not afraid of torture or of death. You have seen to that with your training. Do with me what you will."

"Such brave words from one who is so very vulnerable." The Overlord came to a stop in front of his charge. "You are about to learn that there are many types of torture, one in particular that you are not prepared to endure."

Narian tensed, bracing himself for whatever pain he was about to suffer, but the warlord merely watched him, a smirk curling the corners of his lips.

"I believe this will provide the proper incentive to obey." The Overlord turned toward a door behind and to the left of the dais. "Bring in the prisoner," he called, raising his voice but slightly, for the malice within gave it great resonance.

Narian paled as the door was flung open and a young woman whose face he knew well was pulled into the hall. A single guard accompanied her, grasping the manacles that bound her hands before her.

The Overlord strode to the girl and seized her by her tangled hair. She whimpered as he hauled her across the floor toward Narian, and a tear slid down her cheek.

"Don't hurt her," Narian said, shaking his head, and for the first time, there was a slight tremor in his voice. "Please, don't hurt her."

"Really, Narian. Begging doesn't become you."

Releasing his hold upon the young woman's hair, he hit her across the face. She collapsed to the floor, sobbing, hand to her mouth where blood had begun to trickle.

"No!" Narian shouted. "I said don't hurt her!" His eyes flicked between his master and the girl while his mind raced, for this was something he had not anticipated. Then he took hold of his emotions and steadied his voice. "We can come to terms. Just don't do her harm."

"Terms?" the Overlord repeated, mulling over the concept. "You would gamble with her life?"

"No, I would gamble with your victory. If she is injured or killed, then nothing on hell or earth will persuade me to do your bidding." Narian paused, expecting a reprisal, then continued when none was forthcoming. "My demands are simple. Give me your assurance that she will not be harmed, and guarantee that the Hytanican people will not be needlessly slaughtered."

After a moment's contemplation, the Overlord nodded. "Though I do not view you as in a position to negotiate, I will accept these *terms* in exchange for your willing submission to my authority." He glanced at the prisoner, then motioned to the guard to retrieve her. "I knew you would once again see things as I do."

The guard scurried to where the girl lay sobbing and attempted to pull her to her feet, but she cried out and jerked from his grasp. She reached toward Narian and tried to move in his direction, weeping and whispering his name, but he could only shake his head in silent apology. At a pointed glance from the warlord, the guard grabbed the prisoner by her upper arms and dragged her away. The Overlord then considered his charge once more.

"There are a number of offenses for which you should be punished—insolence, disobedience, flight—but I am willing to overlook those things. I fear, however, that you have forgotten the extent of my power, so for that reason alone, a reminder is in order."

The Overlord stretched out his arm toward Narian and the young man stiffened, steeling himself against what was to come. Then he fell to his hands and knees, convulsing in pain, his body battered by his master's magic. Although he struggled not to scream, his efforts in the end were futile, and his cries continued until the warlord relented, lowering his hand.

"That's enough," the Overlord admonished, as though Narian were accountable for his own agony. "Just remember when we resume your training that this is just the beginning of what you, as well as the girl, will suffer if you fail to accomplish the task that I have set before you."

CHAPTER 1

SUCCESSOR

PALACE GUARDS LINED BOTH SIDES OF THE Throne Room, standing at attention in their royal-blue tunics with gold center panels, each holding in his left hand a flagstaff from which hung silks in the same colors. At the front of the hall on the marble dais, the King's Elite Guard formed a double arc on each side of the thrones, with Cannan, clad in the black jerkin he wore as Captain of the Guard, standing closest to the right side of the King's throne. The benches that had been placed in rows with a wide aisle between were filled with the opulently attired members of Hytanica's nobility. Late-afternoon sunlight filtered through the high windows of the northern wall, casting a glow over the front of the hall as if extending an invitation. Except for the occasional sound of someone shifting position or a bench scraping the stone floor, the room was silent, as everyone waited for the coronation ceremony to begin.

Steldor and I, along with the other members of the royal family, were likewise silent. Although the antechamber provided ample seating, excitement kept us on our feet. At the opening of one of the doors leading into the Throne Room, we shifted simultaneously to watch Lanek, the King's herald and personal secretary, step into our midst.

"The priest is ready to begin," he informed us.

My dark eyes briefly met Steldor's, but I saw none of the nervousness I was feeling reflected on his face. His composure surprised me until I realized that the stress of this ceremony was probably nothing compared to the pressures he would have coped with as a field commander leading troops in battle.

At the King's nod, Palace Guards swung the heavy double doors open, enabling my mother and father to stand side by side on the threshold. They would be preceded by heralds, one of whom bore the kingdom's standard, another a flag embroidered with the royal family's coat of arms.

My father was dressed in gold and shouldered the Sovereign's Robe of royal-blue velvet with an ermine collar. Upon his salt-and-pepper hair rested the Crown of the King, a diamond-embedded circlet of gold with four bejeweled crosses spaced evenly around its circumference. He carried the royal scepter in his left hand, on his right hand he wore the King's signet ring, and the royal sword rested in the scabbard on his left hip.

Atop my mother's honey-blond hair sat the Crown of the Queen, a golden band to match the King's, but with a single bejeweled cross at the front. From the shoulders of her gold brocade gown swept a royal-blue velvet cape.

The assembled nobility rose to their feet as the trumpets sounded and Lanek stepped forward to announce the King and Queen. Although his short, stocky build made him difficult to see in a crowd, his booming voice always ensured he was heard.

"All hail King Adrik and his Queen, the Lady Elissia!"

My father's soft brown eyes met my mother's serious blue

ones, and I saw him squeeze her hand affectionately before extending his arm to her for the processional. He then made his last entrance into the Throne Room as Hytanica's ruler, his wife at his side. The aged priest who stood in front of the dais in anticipation of administering the oath to the King's successor moved to the right to make way for their coming, and my father and mother mounted the steps to stand before their thrones, turning to face their subjects.

My sister, Princess Miranna, her blue eyes sparkling, entered next, clothed in a gown to match our mother's with a tiara of gold and pearls encircling her strawberry blond hair. She curtsied to the sovereign before likewise climbing the steps to stand in front of the farthest of three regal armchairs that had been placed to the left of the Queen.

I waited for my sister to take her position and then began the slow walk down the aisle. Despite my efforts to quiet them, my hands were shaking, for my heart was laden with dread at the thought of the power Steldor would soon wield as King. I was clothed in the dress I had worn for my wedding but a week ago on the tenth of May, although a crimson robe was now attached at the shoulders to sweep the floor in my wake. Like Miranna, I wore a tiara of gold and pearls upon my head, my dark brown hair drawn up off my shoulders.

As I approached the thrones, a smile flitted across my countenance at a sudden mental image of what London would have looked like had he been standing among the Elite Guards. My former bodyguard had not yet returned from his search for Narian in the mountains, but I knew if he had been present, he would not have worn the requisite uniform. The thought of him standing in his leather jerkin among this ostentatious company struck me as comical. Reaching the dais, I curtsied to my parents before stepping up to stand in front of the armchair immediately to the Queen's left.

The anticipation in the room heightened as I gazed at Steldor where he waited at the head of the aisle, magnificent in a black dress coat over a gold doublet that emphasized his muscular build and set off his dark hair and eyes. The scabbard that hung at his left hip was empty, but the dagger I had given him three months ago for his twenty-first birthday was sheathed on his right. A crimson cape, secured to the shoulders by gold clasps, pooled on the floor at his heels.

At the sounding of the trumpets, Steldor began the long march down the aisle, his boots beating a slow and steady cadence. He focused straight ahead, seemingly oblivious to the gathered throng, his expression as fixed as those of the past kings in the portraits lining the walls to his left and right. Regardless of his demeanor, I knew from the tilt of his head that he was relishing this moment.

As Steldor drew closer to the thrones, the priest moved into the aisle, not speaking until my husband had halted ten paces from him.

"Lords and ladies of Hytanica," he said, raising the volume of his nasal, tremulous voice so that all might hear. "I present unto you Lord Steldor, son of the Baron Cannan and husband of the heir to the throne, Princess Alera, who comes before you to be crowned rightful King over all the lands and peoples of Hytanica. Are all you assembled here this day willing to recognize him as such?"

A resounding "Aye" echoed throughout the Throne Room.

"And are you, Lord Steldor, willing to take the King's Oath?"

"I am willing."

The priest surveyed the nobility and, when he was satisfied that everyone was listening, nodded to Steldor, who dropped to one knee.

"Will you solemnly promise to govern the peoples of the Kingdom of Hytanica with justice, mercy and wisdom?" the priest inquired.

"I solemnly promise so to do."

"Will you promise to enforce and maintain the laws of God?"

"I do so promise."

"Will you restore the things that are gone to decay, punish and reform what is amiss, and confirm what is in good order?"

"All this I promise so to do."

"Then arise and approach the throne."

Steldor stood as the priest yielded the aisle. After tendering one last bow to his King and Queen, he mounted the steps of the dais, and Cannan advanced to remove the crimson robe that marked his son as the successor to the throne. My mother thereupon took the Sovereign's Robe from the King's shoulders. She waited as Steldor turned to face the nobility and then draped it over his powerful frame. As my parents moved to stand next to the Captain of the Guard, Cannan tendered the crimson robe to my mother so that she could place it upon my father's back.

Steldor now cast his eyes over the nobility, poised to make his final pledge.

"The things that I have here promised, I will perform and keep, so help me God," he declared, his voice impassioned.

He held out a hand to me, and I moved to his side. After detaching the crimson robe from my gown, he passed it to my mother in exchange for the Queen's royal-blue cape. He then laid the raiment upon my shoulders, and for the first time we took our places upon the thrones.

The priest now came before us with a small vial of oil for the Anointing.

"So be thou anointed, blessed and consecrated King over the peoples of Hytanica," he intoned, dipping his fingers into the vial and making the mark of the cross on Steldor's hands and forehead. "May you govern and preserve us in wealth and peace, and may you rule wisely, justly and mercifully."

Turning to me, he again dipped his fingers in the oil.

"So be thou anointed Queen of Hytanica, to support and assist your King in the performance of his charge," he said, likewise placing the mark of the cross upon me.

After administering a blessing, the priest moved to the far right of the thrones to sit in the chair that had been provided for him.

My father would now relinquish his authority as King and invest it in his successor. He stepped forward, and Steldor rose to accept the accoutrements of the monarchy.

"Receive the Rod of Wisdom," my father said, pressing the royal scepter into Steldor's left hand. "Honor the faithful, provide for the weak, cherish the just and lead your people in the way wherein they should go."

The King then drew the royal sword. "Do not bear this sword in vain, but use it for the terror and punishment of evildoers, and for the protection and encouragement of those who do well."

Steldor accepted the sword, briefly holding it aloft before placing it in his scabbard.

Removing the royal ring, the King slid it onto the third finger of Steldor's right hand.

"Receive the Ring of Kingly Dignity so that all may recognize your sovereignty, and so that you may remember the oaths you have here taken this day."

The time for the final act had arrived, and I watched somewhat sadly as my father removed the crown from his own head and held it high for all to see. He then fervently made his last pronouncement.

"Receive this crown as a sign of royal majesty and as the rightful King of Hytanica."

He placed the diadem upon Steldor, and enthusiastic shouts erupted from the gathered throng.

"Hail to the King! Hail to King Steldor!"

My father, no longer Hytanica's ruler, waited for the noise to abate and then humbly knelt before his King to pledge his allegiance.

"I will be faithful and true unto you, my Sovereign Lord, King of Hytanica, and unto your heirs."

After kissing the royal ring, my father stood and took up position in front of the chair that had originally been provided for me. I came to my feet and removed my tiara, passing it to my mother, who had come before Steldor so that he could remove the Queen's crown. She gave him a curtsey, then crossed the dais to stand between her husband and her younger daughter.

"Be thou rightfully crowned Queen of Hytanica," Steldor proclaimed, placing the golden band upon my head, and another cheer ricocheted off the stone walls and wood-beamed ceiling.

The weight of responsibility descended upon me along with the crown, and I suddenly felt eighteen was far too young an age at which to assume such a role. Seized with panic, I glanced at my mother, and she offered the only assistance she could—a reassuring smile. As Steldor and I once more occupied the thrones, the rest of the royal family and Hytanica's nobility took their seats. Cannan then strode forward to kneel before his son and pledge his service.

"I, Baron Cannan, Captain of the Guard and head of Hytanica's military, do become your man of life and limb, and faith and truth will I bear unto you, to live and die in defense of you, against all manner of threat."

After kissing the royal ring, the captain returned to his position on the King's right. I followed him with my eyes, wondering what he was feeling at this moment, but his countenance was as impassive as always.

Homage then continued to be paid, with each male member of the nobility coming forward to kneel and make a pledge of faith and truth unto his King before returning to his seat. When the last person had approached, Steldor and I came to our feet, and the others in the room rose as one. With the royal scepter in his right hand and my hand upon his left, Steldor nodded to Lanek, who announced Hytanica's new ruler.

"All hail His Royal Majesty King Steldor and his Queen, the Lady Alera."

The trumpets sounded, and the heralds bearing the flags of the royal family and the kingdom led us down the aisle to exit the Hall of Kings, followed by Cannan and the Elite Guards, my parents and Miranna. My eyes briefly met Steldor's as we entered the antechamber, and the feverish gleam within his gave me pause. I knew he had probably envisioned this coronation from the moment we had first formally met almost ten years ago, and I could not fathom the satisfaction he had to be feeling at having won his coveted prize. We did not dally, but followed the heralds, accompanied by the guards, through the doors into the Grand Entry Hall, then up the Grand Staircase, leaving my parents and sister behind. From there, we entered the Royal Ballroom, crossing its expanse to step onto the balcony, where the trumpets were again sounded to draw to us the attention of the thousands of people gathered outside the courtyard walls.

"All hail King Steldor and his Queen, the Lady Alera," Lanek again shouted, and the cry was echoed by the Palace Guards at the gates. Soon thunderous applause and repetitive shouts of "Hail to the King" reached our ears, and Steldor began to wave to the citizenry, quite in his element.

I could not have said how long we stood on the balcony, but given the length of the coronation ceremony, my high level of anxiety and the time that had passed since my last meal, I was exhausted. Steldor, on the other hand, was exhilarated and seemed ready to bask in the acclamation of the people for the rest of time. As the dizzying reality that I was now married to the King of Hytanica settled upon me, I swayed against him, clutching at his shoulder. He looked at me, startled, and then scooped me into his arms, cradling me so that my head fell against his chest.

"It would appear you have had enough excitement," he remarked, then carried me back through the ballroom and on to our quarters, waving away his father and the guards. Bearing me into my room, he lowered me onto the bed and removed my crown and cape, then undid the laces of my gown, sliding it down my arms and assisting me to take it off. I slumped sideways onto the pillows in my undergarments, feeling too tired to resist him, and he lifted my legs onto the bed, removing my shoes and folding a blanket over me. To my surprise, he kissed me on the forehead.

"Relax and sleep. I will bring food later to help you regain your strength." He touched my cheek, then turned and departed, and my eyelids fell like heavy drapes.

Memories of Narian, as always, haunted my dreams. We were standing in the clearing in the woods on his father's estate, the sun hot upon my back, birds chirping in the trees.

"Here, see? I have them," I said, holding up a pair of breeches for Narian's inspection. "Now you have no basis upon which to object to teaching me self-defense."

"I can object as long as you're not wearing them." His voice was steady, with a faint but pleasing accent, and his golden hair ruffled in the breeze.

Then the image shifted, and I was wearing the breeches and a white shirt, standing at the side of a dark bay gelding.

"Surely women in Cokyri don't ride horses," I said.

"The woman who raised me is one of the best riders in the empire," Narian responded from where he stood by the horse's head, and any will to resist left me as I gazed into his compelling blue eyes.

He came to my side and bent his knee toward me, offering his leg as a step so that I could mount the animal by myself. I gracelessly complied, and he smiled up at me, his cheeks flushed with happiness, his expression unguarded. Then he swung up behind me on the horse's back.

Now we were riding through the darkened city, the horse's hooves sometimes clacking against cobblestone, other times muffled on a dirt street, the moon and stars reflecting off the dusting of snow upon the ground. I leaned back against him, warmed by his body, at one with him and at peace with the world. We gradually circled around to return to the Royal Stables, where he dismounted, then looked up at me. I slid off the horse into his arms, and I could see the love in his eyes; then his lips met mine and I melted against him, a thrill sweeping through me.

The scene changed once more…

We were in my parlor, sitting in front of the glowing embers of the fireplace. I nestled against him, secure in his arms, listening to the steady cadence of his voice as he described to me the raw beauty of Cokyri, the land in which he had been raised.

Then London appeared, pulling Narian from me.

"You will keep away from Alera or you will deal with me," he growled before locking his eyes upon mine. "We cannot control our hearts, Alera, but we must control our minds and bodies. You cannot marry him. It is best that you keep away from him, so that these feelings will disappear." I stared at London, an ache in every fiber of my being, tears falling freely.

It was dark outside when I awoke, my slumber disturbed by sounds from the parlor, my pillow and cheeks damp. I contemplated the light filtering through my open door, then decided to investigate, slipping on my robe.

The parlor had not changed much since my parents had lived here, and yet Steldor had made his mark. The cream brocade armchairs that my mother had favored were still grouped near the window that offered a view of the garden and, beyond that, of the Kilwin Forest that spread toward the Niñeyre Mountain Range to the north. The sofa, however, had been replaced by one of brown leather, reflective of Steldor's tastes. The fireplace on the eastern wall that had always been bounded by bookshelves and fronted by a bench now also served as a backdrop for leather armchairs and a gaming table. The desk that my father had rarely used had been stocked with quills, ink, parchment and account books, a pair of armchairs and an elaborately carved sideboard added nearby. Tapestries continued to adorn the walls and cushion the floors, with oil lamps providing soft lighting. My touch seemed to be the only one missing from the room, and it felt odd to be absent thus from my own home.

Steldor was placing a tray upon the low table that sat in front of the sofa when his eyes caught my movement.

"Feeling better?" he asked, pouring himself a glass of wine.

I nodded, debating whether or not I should join him.

"Then come—I have brought something for you to eat."

Despite his invitation, I stayed in place while he filled a second goblet for me. He glanced up and, noting my reluctance to approach, stepped toward the fireplace, where his coat, doublet and weapons lay on the hearth bench.

"I promise to let you eat in peace," he said with a chuckle, making a sweeping motion with his arm toward the meal he had brought.

My cheeks bloomed, but I walked forward nonetheless, the smell of food irresistible. Steldor relaxed in an armchair with his goblet and jug of wine, and I sank onto the sofa to devour the meat, bread and fruit. When the hollow feeling in my stomach had at last receded, I glanced at my husband, whose bemused expression brought another blush to my cheeks.

"Don't let me stop you," he said, as if realizing he was upsetting me. "I ate just as hungrily about an hour ago."

I took a few additional bites, albeit a bit more daintily, then put down my tableware.

"How long did I sleep?" I asked.

"At last I hear your sweet voice," Steldor teased, his spirits obviously running high. He poured himself another glass of wine before returning to my question. "You've managed to dream away almost three hours."

I stared at him, surprised and appalled by the possibility that I had slept through my first duties as Queen of Hytanica.

"Are the celebrations over then?"

"Yes, unless we wish to have a private celebration of our own." He stood with a roguish grin and carried the wine toward me. "But don't feel guilty. I suspect I enjoyed the revelry to a much greater extent than you would have."

Returning his own glass and the wine jug to the tray-laden table, he picked up my goblet and handed it to me. I took a sip, aware that his eyes were upon me and unsure of his intentions. After an awkward moment, he stepped around the table and sat beside me. I immediately stood, as if his weight had propelled me upward.

"I believe I will retire for the night. Pray excuse me, my lord."

He gave a short, cynical laugh. "Sleep…food…drink… You surely have recovered enough to keep me company for a short time."

"If you wish it."

I sat down stiffly on the edge of the sofa, my hands wrapped around my glass of wine. Without a word, Steldor took the goblet and set it on the tray, then pulled the pins from my hair, letting my tresses cascade about my shoulders.

"A week ago, you asked me to take things slowly, and I agreed and kept my distance," he said, examining my face. "I even slept on the floor in my soldier's bedroll the last few nights of our stay in the guest room."

He paused, twirling a strand of my silky hair around his forefinger.

"I fail to understand how you will become physically comfortable with me when you will not even let me kiss you, let alone touch you."

Though his voice was light, I could see the longing in his eyes. I bowed my head in misery, knowing that he had the right to expect more, that I had no excuse. Shifting closer, he cupped my chin, then leaned forward to tenderly and sensually press his lips against mine. Despite my desire to escape, I was enticed by his gentle advance and captured, as always, by his provocative scent. He pulled back to assess my reaction and then opened my robe. Glancing again in my eyes, he rested the fingers of his right hand upon the hollow of my throat, then traced the line of my collarbone, gradually dropping lower to sweep across the swell of my breasts.

"Please, don't," I breathlessly asserted, unable to stem my deepening blush or calm the rapid beating of my heart.

"You must accept my touch," he murmured, repeating the path of his fingers with his lips.

"Stop," I tried again, but his mouth found mine, muffling my words, while his hands followed the curves of my body, sending heat coursing through me. Hating that he could affect me in this way against my will, I pushed against his chest. For one horrible moment, I thought he might not yield, but he straightened, his hands settling on my waist, an exasperated frown upon his handsome features.

"Your lips respond favorably to mine, so perhaps it is your heart that is unwilling," he said, deliberately drawing me toward him. "As your husband, I have the right to your body, with or without your heart."

"If you love me at all, if you have any hope that I will one day love you, you will not do this," I beseeched, knowing how helpless I would be against him.

He held me a moment longer, his deep brown eyes boring into my own, then released me to stalk toward the fireplace. Although my heart still pounded, I felt a wave of dizzying relief as he grabbed his doublet from the hearth bench, shrugging it on. After seizing his weapons and strapping them about his hips, he strode to the door without a word or even a passing glance.

"Where are you going?" I asked.

"Out," he snapped. With one last withering look at me, he disappeared into the hallway, leaving me to contemplate the vagaries of his personality as well as the contradictory impulses of my body and my heart.

★★★

The following day, I became aware even before I saw him that Steldor's displeasure with me had not diminished. While he usually left our quarters quietly before I was awake, this morning he had taken special care to disturb me, even slamming the parlor door on his way out. Sighing, I dressed and breakfasted, then left the room to begin my first official day as Queen.

I made my way to the Grand Staircase, feeling incomplete without a personal bodyguard. During my father's reign, he had ordered that my mother, my younger sister and I be constantly guarded, probably due to the wariness instilled in him by the war with Cokyri. Steldor had decided that there was little need for such measures while we were within the heavily protected palace, and Cannan had reassigned the men who served in such a capacity. To placate my father, however, Steldor had left Halias, the Elite Guard who had been safeguarding my sister since the day of her birth, in place as Miranna's guard.

My first order of business was to meet with the heads of the household staff in the Queen's Drawing Room, located on the first floor in the palace's East Wing. After discussing the menu for the upcoming days with the cook and determining which rooms were to be cleaned by the maids that week, the head housekeeper informed me that two servants needed to be replaced and that she had several candidates for me to consider. I stared at her from where I sat behind the desk that had always served my mother, alarmed at the request. This was the first time I had been expected to hire someone.

"What purposes would these maids serve?" I inquired.

"One would do general cleaning, Your Highness," the

housekeeper replied. "The other would serve Princess Miranna, as Ailith has left to marry."

"And the women are with you?"

"Yes, my lady, they're in the corridor."

"Well, I suppose I should talk with them."

"Yes, my lady."

I shifted uneasily while I waited for the housekeeper to bring forth the applicants, trying to determine the basis upon which such a decision was to be made. Four women of varying ages, shapes and sizes came into the room to line up before me, and I asked the only question that came to mind.

"Have any of you previously held a position as a maid?"

Unfortunately, they all replied in the negative. There was a tense moment as I struggled for something more to ask, then I spoke to the youngest and best groomed of the four.

"What is your name?"

"Ryla, Your Majesty," she replied with a bright smile, and my intuition told me that her personality would blend well with my sister's.

"Do you believe you could carry out the duties of a personal maid?"

"Yes, Your Highness. I'm a quick learner and would be honored to fill such a position."

"Very well, you will serve Princess Miranna."

At a loss as to how to distinguish among the remaining three candidates, I turned to the housekeeper.

"I shall leave the final decisions to you," I said, hoping I sounded more confident than I felt. "You are no doubt better able to judge the abilities of these women than am I."

The housekeeper nodded and ushered all four from the room. As a maid entered with lunch, I dismissed the rest of the staff to attend to their duties, and moved to one of the rose velvet armchairs beside the bay window. While I ate, my thoughts turned to the first official gathering I would plan as Queen: a small celebration on the nineteenth of June in honor of Miranna's seventeenth birthday.

The head cook returned in the afternoon, along with a palace scribe, and I began to discuss the ideas I had formed for a dinner party. Over the next few hours, I decided on a menu and a guest list, charging the scribe with preparing the invitations. The guests would include my parents; Lord Temerson, the young man my sister favored, and his parents; Miranna's best friend, Lady Semari, and her parents; Cannan and his wife, Baroness Faramay; Steldor's best friend, Lord Galen, and whomever Galen asked to accompany him; and Lord Baelic, Cannan's younger brother, with his wife and two eldest daughters, for his girls were among my sister's circle of friends.

After joining my family for dinner, I was so worn-out from the day's stresses that I would have liked to return to my quarters, but I hesitated in light of the mood Steldor had presented that morning. Since he had not shared the evening meal with us, I assumed his disposition had not improved and feared an encounter with him in our parlor. I thus went to the library instead. An hour later, I left with my book, hoping to avoid my husband and his antagonistic attitude by going straight to bed.

To my dismay, I entered the parlor to discover Galen and Steldor sitting in armchairs across from each other with the gaming table in between, deeply enmeshed in a chess match. Galen had recently been appointed Sergeant at Arms, the former sergeant Kade having willingly passed to the younger man the responsibility of commanding the Palace Guard. As Galen was quickly discovering, this also cast him in the role of Cannan's official lackey, and he was finding it necessary to spend long days, and sometimes nights, in the palace.

I examined the two friends, noticing again how alike they were in appearance. Only a year older than Steldor, Galen was of similar height and build and even had the same taste in clothing. I had always thought their personalities to be similar, too, but had recently started to consider that Galen's nature, like his brown hair and eyes, was not as dark as Steldor's.

Galen glanced in my direction and hastened to his feet.

"My Queen," he said with a slight bow, whereupon Steldor took note of me, although he did not rise. I inclined my head toward the sergeant, at the same time stealing a peek at my husband, unsure whether or not I was welcome.

"Perhaps I should take my leave," Galen said, feeling the tension that now permeated the room. "We can finish our chess game another time."

"Just sit down," Steldor gruffly directed. "Alera won't mind. She like's it when some*thing* or some*one* comes between us."

Ignoring the King's remark, I held up my book and spoke sweetly to Galen.

"Please, do stay. I was planning to read anyway."

"Trust me," Steldor added, indicating the chessboard. "*This* will be the best part of my evening."

While it had not been my original intent to remain in the parlor, I chose to do so now, knowing that my presence would aggravate Steldor and provide some repayment for his rude comments. Although clearly unhappy at having been caught in the cross fire, Galen took his seat, and the two men resumed their match. I crossed to the sofa, stepping around the table that stood before it upon which had been placed the usual goblets and jug of wine. Slipping off my shoes, I tucked my feet beneath me on the padded leather and began to read, only to be pulled from my book about twenty minutes later by Steldor.

"Alera, bring us some wine," he called.

My skin prickled in indignation at the interruption, and I wondered why he was unable to get the wine himself, or why he felt the need to issue an order rather than make a request. As I deliberated, Galen stood and strode toward the table without a word to either of us. He filled one goblet with wine and extended it to me.

"Thank you, kind sir," I said, smiling at his gesture and deriving great satisfaction from my husband's irritated frown.

"Most welcome," Galen rejoined with a smirk.

After filling two additional goblets, he tucked the jug under his arm, then walked back to Steldor. With a feigned look of apology, he handed one of the glasses to his best friend.

"I felt the need to help a damsel in distress," he explained, retaking his seat. To my surprise, Steldor laughed, and Galen placed the jug upon the floor so that they could continue their game.

A few minutes later, I set my full goblet down on the low sofa table, still not having cultivated a taste for the drink, then stood and walked toward the two friends.

"Good night, gentle*man,*" I said pointedly, looking at Galen before directing my attention to Steldor. "And good night, husband. I believe I will retire." As they looked up at me, I warmly addressed our guest. "It was nice to see you again. You were most assuredly the best part of my evening, as well."

With a final glance at Steldor, I disappeared into my

bedroom, pleased with the consternation I had seen upon his face.

"She's a bit feisty, isn't she?" I heard Galen say almost approvingly as I closed the door behind me. I remained next to it, listening for my husband's response.

"Yes, she is quite a challenge. I'd break her of her impudence, but I'm afraid that may be her best quality."

The two men chuckled, and I leaned back against the wood, angry at Steldor for belittling me in front of his best friend and disappointed in myself for caring.

I prepared for bed, railing in my head against the circumstances in which I found myself. Had it not been for my father's selfishness and his inability to see me as anything but a device in the plans of men, I would not now be married to Steldor. The former King had long ago determined that the Captain of the Guard's son should be his successor in the absence of a male heir, not caring about my happiness—not caring that I had given my heart to another.

Feeling empty inside, I sat upon the bed and unwisely let my mind drift to Narian, the enigmatic son of the Baron Koranis and Baroness Alantonya. My father had feared the young man and the questions regarding his loyalties—Narian had been abducted as an infant and raised in Cokyri, the ruthless mountain empire that had for a century been our enemy. When he had returned to his Hytanican family ten months ago, it had seemed that my eyes alone were not clouded by hatred and bigotry. I had been able to see Narian for who he truly was: a young man with courage and an independent mind, who had been made to pay for so much that was outside his control. He couldn't help his past any more than he could help the way those intense, deep blue eyes pierced me and held me captive. I trusted him, and he respected and trusted me.

With a heavy sigh and a heavier heart, I crawled beneath my covers, deciding to read in the hope of suppressing further memories. But as the candle in my lantern slowly burned down, I concentrated less on the words and more on the question of whether any eventuality could restore hope for the life of which I had dreamed.

CHAPTER 2

RETRIBUTION

"MY LADY? MY LADY."

As the voice penetrated my slumber, I slowly opened my eyes, rolling onto my back to see who had spoken.

"My apologies, Your Highness," murmured my golden-haired, round-faced personal maid, Sahdienne, from my bedroom door.

"What is the hour?" I asked, glancing toward the heavy drapes that blocked the sunlight from my room.

"Half past nine, my lady."

"Half past nine?" I repeated, jarring fully awake and swinging my feet to the floor. "I've overslept. Hurry and help me dress."

Sahdienne rushed to the window, and I squinted when she let the light of day shine brilliantly through the glass.

"A guard was sent here with a message, Your Majesty," she hesitantly continued, as though still apologizing for her presumptuous action in rousing the Queen, however prolonged her sleep may have been.

"What was the message?"

"You've been asked to report to the Captain of the Guard's office as soon as possible."

I frowned, perplexed, and Sahdienne moved toward my wardrobe to assist in the selection of my attire.

"Did the messenger give a reason?"

"No, my lady."

She helped me into the gown I had indicated and then brushed my dark brown hair while I sat in front of the mirror that graced the top of my dressing table. As she began to fashion my tresses, intending to pull them up off my shoulders, I shooed her away.

"Don't fuss further. I shouldn't keep Cannan waiting."

Foregoing breakfast, I hastened into the corridor, not slowing until I reached the landing of the double staircase. Smoothing my skirt, I more sedately descended the flight to my left, turning to walk underneath it in order to enter the Throne Room by means of the antechamber. The Captain of the Guard's office opened off the eastern wall, and a Palace Guard knocked upon its door at my approach. Without waiting for an answer, he opened the door. Overcome with foreboding at sight of the men who were talking with the captain, I stopped on the threshold.

I had expected that Cannan desired to speak with me alone, although to what end I could not fathom, but Steldor, Galen, Destari and my father were also present. This placed me in the company of the Captain of the Guard, the King, the Sergeant at Arms, a deputy captain in the Elite Guard and the former King, men who were not only imposing, but intensely dark in coloring. As everyone's expressions were somber, I felt as if I was stepping into a room full of storm clouds.

Cannan was seated behind his desk, with Steldor on his left so that he likewise faced the others. Everyone came respectfully to their feet, but I continued to stand still, unnerved.

"Come in, Your Majesty. Have a seat."

Cannan motioned to a spare wooden chair in front of his desk, which looked to me to be an interrogation chair, for it was not designed for comfort. Galen and my father—who was still addressed as King Adrik, though he no longer ruled—took up seats in similar chairs to my left. Destari, the towering Elite Guard who had at times replaced London as my bodyguard, stood on my right, unaccustomed, I supposed, to relaxing while within his captain's office. Father and son had reseated themselves in leather armchairs, and I eyed Cannan, unable to imagine the reason he had sent for me; women in Hytanica, including the Queen, were not consulted in financial, political or military matters.

"We've been updating Steldor regarding our efforts to hold the Cokyrians at the river," the captain explained. "It's time to inform him of Narian's significance to the enemy."

My breath caught, and I fervently hoped I had not yet awakened—that this was just a nightmare. I did not want to have to discuss Narian in the presence of any of these men; that was doubly true when it came to my father and Steldor.

"London has not yet returned to Hytanica," Cannan continued in his businesslike manner. "It is incumbent upon you and Destari to tell us to the best of your abilities about the Legend of the Bleeding Moon."

"Then let Destari speak," I blurted. "He knows as much if not more about the legend than do I."

Cannan, I was certain, knew what I was doing, but he let it pass and turned to the deputy captain, who came to attention.

"Stand at ease, and tell us what you know."

"Yes, sir. On the day of the tournament last October,

London met with Alera and me to discuss an urgent matter. He told us that he had become suspicious of Narian and had gone to Cokyri to learn what he could about his upbringing."

My father seemed shocked by this news, and even the military men seemed taken aback by London's bold and dangerous initiative, leading me to believe that no one else would have dared to venture into the enemy's stronghold.

"While he was there," Destari continued in his deep, resonating voice, "he discovered an account of an ancient legend, the Legend of the Bleeding Moon, which foretold of our kingdom's downfall. The account repeated our own lore about how our first King hallowed our land with the blood of his infant son to give Hytanica abiding protection from her enemies. The legend held, however, that a Hytanican boy would be born under a bleeding moon, and that this boy would be marked by the moon and given the power to overthrow his kingdom.

"In the final months of the war seventeen years ago, a blood-red moon dominated the night, and the Cokyrians snatched our infant boys from their homes. All those taken were murdered except for one, the young man now known to us as Narian. I'm sure you are all aware of his unusual crescent-shaped birthmark, for it was the basis of his identification as the Baron Koranis's son. London believes that Narian is the one of whom the legend speaks—that Narian has been trained by the Overlord to destroy Hytanica."

A lengthy silence followed Destari's revelations, and I was thankful to see that the others were focused on the King, who was absorbing this information with no more than a crease in his brow.

"And when did you and King Adrik learn of this?" Steldor finally asked, directing his question to his father, having inferred that London, Destari and I had withheld this information for quite some time.

"Three months later, on the day Narian left Hytanica," Cannan responded. "We sent for him shortly after London met with us, at which time we discovered that the boy had fled."

Steldor glanced at me in confusion, though his next question was directed to Destari. "Why did London bring this information to Alera?"

"He did not believe the captain or the King would trust what he had to say since he had been dismissed from his post. He also wanted to warn her against befriending the young man."

"And *did* she stay away from him?" Steldor pressed, his eyes narrowing, and I suspected he already knew the answer.

Destari wavered for an instant, reading Steldor's expression, but in the end answered straightforwardly.

"No, Your Majesty, she did not."

Not wanting to look at any of the men in the room, I focused on stilling my fidgety hands, for this habit revealed my level of discomfort, and my anxiety was now nearing panic proportions. I couldn't remember a time when I had so desperately wanted to escape from a situation, but the captain had no intention of granting me a reprieve.

"It is imperative for us to know where Narian's loyalties lie. Alera, you and he appeared to be friends. What can you tell us?"

I concentrated on Cannan as words tumbled from my mouth without passing through my brain. In my extreme desire to end this conversation, I told him what I could, as rapidly as I could, painfully aware that Steldor's eyes were upon me.

"He rarely spoke about his life in Cokyri, and I always

felt that it must have been very harsh. In any case, I know he did not want to return. He once told me that he despised having his life laid out for him, but he also told me that if ever he did return to Cokyri, the Overlord would be difficult to refuse. Still, I think he will turn from the legend if he can—"

"He spoke with you about the Overlord?"

The captain interrupted my monologue, lifting one eyebrow, the only trace of surprise that ever showed on the imperturbable man's face.

"Yes…but we didn't *talk* about the Overlord. He just mentioned him."

"I see."

Cannan considered me, and my empty stomach felt as though it were shriveling. I had unwittingly made my position more precarious, for Narian had spoken to no one but me about his relationship to Cokyri's powerful warlord. I was the only person in whom Narian had confided; I alone knew that the Overlord had been his teacher.

"I take it the two of you became quite close," Cannan finally concluded.

I shot Destari a quick look, fearful that the captain might bring to light my relationship with Koranis's son, which had far exceeded the bounds of friendship. I had a feeble hope that he could somehow deter his commander from further pursuit of the matter, but Cannan's keen eyes caught my glance and he turned to his Elite Guard.

"You were her bodyguard at the time. What was the nature of their relationship?"

Destari shifted uncomfortably, his thick, dark eyebrows shrouding his black eyes, and the fact that he was attempting to protect a secret of mine seemed to echo in the room.

"She had become his…closest friend."

The tension in the office heightened, as if the air had been sucked out through the doors and every person inside was now silently battling to draw breath. Steldor had gone rigid in his chair, jaw clenched, and I thought the animosity burning in his eyes would set the room aflame. Galen was watching the King, plainly worried that he would not be able to contain his famous temper. My father's usually kind gaze roved the room as he undoubtedly tried to determine whether or not his mind had jumped to ridiculous conclusions.

"Ahhh..." Cannan's monosyllabic utterance told me that he had grasped the situation, but my heart sank when I realized he was not yet ready to let the matter drop. "And had this friendship led to intimacy?"

I could feel myself blushing, for all of the men except Cannan had shifted their attention to me. The captain continued to wait for a response from Destari, but when none was forthcoming, his countenance grew grim. Concern for the guard who was struggling to defend me finally compelled me to speak.

"Narian had fallen in love with me," I said, eyes cast downward.

I heard Steldor's chair scrape against the floor as he stood, and looked up to see him move behind me, apparently unable to tolerate the sight of me. For an instant, I thought he was going to storm out of the office, but instead he leaned his shoulder against the wall next to a glass-fronted weapons cabinet, crossing his arms over his chest. Galen showed no reaction to my confession but monitored Steldor warily. Cannan hadn't moved, continuing to scrutinize me despite his son's fractious reaction. My father's eyes were unfocused, his lips parted in shock. I could only presume he was remembering a conversation in which I had let him believe that Narian and I were just friends, and that he was feeling deceived.

Now that the truth was out, Cannan returned to the original subject. "What was Narian's behavior like in the weeks preceding his departure?"

I opened my mouth to answer, then recalled that London and Destari had kept me from Narian during that time. They had discovered that the young man had been sneaking me out of the palace late at night—in disregard of my courtship with Steldor, without my father's knowledge or permission and without a chaperone—and had put an end to our illicit escapades. Not wanting to reveal these details, I again looked in the Elite Guard's direction, realizing as I did so that our conduct had begun to annoy Cannan, who had little if any patience for games.

"Circumstances are too desperate to withhold information," the captain warned Destari, his aspect stern. "You *will* tell me what you know, regardless of your desire to shield Alera's judgments from scrutiny."

"Yes, Captain," Destari relented, with an almost imperceptible shrug of apology for me. "London and I prevented her from having contact with Narian in the two weeks preceding his disappearance. We thought it best that she end her relationship with him. When she could not seem to do so, we took matters into our own hands."

"So our hope that Narian does not return to Cokyri is based on his relationship with Alera," Cannan concluded. His next question was addressed to me. "Is there anything else we should know that would help us to judge his intentions?"

I hung my head in humiliation at the pieces of my personal life that had come into the open, knowing that what I was about to say would only make the situation worse.

"He pledged that he would never harm me, and I do not think he would break his word." My voice was meek, for I did not want to speak louder than was necessary for the captain's ears, in the hope that Steldor would not hear.

Cannan studied me for a demoralizing moment, though I could not imagine what he was thinking. Finally, he stood and motioned toward the door.

"That is all I need from you, Your Highness. You may go."

I came to my feet, not knowing at whom it would be safe to look. My father was frowning in undisguised disappointment, and Galen's eyes were flicking uneasily between the King and me. Destari had targeted a spot on the wall and was refusing to look at anything else in the room. Cannan, now that he had finished with me, was studying Steldor, perhaps also thinking of his son's volatile temperament.

The men rose as I started toward the door, observing protocol even though it was debatable whether or not I still had their respect. Just before I stepped over the threshold and into the Throne Room, I glanced at my husband, and the murderous glint in his eyes told me all I needed to know about the conclusions he had reached.

I halted outside the door to the captain's office as it closed behind me, for I did not know where to go from there. There were two things of which I was certain: Steldor would come searching for me, and there was no way I could avoid him. Sighing, I crossed the floor to exit the Hall of Kings through the King's Drawing Room, reluctantly heading to the royal family's private staircase to climb to my quarters on the second floor. The time to pay for my sins had come at last.

Hours passed without Steldor coming to our rooms. I tried to fill the time by reading in the parlor but eventually moved into my bedroom to lie down, for the tension had given me a dull headache.

I now occupied the room that had been my mother's, but I had taken the feather pillows and cream-colored spread from my childhood bedroom with me. The feel and familiarity of these items brought me some measure of comfort, even though everything else in my former quarters, other than my clothing, had been left behind. I wished I could have as easily left behind my memories of Narian. While I no longer had the balcony off my other bedroom as a daily reminder of the nights he had surreptitiously visited me, images of him continued to plague me, unbidden and cruelly tantalizing: the mesmerizing blue eyes that compelled me to share with him my most private fears; the feel of his thick, untidy hair as the sunlight split it into myriad shades of gold; the soft laugh that touched my soul; his aloof but unpretentious manner; his confident assurance that I could make my own choices. I shuddered at the thought of Steldor's attitude toward me, for he saw me as only a woman, relegated to supervising the household, planning and executing the social events and raising the children. All he really wanted was my presence in his bed, which made me all the more unwilling to comply. Steldor's glance made me uncomfortable, his patronizing laugh made me cringe, his condescension frequently led to my humiliation. In Narian's arms, I had felt extraordinary happiness; in Steldor's, I felt trapped.

Gripped by restlessness, I returned to the parlor and walked aimlessly through it, stopping at the closed door to Steldor's bedroom. I had not yet visited his private domain—primarily because I had so far resisted his attempts to entice me into it. I put a hand to the door, curiosity urging me forward, but the wild thudding of my heart caused me to pause. I did not know what would happen if Steldor returned while I was within the very room into which he endeavored to lure me.

I crossed the parlor once more and slowly sat down on the sofa, the reality of my life falling like a heavy weight upon my shoulders. Of the rooms Steldor and I occupied, I was afraid to enter his bedroom and was always jittery when he and I found ourselves together in the parlor. The only room in which I felt safe was my bedroom, and even there I fretted that Steldor would pursue me.

As the afternoon waned, hunger got the best of me, and I left to join my family for the evening meal in our private dining room. My father was there, although in a much less jovial frame of mind than usual. Throughout the stilted dinner conversation, he barely made eye contact with me, and I felt awash in shame. Just when we were concluding the meal, Steldor appeared in the doorway, his stony gaze immediately finding me.

"Join us," my mother said with a hesitant smile. "I will have the servants refill the platters."

"No, thank you," Steldor responded without taking his eyes off me. "I have just come for Alera."

"Of course," my mother said lightly, although I knew from her expression that she could feel the enmity radiating from the King.

I stood, then walked past my husband into the corridor, my stomach churning. Steldor walked behind me, not speaking, as we proceeded to our quarters. I entered the parlor first but was barely over the threshold when he caught my arm, spinning me around to face him and slamming the door behind us.

"I think I have a right to know how far your relationship with Narian went," he said to me, his voice calm despite the crazed glint in his eyes.

"What do you mean?" I cautiously asked, even though I understood what he wanted to know.

"I mean," he snarled, "did I marry a whore?"

I stared at him, mortified, then without thought slapped him hard across the face. My hand stung from the force of my blow, and I stumbled back from him, my body suddenly cold as fear of how he might respond settled over me like a pall.

He rubbed his cheek, astonishment playing upon his features, then he grabbed my arm above the elbow.

"You didn't answer my question," he said.

With no escape, and knowing that continued effort on my part to evade him would only anger him further, I gave as vague an answer as I dared.

"We…kissed. That was all."

"You kissed?" He placed one hand upon my back, pulling me against him, then ran his other hand roughly up and down my body. "Or did you caress?"

"Unlike some, Narian was always a perfect gentleman," I said caustically, pushing hard against his muscular chest. "Now let me go!"

Still he held me in place, and I knew how futile my attempts to thwart him would be if he ignored my plea. Emboldened by the peril of my position, I tried once more to shame him into releasing me.

"Narian did not press me for anything I was not willing to give!"

"Then the question becomes, what were you willing to give?"

Once again, shock reverberated through me at his insinuation. Just as I felt certain that he would harm me, no longer caring whether I came willingly to his bed, he thrust me from him. As fear left me, indignation swelled, and words burst from my mouth.

"You have certainly kissed women other than me."

"Of course I have," he said with a mirthless laugh. "But I did not pursue any of them after *we* began courting."

His glower returned, and he again advanced on me, and I realized how foolish I had been to engage him further. I backed away until I collided with the wall.

"The problem with you, Alera," he said, leaning toward me, one hand against the wall on each side of me, "is that you have been keeping the wrong man at bay."

Unable to bear his accusatory eyes, I turned my head away. After a moment that felt like a lifetime, he pushed himself upright, then stalked to the parlor door, where he turned to me one last time.

"You will never be with Narian. You are, and always will be, mine."

He disappeared into the corridor, leaving me trembling and so weak that I felt I would faint. I stumbled to the sofa and sank upon it, sobbing. I thought of how Narian had once defended me from Steldor's ungentlemanly conduct; he would never have stood by while Steldor treated me in such a manner. It was painful to think of Narian under any circumstances but doubly so in light of my husband's behavior.

I rose to my feet, not wanting to remain in this room alone. I left my quarters and stumbled down the length of the corridor, bowing my head to hide my swollen eyes from the guards and servants I met. I stopped outside my sister's door and knocked, trying not to look at her bodyguard, Halias, and barely able to keep my tears in check.

Miranna appeared in the doorway and, at sight of me, drew me in and closed the door behind me, then wrapped me in her comforting embrace. With an arm around my shoulders, she guided me to the sofa, and we huddled together as my eyes overflowed.

"What happened?" she asked gently.

"He was so angry, Mira," I choked, and I began to tremble.

"Steldor?"

I nodded, sitting upright. "He called me a…a whore."

I struggled to say the word, not understanding how he could have used it, yet knowing that my confessions in Cannan's office must have led him to this belief.

"What?" breathed Miranna, her eyes large and round.

At the thought that everyone else at the meeting might have reached the same conclusion, I hurried to tell Miranna the entire story, beginning with the interrogation I had undergone in the captain's office.

"Miranna, what must everyone think of me? Cannan, Galen, Destari? And Father, he hardly acknowledged me during dinner. Perhaps they, too, think I'm a…" I broke off and buried my face in my hands. "I am so ashamed."

"But Steldor didn't mean it, Alera. He couldn't really think that. It's just—well, we know he has a temper. He'll calm down, and then everything will be all right." Her tone was soothing, and she brushed my hair over my shoulders. "And don't worry about everyone else—not one among them would think that way, I know it."

"But I deceived him. He didn't know until now that I had a relationship with Narian. I don't think he'll ever forgive me." I met her earnest blue eyes, knowing she would not grasp the full meaning of my words. She did not know that I was refusing to let Steldor bed me, that I had led him to believe I was not yet ready to have a physical relationship, when the true reason for my reluctance was that my heart belonged to someone else. I doubted that Steldor would ever get past my betrayal.

"I suppose you did, and Narian's been a sore subject ever since he got the better of Steldor at the tournament last year." Distractedly twirling a strand of strawberry blond hair around the fingers of her left hand, she added, "But I'm sure if you apologize, he will come around. After all, Narian is gone. Steldor can't feel threatened by him anymore."

"He frightens me," I admitted, and she again put her arms around me.

"But he didn't strike you, Alera—even though he was furious, he didn't hit you. I don't think you need to be afraid of him—you saw him at his worst and he didn't lay a hand on you."

I found some solace in her words, for Miranna was right. He had not struck me, although most men probably would have, especially considering that *I* had struck *him*.

I stayed with her for as long as I dared, not wanting to return to my quarters but knowing that I must. When fatigue threatened to immobilize me, I made my way to my rooms, praying I would not encounter Steldor. I didn't think I could withstand another assault, whether verbal or physical. I was relieved to see that his weapons were not hanging on the pegs in the wall next to the fireplace. Though I wondered where he was and when he would be back, in the end all I wanted was to cherish whatever time I had alone.

CHAPTER 3

ROYAL PAINS

I AWOKE THE NEXT DAY FEELING ANXIOUS AND restless, with a strong desire to escape the confines of the palace and the city. The activities of my morning, which consisted of a series of mundane meetings with my household staff, did not improve my mood. The afternoon was even less promising, and I was considering whether I should cancel the remainder of my appointments when my thoughts were interrupted by a knock on my drawing room door. I frowned, certain I had no other business until after lunch. Nonetheless, I bade my visitor enter. To my surprise, Cannan opened the door and came to stand before my desk. I sprang to my feet, and he inclined his head in a respectful yet understated greeting. Unable to meet his gaze, I began to fuss with the papers that were strewn on the wood before me, the disgrace of the previous day haunting me.

"Are you all right, Alera?" Cannan inquired, frank as ever, his dark eyes never leaving my reddening face.

I nodded, struggling to compose myself.

"We should sit," he said, motioning toward the stately, yet decidedly feminine furniture that sat bathed in sunlight on the far side of the room. Cannan stepped aside to permit me around my desk, and I glanced out the bay window into the East Courtyard, certain that the flowers and trees were urging me to escape. As that was not an option, I perched on a rose velvet armchair, dreading whatever the captain had come to say.

He sat on a cream brocade sofa, his dark features and serious demeanor causing me to wonder if I would once again be under interrogation. That thought was quickly followed by the slightly hopeful one that if he had wanted to rebuke me, he would have summoned me to *his* office, rather than coming to mine.

As the seconds passed, I searched for something appropriate to say. Did he want me to express remorse for my crimes? Did he expect me to defend myself? Was he here on my father's behalf? Try as I might, I could think of no reason other than the disastrous meeting that would explain his presence in my drawing room.

It was Cannan who finally opened the conversation.

"I know yesterday was a trying day for you," he said, and I thought I detected a note of sympathy behind his words. Despite this, I fidgeted with the folds of my gown.

"You are no doubt concerned about the reactions of those who attended the meeting. You need not be."

I was dumbfounded by this assertion, for though he had not yet expressed disapproval or accusation, I had been expecting criticism of some sort.

"I don't understand," I managed, certain my ears had tricked me.

"You are the Queen, Alera. The only person to whom you answer is the King."

Still unable to discern his meaning, my thoughts flew unbidden to my father, who had not spoken to me since the meeting. Regret rose as I recalled the disappointment in his eyes.

"But my father..." I ventured, unable to exorcise that last, wretched thought.

"Listen to me," Cannan more firmly stated. "You no longer answer to your father. You are the *Queen,* and that puts you beyond reproach from anyone other than Steldor. Your father is now one of your subjects, and he owes you the same respect as do all Hytanican citizens." He waited for his words to penetrate my brain before continuing. "Everyone has regrets, from peasants to nobility to military officers to kings. You are not exempt simply by virtue of birthright. Hold your head high—there is no need for shame."

Time elapsed in silence. Cannan's advice made sense—however strange it was to think that my status was above my father's—and yet I remained troubled. I had confessed some of my worries to Miranna, but she was not well equipped to advise me, for she did not know Steldor well. Cannan, on the other hand, would be able to offer insight into his son's disposition. The captain watched me patiently, as if knowing there was something else I wished to discuss, and I decided to risk his displeasure by raising the subject.

"Last night, Steldor was so livid that I don't even know how to describe it," I put forth, not wanting to divulge the specifics of my clash with his son. "It felt like...hatred. The intensity of it was frightening."

Cannan nodded, showing no curiosity about what had transpired, providing yet another reason for me to feel beholden to him.

"Steldor is, unfortunately, well-known for his temper. Galen and I expended considerable effort settling him down before he sought you out."

I considered his words, twining my hands together. Was

he really implying that the rant I had endured was a mild version of what it could have been?

"Steldor doesn't hate you, Alera," he said, trying again, now gazing through the window, his manner suggesting that his next words would be more insightful. "My son is a very passionate person, about many things, and when a passionate person is hurt, love can express itself as anger."

Something in the captain's phrasing caught my attention, and it occurred to me that he might be speaking not only of Steldor, but of himself. He had once told me that in his youth, he had been much like his son. I tried to imagine Cannan with the temper, willfulness and ego of my husband, but found it to be as difficult as picturing Steldor with his father's qualities.

"I tell you this so you can better understand him, not in an attempt to excuse any particular conduct. Although to the extent he hurt you, I am confident it was through his words and not by his hand."

I nodded, marveling at how well Cannan knew his son. Relief flowed through me, but there was one last question that I was certain the captain would be able to address, for he had served as a father to Galen in addition to Steldor. Knowing how close the two young men were, I feared that the burgeoning relationship between Galen and I had been irrevocably damaged.

"And what of Galen? Steldor said some things to me that I hope he didn't mean. I can't help but think they are in Galen's mind, as well."

"Contrary to popular belief, Galen and Steldor are not the same person," Cannan said, raising one eyebrow. "When Steldor is angry, he has a tendency to draw the worst conclusions. Galen does not have the same temperament and usually assumes the best of people."

At last I graced my father-in-law with a genuine smile.

"Thank you," I said, more grateful than I could express that he had come to see me.

He rose from his seat and nodded.

"I will let you continue with your day." After taking a few steps toward the door, he turned to offer one last encouraging thought. "I have confidence in you, Alera. You will be good for my son. If you refuse, as you have been, to let him have everything his way, he may even learn a little humility."

Before I could respond, Cannan disappeared into the corridor, leaving me utterly bemused.

I ate a lunch of vegetable soup and bread in my quarters, having declined to join my family in our dining room on the second floor. Although my spirits had improved following my discussion with the captain, I still did not feel ready to face my father, Steldor or Galen. I also thought my parlor would provide a welcome break from prying eyes, as there was a definite buzz about the palace that the King and Queen were not on speaking terms.

After I had finished eating, I left my quarters and returned to my drawing room to slog through the afternoon. I moved quietly down the corridor toward the spiral staircase, not wanting to attract the notice of anyone tarrying at lunch, only to be intercepted by a Palace Guard.

"Your Highness, King Adrik wishes to speak with you. He has asked that you meet him in his parlor on the third floor."

My confidence level, which had been bolstered by Cannan, plummeted along with my stomach. I had anticipated that my father would desire a word or two with me, but could not envision exactly what I might encounter. I needed additional time to collect my thoughts; I needed a chance to dredge up some kind of explanation.

"Kindly inform my father that for the remainder of the day, I shall be occupied with other activities. Tell him I will see him in the morning."

The guard nodded and left to deliver my message. Knowing that my father would be displeased with my response and might decide to seek me out regardless, I hurried back toward my rooms, an escape plan forming in my mind. I addressed the first Palace Guard I met, instructing him to send word to Lanek, Steldor's personal secretary, that I was afflicted with a headache and needed my afternoon schedule cleared. I knew Lanek would also inform Steldor of my condition, which would ensure that he would not try to see me, although I doubted this measure was necessary given his current state of mind. Having freed my day, I sent another servant to the Royal Stables to have my father's favorite mount, a steady and well-trained former cavalry horse, brought to the courtyard gates, readied for riding. While the request to the stable was coming from me, it would not occur to anyone that my father would not be the rider, and I hoped to be well away from the city before anyone could report the unorthodox nature of my activities.

I prepared for my excursion, donning a skirt and a white blouse, and tying my hair at the base of my neck in the style Halias, Miranna's easygoing bodyguard, wore his. It was my intention to imitate a man as well as I could in order to be less conspicuous while out and about mounted on a horse. But now I had a challenge, for no man wore a skirt, and I therefore needed a pair of breeches. Unfortunately, I no longer had the pair I had used when Narian secretly taught me to ride, an activity that was totally inappropriate for a Hytanican woman. I had thrown them in with the servant's laundry to prevent them from being found when my belongings had been transferred to my new quarters, for their discovery would have raised questions and fed palace gossip. I furrowed my brow as I confronted this problem, for I had little time in which to come up with a pair. Believing that Steldor could not possibly become more upset with me, I decided his trousers could meet my needs. With a great breath, I strode to his bedroom door and pushed it open, glimpsing for the first time his inner domain.

I don't know what I expected to find, but what I did see was a fascinating conglomeration, some of the items in keeping with the Steldor I knew and some out of character. The room contained the usual furnishings, albeit masculine in design: an ample four-poster bed; heavy, leather-padded armchairs near the hearth; a sturdy trunk and wardrobe; two large bookcases; and a sidebar topped with goblets and mugs that were often accompanied, I presumed, by flasks of wine and ale. My husband's familiar scent also hung in the air, heavier than it should have been considering how long he had been gone this day. I glanced around and noticed a bowl on the mantel of the fireplace, from which the fragrance seemed to emanate, and realized that the wolf's head talisman he always wore contained the same mixture.

It was the personal aspects of the room that I found intriguing. Contrary to what I knew of his disposition, the style of the furniture was simple, containing none of the usual carvings, and the color that dominated the room was a deep wine—not quite burgundy, not quite red, but somehow subtly warmer and more inviting than those stronger hues. Thick tapestries covered the floor and hung on the walls. Numerous weapons of various types and sizes were mounted above the fireplace, including a collection of daggers. The neatly shelved books were of the expected variety:

weaponry, falconry, military history and military strategy. There was not an item out of order, and yet the room felt relaxed and comfortable.

As I glanced around, I tried to reconcile what I was seeing with the military man I knew Steldor to be and was suddenly struck by the answer. The room, of course, was befitting a man, but also sensuous and elegant, perfectly suited for coaxing a woman into his arms.

I crossed to the wardrobe, rifling through it until I found my husband's breeches. I pulled out a pair and put them on under my skirt, adding one of his belts in the hope of keeping the trousers from falling to my ankles. Scanning his tidy room one last time, I snatched an empty flask, filling it with water from the pitcher that stood on the bedside table and attaching it to my borrowed belt. I left his bedroom, bending my left arm over my abdomen to hide my strange bump. Thus equipped, I summoned my mettle and walked through the corridors to flee the palace, my father and my humiliation.

It wasn't until I reached the courtyard gates that my behavior began to raise eyebrows. The groom holding my father's chestnut gelding was just short of shocked when I took the reins from his hands to lead the animal down the cobblestone thoroughfare that cut through the center of the city. He did not, of course, dare question me, nor did the equally confused Palace Guards who were standing sentry, but I suspected that my behavior would at some point reach the ears of my father, Cannan, Steldor or Galen. Pulling the horse onto a side street in the Market District, I hastily removed my skirt and abandoned it between two shops.

I mounted the large but sedate animal and guided him onto the busy thoroughfare. Although it had been over three months since I had last ridden, it did not take me long to feel at home in the saddle. Without a backward glance, I urged the horse into an easy trot, wanting to put distance between myself and the palace, afraid of pursuit.

The city thrummed with activity as I trotted onward, and I began to enjoy the freedom I had stolen, praying that it would not be short-lived. The May sun made the afternoon pleasantly warm, although I knew it would cool come evening and that I would need to be home before the day was out.

My meager disguise was less than convincing, for I was drawing incredulous stares and a few double takes from passersby, some of whom gave an astonished bow or curtsey to their Queen. As I approached the point of entry into the walled city, I could feel the watchful eyes of the sentries upon me, but again no one dared question me, and I passed unhindered beneath the raised iron gate. I cared not about the reactions of the guards, only about the possibility that they would inform the King, and urged my mount into a canter, a gait I was certain it had not been asked to employ in years.

By this time, I had decided on a destination. I reined the gelding off the thoroughfare onto a narrower road, traveling east toward Baron Koranis's country home, which was about an hour and a half farther at a brisk trot or easy canter. Although London had left to search for Narian ten days previously, I wanted to check the estate myself on the slim chance that he might have returned to his family's property. Koranis had vacated the estate in favor of his manor house in the city when the Cokyrians had begun threatening our borders, and I knew Narian would have the ability to move about his father's lands undetected by our patrols if that were his desire.

While I felt some urgency about reaching my destination, my father's horse clearly did not, refusing to maintain the gait of my choosing, dropping continually down into a rough and uncomfortable trot. In the midst of my frustration in dealing with the stubborn animal, I became aware of the sound of approaching hoofbeats, although it took a moment for my brain to comprehend that a rider was overtaking me. I looked over my shoulder, recognizing the powerful gray steed that was in pursuit, and released a groan, for if Steldor was coming after me himself, he must be angry indeed. Refusing to acknowledge him, I continued down the road, disappointed by how quickly he had caught up to me. I had left the palace barely an hour ago, and already he was upon me.

Steldor rode past me and pulled his charger to an abrupt halt in front of my considerably smaller mount, the stallion half rearing in protest. It had been enjoying the run, and continued tossing its head and flaring its nostrils, indicating its desire to continue. Startled, I tried to move my father's gelding away, but Steldor leaned forward to snatch my reins.

"Release my horse!" I ordered, infuriated with him and wary of both the large, energetic beast and its rider.

"No," Steldor snapped. "You're coming back with me."

Gripping my reins, he permitted his stallion to move forward in the direction of the city, my mount obediently following. Unwilling to give in to him, I slid from my horse's back.

"I don't think I will return just yet, Your Majesty."

With an exasperated sigh, he dismounted and strode toward me. As he did, he took in my preposterous appearance.

"What *are* you doing?" he demanded, stopping in his tracks. "You're out in the middle of nowhere, by yourself, dressed like a man and riding your father's horse! Have you gone *mad,* woman?" He continued to scrutinize me, and his incredulity transformed itself into a frown. "And just where did you get the belt and breeches?" As realization struck, he sarcastically added, "Just my luck that you would decide to get into my trousers when I wasn't there to enjoy it."

My cheeks burned at his crude comment, and had I been a little closer, I would likely have dealt him a second slap. At the same time, I knew his assessment was accurate.

"I was just going for a ride. I have the right to some fresh air," I asserted, hands upon my hips.

Steldor gave a short, scathing laugh. "Not like this you don't. Now get on your horse."

Incensed by his dictatorial tone, I turned away without a thought as to how he might react, and set off once more on my original course, not bothered in the least that I was leaving my means of transportation behind. It wasn't long before I heard his boots scraping against the rocky surface of the road, and the back of my neck prickled in alarm. Before I could think how best to handle him, he stepped in front of me to block my path.

"You *will* return with me," he growled, jaw set.

"No, I will *not!*"

He ran both hands through his hair, and I thought that he might bellow in frustration. Then he stepped forward and wrapped an arm about my waist, pulling me to him. With a scowl, he threw me over his shoulder and carried me toward the horses.

"Put me down!" I shrieked, struggling fiercely, but he did not even acknowledge me. Although I knew I could not break free, I continued to shout and kick my legs, then resorted to hitting him on the back with my fists to cause him as much discomfort as possible.

When we reached the horses, he thrust me into his saddle, then released me to mount himself. Taking advantage of his small lapse, I swung my left leg over the stallion's withers in an attempt to slide off the opposite side. Unfortunately, Steldor was quick to swing onto the horse's back, and he caught me with an arm across my chest. Desperate to get away from him, I tucked my chin and sank my teeth into his forearm, biting down hard.

He cried out in pain, dropping me at once. I landed in an undignified heap upon the ground, then triumphantly scrambled to my feet, looking up at my husband, who was examining his wound in disbelief. I seemed to have rendered him speechless, and it occurred to me that I had twice in the past day and a half caused him an injury. With blood trickling down his arm, he glowered at me, almost trembling with rage, eventually finding his voice and its volume.

"Fine!" he yelled, so loudly that my father's languid horse jumped to life and shied away. "Stay out here! But I'm taking the horses, so you can either get on your bloody animal right now, or you can walk back!"

"It's a delightful day for a stroll!" I retorted, making known my choice, whether or not it was a wise one. I did not wait for him to respond but marched off in the direction of Koranis's estate. I didn't look back but heard Steldor's horse whinny in excitement at again being allowed to run, and my father's horse noisily object as it lumbered along behind.

The distance separating me from my destination was longer than I remembered, but then, the previous trips had been in a buggy, requiring no physical exertion on my part. On this day, my father's horse had taken me a little less than half the distance to Koranis's estate; now that I was on foot, I estimated that it would take me roughly three hours to complete the journey. It was absurd, however, to think that

I would be able to maintain a consistent pace or that I would not need to rest. Nonetheless, I had made my decision and so continued resolutely onward. I would not give Steldor the satisfaction of knowing he had ruined my outing, nor would I return to the palace in ignominious defeat.

As I walked, the ground seemed to become harder and more painful to tread upon, and my legs felt the strain of the exercise. With a humorless chuckle, I realized how poorly suited for this activity were both my thin leather shoes and my body. An hour had passed, and already I wanted to lie down on the road and wait for a farmhand to collect me and return me to the city. But I was quite certain that no one would be out in this part of Hytanica, for the threat of the Cokyrians at our borders had led to planting only those fields within a safe distance of the city. To my right and left were croplands that had been abandoned by field hands, the last of whom I had seen on the road long ago. My only hope was that Steldor would send someone after me, but that was a feeble hope at best. I had left him infuriated and bleeding, and the idea that he would be forgiving enough to send a guard to find me was comical.

I kept on trudging, limbs becoming heavier as the minutes went by and several times needing to quench my burning thirst. I praised my own good sense at having brought along a water flask but was now wishing I had brought some food, as well. My stomach grumbled unhappily every so often, but I had no choice other than to ignore it.

Thankfully, the day was not particularly hot, for the spring sun was less intense than it would become in June and July; at the same time, it would grow colder when the day's warmth dissipated in the evening. I was wary of what would happen then, for I had brought no cloak. With a sigh of relief, I remembered that there would be blankets and food stores inside Koranis's home.

I continued for another hour before I again stopped to revive beneath a large, shady tree along the roadside, leaning back against its trunk. I closed my eyes and pressed my hand against my hot, damp forehead, unable to recall the last time I had perspired in such a fashion. My legs ached, and I rubbed them to relieve their stiffness, with poor results.

After about fifteen minutes, I stood and resumed my journey. I believed I would make it to the estate before dusk, but did not want to waste time, not fully trusting my instincts as to how much distance I had yet to cover. My anxiety had been growing with the lengthening shadows, for it was too late to turn back to the secure and friendly city. Trying not to think, I focused on the ground as it moved beneath my feet.

I was enormously relieved when at last I glanced up and saw Koranis's two-story country home taking shape before me. It looked strangely lifeless in its unoccupied state, and the unkempt grounds had an air of desolation about them, but it represented comfort and safety. I was drained of energy, my shoes were tattered and my feet throbbed with every step, my stomach was protesting loudly and my water flask had dried up half an hour ago.

The walk had taken me a good hour longer than I had anticipated, and I stumbled up the path to the front door of the house with an air of wretchedness quite unlike anything I had ever before experienced. I tried the door handle only to discover it was locked, and a strangled cry escaped me. Resisting the urge to collapse then and there, I limped around to the back entrance to find that it also was closed tight. I wrenched at the door, but it would not budge, and I finally leaned against it, giving in to tears. I had been certain that my trials would end once I had reached my goal. Feeling lost and alone, I sank down on the back steps, burying my face in my arms, knowing my crying would serve no purpose other than to vent my despair, for there was no one around to hear me or help me.

I was not aware of the passage of time until the dryness of my throat made me long for a drink and I raised my head to see the purplish blue of evening spreading across the sky. I would have to go soon if I wanted to fill my flask from the river, for darkness would shortly cover the land. After that, I would return to the house, trusting that Steldor would not be so vindictive as to leave me out here through the night.

Despite the tenderness of my legs and feet, I made my way down the sloping hill atop which the home sat to the edge of the forest, where I spotted the path that I had trekked many times with Semari, Miranna and occasionally Narian. I followed the winding trail, now and then stumbling over a tree root hidden by the shadows, until I emerged into the narrow clearing that bordered the Recorah. I hurried to kneel at the river's edge and splashed some of the refreshing liquid into my mouth and over my face to wash away the remnants of sweat and grime, finally drinking from my cupped hands. The water was cold, and after refilling my flask, I sat down and dipped my swollen feet, ragged shoes and all, into its swirling eddies. I immediately felt the pull of the current, surprised by its force even near the Recorah's bank, but the chill brought welcome relief.

The air was losing its warmth with the setting of the sun, and a shiver ran down my back. I knew I should return to the house but could not bring myself to do so, for the memories I found in this place were too strong to ignore. I gazed downriver and saw the spot where Narian had rescued me after my fall into the raging water last summer, pulling me into his arms for the first time. My throat tightened, and I bit my lip to suppress the emotions that were rising inside me. I stood and gingerly walked to the boulders, then hoisted myself atop their craggy surfaces, maintaining a safe distance from the water. Narian would not be here to save me if I fell.

I looked across the Recorah, the rushing and crashing sounds of the mighty river as it tumbled over rocks and broken branches filling my ears. The thinning trees on the opposite bank looked like eerie sentinels in the dwindling light of day, and beyond them, some distance away, I could make out Cokyrian campfires. It was strange to be close enough to see where Hytanica's adversaries ate and slept and watched, awaiting the right moment to strike. The thought that I might be in peril this near to enemy lines flashed through my mind, but the evening was tranquil and it seemed to me that the Cokyrians were enjoying a night of peace.

A noise from the woods at my back startled me, and my sense of security fell away. It was just an animal, I assured myself, only to realize that wild animals presented risk. While I had not spent much time in the forest, I knew that wild boar and bear lived within it. What if an animal attacked me? My instinct was to scoot farther back on the boulder, but I was wary of meeting the river, which was probably more treacherous than whatever foe might be lurking among the trees. When the sound did not repeat itself, I began to relax, only to remember that I needed to walk through those woods to return to the baron's house.

I scrambled down from the boulders to begin my hike back through the forest, finding it much more challenging in the dim light to spot the path. I faltered, reluctant to walk among the looming trees, each of their trunks thicker around than was I and many times as tall, but I could not stay the night without shelter or defense on the banks of the Recorah. With no other choice, I began the trek back to the baron's home, feeling as if the forest was closing in, tightening a net of darkness around me.

As I walked, every noise—the rustle of a branch, the hoot of an owl—sent my pulse racing. I persevered, fear now amplifying the sounds of the night, but though I was moving cautiously lest I fall on the uneven footing, I was making good progress. Just when it seemed that more moonlight was penetrating the gloom, a sign that the trees were beginning to thin, a hand clamped tightly over my mouth. Unable to breathe, unable to scream, with icy terror solidifying the blood in my veins, I fell back against a muscular chest. Then cold steel depressed the tender skin of my neck.

CHAPTER 4

WITHOUT GUARDS

"YOU HAVE TEN SECONDS TO TELL ME WHAT you're doing here," a man snarled into my ear, removing his hand from my mouth to grasp my upper arm.

With death but the slip of a blade away and the gruesome image of my own blood spilling down my chest foremost in my mind, I squeezed words through my constricted throat.

"I—I'm lost," I gasped. "Please, please don't hurt me!"

For one horrifying moment, all was still. Then I felt the dagger lift away from my throat.

"Alera?"

The man's voice was laced with disbelief, but I was too frightened to care. I desperately attempted to pull away, not yet processing that he knew my name. Reaching for me with his other hand, he turned me around.

"Please, I beg of you, let me go," I pleaded, suddenly not only in fear for my life. I cast wildly about, not wanting to see the face of my captor.

"Alera, look at me."

This time when he said my name, his voice compelled me to stop struggling. Mustering my courage, I glanced up to see unkempt silvery bangs framing familiar eyes—eyes that even in the darkness I knew were indigo—and I collapsed against him, light-headed with relief.

The man who had been my bodyguard for most of my life lifted me into his arms and carried me out of the trees and up the hill. I laid my head against his shoulder, enormously grateful to be in his company, for with him I was safe. When we reached the house, he set me on the ground with my back against one of the walls, and a shiver ran through me, which did not pass his notice.

"Put this on," he said, removing his leather jerkin and draping it around my shoulders. The familiar garment, which he wore over a white shirt, was warm from his body, and I nestled into it, comforted by its feel as well as its scent. It smelled of leather, the woods and the smoke of campfires; in short, it smelled like London.

"Eat this," he tersely continued, placing something in my hand that he had taken from the pouch at his belt.

My stomach rumbled at the thought of food, and I shoved whatever he had given me into my mouth. It was chewy and dry, obviously something soldiers carried with them, but I cared not.

"I want you to wait here." London's voice was hushed, but firm. "I'll only be gone a couple of minutes."

I nodded, too worn-out to respond. He studied me, unusually hesitant, then dropped to one knee in front of me. He withdrew a dagger from his boot, pressing it into my hand. With a brief but reassuring touch of my cheek, he walked away along the length of the house to my right, examining the structure. I heard the shattering of glass as he struck a window with the hilt of one of the twin blades that he wore sheathed at his sides, and then he disappeared from view.

While I waited for the Elite Guard to return, fear again crept into my bones. Why had London given me a weapon? Was I truly in peril out here by myself? Needing a distraction, I squinted through the darkness to examine my feet. My shoes were almost destroyed, and my partially exposed skin was red with blisters and from the cold. I leaned my head against the house, sickened by my foolishness, hoping that London would soon come back. I almost jumped up to flee at the touch of his hand on my shoulder, for whether due to my fatigue or his training as a scout, I had not heard him approach.

"Can you walk, or do you need assistance?" he asked, kneeling once more beside me and glancing at the remnants of my shoes.

"Where're we going?" I said, unable to control the slight slur in my speech.

Without further attempt at conversation, London picked me up, correctly interpreting my difficulty with words as exhaustion, and walked around to the front of the house.

He opened the door, evidently having unlocked it from the inside, and carried me to a comfortable armchair in the parlor. I glanced about at the furnishings, for although it was dark, the room was well-known to me. I longed for a servant to bring the tea that was so oft served within its walls. London once more left me, returning a short time later with a blanket from one of the bedrooms.

"You'll be safer in here than outside," he explained, wrapping the blanket around me. "I'm going back into the woods to retrieve my horse."

He went to the archway that separated the parlor from the entrance hall, then looked back at me.

"Keep that dagger with you, just in case…."

I closed my eyes, planning to rest for just a few minutes,

only to be roused by London gently shaking me awake. He took the dagger from my hand and replaced it in his boot, then pulled me into his arms, bearing me out the front door to his horse as I struggled to orient myself. He hoisted me into the saddle, blanket and all, and swung up behind me just as Steldor had done such a seemingly long time ago.

Taking the reins, he muttered, "As soon as we're out of here, you have some explaining to do." He dug his heels into the mare's sides, sending her off at an urgent canter, and I was thrust back against him.

We stayed away from the roads, skirting the edge of the forest to approach the city in a roundabout fashion. I didn't say a word, not even when London turned our mount into the woods and up a rather steep hill, the athletic animal dodging around trees that came out of nowhere in the thick darkness. When the ground began to flatten, he reined in the mare, and I saw a deeply recessed cavity in the rock before us. With a jolt I realized that we had ridden into the foothills of the Niñeyre Mountain Range, a place I had never been allowed to venture, in part because I was a woman and in part because the enemy claimed the high desert area to the north and east of our borders. Despite the rocky terrain and the southerly flowing Recorah River that separated us from Cokyri, my cautious father had never permitted my sister and me to explore this part of our kingdom.

London slid from the horse's back, landing soundlessly on the forest floor, then held out his hands to me. Not wanting to appear helpless, I shook my head and dismounted by myself. I instantly regretted my decision; the moment my battered feet met the hard earth I grimaced in pain, grinding my teeth to keep from crying out.

My former bodyguard secured his horse near the mouth of the hollowed-out area and motioned for me to go ahead, then disappeared from view to return with an armful of dry wood. Bringing it into the center of our shelter, he used his flint and steel to make a comforting fire. There wasn't much room in our refuge, just enough for two people, but I didn't mind, for the fire's light and pleasant warmth were captured within the cozy space.

London and I now sat opposite each other, the flickering flames reflected in his keen eyes, and I pulled the blanket tighter around my shoulders as though to ward off the questions I knew were forthcoming.

"Do you want to tell me what you're doing out here?" he finally asked, his tone gentle, as if he were worried that he might frighten me.

"I walked," I croaked, my words catching in my dry throat.

He stood to retrieve a flask from his saddlebag and tossed it to me. I caught it and took a drink, then scrunched up my nose at the taste of the liquid.

"It's wine," he said, catching my expression. "It will revive you and ease your soreness."

I nodded and took another sip, watching him return to his position across the fire from me. He waited until I had drunk a bit more, then pressed for additional information.

"You walked? From where?"

"From where Steldor took my horse."

Though I had slept some in Koranis's home and had drifted in and out of awareness while we had been riding, I still had little energy to devote to speech. London frowned in confusion.

"Where are your guards?"

"I didn't take any."

"Were you and Steldor out riding together?" he persisted, disapproval creeping into his voice.

"No," I responded, beginning to realize that Steldor was not the only one at fault for my predicament. "I left by myself and he came after me."

"And he took your horse."

"I didn't want to go back, and he got angry with me," I said woefully, wanting the Elite Guard to sympathize and lay the blame on Steldor. He did not.

"And why did you leave the palace in the first place?"

I hung my head, unable to meet London's eyes, and hoping against hope that he wouldn't come to the answer on his own. There was a silence, and I could feel him studying me.

"I understand what this is about," he finally scoffed.

I glanced up to see that he had risen to his feet, too irritated to remain in place.

"You left the palace because of some ridiculous notion that Narian might be at his father's estate."

I averted my gaze, making no attempt to deny his assertion, and he shook his head in exasperation.

"Didn't it occur to you that I would already have searched there? Your longing to find Narian could have gotten you killed! You know better than this, Alera. You've had a bodyguard your entire life. How could you have left without one?"

He ran his hand through his silver hair, and I wasn't entirely certain his next question was directed at me.

"How can we end up with the *Queen,* on her own, in the woods, cold, hungry, scared, with no protection, and only the river separating her from the Cokyrians?"

He laughed, albeit mirthlessly, and I cringed. I had been holding Steldor responsible, but, in retrospect, I had behaved just as rashly as had he. I felt foolish and embarrassed at having assumed I would not be in harm's way. Was I really so desperately naïve? Or was London exaggerating the danger to make an impression on me?

London walked partway around the fire and stopped, his arms crossed over his chest, decidedly displeased. As if he had read my mind, he began to answer my questions.

"Do you have any idea how lucky you are that *I* found you? Most soldiers wouldn't have given you ten seconds—they would have slit your throat without hesitation. And do you honestly believe that while you were sitting on those boulders observing the enemy that they couldn't also see you? Any of their archers could have pierced you through the heart where you sat. Or the Cokyrians could have sent someone to find you, in which case our Queen would now be in their hands."

He continued, making a sweeping motion around our shelter with his arm. "I brought you here because I'm not convinced they failed to see you. And even if you didn't attract the enemy's attention, you would have spent a miserable night with no shelter and no ability to defend yourself. You could have been attacked by an animal, you could have fallen in the river as you did once before, you could have gotten lost!"

I hated how annoyed he was with me but couldn't help noticing how much he sounded like an overwrought parent. That thought threatened to pull up the corners of my mouth, and I bit my lip, knowing that a smile would be absolutely inappropriate under these circumstances. London appeared to be done scolding, but the furrow in his brow told me there was something else he wanted to say. I waited, the shifting shadows cast by the flames playing over his form, giving him an eerie appearance, and he dropped to one knee beside me.

"Listen to me, Alera. Whatever romantic fantasies you

harbor about Narian can never come true. You are a married woman, and Narian is the enemy."

These last words cut me deeply. Hearing it said so matter-of-factly was like having the breath knocked out of me. *Narian is the enemy* repeated in my head, and I recognized for the first time that I was the only one who wanted Narian to return out of a desire for his company and not just because it would be detrimental to our kingdom for him to end up among the enemy.

"I couldn't find him," London said, bringing me back to reality. "But the Cokyrians probably will."

London's dark prediction was still ringing in my ears a half hour later as he doused the fire, satisfied that I was warm and sufficiently restored to enable us to set out again. He did not want to wait until morning to journey back to the city, certain that someone would have noticed my absence, whether or not Steldor had been forthcoming.

We traveled quickly, although it was another two hours before we reached the city, as the route of London's choosing continued to avoid the main thoroughfare. I again slept off and on, secure in the arms of my rescuer. I woke as London brought his horse down to a walk before the gate that restricted access to the city. The massive barrier, which stood open during the day to provide passage in and out, had been lowered, and Cannan's standing order was that it not be lifted until sunrise.

"Halt and identify yourself!" One of the sentries hailed us, hand upon his sword, but then a guard in the tower recognized my companion.

"London!" he shouted, and immediately the message that the deputy captain was back swept through the soldiers on duty. Upon seeing me, the tower guard followed with an additional exclamation. "Queen Alera!"

Recovering from his surprise, the man called for the gate to be raised, for despite Cannan's orders, he would not deny entry to the Queen or to an Elite Guard who was just below the captain in rank. As soon as the barrier was high enough for us to pass underneath, London urged his mount forward into an easy canter, a gait that would normally have been unsafe to employ on such a well-traveled street. The thoroughfare, however, was virtually deserted.

"London, what is the hour?" I inquired, for I had lost track of time completely.

"Just after midnight."

We skirted the Business District, which lay to the east, occasionally hearing loud laughter or singing emanating from a pub, or catching sight of a drunken patron staggering home. The closer we came to the palace, however, the more it quieted, until the clacking of our horse's hooves on the cobblestone was the only sound cutting through the night.

I leaned against the Elite Guard, closing my eyes and allowing myself to imagine I was with Narian, remembering the first time he had come to my balcony to steal me away from the palace. We had ridden together through the quiet streets on that beautiful winter's night, then talked until morning in the Royal Stables, and I had never felt so content with someone or so safe.

I had become so enraptured in my vision that I was disoriented when London brought his horse to a halt and assisted me to the ground. We were not at the palace; instead, the stables loomed before us. At first I was bewildered by this, then surmised there would have been no groom to take charge of the horse had we ridden to the courtyard gates. I waited while London tended to his mount, then walked with him to the front of the palace estate, trying to ignore my throbbing feet, unwilling to request that he carry me.

As we approached the gated entrance into the courtyard, we were hailed by the Palace Guards who stood sentry, but like the City Guards before them, they recognized us and hastened to admit us.

"King Steldor will be relieved you are safe, Your Majesty," one of the men remarked. "He has patrols out searching for you."

London led me forward, and in the light of the torches illuminating the gateway I saw him cock a cynical eyebrow. I was still too tired to display any type of reaction, although inside I seethed.

We walked up the white stone pathway through the Central Courtyard, and I thought the lilac hedges on either side of us had never smelled so sweet. The Palace Guards at the front doors pushed them open for us, and I stepped at last into the light and warmth of the Grand Entry Hall, enormously relieved to be home.

Galen and two of his men stood toward the back of the entryway near the antechamber, speaking in urgent tones. There was little activity in the palace at this hour which allowed their words to easily carry.

"Shouldn't the captain be informed, sir? Surely he—"

"Are you suggesting a breach of the King's specific orders?"

"No, sir."

"Good. Besides, I believe the captain will have gone home by now and I should not like to be the one to rouse him from bed."

It was clear from Galen's words that Steldor had not informed his father that I was alone outside the city, my whereabouts unknown.

"Queen Alera!"

Galen's head snapped around at the call of my name by

one of the guards with whom he was conferring. Worry visibly drained from the sergeant's face, and the tension left his stance as he realized that I was indeed home.

"Thank God." Galen's words were hardly more than an exhale, a quick prayer born of relief. He reflexively moved toward me, but stopped to bark an order to his men.

"Notify the King at once, and then resume your usual duties."

Returning his attention to me, Galen took in my fatigued and disheveled appearance.

"Are you all right?"

To my surprise as well as Galen's, London stepped in front of me. "Is she all right? Let's think. She's just spent hours roaming the countryside, hungry, parched, cold, lonely, scared that she'd never find her way home again, or that the Cokyrians just across the river would come over for some pleasant conversation, but yes, I think she's perfectly fine, don't you?"

Galen was speechless, but he was saved from stuttering out a response by Cannan, who emerged through the guardroom that opened onto his office, presumably having been disturbed by the commotion.

"What is going on out here?" the captain demanded, and although Galen was plainly startled that his commanding officer was still in the palace, he took a step toward him, as if seeking protection from London's wrath.

At that moment, the antechamber doors were pulled open, and Steldor strode into our midst.

"Ask your son," London spat in answer to Cannan's query, tilting his head in the King's direction, displaying his typical lack of regard for protocol or authority.

Cannan turned to Steldor. "What is this about?"

The King stopped in his tracks but did not otherwise react

to finding the captain in the entry; neither did he address the question.

"Oh, Father," he said, with a slightly contrived chuckle. "I didn't know you were here."

"I've been talking with some of my battalion commanders," Cannan volunteered, ignoring for the moment his son's evasive response.

"You needn't have come to investigate," Steldor continued, proceeding toward me. "Everything is well in hand. No need to interrupt your meeting."

Cannan caught Steldor's arm as his son made to pass him by.

"My men can wait until I get an answer to my question."

"And what question was that?" Steldor asked, voice honey sweet and innocent, an attitude belied by his irreverent smirk.

There was silence as the two men stared at each other, a matched pair with hair so dark it was almost black, and deep brown eyes, although Steldor's features otherwise resembled those of his beautiful mother. Galen was on edge, while London, who was leaning against the wall with his arms crossed over his chest, was relishing the voiceless battle of wills. The Palace Guards who stood sentry tried not to look at their King and their captain, never having witnessed father and son at odds, but I could not seem to focus anywhere else, riveted by the confrontation taking place before me.

When Steldor's sly smile had at last faded, Cannan spoke, drawing his son closer, his voice low and ominous.

"Do not play games with me, Your Highness."

Steldor had until this point been matching Cannan's glare, but now his eyes flicked away, showing his wariness of his father.

"Fine," he muttered, disgruntled yet obedient. "Will you let go of me?"

"Very well," the captain said, releasing his son. "Now answer me."

It seemed unnatural for Steldor to be so subdued, and I could tell he did not appreciate that his father was getting the better of him. A slight flush had crept up his neck, but whether this was an indication of embarrassment or anger I could not ascertain.

"Alera left the city. When I went after her, she refused to come back with me. I sent men to find her, but she's only just returned with London."

"And did she leave on foot?" Cannan queried sardonically, taking in my manner of dress along with the remnants of leather that had once been my shoes, and I suspected he had already worked out what his son had done.

"No," Steldor muttered.

"Then what happened to her transportation?" Cannan's tone was terrifyingly controlled, every syllable enunciated perfectly.

"She took King Adrik's horse, and I…I brought it back with me."

The words left Steldor's mouth slowly, as if reluctant to condemn, and Cannan turned to address the Palace Guards who stood sentry.

"Step into the courtyard until I send for you."

The guards departed, caught between wanting to witness the looming altercation and running away from it, but not having a choice either way. After the door had closed behind the men, Cannan stepped to within a foot of his son, and I imagined that it was taking all of Steldor's strength of will not to flee. The captain, always an imposing figure, was particularly fierce, his mounting anger visible in the tightening of his muscles. He seemed to grow taller and darker as the seconds passed. I had only once before seen him like this—when Narian's father, the Baron Koranis, had demanded that his son be removed from the country estate that I had just visited.

"Am I to understand," Cannan said, his voice rumbling with the spine-chilling quality of distant thunder, "that the Queen left the city, *without guards,* the King pursued her, *without guards,* the King then abandoned her, *without guards,* and without a horse, and didn't feel the need to inform the Captain of the Guard, who is charged with the protection of both the King and Queen?"

"Yes, sir," Steldor replied, with hesitant honesty.

"Do you have *any* idea how much danger you put Alera in—you put yourself in? The Cokyrians are pressing our borders—"

Steldor interrupted him with a haughty laugh, surprising me with his audacity. "Surely you know by now that I can take care of myself. I was never in any danger."

Cannan's reply was swift and merciless. "Need I show you the graves of the hundreds of Hytanican soldiers who could *also* take care of themselves? You're not *God,* Steldor. I took an oath to protect you with my life, and I don't want to die defending your arrogance!"

The captain's words echoed in the vast entrance hall, and Steldor bowed his head, attempting no rejoinder.

"It's one thing to compromise your own safety," Cannan continued, dropping his volume, although his tone was no less severe, and I understood that he was reprimanding Steldor not as a father but as the captain charged with his and my defense. "But you put our Queen at the mercy of countless dangers, including that of the Cokyrians! She does not appreciate the risks posed by leaving the city, but you know better than to desert her."

For a moment, it appeared the fight had been won, and Cannan took a step back, presumably to return to his office. But he did not do so, and I wondered if he was anticipating a response from his son.

"Well, what was I supposed to do?" Steldor suddenly shouted, gesturing with his hands in frustration, and I realized that the captain had moved to avoid being hit. "What you've said doesn't change the fact that she *wouldn't* come back with me! Should I have knocked her out or tied her to the horse? She is the most stubborn, most aggravating, most *exasperating* woman I have ever met!"

"That's irrelevant," Cannan contended, without so much as a blink of an eye. "When you were unable to convince her to return, you should have sent guards to protect her. *Immediately,* not several hours later. And you should not have gone after her in the first place without guards to accompany you."

Cannan waited for this to register, and when Steldor attempted no further defense, the captain seemed ready to return to his meeting.

"I've kept my battalion commanders waiting long enough. London, you will come with me." He motioned to the Elite Guard, who pushed off the wall and moved toward the guardroom, for once obeying an order. Then Cannan turned to the Sergeant at Arms.

"Galen, repost your guards. And send one of your men to notify the Royal Physician that the Queen needs tending."

Galen nodded, crossing to the front doors and stepping outside while Cannan addressed his son one last time.

"Steldor, you need to talk with your wife."

I studied my husband from across the entryway as the

captain returned to his office, but he was looking away from me, infuriated, I suspected, with everyone and everything. Guilt nagged at me, though I would have thought seeing Steldor reprimanded would give me pleasure. London had impressed upon me how equally blameworthy I was, but the captain hadn't taken my actions into account. *She does not appreciate the risks posed by leaving the city, but you know better than to desert her.* I did not believe myself to be as ill-informed as did Cannan, and knew full well that, though Steldor had been unreasonable in stranding me, he had expected me to walk back to the city. It had been my obstinacy that had led me to walk all the way to Koranis's estate and practically into the enemy's camp. Steldor was shouldering full responsibility for a dangerous situation that I had helped to create.

Galen reentered, followed by his Palace Guards, who took up their posts on either side of the large double doors. The sergeant then disappeared into the guardroom to send a man to rouse the doctor who attended the royal family.

I faced Steldor, hesitant to talk for fear of igniting his rage, all the while feeling the stares of the sentries upon my back. It seemed, however, that if I did not speak, no one would. I was scrambling to formulate the appropriate words when Galen rejoined us, looking ill at ease. He crossed the entryway, apparently to go home for the night.

"Wait," Steldor bid him, interrupting his friend's exit. "I'm going with you."

Galen nodded and waited by the doors, although he glanced at me as if trying to determine whether he should offer some assistance. In the end, he did not, and the two friends departed, leaving me standing quite dismally alone under the curious eyes of the Palace Guards. Dragging the blanket London had given me, I hobbled up the Grand Staircase in as dignified a manner as I could manage, hoping the doctor would have something more effective than wine to treat my wounds.

CHAPTER 5

THE QUEEN

IT WAS MIDMORNING THE NEXT DAY BEFORE I forced myself out of bed. Sahdienne had prepared a bath, for I had been too exhausted in the aftermath of my misadventures to manage more than a quick wash. I stepped into the warm water, mind replaying all that had happened the previous day. My trials hardly seemed real anymore, but the soreness of my muscles and the tenderness of my feet were reminders that it had been no dream. I soaked in the water, relaxing, until my thoughts went to my morning and I began to fret about the engagements I had missed.

Sahdienne had gone to the bustling kitchens on the first floor, where food was always ready to meet the erratic schedules of the guards, to request that a meal be delivered to me in the tea room in an hour. When she returned, she helped me to dress and applied the salve the doctor had brought for my blistered skin, then enclosed my feet in soft slippers. As my stomach rumbled in an embarrassing fashion, she styled my hair into a single plait down my back. She scrutinized me one last time, then gave me a message.

"The Captain of the Guard stopped by earlier, Your

Highness, before you were awake. He said not to disturb you, but to tell you when you rose that he'd cleared your schedule for the morning."

"Thank you," I said in amazement, wondering how it was that Cannan, one of the busiest men in the kingdom, especially now that we were at war, had the time to worry about modifying the Queen's schedule. I was greatly touched that he had thought to do so and again pondered the contradiction he presented. The strong, intelligent and decisive military commander was respected by everyone and feared by most, yet he had several times shown himself to be more sensitive and caring than my own father or, for that matter, any of the other men in my life. It was strange now to think that I had once been afraid of him.

Ready for the day, I descended the spiral staircase to the first floor, then turned right down the corridor, too preoccupied to glance at the multicolored stone floor or the intricate tapestries that adorned the walls. I entered the tea room and sat at the table nearest the bay window, letting the sunlight warm me through the glass. I did not have long to wait before a servant brought in a plate of food, the delicious aroma reawakening the gnawing in my stomach. My self-restraint greatly challenged, I forced myself to wait until she had departed before attacking the meat pie she had set in front of me. I had a few bites left when the door opened again, and I raised my head to see who was joining me. I stiffened at sight of my father and set down my tableware, feeling as though I had consumed the proverbial last meal of the condemned.

He stood to the right of the door, his hands behind his back, his eyes devoid of their usual sparkle. It felt as if a wintry wind had swept in behind him, and the sun that still shone on the back of my neck seemed to have lost its heat. I had forgotten my promise to see him this morning, which by itself would have cast me in disfavor, but that indiscretion became insignificant in light of my other misdeeds. I held no hope that he did not know what I had done the day before, for any display as public as the one in the entry hall last night would have set the palace gossips buzzing. I stood and moved around the table, trying to prepare myself for the onslaught.

"Alera," my father said, his voice rich with displeasure, "you have shamed me greatly."

I shifted, unable to meet his eyes. I could tell from his manner that had I been younger and unmarried, my offenses would have merited a whipping.

"I had intended to speak with you about your relationship with Koranis's son, but now it appears there are additional egregious matters to address."

He had started pacing across the front of the room, and the fingers of his left hand went automatically to the third finger of his right as if to twist the royal ring that had for years encircled it but that now belonged to Steldor.

"You promised me once that your affection for Narian was purely the fondness of a friend, but I see now that you lied to me. Your dishonesty has hurt me, Alera, and your childishness is hurting the kingdom. Steldor has every right to be furious with you, especially following yesterday's *frolics.* I feared that as a queen you would distract your husband from his duties, and you have done so several times already. You have deceived and embarrassed him, and you have deceived and embarrassed me."

His words stung, and I attempted an apology.

"I don't know what to—"

"It would be considerate of you not to interrupt me," he

said sharply, turning toward me and holding up his hand. "I have no patience for excuses or fabrications."

My mouth clamped shut, and indignation flared at the implication that I was being rude. I had not viewed myself as interrupting him when I'd spoken.

"I do not understand how this happened," my father persisted, resuming his pacing and punctuating his words with his hands as he became more and more engrossed in his speech. "You were raised properly and purposefully, yet your behavior is no better than I would expect of a peasant. You were taught your place, yet you do not keep to it. You know the standards to which you must conform to be a fitting queen, but you refuse to adhere to them." He pulled up short and gazed sternly at me. "I am *appalled* by your affair with the Cokyrian boy."

Indignation was transforming itself into anger at my father's reference to Narian as "the Cokyrian boy." Still, I did not let it show.

"You met with him in secret, without my permission, and I'm certain, without a chaperone, all of which is unacceptable behavior for any young woman in the nobility, let alone a member of the royal family. I had hoped that by the time you were crowned Queen, you would have grown up enough to meet your obligations, but a *queen* does not dress like a man, steal her father's horse and disobey her husband.

"This cannot continue, Alera. Your actions have shamed me, dishonored the King and disgraced the kingdom. I would not fault Steldor for taking you in hand. Nor would I object if he locked you away until you can conform to behavior befitting his wife."

As he uttered his final sentences, I glared at him. The fury building within me seemed to have a life of its own; it felt as if a phantom being was rising, pounding against every pore of my body, clamoring to be released. My father's condemning words echoed in my mind, only to be supplanted by Cannan's: *You are the Queen, Alera. You no longer answer to your father.*

Our identical dark eyes locked together, and I straightened my spine, then words came out of my mouth that, for once, suited the circumstances perfectly.

"If you feel ashamed, perhaps it is because of your own foolhardiness and not due to mine."

My father's eyebrows rose in astonishment. "Do not speak to your father in such a manner!"

"Do not speak to your *Queen* in such a manner!"

The former King was struck dumb, my passion a wall with which he had unexpectedly and painfully collided.

"You have the *gall* to come to me and say that I am immature, that I have disappointed you and that I am incompetent, when it was *you* who were too selfish to allow me additional time before taking the throne, *you* who would not hear that any man I loved could be a suitable king and *you* who pressured me into a marriage for which I was not prepared. All these things for which you are chastising me are of *your* design. I would not have met secretly with Narian had I thought you would accept him. I would not be an inept queen had you not charged me with the throne. And I would not be a distraction to Steldor had you not trapped me into being his wife."

I had crossed the room to my father, who stood with his mouth open as if he desired to argue, to defend himself, but was unable to conjure words.

"I wish, perhaps more than you, that you had given these decisions further thought," I bitingly added. "But I am now your Queen, and *you* will show *me* proper respect. You will never address me in this way again."

His stunned eyes met mine, and I waited a moment while he stuttered incomprehensibly. Then I stepped around him and left the room.

That evening, I waited for Steldor in the parlor we shared, passing the time curled up in one of the leather armchairs with a book of poetry. My husband had missed dinner—along with my father, amusingly enough—and had not yet come to our rooms for the night, though the hour was late, even for him. I knew he was in the palace, for I had seen an oddly pale Galen once or twice throughout the day, and had the King been absent from his duties, the whispers of the servants would have been impossible to suppress. Instead, rumors were circulating to the effect that the sergeant suffered from a self-inflicted malady, although I was not certain what that meant.

I soon found myself reading without comprehension, my thoughts wandering while my eyes continued to scan the pages of the book. I'd been experiencing a strange sense of liberation in the aftermath of the quarrel with my father, for I was free of his judgments and therefore free of his expectations. This notion had bolstered my confidence to the point where I was willing to contend with Steldor in the hope of settling things between us.

In the past hour or so, however, doubt had begun its assault. My father was currently avoiding me, but he resided in the palace, and I would see him nearly every day. What would our relationship be? We would be on civil terms; I was not concerned about that. But would we ever be *friendly* toward one another again? Had I changed things irreversibly? And if I had, was that necessarily something to bemoan?

I laid aside my book, trying to concentrate on the matter

at hand—what to say to Steldor when—if—he returned. It was possible he had either gone with Galen for the second night in a row or was waiting to come to our quarters until he was certain I'd gone to bed. In either case, he surely didn't want to talk to me. Considering his recent fits of rage, perhaps it would be wise to stay out of his way.

As if on cue, Steldor quietly came in—so quietly, in fact, that I was not aware of him until he cleared his throat. I started from my pensive trance and looked to the doorway where he was smirking at me, and I felt like a child who'd been caught daydreaming while her studies awaited her. But when he stepped out of the shadows and into the lantern light, I noticed the abnormal pallor of his skin, tinged gray as if in sickness. He fell heavily onto the sofa, stretching out atop it, his hands clasped behind his head. I was unable to read his mood but thought he could not be feeling well.

"Are you all right?" I inquired.

"I've been better."

"You missed dinner. Perhaps I could get you—"

"Not hungry."

I paused, not certain how to proceed, then my eyes fell upon the jug of ale on the table in front of the sofa.

"Maybe some ale would help," I suggested, wishing he would humor me in some way and tell me what was wrong.

"Ale is most *definitely* not what I need," he pronounced. Before I could make sense of this statement, he asked, "Why were you waiting up for me?"

"To talk to you," I answered, honesty seeming the best course.

"Ah."

I began to understand that this conversation would be mostly one-sided.

"I want to apologize," I continued, swallowing the lump that had risen in my throat, "for several things."

"Apology accepted. You're forgiven."

I frowned, twining my hands together in my lap.

"I haven't even said what I'm apologizing for!" I protested.

He winced and put a hand to his forehead in reaction to my raised voice. As he did, his right shirtsleeve slipped to his elbow, and I caught sight of a bandage wrapped around his forearm.

"You have my attention," he groaned, motioning with his arm in my general direction. "There's no need to be shrill. By all means, explain."

I decided to start at the beginning, hoping I sounded more confident than I felt.

"I'm sorry I didn't tell you about my feelings for Narian. It was wrong of me to keep that from you."

I was hesitant to broach this particular topic, even though I knew it was probably the most important one, but Steldor did not react; rather, he seemed content to simply listen. Courage bolstered, I forged ahead.

"I'm sorry for leaving the palace without telling anyone and for not taking guards. I'm sorry for being unreasonable and refusing to come back with you, and..." I grimaced as a pang of remorse shot through me. "I'm sorry I bit you."

Still Steldor was silent, only now I found it unnerving instead of emboldening. Nevertheless, I persisted.

"And I'm terribly sorry that, due to my obstinacy—" I struggled to avoid blatantly stating that he had been scolded by the captain, finally settling upon "—you and your father had a disagreement."

I was again met with silence and wondered if he had fallen asleep. With a sigh, I rose to go into my bedroom, but his subdued voice arrested my movement.

"You're forgiven," he said, repeating the words, only this time with conviction.

I smiled slightly, then proceeded to my room, not naïve enough to expect a reciprocal apology from him.

"Alera," he said, stopping me, and I turned to see that he had pushed himself into a sitting position, his brown eyes sincere. "In the future, if you would tell me before you leave…"

He paused awkwardly, and I realized that when dealing with women, he was used to charming them, commanding them or ignoring them. I doubted he had ever before employed such a respectful tone to make a request from someone of my gender. In fact, to my knowledge, Steldor had never faltered in speech in his entire lifetime. Something about his unexpected vulnerability melted my heart, his youthful, handsome features made doubly so by the absence of a haughty expression.

"I promise," I said, allowing his sentence to remain unfinished. He again fell back on the sofa, and I stepped into my bedroom, for once having affectionate feelings toward my husband.

Three weeks remained until we would host the celebration for Miranna's birthday, and during that time our lives fell into something of a pattern. When I awoke, I would breakfast in my quarters, proceed to the Royal Chapel for morning prayer and meet with the household staff in my drawing room. When necessary, I would also meet with the palace scribes to arrange for letters, invitations or announcements to be written and dispatched. In the afternoons, I would meet with visitors or host a small palace function, such as a tea party, then do as I wished—go shopping, walk in the garden, read, work on my embroidery or spend time with my sister or mother. I would share the evening meal with my family, my father having finally regained pride enough to sit at the same table with me, although Steldor was always too busy to join us, a fact my parents found baffling. Apparently during my father's reign, the King had never been so consistently occupied. Whether this was a sign that Steldor was inventing excuses to avoid me or that my thickly built father had simply been more devoted to the consumption of food, I could not be certain. I would retire shortly thereafter, to begin the same routine with the rising of the sun.

I knew little of Steldor's daily activities, except that he kept exceedingly irregular hours. He sometimes came to our rooms in midevening to change clothes, only to leave again without a word, never returning before I went to bed and yet already departed when I rose in the morning. At other times, he would not return at all at the close of day, and I would instead hear him enter to change clothes at sunrise, then immediately depart to undertake his duties, as if neglecting to sleep for nights on end were the most natural thing in the world. I saw little of him, and we spoke fleetingly at best when our paths did cross.

Despite our minimal contact, his testiness toward me had noticeably increased since his tender response to my apology—it had begun to seem that, for every nice or sensitive action Steldor took toward me, he felt the need to compensate with a turn for the worse. Needless to say, such fickle behavior did not increase my desire for his company, and he likewise did not, for the time being, seem to yearn for mine. I wondered if he was this variable in temperament with everyone or if he reserved it for me.

Just a few days before Miranna's birthday, I visited my favorite retreat, the garden that extended from the rear of the palace to the northern section of the walled city. At this time of year, the flowers filled the air with a rich fragrance, while the elm, oak, chestnut and mulberry trees offered cooling shade. I walked along one of the footpaths that divided the garden into four sections, listening to the chirping of the birds and letting my mind wander. I stopped to examine one of the four double-tiered marble fountains, its splashing water sparkling in the sunlight, almost hypnotizing in its sound and motion. I became lost in thought, oblivious to my surroundings, until a voice pulled me from my reverie.

"There you are!" Miranna cried, springing down the garden path toward me, looking cheerful. When she reached me, she took my arm and pulled me toward the palace, speaking so quickly that it took all my concentration to understand her.

"I've been searching everywhere for you, Alera! I just spoke to Father, and he hinted that he's going to make an announcement at my birthday dinner. I hardly dare hope, but I think I know what it will be, in which case this is one birthday I'll never forget!"

I didn't bother trying to persuade her to confide her suspicions, for she would tell me if she wanted me to know. Given her enthusiasm, however, it was easy to guess it involved Lord Temerson, the shy young man in whom she had been interested for almost a year.

She led me all the way to her quarters, rambling about the need to choose the perfect gown, how her hair had to be styled impeccably and how she needed to decide on both of these aspects before a tiara could even be considered. Her cheeks were flushed, and her blue eyes danced while she recounted her worries to me. I was amused as she flew about her bedroom, her strawberry blond curls bouncing every which way. She was probably the only person in the entire kingdom who ever thought she could look anything short of beautiful.

After we had sorted through her wardrobe three times, I managed to convince her one of her newest gowns would be most fitting, and it wasn't by chance that the dress I picked went well with only one of her tiaras. The decision about hairstyle would have to wait, as Ryla, the personal maid I had recently hired for her, would be assisting with that aspect of her preparations.

Though Miranna continued to waver over her choices, she was more satisfied than she had been, and we moved into her parlor, where I sat upon her sofa while she settled into an adjacent armchair.

"I don't know how I'll make it until the party," she said, unable to sit still and twirling a strand of hair around her fingers with such earnestness that I feared for her scalp. "I haven't seen Temerson in five weeks! Can you believe it? It feels like five years!"

"The Military Academy has been keeping him busy then?" I asked, though I knew that was the impediment. The school year ran from the beginning of November through the end of June, and the only reason Miranna had been able to see Temerson five weeks previously was because of my wedding. It was odd to think that the wedding might have been Miranna's had I foregone my claim to the throne and refused to marry Steldor, and it was heartbreaking to imagine the effect it would have had on Temerson. He would have had to stand by while the woman of his dreams became the wife of a man who had always outranked, intimidated and eclipsed him, and whom he undoubtedly viewed as more deserving of her companionship than was he.

I wondered if Narian, wherever he was, knew that I had married Steldor. If he did, what must he think of me? I had given Narian my heart but had then pledged myself to a man he knew me to detest, and from whom he'd assured me I could escape. While Narian had been the one to depart, I believed he had good reason and would return to Hytanica when he could. Why hadn't I waited for him? At the very least, he would be disappointed in me; at worst, he might not want to return, unable to bear my betrayal. In the end, if Narian ever did come back, what he thought of me would not matter. I could never be with him, for my marriage vows would eternally divide us.

Miranna had continued to chat away about her "dearest," as she now referred to Temerson, and had not noticed that my mind had wandered. I tried to push my bleak thoughts aside, not wanting my frame of mind to affect hers.

"But the thirtieth of June marks the end of the schooling year," Miranna happily babbled. "Then we'll have the whole summer together!" She stopped playing with her hair, and a touch of anxiety entered her voice. "You do think he'll want to spend it with me, don't you?"

"I have no doubt he'll want to spend every free moment he has with you."

"You're right, of course," she agreed, with a blush. "He's hopelessly in love with me."

"Well, *someone's* hopelessly in love," I said with a laugh.

She sank back in the armchair, face shining with joy, spinning her fantasies out loud.

"Wouldn't it be wonderful? Marrying Temerson, having a beautiful wedding—as beautiful as yours! And then we'd have children, lots of them, and they'd all be beautiful, too, and look just like him." She paused, frowning a little. "Except for one. One will look like me. One can look like me, right?"

"Yes, one can look like you."

"Oh, Alera," she gushed, leaning toward me. "What will *your* children look like? You're lovely, and with Steldor as their father..."

She trailed off, imagining my future offspring with a dreamy expression, but I went red, knowing that the way things were, it would be a very long time before there would be an heir in the offing.

She caught the change in my expression, and her eyes grew wide, drawing a conclusion I did not expect.

"Alera, are you...are you pregnant?"

"Certainly not!" I blurted, a little too vigorously, revealing how appalled I was at the idea.

Miranna sat up, the tiniest bit startled by my reaction, and I tried to smooth it over with a more acceptable response.

"I'm not pregnant, not...not yet."

"Something's wrong, Alera. Is he not treating you well?"

"No, nothing like that. Everything's fine, really." I tried to keep my voice light, although the color in my cheeks was refusing to wane.

"Is this about Narian?" she asked, moving to sit next to me on the sofa, the concern in her eyes making me squirm.

"Steldor's not upset about that anymore," I said, averting my gaze, for the problem was with me, not my husband. "I just don't think I'm the wife he envisioned."

"But you *are* the wife he envisioned," Miranna insisted. She sat in silence for a moment, contemplating me, then her skin flushed to match mine. "You are *acting* as a wife, I mean in every way, are you not?"

I was disconcerted by her boldness, but my lack of denial was answer enough.

"You aren't! Oh, my, you aren't!"

I put a finger to my lips, glancing toward the door, not

wanting that piece of information to hit the palace gossip mill, and her voice dropped to a whisper.

"Alera, what can you be thinking? It's his right, and it—it's your obligation as a married woman!"

I stared at the rug, extraordinarily uncomfortable, knowing that no reason I could give would justify my refusal.

"And he hasn't…he hasn't *forced* you?"

"No," I said, my voice trembling as she raised one of my greatest fears. My next words served more to convince myself than to explain his actions. "He loves me. He wants me to be willing, and…he has never raised a hand to me."

"But he can't just be…" My sister was having difficulty completing any sentence, and our flaming cheeks seemed to be heating up the room. "He can't just…not *ever!* A man has…needs." I knew from her expression that another shocking idea had come into her head. "What if there's another woman?"

"Mira, hush!" I admonished, praying there were no inquisitive guards or servants in the hall outside. "There isn't another woman, don't be ridiculous! He wouldn't…"

But my declaration was lost as the notion sank in. Would he?

I thought of the unusual hours Steldor kept. There was no denying the possibility; and the only way I could stop him was to let him bed me instead. So those were my choices: to continue to refuse him, sending him into the arms of a mistress and disgracing myself when the inevitable rumors began to circulate; or to let him bed me, to *touch* me and believe that he *owned* me, an idea I found so revolting it made me feel sick.

"Perhaps…perhaps I should go," I mumbled, mortified by my own situation. We stood, and Miranna clasped my hand.

"Alera, I'll always be here for you, whatever happens. You

know that." She hesitated, then finished, "But your life is with Steldor now, and that's not going to change. I think he could be a good husband, but you…you have to let him."

She blushed again, then led me to the door. Feeling drained, I stepped into the corridor to walk back to my quarters, aware that Miranna's eyes were still upon me. I quickened my pace in a false show of composure, and only when I heard the click of the latch behind me did I succumb to the dreariness that made my heart and limbs heavy. I continued down the hallway, past the library, with my eyes downcast, not wanting to talk to anyone. So immersed was I in my misery that I recoiled at the sound of a male voice emanating from just a few paces in front of me.

"I know feet are fascinating, Alera, but it's much more sensible to pay attention to where you're going."

Steldor stood outside the door to our quarters wearing a cocky and irritating grin, and for the thousandth time that day, I felt myself turning crimson. I stared at him, struggling for a witty rejoinder but unable to produce one.

"Did you want something, my lord?" I finally asked, forcing a smile that felt like a grimace.

"I simply wanted to see my beautiful wife," he said, countenance still smug, although his eyes had softened and I suspected the compliment was sincere. "Your sister's party is in three days, and I took the liberty of having a gown made for you for the occasion. You'll wear it with your gold-and-pearl tiara, and your hair down, as you know I prefer it that way. The seamstress will bring it tonight for the final fitting. Obviously you need to be here."

I gaped at him, stunned that he would have commissioned a gown for me without even consulting me. Had he considered that I might already have something in mind to wear? No. Had he sought my opinion on the appearance of the garment? No. I could feel my ire growing, but before I could reprove him, he brushed past me, continuing down the corridor without a hitch in his stride.

When the seamstress came to my bedroom that evening, the gown she carried with her was like none I'd ever before seen. I had always worn the finest fabrics and most stylish designs that money could provide, but never had I felt as rich and lovely as when I donned the garment for which my husband had made special arrangements.

I guessed from the way the woman nervously drummed the tips of her fingers together that Steldor had personally guided the gown's creation, which meant that his taste was extraordinary. He would have specified the ivory silk of the skirt and bodice, the gold trim and the sleeves that were tight unto my elbows before draping like beautiful bells over my wrists. The fabric barely graced my shoulders, settling almost scandalously low across my bosom. But instead of being improper, it achieved a look that was daring and new, yet quite elegant. It was an ideal fit, gently skimming the curves of my body, then flaring out to sweep the floor. The only thing it lacked was a necklace. When I mentioned this to Sahdienne, she rushed into the parlor to retrieve a box that contained a distinctive gold chain that drew about the hollow of my throat, and from which short strings of pearls hung at intervals over my collarbone.

"His Highness left it for you, my lady," Sahdienne explained, eyes shining with admiration for my spouse. I moved to sit at my dressing table so she could add the finishing touch, crowning me with my gold-and-pearl tiara.

"Your Majesty..." Sahdienne sighed, enchanted by my appearance. "I don't believe I've seen a lovelier gown in all my life. The King is a remarkable man indeed."

She began to fuss with the items on my dressing table,

straightening what did not need to be straightened, flustered by her forward remark.

"That he is," I concurred, with a note of bitterness I could not disguise.

I walked with the seamstress through the parlor, dismissing her with my genuine thanks and assurance that her work was exemplary, then marched back into my bedroom.

"I'm terribly sorry to have upset you, Your Highness," Sahdienne said, obviously believing herself at fault for my crossness. "I was too familiar before."

"Oh, hush, you're not to blame for my bad humor. The King can take credit for that. Now help me out of this dress."

Sahdienne obeyed, muttering additional apologies, then left me alone to examine the gorgeous gown that was laid out upon my bed. I would not wear it. I could not wear it. Suddenly remembering the necklace, I removed it none too gently from around my neck. Even I could not deny that these were magnificent gifts, but they came at a price. This was Steldor's way of gaining dominion over me. If I consented to put on that gown to attend my sister's birthday, he would expect something in return, believing he had won our odd little game. And I certainly could not permit that.

CHAPTER 6

BOYS AND MEN

ON THE NIGHT OF MIRANNA'S DINNER PARTY, I put on a white chemise with long, billowing sleeves underneath a sky-blue dress with a front-laced bodice. It was less formal than the gown Steldor had commissioned for me but attractive nonetheless. Most important, it was as far from ivory and gold as I could get, and so was bound to clash with Steldor's attire, whatever it might be. I glanced slyly at my reflection in the mirror above my dressing table, delighted not only with my gown, but with my hair, artfully transformed into a bouquet of curls at the back of my head and crowned with a silver-and-diamond tiara.

Thoroughly satisfied, I left my bedroom and stepped into the parlor to find Steldor sitting on the sofa, his feet, in freshly shined black boots, crossed at the ankles and resting on the low sofa table. His eyebrows lifted at sight of me, but I met his gaze tenaciously, daring him to challenge my choices.

"Darling," he said. "What have you been doing all this time if not getting ready for your sister's dinner?"

"I am ready to meet our guests whenever you are," I

replied, tone cordial yet firm. I moved across the room to stand beside the door, and Steldor came to his feet, bemused.

"You're not wearing *that,*" he informed me.

"Yes, I am."

"No, you're not."

"Yes, I am."

"You'll look ridiculous."

"I beg your pardon?" I said, affronted.

"There's nothing wrong with your dress, or the way it fits you," he clarified with a roll of his eyes, as if he were explaining the obvious to a simpleton. "But it just won't do."

"And why not?"

"Your attire doesn't complement mine at all."

This was entirely accurate and pleased me greatly. He wore black pants and an ivory shirt under a fitted gold-and-emerald-green doublet, an ensemble that made him appear annoyingly godlike, but which was very near horrendous next to sky blue.

"Then our garb will complement our personalities," I retorted.

He sighed and ran a hand through his dark hair. "Go change."

"I will not." My hands were on my hips, my jaw set.

"Think of it this way, Alera," he began, and I could tell from the glint in his eyes that his next words would be manipulative. "Everyone will assume that you planned our clothing for the evening and that you intended for us to look well together. If we go as is, you will be held accountable for this atrocious misdemeanor against the laws of fashion. On the other hand, if you change into the gown that I provided, I will defer to you, and you will be admired for your magnificent taste. The choice is yours. Either way, I will be faultless. So ask yourself, would you rather take credit for an eyesore or for a work of art?"

His speech complete, he sank onto the sofa, stretching his arms out across its back, a grin spreading across his face. I had not thought this through, that much was evident, but now that I had commenced it, I would not give in to him.

"You could change. More easily than could I."

"True," he acknowledged with a chuckle. "But I look perfect."

"Well, I'm sure you could look perfect in something else."

"Oh, doubtless, but why duplicate what is perfect when one could improve what is not?"

I wanted to kill him. I wanted to close that infuriatingly divine mouth once and for all, and if ending his life were the way to do it, I was willing to take that step. Instead, I took a deep breath and tried again.

"If I change, my hair will be ruined."

"You know, dear, something really should be done about your hair in any case. I told you to wear it down. And mind you switch tiaras."

"We're almost late as it is," I blustered, trying to keep my tone civil, though inside I was burning. "You could change more quickly."

"Not necessarily. You already know the gown into which you will change. I would have to search for something less elegant to match the dress you have on, but still formal enough for the occasion. And honestly, have you ever seen me in anything that might go with *sky blue?*"

I fell silent, for as much as I hated to admit it, he had a valid argument. He generally wore dark or rich colors, nothing similar to my gown. I despised myself for what I was about to do.

"I'll wait," Steldor said, accurately reading my expression.

I stormed back into my bedroom and donned the gold-and-ivory gown, which I was adamant I must detest despite its unparalleled beauty. I clasped the gold-and-pearl chain about my neck and almost brutally let my hair down, jamming the tiara of Steldor's choice onto my head. Then I marched through the parlor and out the door without waiting for him.

I quickened my pace in the corridors, reaching the landing of the Grand Staircase well ahead of Steldor. Recognizing—though I was not on good terms with the knowledge—that the Queen could not waltz into a royal function without the King, I waited irascibly for him. He sauntered after me, pleased at having been the victor in our trivial argument. His attitude changed when he reached me, however, and he extended his arm with a winning smile, slipping on his characteristic charm like someone else would slip on a cloak.

Scowling in return, I tucked my hand into the crook of his elbow, permitting him to guide me down the stairs and to the first-floor dining room, where our guests had already gathered. Lanek awaited us and, at Steldor's nod, stepped into the room to announce our arrival.

"All hail King Steldor and his Queen, the Lady Alera."

I surveyed the small group of guests who bowed or curtsied before us. While I was accustomed to this show of respect, it felt strange for my parents and my sister to be among the crowd. Steldor did not seem to share my discomfort.

Lanek excused himself, and my husband and I moved into the room. Tadark, who had been standing with London next to the doors through which we had just entered, hopped after Steldor, while London stayed in place, arms crossed over his chest, back against the wall. It was customary at these kinds of engagements to devote one Elite Guard to each member of the royal family, even though the possibility of danger was nigh on nonexistent. London was, of course, assigned to me, and I could only assume that Cannan had been feeling vindictive when he'd attached Tadark to Steldor. The baby-faced guard tended to be clingy, overtalkative and rather excitable, despite his self-proclaimed dedication to duty. In short, if trouble brewed, it was far more likely Steldor would end up protecting Tadark than the other way around; if all remained tranquil, the annoying guard was likely to drive Steldor mad. Elite Guards had also been assigned to the rest of my family, with Destari and Orsiett, who had at one time been Miranna's secondary bodyguard, serving my father and mother, and Halias, as always, shadowing my sister.

The lords stood next to the farthest of the double marble fireplaces that served the room, while their wives chatted a few feet from them. My sister and the younger guests were huddled in front of the large bay window that granted a view of the West Courtyard.

My parents were the first to approach to greet us, my father warmly addressing Steldor but offering only a nod to me, my mother dividing her attention between us. Steldor cast me a quizzical glance as the former King stepped away, but I ignored it, concentrating on my mother's lilting voice instead.

"I'm very proud of the way you have adjusted to your new role, darling," she said, apparently oblivious to my recent eyebrow-raising activities. She reached out to stroke my hair, although I suspected her gesture of affection was a way to tame an independent lock without embarrassing me, for I had not glanced in the mirror after adjusting my hairstyle.

"And I commend you on your choice of clothing. You have not always had patience for fashion, but you and Steldor look splendid tonight, and your gown is simply exquisite. You make a stunning couple."

My mother had made the assumption Steldor had known she would, but I couldn't bring myself to acknowledge the compliment. She looked at me, slightly baffled, and Steldor spoke up in my place.

"Alera really does have impeccable taste," he agreed with a slight smirk meant just for me.

My mother moved on, and we continued to offer a few words to our other guests in turn. The men would talk with Steldor, and the women would pay me generous compliments. Although I would not admit it, Steldor had been right to insist on a change in my clothing and was being rather gentlemanly by allowing me to accept the praise.

When the area around us began to clear, Baroness Faramay rushed to her son, leaving Cannan to follow at a normal pace.

"Oh, Steldor, my angel, just look at you," she exclaimed, reaching to unnecessarily straighten the collar of his shirt. Her chocolate-brown curls fell across her shoulders, accenting the arrestingly beautiful features and radiant smile that she had in common with her son.

"Hello, Mother," Steldor replied, a drawl of resignation in his voice. He crossed his arms, his fingers gripping his biceps.

"I haven't seen you since the coronation," Faramay continued, adoration for her only child shining in her blue eyes. "And I do miss you so. I wish you would find time to visit. Surely your wife doesn't deserve all of your attention."

She threw a petulant glance in my direction, and I wasn't certain if I should be offended or amused. Was she jealous of me? The very idea was absurd.

"Actually, Mother, *running the kingdom* has been deserving

of my attention," Steldor said, and this time the bite in his tone was palpable.

Faramay extended a hand to brush the hair from Steldor's forehead, but he jerked away.

"Don't," he snapped.

Cannan came to his wife's side at that moment, acknowledging me with a brief inclination of his head before placing an arm around her waist.

"Faramay, I think you've talked with the boy long enough," he said, attempting to escort her elsewhere, but she ignored him and turned once more to Steldor.

"Come now, love, don't be cross," she implored, laying a delicate hand upon his chest. "You know I don't have a head for politics."

"Yes, of course. I forgive you. Just go."

"But kitten..."

"Mother, everything's fine, but Alera and I have more guests to greet. Perhaps I'll have a chance to speak with you later."

Faramay acquiesced with a sigh and placed her arm around Cannan's. Before they walked away, Steldor shot his father a disgruntled look, as though the captain had broken some agreement by allowing her to come near. Cannan responded with an almost imperceptible shrug, and I pondered what could cause Faramay to behave so obsessively toward Steldor. With a wave of empathy, I recalled that Steldor's younger brother had been snatched from his crib and murdered by the Cokyrians, enough to make any mother overprotective. Still, her pandering seemed excessive, for her remaining son was no longer a little boy in need of her care.

Steldor's charismatic attitude returned as Galen guided his companion, Lady Tiersia, to us. Steldor's cousins, Lady

Dahnath and Lady Shaselle, daughters of Cannan's brother, Lord Baelic, and his wife, Lady Lania, trailed closely behind.

Galen greeted me with a kiss on the hand, then he and Steldor fell into good-natured bickering, while the young women gossiped about recent happenings in the kingdom. Shaselle, bearing a close resemblance to her mother with hazel eyes and thick, straight brown hair, kept inching closer to the young men, apparently finding her cousin and his best friend more interesting than the rest of us. Tiersia's soft green eyes also flicked with frequency in the same direction, although for quite a different reason—Galen looked quite handsome in an amber-colored doublet. I was thankful to find that Dahnath, Shaselle's studious, auburn-haired older sister, had no more interest in the men than did I, and we conversed enjoyably for several minutes.

Miranna flounced over with Temerson and Semari in tow, attired in the iridescent pale blue gown we'd chosen. It seemed to float as she moved and was cut with a more daring bodice than was typical for her, another reminder that she was growing up. Her hair had begun the evening meticulously styled but was now coming loose, its coiling tresses framing her delicate features; somehow, though, her golden tiara mounted with shimmering opals remained in place. I greeted Miranna and her best friend with a kiss on the cheek, while Steldor clapped Temerson on the back so heartily that the poor boy took a stumbling step forward. My sister, excited almost beyond reason, easily became the center of attention as she chatted incessantly until it was time for dinner to be served.

When we moved to the linen-covered table, Steldor, as the King, took his seat at the head, with me on his left and Galen on his right. As the rest of the company took their places, I looked to where my father sat at the far end of the table across from Baron Koranis and his wife, Baroness Alantonya, Semari's parents, an arrangement I favored, for it placed him as far away from me as possible.

Throughout the meal, Steldor was a perfect gentleman, charming our guests with his quick wit. I spoke little, giving the impression of a polite but reserved Queen and, I thought dryly, of a biddable wife. My mother smiled at me often, perhaps convinced that I had taken her advice to *give in to fate* and was, therefore, content in my role, even if I was not happy. As dinner drew to a close, my father caught Steldor's eye, then stood at the King's nod to make an announcement.

"My good friends." He beamed, glancing around the table. "Many of you are my family, by blood or by marriage. Others I have known for so long that should justice be done, you would be counted among their numbers."

At this, Koranis straightened in his chair, as though he and his family had just made an impressive rise in status.

"It is with high spirits on this nineteenth day of June that I announce our hope and intention to welcome the remaining guests into our family. Lieutenant Garrek and I have spoken, and I have granted permission for young Lord Temerson to court my daughter, Princess Miranna."

Miranna gave an unladylike squeal that I would have mimicked had we been in a less formal setting. She quickly covered her mouth, her cheeks turning pink, but the rest of us forgave her lapse in manners in light of the joy in her eyes. She turned to Temerson, meeting his bashful gaze with a brilliant smile, and relief flooded his face, as though he'd been unsure how she would react to this development.

I was delighted for the blissful couple, but there was an undertone to my emotion that took a moment for me to identify, a pang of what could only be envy. London had once told me that the way Narian and I looked at each other made it obvious that we were in love, and I now understood what he had meant.

"Shall we adjourn to the garden?" Steldor asked, rising to his feet.

The mid-June evening was warm but with a refreshing breeze. Steldor extended his arm to escort me, and though simple courtesy dictated he do so, I had the impression that our earlier disagreement was behind us. Before I could assent, however, Faramay came over to clutch at his arm.

"I thought we might walk together, darling," she chirped. "That is, of course, if the Queen doesn't mind."

Somewhat wary of the consequences that might result from denying this besotted mother access to her son, I acceded with an apologetic glance at Steldor. He smiled wryly, succumbing to the inevitable.

I scanned the room, feeling rather lost without the King to escort me, and saw Cannan and Baelic in conversation with each other. My attention was captured by the sight, for the usually stern Captain of the Guard was laughing and joking with his much more affable younger brother. Cannan glanced up at that moment, probably searching for his wife, and his expression soured when he spotted her with Steldor. He pointed this out to Baelic, who patted Cannan on the shoulder with a hearty laugh, muttering something that made his older brother roll his eyes for the second time that evening. To my chagrin, they caught my stare, and I hastily shifted my attention elsewhere.

A moment or two passed before I heard someone approach, and I looked up to see Baelic, dark as the other men in his family, offering me his arm and his friendly grin.

"Unlike the rest of us, Steldor's mother is having some difficulty letting him go," he said puckishly. "May I escort you in his stead?"

"Yes, thank you," I replied, surprised but not disappointed. I had guessed that one of the gentlemanly brothers would come to accompany me but had expected it to be Cannan. Instead, Cannan was with Lania, Baelic's wife, who seemed to be quite content in his company.

I took Baelic's arm and we followed after the others toward the rear of the palace and the garden. As we walked, my new uncle leaned closer to me.

"I have heard from a very reliable source that you on occasion enjoy horseback riding," he confided.

I smiled uneasily, wondering what he intended by this comment.

"Don't jump to conclusions, Your Highness," he chided. "I'm the cavalry officer, remember? I could get you an entire herd of horses, if that were your desire, right under Cannan's and Steldor's noses."

"What are you suggesting?" I queried, caught between skepticism and mirth.

"I simply wish to make it known that, though my dear nephew and my darling brother are trapped within traditional minds, I often go riding with Shaselle and my son, Celdrid. We would be most honored to have the Queen join us someday."

"Shaselle rides?" I asked, my eyes widening at the thought of tasting forbidden fruit, but also curious about his daughter.

"Yes, Lania and I often wonder if she wasn't meant to be a boy." Baelic drew me off to one side of the back entry to finish the discussion before we exited the palace. "Lania hates it that I indulge her, but I'd go mad if someone tried to keep me from riding, so I can't refuse my own daughter."

"She must adore you," I said, for I was feeling giddy at his generous and highly irregular offer. Few men would have been tolerant enough, or interested enough, to provide a daughter with the opportunity he so casually gave to Shaselle.

"She's closer to me than she is to her mother," he allowed. Then his crooked grin signaled a return to the topic with which he had begun. "All you have to do is send word, and you'll be in the saddle—without my nephew in pursuit."

He winked, and I suspected that Cannan, who obviously had a close relationship with his brother, had relayed to him the tale of my horseback riding misadventure. I could hardly be annoyed that my father-in-law had passed the information along to my uncle, considering the result. It also occurred to me that this could be my chance to take advantage of the gift Baelic had extended on my wedding day—his readiness to tell me those things about Steldor that even Cannan didn't know.

"Thank you. Be assured that I will call upon you."

"I will wait breathlessly to hear from you," he teased, motioning me across the threshold and into the garden. With a slight bow, he finished, "If you will grant me leave, I should like to continue antagonizing my brother."

"By all means," I said, laughing out loud, and he went to join Cannan, my father, Koranis and Garrek, who stood a short distance down the path to my right, enjoying the spicy mulled wine that had been served.

The older women had again come together and were likewise enjoying the wine and some pleasant conversation. Down the path that lay ahead of me, Galen, Steldor, Temerson and the young ladies had come together. Steldor's bodyguard for the evening, Tadark, was hanging off his elbow, while Halias more discreetly maintained a polite distance from my sister. Temerson was looking rather dejected; I supposed he'd assumed that once he was courting Miranna,

Steldor would stop toying with her affections, but such was not the case. Galen, too, was flirting shamelessly, and all the young ladies were giggling at their witticisms. Although I knew Temerson had won my sister's heart, doubt nagged at me as to his ability to fulfill the role of her husband, for I did not know if he would ever be able to hold his own among such company.

Finding the prospect of enduring my husband's popularity unappealing, I chose to join my mother, Faramay, Alantonya, Lania and Lady Tanda, who was Lieutenant Garrek's wife and Temerson's mother. I soon regretted my decision, for their topic of conversation was one with which I was not comfortable, but it was too late to turn back without seeming rude.

"Koranis absolutely forbids that we speak his name," Baroness Alantonya was confiding as I neared, sounding sad and worried. "It's worse than before he returned, when we believed him to be dead. But I cannot act like we never had another son, and the knowledge that he's alive somewhere eats at me, and… Your Highness."

Alantonya trailed off as she took note of me, and she dropped into a generous curtsey. The other women did the same, although Faramay's eyes constantly flicked toward Steldor. She appeared to be monitoring his every movement, providing me with a further understanding of Steldor's reaction to her.

"Perhaps Alera could offer you some reassurance," my mother said, picking up the thread of their conversation, and clearly ignorant of my true relationship with Alantonya's eldest son. "She was good friends with Narian, and may be able to ease your mind."

Alantonya's hopeful azure eyes wrenched my heart, and I struggled to maintain a collected front. I didn't want to have to talk of Narian in this company; my lingering feelings for him made it painful to utter his name. Yet I could not ignore the agony on the baroness's face that was so similar to my own.

"Narian… I don't know why Narian left, or where he went," I managed, and her expression faded into disappointment. "But I believe he may yet return to Hytanica—at least we know he hasn't gone to Cokyri. If it's any consolation, he always spoke kindly of you, and I'm certain he knows that you care for him, wherever he is."

My words, unenlightening though they were, seemed to soothe her, and she thanked me wholeheartedly before addressing another of her concerns.

"Koranis also won't permit us to visit our country estate. He says it is too near the Cokyrian border. I realize there may be some danger, but I'm worried the estate will be looted. You remember the raids from the last time we were at war, and it is so close to the river…"

"It is best to keep your family safe," advised Lady Tanda. For the first time, I noticed the resemblance between mother and son, as her hair was just slightly darker than Temerson's cinnamon-brown, and their warm brown eyes were a match.

"Oh, yes, of course. And I am grateful that we have our home within the city. But I had to leave behind some items that are dear to me and would like to send someone after them." Alantonya was fretfully playing with her wedding band. "But Koranis won't allow anyone to return, not even a servant boy. I have no way of knowing how our property is faring, or even if the danger to it is real."

"London was there recently," I revealed, omitting that I had been there, too. "I'll call him over—he may be able to offer reassurance."

I turned, not noticing that something in the air had

changed, and motioned to my indigo-eyed bodyguard, who was leaning against the wall of the palace with his arms crossed, as was his bent. He straightened and began to move toward me, then came to a halt. I cocked my head and frowned, confused by his manner; my frown deepened into a scowl when he shook his head and returned to his position against the wall. I continued to stare at him, unable to believe he would disobey me, but he steadfastly refused to meet my gaze.

"I'm sorry," I said to Alantonya, turning to address her. "I don't know why he's acting like this."

"It's not important, Your Highness," she said, contradicting her earlier statements.

"Of…course," I concurred, baffled by the change in her attitude as well as by London's unusual behavior. I glanced at the other women in the circle: at Faramay, who still seemed to have no interest in anything aside from her son; at Lania, Baelic's wife, who stared at her sister-in-law in irritation; at my mother, whose hand lay gently upon Tanda's upper arm; and at Tanda, who looked oddly sad, perhaps considering those who did not have a safe haven within the city.

"Excuse me for a moment," I said, not knowing how to bridge the awkward silence and wanting to obtain an explanation from my recalcitrant guard.

I left the group and took a few steps toward the palace, only to discover that London had moved. Feeling somewhat foolish for having left the women to end up by myself, I cast about to locate him. Given the dwindling light of evening, it took me a while to discern he had headed toward Steldor, Galen and the young women, all of whom were now standing near one of the double-tiered marble fountains. As I watched, he joined Halias in the shadows of the trees.

Tadark, I noted with a certain sense of satisfaction, was still crowding Steldor, while Temerson appeared to have given up hope and was sitting alone on one of the benches that ringed the fountain's ten-foot diameter base. While it would not be my sister's intention to neglect her suitor, he looked woeful nonetheless.

I marched up the path toward the Elite Guard, who stepped forward to inject himself into Galen and Steldor's conversation, making it harder for me to corner him. He was becoming more confounding with every passing second.

"We've started calling him the Drunk-Gent at Arms," I heard London say brashly to Steldor as I neared.

Steldor cackled and gave his best friend a good-natured shove, which Galen returned with a grin, despite the razzing he was receiving.

"This is your fault, you know! I couldn't very well let the King drink alone!"

Galen gave Steldor another shove, and Tadark stepped behind the sergeant, positioned to grab him if he got too rough, seemingly worried that my husband would be hurt. In reality, Tadark was likely worried that such an incident would prove him an inadequate bodyguard.

Everyone watched in amusement as the King and the Sergeant at Arms pushed at each other like adolescent boys, and I saw that Temerson had perked up, probably surprised to be acting more refined than the men who typically overshadowed him. Tiersia's eyebrows had risen and London smirked at the bedlam he had wrought—at least until he read the determination in my eyes.

I went toward my bodyguard, and he sighed, looking resigned that he could not avoid me. At the same time, Steldor, a mischievous glint in his eyes, gave Galen a tremendous shove that sent him stumbling backward into Tadark, who toppled into the fountain.

The riotous laughter that ensued drew the attention of all the other guests, who filtered over to see what had happened. For a moment, I thought that Steldor and Galen, doubled up from the hilarity of it all, might follow Tadark into the water, but they managed to stay on their feet. Poor Tadark, on the other hand, sputtered and clamored to find dry land, face ruddy with embarrassment. So desperate was he to escape that climbing out became a much greater feat, and he slipped and fell several times. No one thought to help until Steldor found a breath and proffered his hand, hauling the sopping wet guard onto the path just as Cannan came on the scene.

"You're dismissed, Lieutenant," the captain said evenly. "Go to your quarters."

"Yes, sir, thank you, sir," Tadark squeaked, glancing about miserably before sloshing into the palace, his dignity as waterlogged as his boots.

Cannan looked disapprovingly at Steldor and Galen, both of whom had begun to laugh anew, but there was something about his manner that revealed subtle amusement. Steldor countered with a sheepish, but not quite repentant, grin.

With a shake of his head, Cannan turned to assure the other guests that everything was fine, and the group began to break apart. Galen clapped Steldor on the back, then extended his arm to Tiersia, and when she consented to walk with him, they departed down one of the garden paths, escaping without a chaperone. Miranna, apparently deciding to follow their example, bounced over to Temerson, her smile and rosy cheeks exceedingly endearing. Temerson's face lit up, and he took her hand to walk in the same direction as Galen and Tiersia; Halias, however, followed a judicious distance behind. Just before they disappeared from view, I saw Temerson pull a small box from the pocket of his doublet, and I wondered what gift he was preparing to present to her.

Semari, Dahnath and Shaselle went to join their mothers, Dahnath tugging at her sister's sleeve to pull her away from her newly royal cousin, and it was obvious that feminine chatter was of little appeal to the younger girl when Steldor was around. London, of course, had once more dodged me by moving out of my line of sight. This left me alone with the King. I considered going after Semari and the two sisters, but the time had passed when that might have seemed natural. Feeling Steldor's eyes upon me, I shifted uncomfortably, wondering what held him so transfixed.

"Stop staring," I scolded, managing to sound irritated rather than embarrassed.

He strode closer to me without breaking eye contact, so close that my heart began to race.

"I can't," he said, reaching out to play with a strand of my hair. "You take my breath away."

Without waiting for a response, he flashed his perfect white teeth and walked toward his father and uncle, ensuring that this would be one of the most confounding evenings of my life.

When Steldor at length decided to draw the celebration to a close, he and I bid our guests good-night and departed, returning to our quarters. He came into the parlor after me, and I thought I might say something to him, but when I turned he was disappearing into his bedroom. Peeved, I considered knocking on the door, but didn't want him to make the wrong assumption regarding my interest. I waited a moment to see if he would rejoin me of his own accord, feeling silly to be standing in the middle of the room by myself. As I debated whether to take a seat and continue to wait or retire to my bedroom, he reemerged, having changed into something less formal. With a slight nod in my direction, he made to leave, strapping his sword belt around his hips, and my thoughts flew to Miranna's conjecture—that Steldor might seek the company of other women if I would not give him mine.

"Where are you going?" I called.

"Why do you care?" he asked, sounding genuinely curious as he pulled the door wide.

"Because I—I… I'm thinking of the promise you made to commit to me the fidelity of your body." I bit my lip, hoping he would catch on. "I can't help but wonder whose company you keep."

He swiveled to face me, and I glanced up expecting to be confronted with anger or resentment. Instead, he appeared to find my statement comical.

"Worried about my eternal soul, are you?" he queried. I again struggled to speak, but he waved a hand dismissively. "Don't be. My soul won't be in danger until we've shared a bed. Consummation *is* a requirement of the marriage, remember?"

I grimaced and studied the pattern of the rug, wishing I had not raised the subject. A moment passed in silence, then I felt his hand beneath my chin. When I raised my head, he gave me a long and sensual kiss, his enthralling scent washing over me, and I was thrown off balance. He, however, went on his way as though nothing had transpired between us. Reeling from the unexpected feelings of both pleasure and confusion that his kiss had stirred, I stumbled to my room to prepare for bed. The entire evening now seemed surreal—Baelic's offer to take me horseback riding, Alantonya's questions about Narian, London's unusual behavior, the compliment Steldor had earlier paid me, the love I had felt in his kiss, my response to his overture. I smiled drolly, for while I was bone weary, I suspected it would be hours before my restless mind and troubled heart would let me sleep.

CHAPTER 7

CONNECTIONS

IT WASN'T LONG BEFORE I TOOK ADVANTAGE OF Baelic's offer to take me horseback riding. Just a week after the dinner party for Miranna, I sent a request to call upon him through a servant. An hour later, the man returned with a message that I was welcome to come to Baelic's city home that afternoon, and to stay for dinner if I were so inclined.

I enjoyed my day, having something new to anticipate. Miranna, generally my main source of enjoyable companionship, had lately spoken of nothing save the boy who had been given permission to court her, and I had begun to yearn for other topics of conversation. Baelic and his family represented a welcome change.

At midafternoon, I notified the Royal Stables to put a carriage in order and bring it to the front gates. I left my drawing room and returned briefly to my quarters to check my appearance and retrieve a lightweight traveling cloak, then hurried out the front doors of the palace. In the Central Courtyard, lilac bushes were in full bloom and full fragrance, perfectly complementing my mood, and the trees and grass were particularly brilliant shades of green.

What I discovered when I neared the gates was not to my liking. The horse master and a groom were in serious discussion about something and glanced guiltily at me when I approached. I groaned on the inside, knowing something was wrong, but not wanting anything to deflate my happiness or interfere with my outing.

"Why do I not see a carriage?" I questioned the moment I reached them, exasperated that my directive had not been carried out.

The men looked anywhere but at me. It was the horse master who at last spoke up.

"It is not prepared, Your Highness."

"Then have it readied at once or I shall be late, and it will be on your head."

"Indeed, on my head, but I can't prepare a carriage for you, my lady."

"And why is that? What impediment can there possibly be?"

The horse master shifted uncomfortably, reluctant to answer; at my scowl of impatience, the groom tentatively offered an explanation.

"The King has ordered that you not be given a horse or carriage without his express permission, Your Majesty."

My lips parted in surprise, and then anger brewed. The men glanced at each other, and the groom who had broken the news stepped a little behind the horse master for protection.

"One of you, take a message to my uncle, Lord Baelic," I irritably instructed. "Inform him that I have been delayed but will arrive in time for dinner. I'm going to have a word with the King."

I stalked back to the palace and barged through the front doors. Without a word to anyone, I marched through the entryway, the antechamber and the Hall of Kings, straight on to my husband's study, where I barreled through the door without knocking.

My husband did not seem shocked by my unannounced arrival; rather, he looked as though some unexpected entertainment was about to be provided. He was sitting at his desk, booted feet upon its surface, chair pushed back, reading through a few sheets of parchment in his hand, his only discernible reaction the lift in his eyebrows and his ever-widening grin.

"You are unbelievable!" I stormed, hands upon my hips, but he cut me off before I could launch into a full-blown rant.

"I hear that all too often," he said, managing both flippancy and extreme conceit in one short sentence. "If you want to flatter me, try to think of something every other woman in Hytanica *hasn't* told me."

I'd obviously caught him in good humor, and I nearly growled with frustration. Here was I, flustered and infuriated, trying my best to reproach him, and in response, he was reflecting on the praises he had garnered from other women.

"They usually whisper it to me between passionate kisses or in the ecstasy of my embrace," he continued, ignoring the affronted flush warming my skin. "Of course, if you really want to pay me this compliment, then I am ready, willing and able to provide you with the experience." He swung his feet to the floor and stood, motioning to his left. "There's a sofa right over there if you can't wait. I could free up my schedule, then we could—"

"Stop! That has nothing to do with the reason I'm here. Just stop talking!"

He smirked. "There's a way you could make me stop talking."

"You're deplorable! And I demand that you inform the stable hands that I can have a carriage whenever I desire!"

"Ahhh," he said, drawing the sound out in understanding as he resettled in his chair, leaning back. "Going somewhere, were you?"

"Yes, I was!"

"I seem to recollect that you were to tell me before you went out."

Although I hated his supercilious tone, I was reminded that I *had* promised to keep him informed of my whereabouts when I was outside the palace.

"I intended to leave a message with a Palace Guard," I lied, not wanting to admit any wrongdoing and knowing that his actions were far more offensive than mine.

"And did you?"

"That's irrelevant!" I seethed, with a stamp of my foot. "The issue here is the respect I deserve as Queen!"

With a skeptical tilt of his head, he picked the papers up from his desk as though the conversation were over, insulting me further.

"You have no right to take away my authority like this!" I exclaimed, my volume rising. "Do you have any idea how you've humiliated me? What next—are you going to order the entire kingdom to ignore the Queen's commands?"

"Of course not," he said, a touch of boredom creeping into his voice now that our word game had ended. "I'll send a guard to the stables at once to tell the horse master to give you whatever you want."

His response defused me, and I gaped at him, having expected some sharp, arrogant comeback.

"Is there something more you wanted, darling?"

"No," I muttered, and though I wasn't certain why I owed him any gratitude, I added a thank-you as I headed out the door to salvage my day.

Steldor was true to his word, and roughly an hour later, I arrived at Baelic's city home accompanied by the usual contingency of guards. I sent one of the men who had traveled with me to announce my arrival, while another of my escorts helped me from my carriage.

Baelic emerged from his large two-story manor house and approached, offering a courteous bow and his arm so that he might guide me to the front entry, which had a porch topped by a gallery for musicians. I assumed the gallery opened on to a reception room for hosting dinner parties and other galas. The house, sturdily built of stone, had two wings that came forward off its central section and was timber-roofed, although the roofs of the wings were at right angles to that of the main home.

Lania stood near the entry and swept a gracious curtsey when her husband and I drew near. Her straight, light brown hair was tied with a ribbon at the nape of her neck, and her summery white blouse and green skirt were simple, but lovely. Several of the Palace Guards who had accompanied me took positions on either side of the entry, others having gone around to the rear, while grooms took charge of the guards' mounts.

"Your Highness," Lania said respectfully. "Do come inside. Tea will be served in the parlor."

"Actually, I thought I'd show her the horses before tea," Baelic said, intercepting Lania as she began to lead me inside.

While I was pleased with his suggestion, Lania was not. She turned to her husband with an exasperated sigh, disgruntled but not surprised.

"You can hardly take the Queen to our barn, Baelic."

"If you prefer, I could bring the horses into the house," he responded with a wink for me.

"You will do no such thing!"

Lania seemed genuinely distressed, as though she deemed it possible that he would do just that, but I could tell from her soft hazel eyes that she was amused nonetheless.

"I would enjoy seeing the horses," I cut in, despite how entertaining I found their squabble.

"What did I tell you? She would enjoy seeing them," Baelic repeated, offering his arm to take me in the direction of the stable. I accepted, but Lania's almost pained voice stopped us.

"Baelic…do remember that it's almost dinnertime."

"Don't worry—I'll stay clean."

With a shake of her head, Lania disappeared into the house.

Baelic's barn was large enough for several horses, although I could not begin to guess how many head he might actually own. I recognized the animals milling in a small corral nearby as belonging to the Palace Guards, so knew better than to count those as his, but suspected he might keep some of his personal mounts at the military base—just one advantage of being the cavalry officer.

The door of the stone structure was open, and Baelic ushered me inside where it was refreshingly cool and the air smelled of leather and sweet hay. As my eyes adjusted to the dim light filtering through the windows along the side walls, I realized I was standing in a meticulously clean aisle that separated a set of five stalls—three on the left, two on the right, with a tack room at the fore. At the end of the aisle, a door that presumably led to another section of the barn was closed.

Baelic wasted no time, leading me to the first stall on the left where a dark bay mare, tall and well-muscled, stood munching from a hay feeder at the back right corner, displaying the length of her sturdy body. She looked up at the sound of our approach, then let out a contented grumble and turned to greet us.

"This is Briar, my baby," Baelic said, rubbing the mare's nose and ears. "She just turned five."

"She's beautiful."

"Isn't she?"

Baelic leaned his forearms on the top of the wooden stall door, close enough for Briar's breath to tousle his hair, which was the same color as her coat. I laughed, wondering if he had forgotten his promise to his wife or if he were simply choosing to ignore it, and his lopsided grin gave me the answer.

"She secretly likes the horse smell. Otherwise she wouldn't have married me."

He moved toward the second stall, raising a cautionary hand when I began to follow.

"It might be best if you stayed toward the front, and I'll bring the horses into the aisle. Lania will be furious with me already—imagine if I bring the Queen back smelling the same."

I acquiesced, and Baelic stepped around me to disappear into the tack room at my right, reemerging after a minute with a lead rope in hand. As he disappeared into the stall one down from Briar's, I was struck by the contradictions Baelic, Cannan and Steldor presented, and my thoughts burst from my mouth.

"The men in your family are extremely confusing."

I froze, shocked at how forward I sounded. Luckily, I was answered with a loud laugh.

"I do believe I've just been insulted."

"No!" I hastily assured him, blushing scarlet. "I didn't mean it like that—"

Baelic stepped into the aisle with the rope slung around the neck of a gelding as golden as wheat in spring but with white covering the lower portion of each of its legs so that it appeared to be wearing stockings.

"It would have been a compliment, dear niece, but that you bunched me in with the rest of that motley crew."

"You mean to call the King and the Captain of the Guard a 'motley crew'?" I queried with raised eyebrows, enjoying his irreverent sense of humor.

He shrugged, patting the horse's beautifully arched neck. Though I was several feet away, the gelding appeared to be about the same size as Tadark's mount, the animal on which I had initially learned to ride, and I hoped that Baelic had picked this one for me.

"This is Alcander. He's my gentlest horse aside from my son's, but Celdrid's mount would be too small for you."

I took a tiny step forward with the intent to stroke the animal, then remembered Baelic's admonition.

"You can get acquainted with him next time," Baelic assured me, correctly reading my hesitation.

"Of course. He's just hard to resist."

"I suppose that brings us back to the men in my family," he jested, returning Alcander to his stall. "I might be able to clear up a few things for you. Whom shall we address first?"

He crossed the aisle to bring out the next horse, glancing at me with a carefree smile on his face. Although this was the opportunity I had been hoping for, I vacillated, wary of insulting him. He quickly alleviated my concern.

"Don't worry. I have no false notions of my nephew being

an angel, and I know my brother through and through. Ask away."

"Steldor, then," I decided, since the bizarre encounter we'd had immediately before I'd come on this visit put him foremost in my mind. "I know he has a frightful temper—I've already seen it once or twice and, in truth, have even deserved his anger. Yet he's never raised a hand to me." I frowned as I pondered this, then added, "In response to some of my actions, I know my father would not have hesitated to use a strap."

Baelic had stepped out of the stall and was now leaning against the door, giving me his full attention, and though I felt somewhat sheepish, it was a question to which I deeply wanted an answer.

"That's easy to explain. Like father, like son. Steldor will never hit you, because his father never hit him or his mother."

"Cannan never struck Steldor?" I repeated in astonishment.

Beatings were a common form of punishment in Hytanica, so common that a man who didn't strike his wife and children on occasion would have been thought old, feeble or crazy. I myself had endured the occasional beating from my famously lenient father, and I had a hard time believing that Cannan, a tough and prestigious military man, had never employed the method.

"That's not to imply that Steldor was perfectly behaved. He would have earned a few lashings from most fathers, but Cannan never laid a hand on the boy. And that, I suppose, brings us to my brother."

"Yes, it does. Why did he not strike his son?" I moved closer to Baelic as though to read the answer on his face.

"Let's just say that our father employed the method too

liberally, so Cannan refused to use it with his son. He found other ways to handle disobedience, more creative ways that were just as effective, in my opinion. That doesn't mean there weren't times when Cannan wanted to strangle Steldor. The boy definitely earned the only nickname Cannan has for him."

"Nickname?" I said, both my ears and my curiosity perking up.

"I'm not sure Steldor knows about this," Baelic said with a chuckle, "so perhaps I shouldn't tell you."

"All the more reason *to* tell me," I replied with a mischievous grin, coaxing him to reveal what he knew.

"All right then, I suppose you must know. When out of his son's earshot, Cannan sometimes refers to the boy as 'Hell-dor.'"

I laughed, delighted by this new piece of information and already planning the use I might make of it.

Baelic showed me the remaining horses—a sorrel mare that belonged to Shaselle, a smaller bay gelding that was his son, Celdrid's, and, after leading me through the door at the far end of the barn, his prized stallion, who pawed the floor and tossed his head with the pride of a king. Even larger than Briar, the stallion had irregular patches of white and black on his glossy coat, thick, powerful legs and a full, muscular body. Baelic did not have to remind me to keep my distance, although he stroked the majestic animal's neck without trepidation.

We walked back through the barn, discussing the necessary arrangements for a return visit during which Baelic would take me riding, agreeing on a day two weeks hence.

"Shaselle would love to come along, if you don't mind. She hasn't been for a proper ride in quite some time, what with the Cokyrians threatening us at the river. As it is, we'll be able to enjoy the countryside for the first time in a long while."

"Of course I don't mind," I said, quite enthused about the idea of befriending a young woman with whom I seemed to share so many pursuits. Then my tone grew puzzled. "Why is it we're able to go outside the city?"

"The Cokyrians withdrew early this morning," he explained, casting me an odd glance. "I thought you might have heard."

I shook my head, then smiled, at last understanding the reason for both Steldor's high spirits and his lack of concern pertaining to my activities. Could it be that the enemy had decided to leave us in peace? Had they relinquished the search for Narian? Surely we would have known if he were in their custody. A fresh surge of hope lightened my steps as we returned to the house, where Lania came into the large entryway to greet me—and to frown at Baelic in annoyance.

"You smell like a horse."

"Actually, I smell like several of them," he replied, grinning.

With a sigh, she bade him clean up, fondly watching his retreating back as he jogged up the open staircase that marked the separation between the entry and the great room that lay beyond. She then motioned me to the left, down the corridor, and I knew by the tantalizing aromas that filled the air that the kitchen would be found in this wing.

Stopping at the first room, she ushered me through rich, double cherry doors and into a light and airy parlor that provided a view of the front courtyard of the manor house. I glanced at the tapestries decorating the walls and was amused to see they were of horses, some in pastures, some undergoing training, some carrying cavalry soldiers into battle. I took a seat upon a sofa by one of the windows, while Lania chose an armchair, and in a few moments a servant girl brought us rose tea. We sipped and chatted while waiting for Baelic to reappear, and I warmed to her quickly, insisting that she call me by name rather than addressing me formally as Your Highness.

A servant appeared to announce dinner when Baelic had joined us, and Lania instructed her to gather the children from another part of the home. It did not take long for Shaselle, Tulara, Lesette, Ganya and Celdrid, the youngest child at ten and the only son, to come through the dining room door. The eldest daughter, Dahnath, was absent.

"She's dining with Lord Drael," Lania explained, when she noticed my eyes upon the empty chair.

"Yes," said Celdrid, hopping onto his seat while his sisters more properly took theirs. "She thinks he's terribly handsome."

He shared a furtive glance with Lesette and Ganya, the siblings closest to his age, and the girls giggled. I smiled as well, for he seemed identical to Baelic in both looks and behavior.

"Hush, you two," admonished Tulara, who was more proper in manner than Shaselle. "Lord Drael is rich and respectable, and you girls should be lucky to marry a man like him someday."

"And you should be lucky to marry at all," Shaselle muttered, with a grin for her brother.

Tulara appeared quite indignant, but at Lania's stern glower, she shrank back in her chair and adopted a more ladylike demeanor.

As the dinner progressed, I was filled not only with delicious food, but with the warmth generated by such a happy family. I considered the deep-seated connection between Baelic and Lania. Would Steldor and I ever experience such closeness? I thought it highly unlikely; I thought it even less likely that I would ever want to bear a child by him, despite the necessity of producing an heir.

When I left for home, I thanked Lania and Baelic profusely, only to be mystified one more time by my uncle, who extended a wrapped parcel to me.

"I think you'll find this useful," he said, with a wink for me and a shrug for his puzzled wife.

I accepted the package, then rode back to the palace, quite satisfied with my outing. I walked leisurely up the stone path that cut the courtyard in half, continuing through the front doors, almost colliding with London, who was about to depart. He was dressed in his typical fashion, brown leather jerkin with twin long knives at his sides, but this time he also carried a bow and a quiver of arrows.

"Off again, are you?" I teased, noting the pack slung over his shoulder. "Why is it we can't keep a good man in place?"

"I just can't resist the mountains," he responded, running his hand through his unruly silver hair, but despite the lightness of his response, I knew something was wrong.

"To Cokyri?" The tease had slipped from my voice as easily as butter from a hot knife. "What's happened?"

"The Cokyrians withdrew from the river this morning."

"But isn't that a good—" The truth came crashing down, making it difficult to breathe. "It's Narian. They've found him."

"That's what I intend to determine," London offered, concern in his indigo eyes. "At any rate, Cokyri's withdrawal tells us they know he's no longer in Hytanica, despite the measures we've taken to keep that detail hidden. If they don't already have him, they'll engage in an all-out search." London shifted his weight in the manner of a horse that wants to run. "I must go, Alera. You know as well as anyone the consequences that will result if Narian is back in the hands of the Overlord. If he is indeed in Cokyri, we'll need all possible time to make ready."

I nodded, my spirits sinking, but I stopped him once more before he could cross the threshold into the Central Courtyard.

"You will return, won't you?"

"Hytanica depends on it," he said, his eyes resolute. "So, yes, I will."

CHAPTER 8

UNCLE KNOWS BEST

AFTER LONDON HAD DEPARTED THE PALACE for Cokyri, I climbed the Grand Staircase to return to the rooms I shared with Steldor, quite shaken and expecting to be alone. Oddly, I found my husband reclining on the sofa with a book. He looked up as I entered, wearing the impudent smirk I had come to detest.

"Alera, at last you join me," he said, pushing himself upright and dropping the book on the sofa table. "I finally make it to dinner, only to discover that you have not. Can I assume, then, that you enjoyed your day in the city?"

"Yes, I did."

I tried to sound casual, though I was quite flustered by his presence. After weeks of spending nights outside our quarters, why now was he here?

"Shall I request some food for you, or have you eaten?"

"I have already dined, but thank you for asking," I cautiously replied.

"I see."

I moved toward my bedroom, intending to escape the situation, but Steldor's voice brought me to a halt.

"And who received the pleasure of your company?"

Uncertain how he would react to the knowledge that I'd spent the evening with his uncle, I hedged my answer, attempting to change the subject.

"I wouldn't want to bore you with the details of my social outings. But tell me, what is so special about today that you are able to be home?"

"What I find interesting," Steldor replied, bemused, "isn't that you neglect to share the details of your life with me, but that you actually believe you can conceal them."

Unable to meet his gaze, I waited to learn in what direction he would take this conversation.

"Given the nature of some of your secrets that have of late come to light, that disturbs me. So, darling, are you going to tell me how you spent your afternoon?"

Belittled but indignant, I raised my eyes to his and shook my head, and he answered with a condescending laugh.

"No matter. I can find out what I want to know in other ways—perhaps from your carriage driver?"

He studied me, smug beyond belief, and I hated his uncanny ability to always have the last word.

"To answer your earlier question," he drawled, "Cokyri retreated today, giving us a brief reprieve. I thought I would take advantage of it and enjoy some time with my wife. Come and sit with me."

"Allow me a moment to freshen up, my lord," I said, then immediately stepped into my bedroom, wanting to place the package Baelic had given me far from Steldor's prying eyes.

I returned to the parlor a few minutes later, less apprehensive than usual at the thought of being near my husband, as the things Baelic had told me had given me more faith in him. Still, I was not comfortable with the idea that he might try to be intimate, so I chose to sit on the opposite end of the sofa from him. He clearly found this amusing but said nothing, picking up his book from the table and placing it in my hands.

"I would like you to read to me," he said, seeming tired, and it occurred to me that being King might be taking a toll on him. Hytanica did not usually crown its kings until they were at least in their late twenties, so Steldor was exceptionally young to be shouldering the mantle; in fact, he was actually the youngest king ever to take the throne.

I glanced at the book, hoping it would not be about weapons or battle strategy, to discover that it was a history of the royal family, of my family. I opened it, and he again lay back on the sofa, swiveling his body to rest his head in my lap with his eyes closed. While I read, I glanced down at his handsome features, his dark hair falling away from his temples, giving even more definition to his prominent cheekbones. His expression was so peaceful that I felt a desire to touch his hair and face, but I refrained, knowing such a gesture was sure to be misinterpreted.

I read for about fifteen minutes and then stopped, certain he had fallen asleep, but he opened his eyes and sat up. He contemplated me single-mindedly, and the tenderness I had felt toward him was suffused by anxiety, for he was far too close to me.

He reached out and turned my body toward his, gazing into my eyes, then he ran the fingers of one hand along my jaw line. Sliding the same hand under my hair and behind my neck, he leaned toward me and kissed me softly, gently, sweetly, and I felt myself responding. He pulled back to examine my face, playing with a strand of my hair.

"You are driving me mad, Alera," he said huskily. "Your voice, your scent, the way you look, the way you move…I want more than anything to truly be your husband, for you to truly be my wife."

He leaned toward me again and brushed his lips across mine, then gently kissed my neck and the hollow of my throat, sweeping my hair behind my shoulders as he did so.

"Steldor, I'm not ready," I whispered, for some reason finding it difficult to speak.

"I would be gentle," he promised, lips continuing their exploration.

"Please, no," I said, forcing the words from my tightened throat, and he reluctantly pulled away. "Not yet. I'm sorry."

His air of first frustration, then dejection, tugged at me, but before I could speak further, he sighed and stood.

"I'm going out for a while. Don't feel you have to wait up for me."

I nodded, not knowing how else to respond. He paused in the doorway on his way out, hand upon the frame, and glanced back at me.

"Just consider the possibility that you might enjoy my touch," he said, almost lightly, but he could not conceal the ache underlying his words.

An inexplicable feeling of sadness and unease settled upon me as he departed. Where might he be going, and, more important, to whom?

Though the weather changed as spring merged into summer, becoming more hot and humid, there was little change in my relationship with my husband. To my dismay, he continued to leave most evenings, staying out late, and with every passing day, I grew more troubled about the nature of his activities. Needing to know whether I had anything to fear, I considered a different approach to obtaining an answer to my question. If Steldor would not talk with me about where he went, then I would have to ask someone else, and it wasn't hard to identify the person to whom I should turn. Galen, I was sure, knew everything there was to know about Steldor.

After eating an early lunch in the tea room the next day, I returned to the Queen's Drawing Room, sending word to Galen that I wished to meet with him at his earliest convenience. I tried to devote my attention to various household matters while I awaited his arrival, but my ability to concentrate was not what it should have been. Doubts about Steldor and growing concern about London and Narian kept pushing into my thoughts. It was late afternoon when at last the Sergeant at Arms appeared in the doorway.

"You wished to speak with me, Your Highness?"

I nodded and motioned toward a chair adjacent to the sofa upon which I was seated. Although I had a burning desire for an answer to my question, I also felt awkward raising the subject, and so made a clumsy attempt at small talk as he joined me.

"How are things between you and Tiersia these days?"

"Very well," he said with a warm smile. "But I doubt you asked me here to talk about my betrothed."

"That was not my primary reason. Congratulations, though. I did not know your relationship had progressed to that point."

"Thank you," he said, studying me. "Judging by the color in your cheeks, I would guess this has something to do with your husband. Why don't you tell me what is really on your mind?"

"Very well." I took a deep breath, abandoning my pride, and plunged ahead. "Steldor leaves our quarters late in the evenings several times a week, but he will not tell me where he goes or whom he sees. Since you are his best friend, I thought perhaps you could enlighten me."

Galen surprised me by laughing. "If I may ask, what *has* Steldor told you about the nature of his activities?"

"As I said, very little. It is the fact that he is not forthcoming that has me worried."

"And what do you worry he may be doing?"

Again the heat rose in my face, and I cast my eyes about the room, half hoping a Cokyrian would come bursting through the bay window behind me just to put an end to this embarrassing conversation.

"I can't help but wonder if he is spending time with another woman," I confessed.

Again Galen chuckled. "Is that what he has led you to believe?"

"He has not said so directly," I responded, clasping my hands in my lap. "But he evades my questions when I raise the matter with him."

Galen grew serious, and I knew his answer would be honest.

"Well, you need not worry. Steldor spends his time with me or others from the Military Complex. We play cards or dice and, of course, drink some ale. We most often meet at the base, although he and I sometimes play chess in his study."

Tremendous relief washed over me, and I nodded gratefully.

"My lady," Galen teased, "you are married to a man who is content to have you think him a rake, but believe me, he is not. He is in love with one woman to whom few can compare and has lost interest in all others. I have never seen a man so smitten."

My heart lightened and so did my mood. "I think Tiersia had better not let you slip away, as I fear for your safety should other women discover your charm."

"Never fear," he said, his brown eyes sparkling. "That's a very well-kept secret. Now pray excuse me, for duty calls—or at least the captain does."

"Yes, of course, but thank you, both for coming and for your willingness to answer my questions."

"Glad to be of assistance." He stood and swept me a generous bow, then disappeared into the corridor.

That evening, as I walked into the family dining room, I saw that the usually empty seat beside mine was occupied by my husband. His presence caught me off guard, but I nevertheless dined with a cheerful disposition, for Galen had lifted a great worry from my shoulders. This was also the first time in a while that I enjoyed a meal with my entire family: my parents, my sister and my husband. Though my father was still aloof with me, his good-natured attitude was steadily reappearing. Provided I kept at bay the nagging dread of the news London might bring, I found I could actually enjoy myself.

When the meal ended, Miranna skipped out the side door closest to her quarters, while my parents, Steldor and I took the opposite exit. After bidding farewell to my mother and father, who climbed the spiral staircase to reach their rooms on the third floor, I turned toward the King's and Queen's quarters. Steldor, however, started down the hall toward the Grand Staircase.

"Where are you going?" I inquired, emboldened by the information Galen had shared.

"I have a commitment," he replied, flicking a hand glibly in my general direction, intent on causing me strife.

"I thought you were able to join us for dinner because of a lack of commitments."

He stopped and faced me. "Very well. If you must know, I go to seek relaxation elsewhere."

He raised an eyebrow pointedly, and I could no longer permit him to play this game.

"Oh, stop," I said, rolling my eyes. "I know you're only going off with Galen. It's no wonder your father calls you Hell-dor."

He stared at me for a moment with furrowed brow, trying to gauge what I truly knew.

"My father doesn't call me that," he asserted, unable to deny my first statement.

"Oh? Doesn't he?" I was trying desperately not to laugh. "Perhaps you should ask him."

Steldor scrutinized me, and I could tell his confidence in his statement was fading. I smiled sweetly, barely resisting the urge to bat my eyelashes, then cackled with triumph when he spun on his heel and stalked away. I'd gotten the better of him at last.

A few days later, at midmorning on the day Baelic and I had appointed, I donned the breeches my uncle had provided, for such had been the contents of the parcel he had placed in my hands at the end of my last visit. After layering a skirt on top, I pulled my hair back into a bun, then departed to walk to the front gate to await Baelic's arrival. I didn't want to be seen with him in the palace by Steldor or Cannan, certain they would not approve of my intended activity.

Baelic arrived in a carriage, to the back of which were tied two saddled horses: Briar, the beautiful dark bay mare; and the petite sorrel mare that I knew to be Shaselle's. Celdrid rode on a gelding as dark as Briar and held Alcander, the golden gelding meant for me, on a lead line, likewise saddled and ready for use.

I climbed into the coach to join Shaselle, who was boldly wearing breeches that were not hidden by a skirt. It did not take long to fall into easy conversation, for like her mother, she proved to be most engaging. I asked where we were going and received an unexpected answer.

"To my uncle's country estate. The land is beautiful, plus no one dares trespass on the captain's land, so it's perfect from my mother's point of view. She doesn't want anyone to see me out riding."

Traveling in such pleasant company made our journey pass quickly, and we arrived in what felt like very little time. Shaselle opened the door of the carriage and jumped to the ground without waiting for assistance, and then hurried to untie the horses. I removed my skirt so that I wore only the breeches and my blouse, and was helped to the ground by Baelic.

Cannan's country estate was breathtaking, even in its current deserted and unkempt state. It was located by the bend in the river, where the Recorah altered its southerly flow to turn west, thus forming two borders of our kingdom, a scenic location farther from the threat of Cokyri than was Koranis's. The two-story stone manor house that sat among towering oak trees was large and sprawling, and vines covered its northern wall. In addition to the main house, there was a stone guesthouse, wood-framed housing for servants, and a large stable with several fenced pastures.

Baelic unhitched the carriage horses, letting them loose in a small corral, then the four of us mounted our steeds. He led the way across an open field at a slow trot, probably trying to determine my skill as a horsewoman, but Alcander

was very obedient. After we had ridden for about fifteen minutes, he dropped back next to me, and we urged the horses into an easy canter, Shaselle and Celdrid winging out to our sides.

It wasn't until Baelic held up his hand to indicate we should rein the horses down into a walk that it occurred to me I had been on this property before. As I scanned the vast fields, I felt certain that the ill-fated picnic of a year ago with Steldor, Miranna and Temerson had taken place somewhere on this land. After all, my father had taken great care in choosing the location, and where better to send the princesses and their escorts than to a beautiful property Steldor knew like the back of his hand?

Most of the morning passed, to my amusement, with Baelic sharing tales of Steldor's childhood misadventures. While the stories elicited much laughter, I hoped that, if someday I did have children by my husband, they would take after me, for Steldor had truly been a rambunctious child. As Baelic talked about his nephew, the affection he held for him was readily apparent; so was a healthy measure of pride.

We rode for an hour and a half longer, then returned to the manor house to wash and picnic in the shade of one of the oak trees. When the sun began its descent toward the western horizon, we gathered our things for the journey home, and I again put my skirt on over my breeches.

Upon our return to the palace estate in the late afternoon, Baelic offered to escort me up the path through the Central Courtyard, but I declined, still not wanting to be seen with him. Normally I would have had contact with my uncle only through Steldor, and I did not want questions to arise as to our relationship, especially since my husband would not approve of my new pastime. I stepped through the palace's double entry doors, tired but happy, and was just about to tread on the Grand Staircase when Steldor emerged from the antechamber. He studied me for a moment, then made an observation that would have been rude but for the fact that it was true.

"I do believe you smell like a horse."

"Just a new perfume," I tossed back, quickly moving up a few steps, hoping he was not downwind.

"I think I prefer the smell of soap."

"I usually smell of soap?" I asked, not sure whether I should feel insulted.

"There's nothing wrong with the smell of soap," he said. "It's a nice, clean smell. But if this is your idea of perfume, I'm going to have to make choices for you in this area, as well."

With one last puzzled look my way, he walked out the front doors, joined by a pair of Elite Guards, and I continued on to our quarters. I would have been angry at his presumptuous conclusion that he could do a better job than I of choosing perfume, but was instead grateful that he had dropped the subject. With a grin, I vowed to myself that from now on I would spend more time washing before we began the journey home.

The next few weeks passed pleasantly enough, as I resumed my daily routine and gradually learned more about Steldor's. He would rise early and meet first thing with Cannan to discuss scouting reports, security issues and defense of the kingdom. He would then spend the rest of the morning meeting with other advisers and overseeing the day-to-day business of the palace. After lunch, he would conduct audiences and hear petitions from the citizenry, then meet with the scribes to issue any necessary letters, dispatches or decrees. Often in the late afternoons, he would ride out of the city on his gray stallion, generally accompanied by Galen and always with a contingency of Elite Guards. He would view the royal family's holdings, inspect the Military Complex or the troops and on occasion go hunting, although I suspected some of these activities were just an excuse to get away from the demands of being King. He had been a very active military man and no doubt felt confined by all the meetings he had to attend and the administrative matters with which he had to deal. He generally returned to the palace midevening, dining after my family and I had finished, then coming to our quarters to change and depart. In truth, I did not see very much of him, but for the time being, that seemed to suit us both.

Despite the hot weather, I went riding with Baelic twice more during the month of July, again with Shaselle and Celdrid. We continued to make use of Cannan's property, and I came to feel that I was getting to know my husband more through Baelic's stories than through time spent with the actual man. Surprisingly, my greatest worry was that Steldor and I would cross paths someday. I could imagine my husband riding out for the afternoon and meeting up with us as we were returning. I tried to picture how that encounter would go but always came back to the conclusion that if anyone could handle Steldor in such a situation, it would be Baelic. In any case, I enjoyed the stolen pleasure of riding too much to give it up, despite the risk of being discovered. And I derived more satisfaction than I should have from the thought that I was engaged in something of which my husband would not approve.

CHAPTER 9

A PINK ROSE

"ALERA!"

An eager voice halted me as I was about to enter my parlor and I turned to see Miranna standing at the corner just outside her quarters, motioning for me to join her. I walked down the lengthy corridor, beginning to feel stiff and thinking longingly of a nice warm bath after my first August afternoon of riding with Baelic. I nodded to Halias, who stood in the hall, then let my sister pull me through the doorway, her rosy cheeks indicating her level of excitement.

"You're certainly lively today," I remarked as she bounded to the sofa, dragging me along with her.

"I'm so utterly, desperately, unbelievably thrilled!" she breathed when we both were sitting, clutching my hands and bouncing up and down.

"I can see that." I laughed. "Would you like to share the reason?"

"I so badly want to, but I'm not supposed to say anything to anyone. If I tell you, you must promise not to repeat my words to another living soul!"

"I promise. Now what is it?"

"It's Temerson! He wants to meet me tonight in the Royal Chapel. I think he might propose marriage!"

I gasped, more because she would be expecting such a reaction than out of true shock, and she clapped her hands together joyfully.

"I'm to meet him right after dark. And he wants me to come alone, which is just too romantic. Oh, Alera, I've had the feeling since my birthday that he wants to ask me something, and tonight I'll find out what it is!"

I smiled, for her excitement was contagious. Then a possible obstacle came to mind.

"But what about Halias? He won't let you go by yourself."

"I have to go without him. Temerson would never be able to speak of something so important and personal around Halias!"

"That's true enough," I agreed, trying to picture the shy young man stuttering out a proposal in front of an Elite Guard. "But how will you elude him? And even if you do, one of the Palace Guards on night patrol will insist on accompanying you."

"I have a plan," she said with a devious smile. "I'll simply tell Halias that I am retiring early and dismiss him before the night guards come on duty, then go to the chapel and await my dearest." She sighed, then laid her hands over her heart, her expression dreamy. "Did I tell you he sent a pink rose along with the note Ryla delivered? He knows pink roses are my favorite. He's so sweet, don't you think?"

"That he is," I concurred, then couldn't resist teasing her. "And have you given thought as to what your answer will be?"

"I will say yes, of course!" she exclaimed in a near squeal.

"Then I'll stay up late tonight. You must come to my

quarters, *quietly,* the moment you've left Temerson's side and tell me all the details."

She nodded her head eagerly. "I will, and then we can begin to discuss wedding plans!"

While it was easy to get swept along in her enthusiasm, something else occurred to me as I looked at her beaming countenance.

"Mira…don't be too disappointed if he doesn't propose to you. Perhaps he merely wishes to give you a gift."

"Oh, don't be silly," she replied, reaching to give my hands a reassuring squeeze. "He gave me an absolutely beautiful locket for my birthday, filled with forget-me-nots, so there is no need for a gift." She sprang to her feet, eyes dancing. "Besides, if he doesn't, I shall simply propose to him!"

We burst into laughter at the idea, although I wasn't entirely certain Miranna was joking.

That evening, after I had bathed and changed clothes, I sat fidgeting in an armchair in my parlor. Had Miranna's plan to evade the guards gone smoothly? Had Temerson arrived? And what might they be discussing?

Steldor was out, and I did not expect him to return anytime soon. I became certain that he would spend the entire night away with the appearance of stars in the darkening sky, which suited me perfectly. I paced the room, a queasy sensation of nervous exhilaration making it hard to sit still. Temerson must have proposed or she would be back by now. I considered revisiting Steldor's bedroom to divert my attention, curious as to what else it might reveal about my husband, and stopped before it at my third pass around the room's perimeter. Someone opened the parlor door at that moment, and I swiveled toward it.

"Mira—"

But it wasn't Miranna standing just over the threshold, and I clamped my mouth shut, feeling my face flame.

"What are you doing?" Steldor asked, his eyes narrowing at the sight of where I was standing.

"I was pacing," I said, knowing that would be a satisfactory reason for me to be so close to his bedroom door.

"I see."

He took off his sword belt, hanging his weapons in their customary place by the hearth. Glancing at me suspiciously, he stripped off his jerkin and tossed it across an armchair.

"Why are you still up? It's close to midnight."

"I suppose I'm just not sleepy yet," I replied, fingering the folds of my skirt. "In any case, I do believe the parlor belongs to the both of us, so I ought to be free to make use of it, no matter the hour."

"True enough. Perhaps I'll stay up with you."

I cringed, for I should have anticipated this problem. If Miranna returned while Steldor was awake, he would know I had not been forthcoming with him. His comment in the aftermath of my first visit to Baelic's, that I tried to conceal things from him, rang in my head, and I knew he would add this to the reasons he should not trust me. Yet I did not want to tell him. If Halias or my father found out what my sister had done, it would cause her strife.

"You've surely had a long day, my lord," I suggested. "There is no need to keep me company."

Steldor sat on the sofa, placing his feet on the low table.

"No need, to be sure. But you are rarely up when I return, and I don't want to miss the opportunity to enjoy your company."

I bit my lip, trying to think of a way out of this, and the silence between us lengthened.

"Given the lateness of the hour," I finally responded,

aware that his dark eyes were continuing to dissect me, "I believe I will retire after all. I bid you good-night."

I walked into my bedroom, hoping he would likewise retreat into his. I was confident that he had only been staying up to irritate me, as he did seem rather weary. I closed the door and waited, listening until I heard him walk toward his room. After a few more minutes, I slowly opened the door to scan the seating area. Seeing no one, I crept toward the sofa.

"Does this sort of ploy work on other people?"

I jumped and wheeled about, then spied Steldor leaning against the wall to my right. This time, my entire body burned with embarrassment, both because I had thought I'd successfully fooled him and because I'd been so startled by his voice.

He came toward me and tapped me under the chin with his index finger, forcing me to meet his patronizing gaze.

"Why don't you tell me what's *really* going on."

Annoyed by his lofty manner, I pulled away and took a few steps back.

"I'm waiting for Miranna," I admitted, moving to a cream brocade armchair near the sofa, all the while shooting him daggers with my gaze.

He followed, coming to lean against the back of the chair, where he began to play with the hair that tumbled down my back.

"And *why* are you waiting for her?"

I let out a frustrated breath and stood, pulling my hair out of his grasp. "She was meeting Temerson in the chapel."

He looked at me expectantly, enjoying our exchange, his hands resting on the high back of the chair. "And she was meeting him because...?"

"He sent a note through her maid asking to see her tonight. It was all very romantic and mysterious—she thought he might propose marriage."

Though I would have liked to have told him this was none of his business, I hoped that if I simply confessed, he might leave me in peace. Instead, his aspect changed, becoming less smug and more intense.

He pushed off the chair back and observed me critically. "How was Temerson going to get into the palace?"

"I don't know. I hadn't thought about that. He must have found some way, though."

"Is Halias with her?" Steldor demanded, and I frowned, unable to understand his interest.

"No, Temerson said she should come alone. Please don't tell Halias. Miranna only wanted to give him—"

"The chapel, you said?" The urgency in his voice alarmed me, and I nodded, suddenly fearful, although about what I did not know.

Steldor snatched up his sword and dagger, strapping the weapons belt around his hips as he strode to the parlor door to fling it open.

"Guards!" he shouted, breaking into a run down the corridor toward the Grand Staircase.

I rushed after him, jostled about by the four or five men who had answered his call. I came to the forefront of the group as Steldor stepped off the final stair tread into the Grand Entry below me.

"Wait!" I cried, hurrying after him. He stopped by the guardroom that led to Cannan's office to summon more soldiers, and I caught his arm.

"Where are you going?" I tried again, a note of desperation in my voice.

He pulled away from me, not offering an answer, then continued into the East Wing, toward the double wooden doors of the Royal Chapel at the end of the corridor. A few Elite Guards, awakened by the commotion, hurried into our midst from the northern corridor that led to their living quarters. Among them was Destari, who pushed his way toward me.

Steldor stopped before the doors and drew his sword, nodding to those gathered around him. They likewise drew weapons, and he tried the latch, pushing against the wood with his shoulder, but it would not yield.

"Barred from the inside," a guard muttered, and he began to organize men to break it down.

The sound of splintering wood rent the air as a savage kick from the King knocked the door inward, snapping the wooden bar that had held it closed. The chapel lay before us in near darkness, forbidding. Miranna could not be here, nor could Temerson, not without light from a lantern or candle. Nausea crawled through my stomach, tempered by reason. Perhaps they had been and gone; perhaps they were taking a stroll in the moonlight. The entrance to the East Courtyard was nearby—they might have decided to appreciate the refreshing evening air.

I moved closer to Steldor, who stood on the threshold awaiting a torch, wanting him to tell me not to worry. I stopped short, however, as a heavy metallic smell assaulted me, and I covered my nose and mouth with my hand.

"What is that?" I muttered, squinting into the darkness, nausea hitting full-force.

Before Steldor could answer, a cloud outside shifted, giving the moon freedom to gleam through the stained-glass windows and lend pale, colored light to the scene. Sprawled facedown in the aisle between the pews, amid a dark pool that spread across the blue-gray stone like a predator creeping forth, lay a person, limbs too awkwardly positioned for sleep, body too still for life.

A painful scream tore from my throat, and the image before me grew hazy, as though mist were obscuring my eyes. My knees gave out, but Steldor's strong arm wrapped about my waist, shoring me up. The room again came into focus, and I saw that the wooden altar had been ripped apart, pieces of wood widely flung, the cross, now broken, upon the floor. My eyes dropped once more to the stone, taking in the thick texture of the blood, the odd angle of the neck from which it had poured, the frozen quality of death.

"Miranna…" I croaked.

"Take her," Steldor said to someone, but I struggled against my husband, wanting to go to my sister, refusing to let him brush me aside.

"Look at me," he said, turning me away from the scene. "That is not your sister. Now you must move out of the way."

Destari stepped forward to shine torchlight upon the chapel's interior, and I finally took in the thin white hair that covered the victim's head and the priest's robe upon the body. Guilty relief rushed through me, for although a life had been lost, it was not the one most precious to me.

With some rationality restored, I was about to permit Steldor to pass me into the arms of one of the Palace Guards when a new terror stopped my breathing. The desecrated altar had not been random destruction—there was a tunnel. A tunnel about which only one person outside the royal family and its most trusted guards knew. I lunged back toward the chapel, but Steldor held me tight.

"Where is my sister?" I shrieked, tears clogging my throat.

Over my wretched sobs, I heard Steldor issuing orders.

"Send for my father and Galen. Rouse every guard and

raze this place to the ground, searching for intruders. Check the stables—we might yet be able to track them. And sound the alarm to close the city."

Handing me off to a guard, Steldor ventured into the chapel, accompanied by Destari and several additional men, sidestepping the body. Seeming to decide that immediate action was more important than his own safety, my husband sheathed his sword and approached the altar, preparing to drop into the gaping hole beneath. Destari gripped his shoulder to stop him, one of them at least recognizing that the King should not put himself at risk, and Steldor acceded, motioning several other guards forward to explore the tunnel in his place. He came back through the chapel into the corridor, and I barely felt it as he pulled me into his embrace, obscuring my view of the murdered priest and of the entrance to the tunnel through which I knew the Cokyrians, however they had managed to infiltrate the palace, had taken Miranna.

The Captain of the Guard and the Sergeant at Arms arrived within the hour, both aware of the abduction, though I doubted either of them had garnered many details. Cannan took Steldor and me, along with Galen and Destari, into his office for a status report. He sat behind his desk, Galen and Destari to his right, while Steldor settled me into a leather armchair, supporting me all the way as I was shaking uncontrollably. The moment I was seated, the captain took charge.

"I understand that Princess Miranna is missing. I need to know exactly what transpired here tonight."

"I know that Miranna received a note through her maid, and that she went to the Royal Chapel believing she would be meeting Temerson," Steldor volunteered from where he stood beside me.

“Who is Miranna’s maid? How long ago did the princess receive the note?” Cannan firmly but calmly inquired.

I had been staring at the floor, cheeks cold and wet, and Steldor dropped to one knee in front of me to gain my attention. He took my hands, his brow furrowed with worry.

“Who is Miranna’s maid? I need the name.”

Barely comprehending his words through my numbness, I tried to move my lips, but they refused to comply.

“You have to help us, Alera. Miranna’s…safety…depends upon it.”

Even in my disoriented state, I knew he had purposely avoided suggesting that Miranna’s life was in danger, or perhaps already taken. A sob choked me at the horrific thought that my sister, my baby sister, might be dead somewhere, her smile, her innocent giggle, her carefree manner gone forever.

“Ryla,” I rasped.

“Does Ryla live in the palace?” Cannan pressed, and I nodded.

The captain turned to address Galen. “Send a guard to bring Temerson here, and find the maid.”

The sergeant nodded curtly and departed. Steldor stood, but I found myself clasping his hand, searching for something to keep me grounded, and he remained at my side.

“Now, what time—”

Cannan was interrupted by the slamming of his office door against the wall as Halias stormed inside, his blue eyes wild.

“Where is Miranna?” he challenged, placing both palms upon Cannan’s desk, glaring down at his captain.

A shadow of a frown fell upon Cannan, and he rose to his feet to address his Elite Guard.

“Stand down, Deputy. The princess’s whereabouts remain

to be determined, but everything that can be done is being done."

There was a strained silence, during which it seemed that Miranna's bodyguard would fail to comply, but then he pushed off the desk and went to lean against the back wall, every muscle in his body flexed. Destari moved to stand beside him, placing a hand on his shoulder, while the captain again sat down.

"What time did Miranna go to meet Temerson?" Cannan queried, finally having the chance to finish his question.

"She dismissed me for the night right after dinner," Halias said, his eyes darting toward the door every so often as though he might pursue Miranna without delay. "She probably left her quarters shortly after that, before the night guards began patrolling the corridors."

Steldor gave my hand a squeeze.

"Is that right, Alera?" At my weak nod, he persisted, "Can you tell us what time she was to meet Temerson?"

"Right after dark," I said, salty tears finding the corners of my mouth as I spoke.

"That means she was taken several hours ago," Cannan grimly surmised. "If the Cokyrians are behind this, we won't find her in the city anymore."

He looked to Destari and issued an order. "Alert our border patrols. It's possible her abductors have not yet left our lands."

I made a noise that was halfway between a scream and a sob. Destari looked sympathetically at me before he departed, while Steldor again dropped to his knees and pulled me into his arms. I clung to his shirt as if it represented life itself. Over the sound of my weeping, I heard Galen return, and I looked up to see if Ryla was with him.

"The maid is not in her room," he reported. "She hasn't

been seen since early evening, and no one could tell me anything about her background."

"What *do* we know about this maid?" Cannan demanded.

Halias began to tap his foot with impatience as I raised my head from Steldor's shoulder, comprehension depressing my chest with such force that my heart could barely beat, and staying my tears like a dam.

"I hired her almost three months ago, in mid-May," I revealed.

There was a knock on the office door, and a guard ushered an unkempt and terrified Temerson, along with his father, Lieutenant Garrek, into the room.

"Did you send a note to Miranna earlier today?" the captain inquired, without any preliminaries.

"N-n-no, sir," Temerson replied, frightened eyes roving over everyone present: Halias, who appeared almost crazed; Steldor, on the floor with his arms wrapped about me; Galen, troubled and suspicious; and finally back to Cannan, whose slightly drawn eyebrows were the only sign of distress he ever showed.

"So you had no plans to meet her tonight?"

"N-no, sir. What's happened, is Miranna all right?"

"Wait in the Sergeant at Arms' office," the captain said, waving a hand in dismissal. As Temerson and his father were on their way out, Destari reentered, having sent the urgent message to our patrols, and Cannan turned to Galen once more.

"Summon King Adrik and Lady Elissia. Tell them nothing of what has happened—I will deliver the news myself. Also, send for the doctor. I imagine many people will have difficulty sleeping tonight."

Galen left, and a restless Halias pushed away from the

wall and began to pace across the back of the room. Cannan silently observed him for a moment.

"Sit down, Halias," he finally said. "There's nothing you can do."

"I could go after her," Halias spat back, ignoring his captain's directive. "We all know they've crossed the river by now. We could catch them before they reach Cokyri."

"They have an enormous advantage," Cannan said reasonably, eyes following his deputy captain. "They can travel much faster in the dark than we can track." After a few beats of silence, the captain repeated, "Sit down. That's an order."

Stealing a glance at the wooden chair in front of the desk that Cannan had indicated, Halias kicked it, sending it careening past Steldor and me to crash into the wall. Steldor released me and stood, suddenly on guard, posture mirrored by Destari, but the captain was unfazed.

"You could at least let me try to go after her!" Halias shouted, prompting Destari to take a wary step closer. "I'm her bodyguard—it was my duty to protect her, and I've already failed. I've always been willing to give my life for her, and tonight I should have kept her safe or died in the attempt." His voice became more tortured as he made one last plea. "London is in Cokyri. Let me find him, and together we might be able to bring her home."

"No. We won't blindly pursue her into enemy lands." He considered his distraught deputy captain for a moment. "Recognize that if the Cokyrians had intended to kill Miranna, they would have done so without removing her from the palace. Nor would they have planted a Cokyrian as her maid for months preceding the deed. They have some purpose beyond taking her life, which gives us time to react more rationally."

"Perhaps *you* won't pursue them," Halias said through

gritted teeth. He turned and stomped from the office, his threat of insubordination echoing in his wake. Cannan glanced sharply at Destari, who followed Halias from the room.

That left only Cannan, Steldor and me in the captain's office. Steldor retrieved the chair Halias had mistreated and restored it to its place in front of his father's desk.

"What should be done about the tunnel?" he asked.

"It's compromised," Cannan stated. "We'll have to close it off. Somehow the Cokyrians learned of it. I've sent men to investigate the other tunnel that leads outside our city's walls—if the Cokyrians have discovered that one as well, we have a major security breach on our hands, not to mention we'll be deprived of both potential escape routes in the event we need them."

"How could they have learned of it?" Steldor queried with a frown.

There was a pause but not one of contemplation.

"Narian must have told them," Cannan said. "That's the only logical explanation."

"Did Narian *have* such information?" Steldor astutely posed the question to me, and helpless tears again welled in my eyes.

"I told him," I whispered, examining the dark features of the two capable military men who were now part of my family, praying they would not condemn me.

Neither man showed a reaction to my revelation. The room was silent, no scuff of shoe nor sound of breath breaking it. Finally, Cannan ended the oppressive hush.

"You *told* him?" he repeated, his implacability for once fractured by incredulity. "You told a *Cokyrian* about a tunnel leading into the *Palace of Hytanica,* and didn't think it important to inform me or anyone else?"

Hot tears poured from my eyes, and I wiped my face, nose and all on the sleeve of my chemise.

"Father…" Steldor said tentatively, perhaps thinking that I could not handle accusations or blame, but I interrupted him, needing to defend my actions.

"He discovered it." My voice was strained with fatigue and misery as I tried to dredge up the details of my conversation with Narian so many months ago in the Royal Stables. "He found the tunnel himself, or what he thought to be a tunnel, and asked me where it opened. And I told him. But he would never have repeated the information to harm us. He couldn't have known this would happen!"

Cannan looked ready to issue a harsh retort but settled on demanding if Narian knew of the second tunnel, to which I had no sure answer. As if to save me further rebuke from the captain, the office door swung open, cutting him off, and my parents entered, followed by Galen. Cannan closed his eyes and took a steadying breath, preparing to deliver the gut-wrenching news.

My father stepped toward the desk, Steldor moving aside to make way for him, while my mother, seeing that I was crying, came to me. She put a hand on my shoulder and stroked my hair, though she knew not what caused my suffering.

"What has happened?" my father asked, disturbed. "The whole palace is in an uproar."

"You should sit," Cannan advised, and my father obeyed, sinking into one of the three hardwood chairs that stood before the captain's desk. Galen moved one of the others closer to mine, and my mother likewise sat, although she kept a hand upon my arm. The sergeant then moved to stand in the back of the office, and my parents stared at Cannan, knowing they were about to hear something horrific.

"There is no easy way for this to be said," the captain began, utterly collected even as I started to shake with sobs. "Cokyrians, we know not how many, infiltrated the palace tonight and abducted Princess Miranna."

My mother let out an anguished cry that caused my tears to flow with renewed vigor. She wrapped her arms around me, composure shattered, hugging me close. My father appeared to shrink in his chair, growing paler and seemingly older. He mouthed *no,* but could muster no sound, his breath stolen by the captain's words.

"The city was closed down as quickly as possible," Steldor informed my parents, glancing at his father for reassurance before finishing. "But we have reason to believe that she was removed from the palace several hours before we were aware that she was in danger."

"No!" my mother wailed. "No, not my baby..."

Her sorrow ripped at my heart, diminishing my own and stopping my rain of tears, and I became the one attempting to offer comfort. My father's feelings, on the other hand, were apparent from his posture, for he sat still, pale and uncommunicative.

"If it's any consolation, I do not think the Cokyrians would have gone through the effort of taking Miranna from the palace if their intent were to kill her," Cannan said, repeating what he had earlier told Halias. "I believe she is safe for now, although all possible measures will be taken to bring her home."

"Why Miranna?" my father rasped, finally managing sound, his eyes wide and red-rimmed.

"She was the easiest target, the least heavily protected and most naïve member of the royal family," Cannan explained. His next words were meant to offer some measure of comfort. "If we are unable to apprehend her captors, I'm certain the Cokyrians will negotiate for her release. What they'll demand, I cannot say."

A knock on the office door announced Bhadran's arrival, and Galen granted him entry. The graying doctor, who had treated my family for as long as I could remember, scanned the room in confusion, not yet understanding what had happened. The captain gave him the details, instructing him to supply my parents and me with something to help us sleep. Bhadran, shocked by the news himself, administered a sedative to each of us, and Cannan suggested that we all retire, for there was nothing more to be done this night. My father pulled my weeping mother to him and led her from the room, and Steldor helped me to my feet, only to discover that my legs would not hold me. He lifted me easily into his arms and carried me from the office and toward the Grand Staircase, though exhaustion defeated me before he reached the first step.

CHAPTER 10

DARK DAWN

WHEN I AWOKE, THE GROWING LIGHT OF EARLY morning was filtering through my partially open drapes, attempting to conquer the dark corners of the room. I lay curled on my side beneath the covers of my bed, examining my pale hands where they rested on the pillow, trying to recall the previous evening's events. I thought of the bizarre dream through which I'd seemingly journeyed, the lingering effects of the sedative making me feel strangely disconnected. I ran my fingers over my face and found it rough with dried tears, and then, as though I had rushed headlong into a wall, I remembered.

Images of Miranna's overly feminine bedroom flashed in my head, her beribboned canopy bed, the pastel banners that adorned her walls, her legions of dolls. At the thought that she might never sleep there again, my throat stung, and I squeezed my eyes shut in an effort to close out the memories. Only when I reopened them did I notice Steldor in the chair to my left, sound asleep, apparently having stayed with me all night. His head was turned away from me, tucked against his shoulder and the chair's back, one arm dangling over the side so his fingers grazed the floor. His dark hair and clothing were atypically mussed, but he appeared every bit as angelic as people were rumored to look when they slept, his long ebony lashes dusting his smooth cheeks. Somehow the peaceful expression upon his handsome face comforted me.

I pulled the covers tighter and watched him for a time, his chest methodically rising and falling with his soft breathing. I willed him not to wake up, not to break this spell that kept back time. I knew that when he roused, we would go to find Cannan and learn if anything had come of the searches that had continued through the night. We would also have to decide what to do in order to survive this nightmare, and at the moment, I was content to block it from thought altogether.

It seemed, however, that my gaze was penetrating Steldor's layers of sleep, and he shifted, his head lolling to the other side. After raising a hand to his furrowed brow, he finally lifted his lids, instantly focusing on me. He observed me almost apprehensively, as though uncertain what my mental state might be or how I might feel about his presence in my room. Eventually, he stood and cleared his throat.

"My father will want to see us. I'll send for your maid to help you dress."

I sat up, nodding, following him with my eyes as he moved toward the door, not wanting him to leave but knowing that he must.

"Thank you for staying with me," I said.

He stopped with his hand on the open door, turning to give me a slight nod before continuing on his way.

Sahdienne arrived shortly thereafter and assisted me into a simple cream gown. She brushed my hair as she did every morning, and the mundane nature of her actions made me ache, for Miranna's morning would be anything but normal. After she had twisted my dark hair into a loose bun, she stood behind me, continuing to fuss needlessly with a few stray strands.

"Your Majesty, I heard..." she murmured, but I was too numb to react. I stared at myself in the mirror above my dressing table, face blank and pale, dark circles dominating the skin beneath my eyes. I silently prayed for Sahdienne to stop, but she wanted affirmation, despite the sensitive nature of the issue.

"Is—is it true?" she stammered, at last getting her thoughts out into the open.

"It is."

"And—and it was her maid? Ryla was involved?"

"Yes."

The maid I had hired, the maid I had placed within Miranna's rooms, the maid who had fooled us both into thinking last night would be the best of my sister's life. Surely there had been some sign of her falseness that passed my notice that very first day. And why hadn't I recognized the danger the minute Miranna had told me about Temerson's note? If only I had been as astute as Steldor, I might have saved her. If I had just paid more attention, I could have prevented everything.

"I have to go," I announced, rising from my seat at the dressing table, and Sahdienne shied away, bowing her head respectfully.

I entered the parlor where Steldor awaited me in a fresh change of clothes, his hair restored to its usual, perfectly casual style, managing his restlessness by flipping his dagger over and over in his hand. He sheathed the weapon and escorted me into the corridor. As we walked, he informed me that while I'd been dressing, he'd gone to speak with his father.

"The searches during the night were unsuccessful," he said. I struggled not to cry, and he attempted to offer some comfort. "There is still hope, Alera. My father is convening a meeting to discuss what action should be taken."

"When?"

"Now. He sent for the others when he learned you were awake." At my puzzled glance, he elaborated. "He assumed there would be no keeping you from the meeting, and since you were involved in the incident, it's potentially imperative that you attend."

I nodded, but could not refrain from asking the one question that throbbed within my skull as steadily as my heartbeat. I gripped Steldor's shirtsleeve to bring him to a standstill.

"Will we get her back?"

His hesitation was answer enough and diluted any confidence I might have gained at his next words.

"We'll do everything within our power."

He stood still, waiting without complaint for me to regain my composure. After a few deep breaths, I took his arm and he led me down the spiral staircase to the first floor.

I expected him to take me to the Captain of the Guard's office, but instead we walked through the King's Drawing Room directly opposite the stairway and into the Throne Room, crossing to the strategy room on the eastern side, which fell between Cannan's office and the King's study. Inside the vast rectangular room was a large oaken table at which twelve men sat. Cannan was at the head, for he would preside over the meeting, and there were two empty chairs at his immediate left for Steldor and me. Next came my father, Galen, Destari and Halias. To Cannan's right sat

Cargon, who was the major in command of the Reconnaissance Unit, and Marcail, the Master at Arms in charge of the City Guard. The remaining seats were occupied by five other deputy captains. Cannan, Galen, Halias and Destari all looked as though they hadn't closed their eyes since the beginning of this ordeal, though behind their grimness lurked determination.

All pairs of eyes turned our way, then the men rose, bowing as Steldor and I joined them. I followed the King to our seats, aware that most of the men would find my presence odd, but too emotionally drained to feel self-conscious at being the only woman present. After we had taken our places, Cannan began.

"Not all of you are aware of the events of last night, so I will brief you. Sometime during the twilight hours, Princess Miranna was abducted from the palace by what we have determined to be Cokyrian intruders."

Mutterings traveled round the table at this news, but Cannan pressed on without waiting for the sound to die out.

"We believe that the enemy managed to place a young Cokyrian woman as the princess's personal maid. We have yet to locate this servant, and very little is known about her past. It appears she tricked Her Highness into going to the Royal Chapel, where she was seized and taken through the tunnel that leads to the Royal Stables.

"Searches were conducted throughout the night, but those involved have not been found. We are continuing to sweep the foothills and our border patrols are on alert, but the princess was probably outside the city by the time the situation was discovered, possibly even outside the kingdom. I have no hope she will be recovered in this fashion. My men believe they have found the spot where the Cokyrians crossed the river, which makes it probable they are already in the mountains.

"The purpose of this meeting is to determine our course of action. I deem there to be three conceivable options. One, we send men after her. As this would involve going into Cokyri, it would be complex. London's expertise would be invaluable for this purpose, and he is currently in the field doing reconnaissance work.

"Two, we wait to hear from the Cokyrians. The enemy has some purpose in stealing our princess, and I believe they will attempt to negotiate terms with us. This would necessitate that we seriously consider what concessions we would be willing to make in exchange for her life."

My father made a small, piteous noise and put a hand to his mouth, unable to endure the thought of his younger daughter's death. Cannan glanced at him, but not in an empathetic way, purely as if the sound had caught his notice. The captain was in that moment precisely how he had always seemed to me: a man of incalculable strength who acted, not a man who worried or sorrowed.

"Our third and, as I see it, final option is to initiate negotiations with Cokyri. This would give us the advantage of being on the offensive, but we must all remember that Cokyri is not known for treating our ambassadors well. I, therefore, do not favor this approach."

Everyone at the table knew the history of the war with Cokyri: over a century ago, Hytanica had sent its Crown Prince to discuss a trade treaty with the Cokyrian Empress, and she had taken insult at his ignorance of their culture. She'd had him executed, and when word had reached the ears of the Hytanican King, he had launched the war that would span almost a hundred years. No one would be eager to send another valuable man into the midst of the enemy.

"I open this issue for discussion," Cannan finished.

"We should go after her," Halias asserted, the first to open his mouth, and my father earnestly bobbed his head in concurrence. "We should have gone after her last night—she is in danger and is relying on us to save her."

"That would be suicide," Destari responded tiredly, and I had the feeling he'd been arguing similarly all night. "Especially without the aid of our neighboring kingdoms, who we know will not cross Cokyri. We need London's knowledge of Cokyrian territory to develop a suitable plan. I say we wait, at least until London comes back."

"But who knows when that will be?" my father blustered, drumming his fingers on the table, panic pulsating in his voice. "He might be gone for weeks, and by then Miranna could be…could be…"

"Dead," Halias ended harshly.

"Then let us send someone to search for London," Steldor suggested, directing a frown at Halias. "I agree with Destari that an attempt to blindly infiltrate Cokyri would be disastrous, but we don't have to sit back and wait for London to return of his own accord. Perhaps Cargon could dispatch some scouts into the foothills to see if he can be found."

"I'll do so at once," Major Cargon said, and Steldor and Cannan both nodded their approval. "I'll also have my men survey the Cokyrian stronghold for its easiest access points."

"Are we agreed on that much then?" Cannan asked, glancing around the table at everyone. "We'll send scouts to search for London, but until and unless he is found, we will not attempt a rescue. It will be just as perilous for the princess if we go in without a well-developed plan as if we wait. I think it's safe to say that she is not in immediate mortal danger, and if Cokyri brings forth terms before a rescue plan is in place, we will evaluate then."

All but two heads nodded in accordance. My father's anxious brown eyes met Halias's enraged ones of light blue, revealing that neither man was pleased with the decision. Though I was undergoing stabs of fear, I made myself trust the judgment of the majority. Halias was wallowing in guilt, and my father was not a military man, but the rest, with their clear heads, believed Miranna was not at significant risk of harm. Still, I could not stave off a rise of queasiness at Cannan's supposition that Miranna was not in "immediate *mortal* danger." How many kinds of danger were there? And if not in danger of her life, then in what way might she be threatened?

"How long do you think it will be before the Cokyrians contact us to set up a meeting?" Galen asked, forcing me to focus again on the discussion.

"I do not know," Cannan responded. "But the Cokyrians like to create terror and uncertainty, and time is on their side. They will want us to be in the proper frame of mind to make concessions, so they will contact us later rather than sooner. While we do not need to decide this today, we each should give thought to what we would be willing to offer for her safe return."

Cannan paused, his eyes meeting each man's in turn, emphasizing the importance of his last statement.

"There is a second matter that we must address. We've had an enormous security breach, one that must be dealt with promptly. I've already commissioned men to collapse the tunnel through which the princess was taken, but there are several other measures that must be put into place.

"First, any member of the palace staff hired within the past year must be investigated. I won't give Cokyri the benefit of the doubt in terms of planning ahead. Galen, I'm putting you in charge of arranging the inquiries. I want places of birth, families, life histories, whatever proves them to be loyal Hytanicans. If anything seems even remotely out of place, I am to be notified at once. In addition, any staff members hired in the future will be likewise scrutinized.

"Henceforth, any note or invitation intended for a member of the royal family, however casual, innocent or expected, will be brought to me. I don't care if it's a note to Queen Alera from her mother, in her mother's handwriting, asking her to tea—it will be reviewed by me before any response is made.

"Third, the number of guards throughout the palace needs to be increased substantially. From now on, everyone entering the palace will be checked in by a Palace Guard who will also be accountable for overseeing that party's departure. This includes any guests, men delivering supplies through the servants' entrance and even members of the military who are not stationed within these walls. Records of those who come and go will be kept at the courtyard gates and at every palace entrance, and any suspicious behavior will be reported to me. On the off chance that information of this nature is delayed in reaching me, the man responsible will be subject to inquiry on the grounds of insubordination. Galen, I leave it to you to place your men and make them aware of this new procedure."

"Yes, sir," Galen said with a quick nod.

Though everyone seemed a bit taken aback by the captain's intensity, no one said a word. A princess had been taken from the palace, by the enemy, who had, unbeknownst to all, been living amongst us for months, gathering knowledge, spying on everyone. Who knew what secrets the Cokyrian woman might have taken back to her homeland? Who knew how many of her kinsmen might yet be within the city?

"Similar checkpoint procedures will be implemented at the city gates," Cannan continued, turning to the Master at Arms. "Marcail, I leave it to you to inform and assign your men."

"Yes, sir."

"Good. Now, for the final change, I will be appointing a deputy captain as a personal bodyguard to each member of the royal family, including the former King and Queen. Destari, you will return to your post as Queen Alera's guard. Davan and Orsiett, you will guard King Adrik and Lady Elissia, and Casimir, I'm assigning you to the King."

Steldor, who had evidently excluded himself from the royal family to which Cannan referred, sat up straight, a protest on his lips.

"But—"

"Don't," the captain interrupted, holding up a finger without sparing a glance at his son. Steldor sank back in his chair, somewhat stunned, but he did not raise an argument.

"That concludes this meeting," Cannan declared, rising to his feet. To Galen and Marcail, he added, "I expect to hear from both of you by the end of the day."

Steldor and I left the strategy room first, followed by Destari and Casimir, who had already assumed their new assignments. Casimir's manner was stoic, and I knew he would try to be unobtrusive, but still I couldn't say how Steldor would deal with having someone perpetually at his heels. In the short time it took us to cross the Throne Room, my husband cast several disgruntled looks over his shoulder.

Though not as tall as his fellow deputy captain, which was true of almost all of the Elite Guards, Casimir was equal in height to my husband and had the well-muscled build of a soldier. With medium brown hair and smoky gray eyes, he was younger than Destari, London and Halias, but I did not know him well, for he generally took care of business for Cannan in other kingdoms.

I climbed the first two steps of the Grand Staircase, then realized that Steldor had stopped at the bottom.

"I need to discuss a few matters with my father," he explained, and I wondered if he was going to revisit the question of whether he needed a bodyguard.

I was surprised at the nervous flutter in my stomach at the thought that he might leave me. I inhaled deeply, trying to think sensibly, but I could not quash my initial reaction, and it persisted even as I nodded. He stepped forward and brushed a lock of my hair behind my ear, apparently seeing something of my emotions in my face, and I closed my eyes at his touch, trying to soak up his confidence and the security that came with it. Then he was gone, Casimir with him.

I glanced at Destari, then hastened up the remaining stairs, for the sympathy in his inky eyes was too much to bear. I didn't want anyone's pity. I wanted everyone to pretend that none of this had happened, that it was a giant charade. I hated every compassionate glance for its jolting reminder that this horror was reality, that my sister was in Cokyri where the High Priestess and the ruthless Overlord dwelled, that Miranna was at their mercy.

Destari hovered at the parlor door, uncertain whether he should join me so that I would not be alone, and I beckoned him inside. Though I was not in a mood to talk, I could not pretend that I felt no fear. Miranna had been taken against her will from our well-protected and presumably inviolable home. Who could give assurance the same would not happen to me? Was there any place that the enemy could not reach?

I retreated to my bedroom, leaving Destari in the parlor,

where I shut the door and drew the heavy curtains over my window to block out the sunlight. I stumbled back to my bed and burrowed under the covers without taking off my gown, staying there for hours, drifting in and out of sleep, wanting to lock out the world so I would cease to be a part of its complete and utter wrongness.

It was much later that muffled voices from the parlor reached my ears, and I tried to concentrate, to turn the sounds into words, with no success. I heard the parlor door open and close, then footsteps approaching my bedroom.

"Alera," Steldor called, with a gentle rap upon the door.

I threw back the covers, eager to see him, scrambling out of bed to open the door. His eyes swept my form and the room behind, taking in my rumpled state, the drawn drapes and the untidy bedclothes.

"Have you been asleep all day?" he asked.

"Sometimes I slept," I said guardedly. "Mostly I just rested."

A shadow of concern fell upon him, but he did not question me further.

"I have something for you," he said, inviting me to follow him, and I saw that Destari had left the parlor to join Casimir in the corridor.

Like a scared animal being coaxed from its den, I went to the sofa and sat upon it, reaching for the covered basket Steldor had placed on the table in front of it. He watched from near the hearth while I lifted the basket's lid.

The moment there was an opening, a tiny gray-and-black tabby kitten poked his head out and mewed at me with surprising volume, his gray eyes round with curiosity. As he struggled to escape the basket, I saw that all four of his paws and his stomach were white. Before long, one back leg found its way over the basket's lip, and the tiny fur ball tumbled into my lap, where he mewed again and got unsteadily to his feet, arching his back so that the roundness of his tummy was even more apparent.

I took the kitten into my arms, nestling him against my neck until he squirmed onto my shoulder, balancing precariously. He buried his head in my long hair, batting at it with his miniature paws, apparently thinking it some kind of strange prey. Steldor came to my side and picked up the fluffy baby, which fit into his palm.

"It's going to be chaotic around here for some time," he said, scratching the kitten behind the ears before placing it on my knees. "I don't want you to spend too much time alone and thought perhaps a companion, even such a small one, might be a good distraction."

"Thank you," I said, gazing at him gratefully. In the midst of all the military activity, Steldor had thought of me, not wanting me to feel abandoned, trying to offer reassurance. Although he had never said the words, his actions affirmed that he loved me.

I spent the next few days in my quarters with my new pet. I did not want to venture out, my usually insatiable curiosity for palace politics having vanished with my sister. I took my meals in the parlor, knowing that if I went to the family dining room, Miranna would not be there. I stayed away from the corridors, since there was no possibility of bumping into her. It was easier to contend with my guilt and sorrow when I did not have to endure reminders of her absence.

Steldor would come and go, but I knew from snippets of conversation he had with Destari that my self-imposed isolation bothered him. He was, however, somewhat placated by the fact that my bodyguard kept company with me in the parlor rather than standing guard in the corridor.

One week after Miranna's abduction, in the afternoon, my mother came to see me. The dark circles beneath her blue eyes gave me reason to think she had not slept since this ordeal had begun, and I wondered if I showed signs of the same fatigue. I had not given my appearance much thought over the past few days, and apprehension and grief seemed to have taken over as my only emotions. She sat next to me on the sofa, smiling slightly at the kitten gamboling at her feet, and then took my hands in hers.

"How are you doing, my dear?" she asked, her voice bleaker than was customary.

"I'm trying, Mother. Steldor is doing what he can to help me." I motioned to the kitten, then added, "He doesn't want me to be alone."

She nodded, but I knew the worry on her face was for me. The thought that I was causing her additional distress was almost more than I could stand, and I scrambled to find words of reassurance. But before I could think what to say, she spoke once more.

"I'm going to make a request of you, Alera, one that will be difficult for you to undertake, but that is important for you to attempt."

"Yes, Mother, anything."

"Until and unless we learn, God forbid, that your sister is dead, we must act as though she is alive. We must not give in to despair, and even when we do, we must not let it show in our actions. Our guards and military leaders must know they have our confidence, and the people of the kingdom must believe that we are strong."

Her tired eyes had a spark of determination in them, and I could feel an unexpected fortitude within her.

"Alera, I am asking you to resume your normal routines,

to carry out your duties. I am asking you to try to live a normal life."

"I have not given up hope," I assured her, then softly added, "but I do not know if I can do what you ask."

She gazed out the window for a long moment, as if trying to decide how to convince me that I was capable of accomplishing the impossible. Finally, she returned her attention to me, her eyes melancholy.

"I have been through trying times before. That does not make these circumstances easier to bear, but it does make them easier to survive. You have long known that my family was killed during a Cokyrian raid when I was a young woman and that I came to live in the palace until the time came for me to wed the King's son. While I lived here, awaiting the wedding, I fell passionately and irrevocably in love with him. What you may not know is that I was betrothed to the Crown Prince, Andrius, and not to your father."

I sat mutely beside her, my heart rate increasing, both shocked and intrigued by the information she was sharing. I had always known that my father had ascended to the throne upon the death of his older brother, but I had never considered how my mother had come to be his wife. Had she, like me, suffered the loss of the man she loved, only to marry another out of duty? The thought of the tragedies she had endured was enough to overwhelm me; yet the strength she was showing was awe-inspiring, and I waited to hear more.

"You never knew your uncle, but he was much like Cannan," she added with a fleeting smile, and I thought a glimmer of longing crossed her face. "Only with a more ready sense of humor."

She reached out to brush a lock of hair off my forehead, perhaps reading some of my reactions in my expression.

"But we were at war, and all the young men went off to fight. Andrius convinced the King to let him join the effort. He lost his life, and I wanted to die, as well. But I gradually recovered and was betrothed to your father, for I had, after all, been raised to be a queen."

My thoughts flew in another direction. Andrius had been raised his entire life believing he would be king; my father would have known it only upon his brother's death. He would have been like Miranna, who as a second-born was more carefree, having been raised with fewer expectations. While he had proven himself to be a good king, I wondered, would Andrius have been a *great* king? Although I was now almost bursting with questions, I forced myself to listen, knowing there was a reason my mother was sharing her history with me.

"I tell you this because tragedy comes to everyone at some time. What separates people is how they handle it. You remind me of Andrius—that's why I know what strength lies within you. What I am asking of you will be grueling, but you are Hytanica's Queen. The people look to you for faith and courage, the same as they look to the King. And each time you show it, whether you truly feel it or not, will make the next time a little easier."

I examined my beautiful mother, appreciating for the first time that much of her grace had been born out of tragedy. My father's tendency toward paranoia was in contrast to her calm, and I gathered my pride, wondering how truly I resembled the first man she had loved.

"I will try," I promised, and she took me in her arms, clasping me close just as she used to when I was young, letting some of her determination flow into me.

CHAPTER 11

BROTHERS IN ARMS

INTERRUPTED BY A KNOCK ON MY PARLOR door, I glanced up at Destari from where I was sitting on the sofa, waggling a ribbon in front of my kitten. Having coaxed myself into making several appearances with Steldor in the few days since my mother's visit, I had returned to my quarters to rest and was not expecting any guests. In response to my nod, my bodyguard pulled the door open, granting entrance to a sergeant in the Elite Guard.

"Your Majesty, I've come to replace Destari as your bodyguard for the time being," he said with a bow. "The captain needs to speak with him and did not want you to be left unprotected."

I sprang up, my anxiety level vaulting at the mere suggestion of Destari's departure. I examined the man Cannan had sent as a substitute for the guard so tall and well-muscled that he made me appear child-sized. After taking in the sergeant's lean stature, his height just a couple of inches beyond my own, and his youthful appearance, I knew I could not feel safe with him. I needed Destari, whom I trusted, whom I had grown up trusting, whose skill and ability were unquestionable.

Destari took note of my expression and spoke up on my behalf.

"The Queen and I would both prefer if I stayed here. Did the captain say why I'm needed?"

The sergeant's eyes darted toward me, uncertain to what extent he should speak candidly in my presence. Then he pulled Destari aside.

"The scouts found a horse," he confided in a hushed, but nonetheless flawlessly audible, voice.

"A horse?" Destari repeated uneasily, and I frowned, unable to fathom the significance of this information.

"One of ours, riderless, roaming the countryside. Caked in blood."

"Could they identify it?"

At the sergeant's grim nod, Destari's heavy black eyebrows fell as though he had learned the worst.

"Whose horse was it?" I demanded, besieged with dread.

The guard glanced between Destari and me, wondering if he should answer, but my bodyguard was too lost in thought to pay him mind.

"London's," the sergeant answered, not bold enough to ignore his Queen.

My stomach roiled, and I fought back the urge to vomit. My knees threatened to give out and Destari put a steadying arm around me, but I pushed against him, knowing he would leave me if he could.

"I'm going with you to Cannan," I choked.

Destari gave a brisk nod, and we left my quarters to descend the spiral stairway to the first floor, the sergeant following. Entering the Throne Room through the King's Drawing Room, we saw Galen, Casimir, Cargon and several other Elite Guards grouped near the dais, talking rapidly among themselves. Steldor occupied the throne, looking weary, while Cannan stood beside him.

Surprise flicked across the King's face as he saw that I was with Destari. Though the other men frowned at my presence, they resumed their discussion until Steldor held up a hand to stay their talk.

"Alera, I know you are concerned about London, but these are military matters. I can either have someone escort you to your drawing room or you can wait for me in my study."

I examined him, hardly believing my ears, for I had expected that he might force me to leave. Instead he was giving me the opportunity to eavesdrop. As our brown eyes met, I knew that this had been his purpose.

"I will go to your study, Your Highness," I said with a curtsey.

I moved to the right of the dais and into the King's study, leaving the door half-open so I would be able to hear every word that was spoken. I dragged one of the padded armchairs away from the fireplace and settled in to listen.

"We have to assume from the amount of blood staining the animal that London was bleeding profusely as he rode toward Hytanica." Cannan's full voice carried into the study. "It's likely that he fell from his mount on our land, for the horse had almost made its way to the city. Cargon's men have since scoured the area where the animal was found, but they saw no sign of London. The question before us now is whether or not to send out a search party." The captain paused before resuming his analysis. "Frankly, it is probable that London is dead."

Cannan's words felt like a kick in the stomach, but I forced myself to continue listening.

"He must have been seriously injured, and it is impossible to say when his wounds were inflicted, for we do not know how long his horse wandered. Dispatching a search party might needlessly put the lives of our men in danger."

It was Steldor who reacted first to Cannan's assessment of the situation.

"But if London is alive, his information could be vital in dealing with Miranna's abduction or in defending against a Cokyrian onslaught."

"A search on our side of the Recorah could be done with little danger to our soldiers," Galen pointed out.

"True," said a man whose voice I did not recognize. "But if he is not found on our lands, is it wise to send men into Cokyrian-held territory?"

"That would put them at significant risk, and I'm against doing so when there is such a small chance that London is alive," Galen answered.

"It seems we should at least search the lands on our side of the Recorah," Steldor determined, closing one issue. He paused, then seemed to address an individual. "You have not yet voiced an opinion on the matter of searching on the other side of the Recorah."

"That is because I will search for him there, regardless of whatever decision is made," Destari said, displaying the unreserved loyalty he'd always had for his best friend and comrade. "I don't ask that you send anyone with me, but I must go, simply because nothing would keep London from looking for me were our circumstances reversed."

"I suspect there are others who would willingly accompany Destari," Cannan noted. "Is there anyone here who would choose to do so?"

A chorus of voices arose, prompting Steldor to again close the discussion.

"We have our resolution then. I will not order men to cross the Recorah to search for London but will not prevent a small number of volunteers from doing so."

"I would require only one or two men," Destari declared. "The smaller our number, the better our odds of passing unnoticed into enemy territory."

"Then let me go," Galen said unexpectedly, and I imagined that in the silence all eyes had shifted to the Sergeant at Arms. Indeed, when next Galen spoke, he sounded defensive. "I have the training necessary for this assignment, I am young enough to believe we will be successful and, if the plan is indeed for me to become Captain of the Guard someday, I ultimately cannot expect men to follow me as they do Cannan unless I have some frontline experience."

"Then it's decided," Steldor decreed, taking the side of the friend whom he had always viewed as a brother.

Cannan left it to Destari to organize and deploy a search party for the Hytanican side of the river. If London were not found, the men would return, and only Destari and Galen would venture into Cokyrian lands to continue the effort.

The discussion having ended, I returned my armchair to its original location just as Steldor pushed the study door fully open.

"I assume you heard," he said, stepping across the threshold.

"Yes."

He seemed exhausted, even though he'd lately been returning to our quarters at a reasonable time to talk with me and then go to bed. I supposed that, though I had been sleeping an excessive amount of late, his workload had dramatically increased, and a measure of guilt to add to all the rest swelled within me.

"We probably won't hear anything for a few days. You'll

be given a new bodyguard, or three, or however many you want. Whatever you need to feel safe in Destari's absence—"

"I want a weapon."

This escaped me without real thought, but as I pictured the slim guard who had been sent to replace Destari and thought of the incident a year ago with Narian at the river, when Tadark had been too far away to prevent him from cutting off the bottom of my skirt, I knew that this was the only way I could feel secure. Bodyguards were effective only to a certain extent. Had Halias gone with Miranna to the chapel but waited in the corridor, she still would have been alone to protect herself. If someone near me drew a dagger with the intent to harm me, I would need to be able to do more than scream.

"A weapon?" Steldor repeated, eyebrows high, a bit of the condescension that had of late been so delightfully missing from his manner creeping into his words. "Really, Alera, I know you're frightened, but you'll either end up causing yourself harm or having the weapon turned on you. You don't know how to handle…"

He trailed off, and I cast my eyes to the floor. I knew his mind had gone to my short-lived self-defense lessons with Narian, which he had somehow discovered. I was by no means well learned in the art, but I did know the proper way to handle a weapon, which should have negated Steldor's main reason for objection. Even so, anything to do with Narian was a touchy subject, and I wasn't sure what to expect from him now.

"You should continue with your day," he said, his voice carefully controlled.

I left the room without further comment, grateful to have escaped unscathed, to be joined by two Elite Guards who had apparently been assigned to me by Steldor. I departed the Throne Room, leaving Casimir to await the King.

Over the next few days, my hope and whatever happiness I'd managed to reclaim decayed. I longed for the sound of my sister's voice, the flash of her smile, the sight of her strawberry blond curls bouncing upon her back; but now thoughts of London, who, if alive, was alone and grievously injured in the wilderness, also haunted me. On top of it all, fear clung to me like a second skin, always with me, as were the two bodyguards who every moment failed to make me feel safe.

By this time, Cannan had granted Destari and Galen permission to cross the river into Cokyrian lands to search for London. With the likelihood of locating him continuing to lessen, my constant worry shifted into premature mourning. London had risked and evaded death many times, but his luck could not last forever. Perhaps he'd been given all the chances fate was willing to allow. I struggled to accept the fact that he might never be found, might never be buried by those who loved him, the tale of his demise never to be known.

In my present frame of mind, I yearned for Steldor's company in the evenings, as I felt protected when I was with him. He was, however, steadily growing more irritable, worry and the pressures of his position taking their toll. Even though I understood this, I couldn't prevent a small flare of indignation every time he lost his patience with me for no apparent reason, especially when it came to Kitten, with whom he had one recurring problem.

"Will you just give it a name?" he said in exasperation one night as he hung his weapons on the hook by the hearth.

"What's wrong with calling a kitten Kitten?" I demanded

from where I sat on the floor, playing with the cuddly fluff ball.

"It's emasculating, that's what," Steldor informed me, moving to the sofa where he rested his booted feet, ankles crossed, on the low table. "The cat needs a *name,* before he becomes a milksop."

"I don't think *Kitten* cares about being a milksop, since he literally is one," I pointed out, scooping the little animal into my lap. "Why does this upset you so much?"

"I'm not upset," he snapped, running a hand through his dark hair. He closed his eyes and took a deep breath. Then he stood and, despite the fact that he had just returned to our quarters, retrieved his weapons.

"I need to go," he said, without looking at me. "I need to work off some energy."

I nodded, and he went to the door, intending to leave, but when he opened it and saw Casimir waiting for him in the corridor, he growled in aggravation and slammed it shut. He withdrew instead to his bedroom, closing that door with the same brutality.

"Someone's testy," I muttered under my breath, but a measure of concern for Steldor's state of mind had taken hold.

Two nights later, I was drawn awake from the strange dreams that had become my nighttime companions by a muted yet repetitive pounding. I rose from bed, slipping on my robe, and opened my door to see Steldor talking with an Elite Guard, his bare chest telling me he had also been roused from sleep. The guard departed, and Steldor spun on his heel, catching sight of me.

"Destari and Galen have returned," he said as he crossed to enter his room, reappearing a moment later fully clothed.

"Is London with them?" I asked, my heart hammering.

"Yes, although I do not know his condition."

"But he's alive?"

Steldor nodded, strapping on his weapon's belt, and instantaneous relief warmed me like sweet tea.

"Where is he? Can I see him?" I exclaimed, the pitch of my voice rising along with my elation.

"He's been taken to a guest room on the third floor, but Alera..." He trailed off, and his demeanor was grave. "He won't be well, Alera. You need to understand—just because he's been brought home doesn't mean death can't claim him."

I nodded, then repeated my question, determination in my voice. "Can I see him?"

I had no idea how horrible his wounds might be or how I would handle his condition. But I knew I had to go to him.

Steldor evaluated me as he weighed the options. "I advise against it but won't forbid you," he finally said, moving toward the door to depart.

I thanked him and retreated to my bedroom to dress. I then hurried to the spiral staircase used by the royal family, trailed by my two bodyguards, and climbed to the third floor. As I reached the top, I heard voices and saw dim light emanating from an open guest room door at the rear of the palace, on the opposite side of the floor from my parents' quarters. I approached and stepped inside without knocking.

Cannan, Galen, Steldor and Destari were talking a few feet from the injured Elite Guard, blocking my view of the bed where he lay, which was perhaps fortunate in light of the severe injuries that afflicted him. Hearing my approach, Steldor turned and ushered me to an armchair next to the roaring fireplace on the other side of the room, from where

I could see Bhadran, the longtime Royal Physician, leaning over the bed.

"He is alive but has been pierced by several arrows," Steldor said softly, obviously unsure of how I would cope with the information. "He has lost an immense amount of blood and is very weak. The doctor is determining whether any attempt should be made to remove the arrows."

I blanched, then tried to move around him.

"You don't want to see this," he said, catching my arm. "Just sit here. London won't be aware of you anyway—he's unconscious from pain and shock."

I obeyed, trying to keep my emotions in check. If I had the chance to talk to London, I had to be strong for him, just as he had always been strong for me. Steldor returned to the other men and rejoined their conversation, which had become more hushed since I'd arrived. I waited, along with everyone else, for Bhadran's assessment, London lying immobile and so silent that the entire situation struck me as some elaborate farce. Almost in confirmation of my thoughts, I heard London's voice, weak and strained, but unmistakable nonetheless.

"Isn't anyone going to take these damnable arrows out of me?"

I sprang from my seat, wanting to see him, only to be confronted with Steldor's raised hand. Destari had moved at the same moment to London's side, and I grudgingly sat once more, albeit on the edge of the chair, certain it was a good sign that he was awake.

"Lie still," Destari advised his friend. "The doctor will decide what should be done."

Cannan also stepped closer to the bed, but for a different purpose.

"What is the news from Cokyri?" he asked.

"Always a man of few words," London replied, speaking slowly and with great effort. "Afraid I might die, I suppose. Better get the information from me right away."

He gave a soft laugh, which turned into a cough, and I noticed with a tightening stomach that a strange gurgling sound dominated his breathing. After a moment, his gasping ceased, and he forced himself to continue.

"The Cokyrians are mustering their troops, preparing for a full-scale assault. Their numbers are far greater than ours… and they have Narian. He will lead the attack."

"No!" I cried, jumping to my feet and rushing forward, London's words too horrific to be true. Steldor caught me as I neared the bed, pulling me against his chest, but not quickly enough to prevent me from seeing the wounds.

London was on his back, his face pallid, sweaty and grimy. His shirt had been cut down the center but not fully stripped away, displaying, amidst dried blood and filth, the broken shafts of three arrows, one in his shoulder, one in his chest and one protruding from his stomach, all like oddly angled pegs. Around the shafts, the visible skin was swollen, bruised and clinging like strange spiderwebs to the wood.

My breath caught in my throat, and I clutched at Steldor, nauseated by London's injuries. My husband wrapped his arms more tightly about me, and I buried my head in his shoulder, not wanting to see more.

"I am only stating what I observed," London added, and I knew his words were meant for me.

Cannan returned to the matter at hand, disregarding my reaction. "How long until they are fit to march on us?"

I peered out, careful to set eyes only on London's face, to watch him try to adjust his position, to hear his sharp cry before he stilled. He paled, near to passing out again but, after a moment of labored breathing, answered the question.

"They were preparing to move troops when I left," he said, his voice even more strained. "I had a bit of trouble making a clean departure. We have little more than a week before they'll be on the other side of the Recorah."

Silence fell as the military men absorbed this. After a few moments, Cannan motioned to the doctor to step away with him, but London halted them both.

"Just let him say what he thinks. I have the right to know how badly I am hurt."

Bhadran looked almost pleadingly at Cannan, clearly not wanting to deliver the bad news directly to the dying man.

"London's right," the captain said gruffly. "What have you concluded?"

With a sigh and a quick rub of the back of his neck, the wizened doctor gave his report.

"One arrow shattered his left shoulder blade, and he has lost use of the arm. The second arrow pierced his lung, hence his labored breathing. The third is embedded in his abdomen, causing much internal bleeding. The only reason he is alive is because all three miraculously missed vital organs. By all indications he should have bled to death regardless, but the wounds have closed around the shafts, damming the blood flow. But infection is building within, as evidenced by the swelling and redness, and by his fever."

Glancing at London with deep sympathy, Bhadran concluded his assessment.

"The arrowheads cannot be pulled. The only way to remove them would be to cut them out, which would not only reopen the wounds but cause further damage and excruciating pain. This would be pointless, for he would bleed to death in the process. The best advice I can give is to make him as comfortable as possible until he succumbs to the infection, internal bleeding or tetanus."

Again there was a hush, then London smiled crookedly. "Apparently he agrees with you, Cannan. He thinks I'm going to die."

I struggled to pull air into my lungs, and only then did I realize that tears were running down my cheeks. I clenched my jaw, feeling pathetic and weak, knowing there was nothing I could do to help. London gazed at me with hazy indigo eyes that relayed a struggle to preserve focus.

"I want these arrows out now," he ordered, with surprising resolve.

The doctor stared in disbelief at him, then turned to the other men in the room.

"Try to talk sense into him. I will give him something for the pain and to help him rest, but I am not a cruel man. That is all I am willing to do."

Bhadran placed a vial on the bedside table, bowed to Steldor and me, then took his leave. Steldor guided me back to the chair by the hearth, shoring me up, for my legs refused to work properly. I sat, trying to breathe slowly to dispel my dizziness, and I was grateful that he stayed beside me, his hand upon my arm.

London was going to die. Those hideous wounds that had been inflicted by the Cokyrians, the wounds I fervently wished I had not seen, would cause his death. A deep sense of abandonment filled me. Soon, my two constant lifelong companions would have vanished from my life, first Miranna, then London. In addition, the man I loved had long since left and would now fight for his ruthless master. I wanted to scream, to strike out at fate, for everything about my world was amiss.

"Destari," London said, calling his friend forward. "Destari, if the doctor won't take them out, then you must."

The large Elite Guard recoiled at the idea, taking a backward step. "The pain would be intolerable, London. I'm sorry, I can't be the cause of—"

"The pain will ease after they are out, and, despite the doctor's opinion, I intend to recover," London growled. "I can't... I'm going to pass out again soon, so I won't feel much anyway. I need you to do this for me."

Destari hesitated, facing a horrible dilemma—cause his friend inestimable agony, or ignore his request, perhaps the last he would ever make.

"There's no point in waiting," London said. "If I'm going to die, let me die trying to survive."

Going tense, Destari yielded. "So be it." He then addressed Cannan. "Sir, I'll need lots of alcohol and cloths to stem the bleeding. I will also need a couple of people to hold him down—I'll have to dig out the arrowheads. If he makes it through that, I'll need bandages and clean bed linens."

"Galen and I will assist you," Steldor volunteered, and though Galen looked at him with raised eyebrows, the Sergeant at Arms did not object. With a glance at his father, Steldor added, "And Alera should be taken from the room."

"I'll see to everything," the captain replied.

I had already gotten to my feet by the time Cannan came toward me, and I walked ahead of him into the corridor. I stopped so he could pass by me and send Casimir for the needed supplies. Unwilling to leave, I sank to the floor, leaning against the wall just outside the room. I would not be able to sleep if I returned to my quarters, and should things go poorly for London, I wanted to be near him when death came. Cannan cast me a sympathetic glance before descending the staircase, taking Casimir with him to collect the requested supplies.

Casimir returned, along with a servant girl, and between them they carried the items Destari had requested. Only the

King's bodyguard went into the room, however, making a second trip to deliver everything that was needed. The servant girl exited, leaving me alone in the corridor with Casimir and my bodyguards, all of whom kept their distance to give me privacy.

I heard London groan and assumed Destari was disinfecting the wounds before beginning, then oppressive silence fell. A moment later I would have gladly given anything to have the silence back as a half-muffled scream shredded the stillness. I hugged my knees to my chest, biting my lip until I was sure it would bleed, and resisted the urge to bury my head in my arms so I could hear no more. There was another agonized cry, then another, until the sounds made my own sobbing inaudible. I longed for the torment to stop, but when at last the cries diminished, I was seized with dread, wondering whether Destari had discontinued this butchery, or London had finally given in to it.

An hour passed, the guards and the shadows in the dimly lit hallway my sole companions. I shivered, for only the heat rising from the rooms below warmed this part of the third floor, and I had not thought to bring a cloak. I almost welcomed the chill, however, as it helped to subdue my queasiness.

Eventually the door opened, and Galen emerged, followed by Steldor, both with blood spattered across their hands, arms and shirts. The sergeant stumbled across the corridor to buttress himself on the opposite wall, leaving a red smear where his hand touched, then doubled over to retch on the wood floor.

I rose to my feet as Galen dabbed at his mouth, face tinged green. Steldor stepped forward and put a hand on his friend's shoulder, then looked at me regretfully.

"Alera, you should not have stayed. There was no need for you to hear that."

"How is he?"

Just then Destari came into the corridor, not spattered like the other two but covered in blood, so much so that I gagged and had to close my eyes to avoid copying Galen. By the time my stomach had calmed, Destari had pulled off his shirt and was wiping the blood from his forearms and hands. His complexion was ashen, his posture tense, and he appeared to have forgotten I was there, though he probably was dealing with too many images from the past hour and a half to care about my sensibilities.

"Destari, how is he?" I asked, readdressing my question to the man who was probably best able to answer.

The Elite Guard gazed questioningly at Steldor and Galen, neither of whom spoke, and in frustration I made to shove my way past them and into London's room.

"Alera, no," Steldor said, catching me around the waist and pulling me back. "He's still alive, but…"

"It's a mess in there," Destari told me, looking as if he had been to hell and back. "At least let us clean things up."

At my nod, Destari and Galen reentered the room, but Steldor was disinclined to leave me in the hallway, once more alone other than for the bodyguards that I barely knew.

"Why don't you find a maid to clean up after Galen?" he suggested, wanting to give me a task. "Waiting is the only thing to be done now."

He kissed me on the cheek, then followed after the other two men. I went down the spiral stairway to summon a maid, noticing as I did so that the sun was rising. I returned to the corridor outside London's room, pacing while the maid scrubbed the floor, wishing there were some other way

I could be of assistance. After what felt like hours, Steldor opened the door and motioned me inside.

London lay unconscious on the bed, chest almost indiscernibly rising and falling. His shirt had been fully removed, and his torso was wrapped tightly in white bandaging, his skin almost matching its hue. The bedding had been changed, and the flames of the fire in the hearth were consuming the remnants of the old sheets.

I went to him, Destari drawing a chair next to the bed for me, and then placed my palm upon his forehead. The heat radiating from him surprised me, for I had expected from the pallor of his skin that he would be cold to the touch. The doctor had been right when he had said London was fevered. I brushed his silver bangs away from his eyes, knowing that, wherever he was in his mind, he was not at this moment aware of his tattered body or of the fact that when he awoke, if he awoke, he might never be the same.

CHAPTER 12

ANSWERS

I STAYED AT LONDON'S SIDE ALL DAY, DEPARTING but briefly to get some books from the library. Steldor and Galen had removed themselves to attend to their duties, although my husband had considerately arranged for meals to be sent to London's room for me. Destari kept me company throughout the many hours, occasionally stoking the fire. Few words passed between us as we waited for our friend to show some sign of life other than his shallow breathing. I eventually rested my head on the edge of the mattress, falling asleep with one hand upon London's arm, praying that he would stir.

I awoke early the following morning, slowly becoming aware that someone had positioned me more comfortably in the chair and covered me with a blanket. I was disoriented until a slight moan from London brought everything into sharp focus. His eyes were still closed, but his brow was furrowed, and I checked for fever, pleased that he was much cooler to the touch than he had been the day before.

Destari was at my side as I called London's name, trying to bring him to consciousness. Before long, his lids laboriously lifted, and his bleary eyes found me. He smiled faintly at my worried expression, but even this small gesture seemed to be a great exertion for him.

"How do you feel?" I asked, prompted by the hope I'd experienced when I'd discovered that his fever had diminished.

Without thought, London tried to shrug, then cried out, his face contorting into a grimace of pain.

"London…" I said helplessly, pushing back his hair, wanting to make the pain go away.

"Just relax," Destari advised. "You don't have to go anywhere today."

Nodding almost imperceptibly, London gazed once more at me, and a spark of his sardonic wit returned despite his condition.

"Alera, you should go and rest. You look terrible."

I let out a laugh, grateful for some way to break the crushing, somber intensity in the room.

"*I* look terrible," I repeated, shaking my head, noticing that I had dried blood on my clothing from where I had brushed against Steldor. "That hurts, coming from you."

He gave a quiet chuckle, but it was interrupted by a second spasm of pain. He caught my anxious expression and attempted to reassure me.

"I'm going to be all right, Alera." His eyes flicked to his fellow Elite Guard as he added, "Destari is a surprisingly good surgeon." He seemed to lose focus for a moment, then forced himself to finish. "You should go and come back tomorrow. I will most likely sleep this day away."

His eyes closed, but I stayed in place, not wanting to leave him alone. Cannan entered a short time later to check on his wounded deputy captain, and he stepped aside with Destari to exchange a few words before addressing me.

"I will talk to Bhadran, Alera, and arrange for one of his

healers to monitor London. Then you should leave and take care of yourself. If he develops any problems, I will make sure you are notified."

I nodded my thanks, and Cannan departed, but I remained at London's bedside until the promised healer arrived to care for him. Destari left with me, having been reassigned as my bodyguard, and we returned to my quarters. He took up position in the parlor, and I changed into a nightgown to crawl, exhausted, into bed. I did not stir until late afternoon, when I freshened up and went to the family dining room.

I had not shared a meal with my mother and father since Miranna's abduction, for I had not wanted to see my sister's empty chair. My parents came into the room a few minutes after I did, my father's hair grayer than it had been before this ordeal had begun, his face haggard; in contrast, my mother's heartache made her even more dignified.

After the servants had brought in platters of food, a hush fell upon us. None of us seemed to have the energy for simple, pleasant conversation. As we began to eat, we let the chink of our tableware against our plates fill the deathly silent room, the dull, repetitive noise gradually settling into me, and I knew I would hear it long after this meal had ended.

When dinner closed, my father announced that he would retire, moving more slowly than usual from the room to make his way to the third floor.

"It's good to have you join us, darling," my mother said, preparing to follow her husband. She gave me a small smile, then added, "I hear London is improving."

"Yes, he is, and as he grows stronger, so does hope for Miranna's rescue."

I wanted, in some small way, to ease her anguish and sadness, but instead she eased mine.

"I have not lost hope, only time that could have been spent with her. I'm so glad that you are back among us—I do not want to lose time with you, as well."

She gave me a light embrace, then left me to my thoughts. I returned to my quarters, my spirits having improved with rest and with the knowledge that London was on the road to good health. Kitten greeted me happily, and I passed the evening curled up with my fluffy pet and a good book in one of the leather armchairs near the hearth.

By the next day, London was markedly improved, his voice more robust and his breathing easier. He still needed much sleep, however, so I planned to keep my visit short. While Destari and I talked with him, Bhadran arrived to assess his patient's condition. Probably thinking he would find a corpse, the mystified physician was compelled to admit that the soldier was on the mend, the infection apparently having bled out with the removal of the arrowheads. When the doctor departed a few minutes later, Destari and I did likewise, leaving London once more in the hands of the healer Bhadran had assigned.

By the next afternoon, London was propped up against the pillows with a piece of parchment and bits of charcoal laid across the quilt that covered his lap. The healer was no longer in the room, an indication that Bhadran had visited him earlier in the day and was confident his patient was doing well. Destari took up position in the corridor, wanting to give me some time alone with my former bodyguard.

"How are you feeling?" I asked as I took a seat at his bedside, curiosity high about what he was doing. When I'd been a little girl, he had often sketched pictures for me, mostly of animals, but I had not laid eyes on a drawing of his since then.

"You need to invent a new question," he said, a welcome tease in his voice. "You ask that every time you come through the door."

"It seems a natural question, considering the circumstances. But if your mood is any indication, you're feeling much better."

"I am, but unfortunately, as my health increases, so does my boredom. I'm afraid I have never learned how to be idle." Unable to resist a slight jab at his captain, he finished, "Of course, Cannan and the doctor are being utterly unreasonable, insisting that I stay in bed."

"You seem to be keeping yourself entertained." I indicated the pieces of parchment atop the spread, ignoring his comment about Bhadran and the captain. "Have you drawn much?"

"A few things. The only fortunate part of all of this is that it's my left arm that's injured."

"May I see them?"

"If you wish," he answered, sounding tired.

I reached for the stack and began to sort through the parchments. As a six-year-old, I had not been able to appreciate the talent behind the drawings made to amuse me, and now gazed in amazement at what I saw. Although they were only sketches, the landscapes and buildings were depicted with startling detail and realism. I more closely examined one of a wide, sprawling city depicted from high above.

"Is this Hytanica?" I asked, thinking the inquiry unnecessary, but his answer was perplexing.

"It's Cokyri."

I nodded, not knowing how to respond, supposing that all the time he had spent in the mountains of late had put the land of the enemy in his mind.

"Most of the pictures are of Cokyri," he said, laying his head back on the pillows.

After examining all of the sketches, I returned the pieces of parchment to their place, a remark about his obvious gift on my lips, when another sheet, isolated from the others on the bedside table, caught my eye.

"What's this?" I asked, reaching for it just as London gave a small exclamation. Once it was in my possession, whatever protest he had intended to utter died, but I could feel his eyes boring into me.

The picture was of a beautiful young woman, perhaps in her early twenties, whose features were oddly familiar.

"London, this is lovely. Who is she?"

"Just someone I used to know." His response was deliberately casual, as well as deliberately unrevealing.

I considered him for a moment, and a conversation with Destari from over a year ago surfaced in my memory. Destari had told me that London had been betrothed to a woman of noble birth before being imprisoned in Cokyri. He had been presumed dead, and her parents had forced her to marry another man. The woman in the portrait, of whose identity I was almost certain, had to be his former betrothed. Of what other woman would he sketch such a stunning likeness?

London fractured my thoughts with a short laugh. "What? You're not the only woman in my life, Alera."

"I know," I said, mildly defensive. "It's just, from the way this is drawn, it seems a fair guess that you were in love with her."

There was a beat of silence, and I flushed at my boldness. Just when I was about to apologize, he gave a half smile and a shake of his head.

"It's only a sketch."

"Of course," I agreed, but there was still one more way that I might be able to affirm my suspicions. "May I keep it?"

At his leery glance, I felt the need to clarify.

"You never draw for me anymore, and this is quite beautiful."

"If you really want it," he said with a casual shrug that was not quite convincing.

We talked for a while longer, then I invited Destari to join us, knowing he would also want to check on London. As the time for the evening meal approached, I bid London farewell with a wish that he enjoy the rest of his day.

"The most enjoyable part of my day has just ended," he replied.

I again ate with my parents, but this time with an ulterior motive. I knew that my mother would be able to answer my questions regarding London, the questions that besieged me out of a combination of curiosity and a desire for distraction. I entered the dining room and took my seat, placing the sketch in my lap. My parents stood at the conclusion of our meal, but my mother graciously obliged when I requested that she stay.

"I'd like to ask you something, Mother."

Her blue eyes, so reminiscent of Miranna's, were inviting but not bright as she nodded and retook her seat. I placed London's drawing on the tabletop in front of her, and she took it into her hands.

"Do you know this woman?" I asked, as though I had no notion of my own.

She examined the parchment, her eyebrows drawn close together in concentration.

"I believe this is Lady Tanda when she was young," she murmured, confirming my suspicion. Lady Tanda and my mother were close friends, so if anyone were capable of making such a judgment, it was the woman sitting before me.

"Where did you get this?" she asked, passing the drawing across the table to me, and I gave her a truthful answer.

"London sketched it and allowed me to take it."

"London drew this?" she repeated, but there was more than bewilderment in her voice. There was disbelief.

I nodded, silently imploring her to tell me more, but she seemed to decide that it was not her place to speak further.

"He has a good memory," she said simply, as if the flawless likeness of Tanda in her youth were the only thing that had astonished her.

"But why would he draw Lady Tanda?"

My mother glanced toward the door, managing simultaneously to reveal her discomfort and make my question seem superfluous.

"It's always been difficult to know what goes on in London's mind," she said, but I had my answer.

When I visited London the next morning, I found him in the company of Cannan and Bhadran. Destari went to join the two men, while I hung back to let them finish their conversation.

"It's just a tingle right now," London was explaining. "But I think I'll be able to move my fingers soon."

"That's impossible!" the physician exclaimed. "Your shoulder blade was shattered—the injury should affect you for the rest of your life!"

"I seem to be managing fairly well," London observed, his customary sarcasm coming back along with his health.

"Fairly," the doctor said with a hoot of laughter. "Indeed. You should be dead—several times over, in fact."

There was momentary silence while everyone recalled

the two previous instances of London's uncanny ability to cheat death. First, when he had escaped seventeen years ago from Cokyri and survived the horrible illness from which he had suffered; and second, when he had been pierced by a poisoned dart just last Christmas. Not to mention the fact that after spending close to a week in the foothills with three arrows plunged deep into his body, he had still been alive for Destari and Galen to find.

"I've been fortunate," London said. With a shake of his head and a small nod to me, Bhadran stepped into the corridor. As I approached London, a puzzled expression settled upon him.

"Where is Miranna? Or is my condition so ghastly you are preventing her from seeing me?"

London's question stole my breath. Cannan and Destari shared a glance, and it occurred to me they had hoped to keep Miranna's plight from him until his recovery was assured. I couldn't meet London's gaze, not certain that I should be the one to respond and doubtful that I could maintain my composure if I tried. He felt the change in atmosphere in the room and repeated his question, to no one in particular.

"Miranna, where is she? Is she ill?"

I looked everywhere but at my former bodyguard, praying that someone else would speak. It was the captain who finally stepped forward to break the news.

"She's not here. The enemy infiltrated the palace, managing to place a young Cokyrian woman in the position of Miranna's personal maid. By the time we had reason to be suspicious, the princess had been lured into a trap and was taken. We believe her to be alive and held in Cokyri."

London's face went pale, and he stared at Cannan with a mixture of frustration and alarm.

"Why were you keeping this from me? And what plans have been made to rescue her?"

Destari moved forward in response to his friend's agitated state, probably to ensure he didn't bound from the bed and reinjure himself, but it was Cannan who replied.

"We're waiting to receive the enemy's demands. They had ample opportunity to kill her if that had been their intention, so I do not believe her life is in jeopardy. They took her for a reason, which they will make known in due time."

"There are far worse fates than death," London spat, his eyes flashing. "Do you not know whose hands she is in?"

The almost imperceptible clenching of the captain's jaw told me that whatever was in London's mind had already occurred to him.

"I'm going back to Cokyri," London declared, trying to push himself into a full sitting position with his right arm.

"You can't, London," Destari countered, gripping his friend's shoulder in restraint. "Don't even suggest it. This is the reason we didn't tell you. We knew the moment you found out that you'd no longer care about your own well-being. And we need you healthy. There is more at stake here than just Miranna's life."

London scowled at Destari, then dropped back on the pillows as if grudgingly admitting the other man's point.

"How long has it been?" he asked.

Cannan supplied the answer. "Eighteen days."

London flinched as though this had been a physical blow. "With no word from Cokyri?"

Silence was the only response needed.

"They will soon communicate with us," London asserted, "for their military is now prepared to back up their demands. Regardless of my recovery, you will need me at that point." Then something else came to him. "Where is Halias?"

"He's confined to quarters," the captain responded. "He has not handled this situation well."

"I want to talk to him."

"That can be arranged." Cannan's voice contained the hope we all felt that London would be able to reach Halias through his layers of irrational guilt.

With nothing more to be said, Cannan turned on his heel and departed, leaving his deputy captains to stare at each other, London obviously still irritated for having been kept in the dark.

"It is my decision as to when I will be able to go to Cokyri," he stiffly informed Destari.

"No, it is the captain's," Destari responded, refusing to yield ground.

London glared at him. "Just leave me."

Destari shook his head, then threw his hands in the air and left the room, the weight of his footfalls revealing his mind-set. I stared uncomfortably at my hands, struggling to decide whether I should remain or likewise exit, and what to say in any case.

"Should I stay?" I asked.

London was tense and brooding, and the fact that I was facing his profile told me he would probably prefer that I did not. His next words, though polite, confirmed my assessment.

"If you wish to stay, you may, but I warn you, I am not feeling conversational."

I nodded, though he wasn't looking at me, and moved toward the door.

"Alera?" His voice arrested me, and I turned to see that

horrible sympathy finally present in his eyes. "I'm sorry. But I promise you, I will find a way to bring her home."

Again I nodded, tears stinging my eyes, and I rushed into the corridor where Destari waited for me, wanting to believe London, but not quite able to do so.

CHAPTER 13

A MESSAGE FOR HER HIGHNESS

LONDON CONTINUED TO HEAL OVER THE NEXT week, regaining almost full use of his left arm. Though it was tender, he could move it normally and flex his fingers; he was also on his feet the majority of the time, too restless to stay in bed. This was to the astonishment of all, Bhadran especially. Indeed, the dignified doctor seemed almost annoyed by London's unprecedented recovery, probably because the Elite Guard had yet again proved him wrong.

While London's improvement was good news, Cokyri's continuing silence was difficult to bear. I had begun to doubt Cannan's judgment that they would offer terms, for if they planned to do so, why were they waiting so long? Still, everyone to whom I spoke—Destari, Steldor, Galen, London, the captain himself—assured me this was how the Cokyrians operated; they wanted to have us so desperate for word that when they came forth, we'd accept any conditions they presented.

I went to see London every day, for he was not permitted to leave his sickroom. In between visits, I began to reintegrate myself into palace life, finding my way to my drawing room every morning and resuming my duties. The household staff with whom I met behaved awkwardly around me at first, but quickly realized that I desired to return to a normal schedule and so acted accordingly.

As cooler September weather arrived to chase the last remnants of summer away, I finally plunged into the daunting task of catching up on my correspondence. I had been at work in my drawing room for nearly two hours, seated at my desk with quill in hand, the stack of letters seeming never to diminish, when there was a knock on the door. Before I could answer, Destari strode into the room.

"Your Highness, you must come with me to your quarters immediately. Captain's orders."

I stood, perplexed by the directive, then went with him into the corridor to discover that two additional guards awaited me.

"What is the meaning of this?" I inquired.

"I'll explain when you are safe in your rooms," Destari responded, guiding me toward the Grand Staircase.

We climbed to the second floor, my apprehension growing with every step and with every moment of my bodyguard's silence. When we reached our destination, the Palace Guards remained in the corridor while Destari and I entered my parlor. When the door had closed behind us, I faced him, thinking that the only other time I had been told to take such action was when the message had come that the High Priestess desired an audience. Had contact at last been made by the Cokyrians?

"Tell me now," I demanded.

"One of our soldiers on patrol at the bridge has brought word that a Cokyrian is on her way to speak to the King."

Light-headed, I sank onto the leather sofa. Kitten jumped

up to join me, rubbing his tiny body against my hand, seeking attention that I was not alert enough to give.

"So this is it? We'll finally know the reason they took Miranna?"

"Most likely," Destari said, and it seemed for a moment that there was more he wished to impart, perhaps words of reassurance, but he did not speak again. Now that the time had come, it was hard to have confidence in promises that had been made before.

An hour painstakingly passed. Destari remained by the hearth, occasionally stirring the fire, while I alternately examined my hands and the rug beneath my feet. A loud knock startled me, and I looked to my bodyguard, suddenly not ready to hear the news the person behind the door carried, for these could be the last seconds I would call myself a sister.

"It's too soon..." Destari muttered, moving to the door to open it, and I stood to see Cannan cross the threshold.

"Your Majesty, we have an unusual situation."

I took a few steps toward him, trying to steady my shaking hands as I waited for him to elaborate. He did not look as if he bore bad tidings. But still, why would he personally come to see me?

"The Cokyrian messenger has arrived and demands to see the Queen. She says her message is for you alone, and that she will relay it to no one else. She has informed us that she has but three hours to return to her encampment on the other side of the river, or the Cokyrians will assume that we have no interest in communicating."

"*I* must speak with her?"

"Yes, and it must be soon. You will meet her in the Throne Room. I will be there, along with Steldor and numerous other guards, but the message will come directly to you. I can't say for certain what it will be, but I believe that the Cokyrian comes to arrange a time and place for negotiation. All you *must* do is hear the message—Steldor and I can take over from there. However, if you can manage more, it might be best if our response comes from you. If she suggests a meeting, and you decide to make answer, try to give us at least three days' time. And Alera, this is key—demand that they bring Miranna."

I dipped my head slightly, unable to even nod, and Cannan glanced at Destari for assistance. The Elite Guard came forward and put a supportive hand on my arm, steering me into the corridor after his captain. We went down the royal family's private stairway rather than the Grand Staircase, since the Cokyrian envoy was waiting in the antechamber, and accessed the Throne Room through the King's Drawing Room. The Hall of Kings was lined with eerily unmoving Palace Guards in their uniforms of royal blue and gold, with the customary arc of Elite Guards to the left and right of the thrones. I noticed London was among them, as always the maverick who did not wear the requisite royal-blue doublet, Cannan and the doctor finally having allowed him to venture forth from his sickroom.

I mounted the dais to stand in front of my throne, certain I was having some strange dream. Destari took up position at my left, and the captain, clad in his black leather military uniform, went to stand at the King's right. Steldor, likewise clad in black and every bit as intimidating as his father, especially with the King's crown upon his dark hair, gave me a supportive glance which did little to convince me that I was capable of doing what they wanted. I wished I were dressed more regally, or at least had my crown, but there had been no chance for preparation or protest.

I tried to repeat Cannan's instructions in my head, at least until the antechamber doors were opened by two Palace Guards, and a petite yet somehow commanding woman walked forward. She was dressed in black, as was typical of Cokyrian soldiers, and carried a sheath at her hip and a bow absent of arrows—she had been disarmed before being permitted entry. Even as she walked, Cannan held up a hand and ordered a guard to remove the pendant from around her neck, which no doubt concealed a smaller blade—the Cokyrians tended to have clever and unusual weaponry. The woman's golden hair was but slightly darker than her skin, falling in graceful waves to her shoulders, and reminding me with a stab of sorrow of my sister.

As the messenger approached, I steadied myself, matching my breathing with every other of her footfalls. She stopped perhaps ten feet in front of the dais and fell briefly to one knee, then stood, directing her attention to me without sparing a glance for the King. I pictured my father and the posture he had assumed when the High Priestess herself had come to the palace, and purposefully mimicked it, my expression stern, my eyes focused on the woman's face.

"Your Majesty, Queen of Hytanica," she began, voice clear and strong, her accent reminiscent of Narian's. "I come to you with a message from my celebrated ruler, the High Priestess of Cokyri."

She paused, and it took me a moment to realize that I needed to give permission for her to continue.

"Then share it as she bids you," I said, hoping my voice would not betray my nervousness.

"The High Priestess will deign to hear your pleas for the release of your princess."

She reached into a pouch at her side, prompting several guards to close ranks, but she held up a hand to assure us of her innocent intentions. Without a word, she withdrew a long lock of curly strawberry blond hair, dangling it high for all to see, and I struggled to contain my surging emotions.

"I bring this so that you may be certain she is in our hands. To ensure her safety, you must follow my instructions exactly. Five days hence, at high noon, the High Priestess will come to the bridge and await you with her guards. She will speak, as I have, only to the Queen. If the Queen does not attend, the High Priestess will not engage in negotiations."

There was a low buzz in the hall following this, but Cannan silenced everyone with a dark glower. Steldor stiffened, but I did not pay him any heed. My mind was working quickly, recalling what Cannan had stressed as most important, and then the approach I should take came to me, along with a profound calmness.

"Very well—I will meet with your ruler. But I will not make the journey unless Princess Miranna does also."

The Cokyrian's lips pursed in displeasure.

"You imperil the princess's life by playing these games," she warned, squeezing the lock of hair to demonstrate the risk I was taking.

"Do not tell me I imperil her life! You have brought me no assurance that she is even alive as we speak—that strand of hair could have been taken from a corpse. I will not negotiate until I have been given surety that my sister lives."

The messenger did not respond for an almost embarrassingly long time, and I wanted desperately to look to Cannan. I refrained, both because I did not want to appear indecisive and because I feared I would not see the reassurance I sought.

"Come to the bridge and attend the meeting, Queen of Hytanica," the Cokyrian finally said, tone intractable.

"I will speak to the High Priestess and inform her of your request."

"See that she grants it."

The woman scowled, then fell to one knee in a final bow before stalking from the hall.

Once the antechamber doors had closed behind her, I began to tremble, all my energy leaving at once. Steldor reached out a hand to steady me, and I sank onto my throne. London came to my side, placing a hand on my arm and giving me a triumphant smile. Cannan also came toward me, his eyebrows raised in a rare show of surprise, while Steldor took his seat, observing me with a peculiar expression.

"You handled yourself very well," the captain praised. "I'm impressed."

"Never a doubt," London added, his pride evident.

Cannan glanced around the Throne Room at the dozens of gathered guards and seemed to decide that we needed a more private place in which to talk.

"We have much to discuss," he said, motioning to the strategy room on the east side.

Cannan, London, Destari, Steldor, Casimir and I stepped down from the dais and moved toward the indicated room. Halias, who like London had been given leave to return to duty, took it upon himself to accompany us. Cannan also gestured for Galen, and the young Sergeant at Arms hastily complied. Once inside, everyone took a seat, and the captain closed the door to block out the babble of those still in the Hall of Kings. He came to the table, once more in charge.

"Now that we have our meeting, we must try to anticipate what the Cokyrians will demand and what concessions we would be willing to make. We must also decide who will represent us at the meeting."

"Alera must go," London declared, before anyone else could speak.

"No, she won't," Steldor interjected, an edge to his words that made me uncomfortable.

London did not appreciate the interruption and continued as though the King had not spoken, failing to recognize his sovereignty and giving him no opportunity to argue his point.

"It is imperative that we meet the Cokyrians' most basic demand. The High Priestess is not bluffing. She will not engage us unless the Queen is present."

"Do you truly believe she'll jeopardize the negotiation because we do not comply with a request that we *know* does not come from her? The Cokyrians have respected our culture in the past and have never requested our Queen. There's only one Cokyrian who would make a stipulation like this, and the High Priestess has good reason to want him happy."

Steldor obviously believed that Narian had been the one behind the demand, and I experienced a strange flutter in my stomach at the thought that he would almost certainly be in attendance. While London had said I *needed* to attend, I suddenly *wanted* to attend. My thoughts and feelings about the young man were so confused, and seeing him would be a chance to find out who he had become. The fact that the request had been for the *Queen* meant he knew I was married, and I realized that Narian might likewise be confused about me.

I expected a hush following Steldor's pointed comment, but Cannan did not allow it.

"It may be that the demand comes from Narian, but whether it does or does not, we must act in the way that will best ensure Miranna's safety. We can't take the chance that the High Priestess will be true to her word, especially when accommodating the request is relatively simple."

"You're right," Steldor said through gritted teeth, making the decision as a king and not a husband. "She'll have to come with us."

Cannan, London and Destari shared a glance, which went unnoticed by Steldor, but I could sense a change in the mood in the room, like the men were bracing for a coming storm.

"It will only be necessary for one member of the royal family to attend. There is no reason to endanger both the King and the Queen."

The room itself seemed to hold its breath in response to Cannan's statement, waiting to see if the fiery temper for which Steldor was famous would erupt.

"I *am* going," Steldor asserted, staring at Cannan in disbelief. "Father?" he prompted when the captain merely met his gaze, his opinion apparent.

"I'm not going," the King concluded. He sat back, and I sensed he was trying not to show how much this development bothered him. As a military man, he wanted to be involved, but on some level, he knew Cannan was making sense.

The captain moved on, ready to leave this prickly issue behind.

"London will act as our negotiator at the meeting," Cannan said, and I knew the deputy captain had already assumed this would be the case. "The issue that remains for us to consider is what the enemy may demand and what we would be willing to concede."

"Nothing," London immediately asserted. "We can give them nothing."

"But what about Miranna?" I burst out, terrified that the

others might agree with him. "We must do something to help her!"

London looked at me with unsettling sympathy before he turned back to the captain.

"Nothing we give will ensure Miranna's return. The Cokyrians are ruthless—everyone here knows this. We could sacrifice our very kingdom, but once they had it, they would feel no obligation to uphold their side of the bargain. The Overlord would kill Miranna regardless and laugh at our folly."

I gasped, horrified, but no one contradicted London's assessment of the situation. It was Destari who finally replied.

"If the Cokyrians do indeed bring Miranna to the negotiation meeting, there's no alternative but to try to rescue her."

London nodded. "Yes. If she is brought to the meeting, we're going to need a plan. Halias and I will undertake that task."

The captain nodded, bringing the discussion to an unsettling close, at least from my point of view, for even the long-awaited negotiation with the Cokyrians seemed to bring my sister no closer to coming home.

I was excluded from the following meetings, which, I was informed, were strategy-focused. Though hope that my sister would return had dwindled, my faith in the men who were planning her rescue ironically had not. Cannan and his deputy captains could seemingly never fail.

During this time, Steldor was incredibly moody. He seemed to blame me for the fact that I had been requested at the negotiation. This probably stemmed, in his mind, from my great mistake—if I had not gotten involved with Narian, my presence would not have been demanded by the Cokyrians. His irritability over Kitten's name, or lack thereof, also continued. All in all, I made a point of rolling my eyes at him when his back was turned, just to keep myself sane.

On the day before the scheduled talks with the enemy, in the early afternoon, London came to my drawing room and explained what my role would be.

"When we go to the bridge, you will be under heavy guard. You will come forward with Cannan, Destari and me, along with other select guards, but will not need to say anything. It must simply be known to the High Priestess that you are there. Then Destari will escort you back to your carriage, and Cannan and I will handle the rest."

"I can ride a horse," I said, thinking of the fierce, confident women of Cokyri and how they would view a queen who arrived in a carriage.

London ran a hand through his hair, considering me.

"My riding lessons have continued," I murmured, anticipating some kind of rebuke. I was grateful when he merely shrugged.

"As long as you have the ability, we should take advantage of it, if only for convenience's sake. Will you need a pair of breeches?"

"No, I have a pair that will work."

"And do they fit?"

I suspected his mind had gone to the baggy breeches I had been wearing when he'd found me at Koranis's estate.

"More or less," I confessed with a blush. "They are borrowed from Baelic's daughter Shaselle."

"In any case, you may need some that will fit the occasion better," he said with a cock of his eyebrow, having figured out who had been taking me riding. "I'll send a seamstress to have you stand for measurements—I suspect they've never designed trousers for you before."

The corners of my mouth lifted at the sparkle of humor in his eyes, but strangely it was then that I began to feel the anxiety that would plague me all night. London must have sensed my sudden unease, for his next words were more serious.

"You have already proven yourself a much stronger person than expected, Alera. I have absolute faith that you will represent us well."

London's words were heartening. He had confidence in me, and I had confidence in him. No matter how frightened and uncertain I was, London would not let me fail.

Deeming his job done, he gave a curt nod, then headed toward the door.

"*I'll* tell Cannan about the breeches," he tossed over his shoulder with a classic smirk before he disappeared from sight.

Almost within the hour, London returned with two seamstresses, who took my measurements and showed me some bolts of cloth. Having no opinion on the style or fabric of trousers, I left the decisions to them. I could tell that they found their task to be quite unorthodox; on the other hand, it presented an interesting challenge. When they had fussed with me to the extent necessary, they gathered up their materials and left, promising to deliver the breeches in the morning. London had waited, gazing politely out the window while the women worked with me.

"I saw Temerson today," he stated casually enough as he turned to face me, but I knew his remark had not merely been conversational.

"How is he doing?" I asked, stung by my own selfishness,

for I had not given a thought to the young man who had been—who *was*—courting my sister.

"He's no worse than anyone else in this mess, but he's no better, either. He's terribly worried, but because he's not in the palace, he's received less information about the situation. I brought him up to date, for which he was very grateful."

"Thank you for that."

"I shall take my leave, then. Try to sleep. Tomorrow will be taxing."

After London's departure, I joined my parents in the dining room, but my churning stomach allowed me only a few bites of the evening's meal. Steldor wasn't present, but I was too distracted to wonder where he was or what he might be doing. When I at last retreated to my quarters, I saw Casimir standing by the door, a sure sign that the King was inside. I slipped into the parlor, wary of my unpredictable husband and not wanting to have an argument on this of all nights.

Steldor sat in one of the leather armchairs near the hearth with a mug of ale, looking as if he desired to be alone. Deciding it was best not to disturb him, I crossed the room with the intention of retiring and leaving him in peace, but he called to me.

"It will be dangerous tomorrow," he said, staring into the embers of the fireplace. "It wasn't just because of Narian that I wanted to go in your stead."

"I know. I'll be careful."

He turned to me, and I waited, thinking there was something more he wanted to say, but whatever it was, he couldn't quite give it voice.

"Good night then," he finally murmured, returning his attention to the fire.

"Good night," I echoed, entering my bedroom with a prayer that the night would be followed by a good day.

CHAPTER 14

GAMBLE

I DID NOT FEEL TIRED THE NEXT DAY, DESPITE my restless night. I got out of bed as the sun was rising and paced my room, listening to the sounds of Steldor's departure, knowing I had much time to squander. Sahdienne arrived an hour later with my breakfast, assisting me to dress in a simple skirt and blouse and fashioning my hair into a long braid down my back. The shirt of my choice was simple but elegant, and I planned to wear it along with a rich royal-blue-and-gold cloak embroidered with the crest of the royal family.

I dismissed my personal maid and moved into the parlor to pick at my food and wait for the servant who would deliver my breeches. After another hour, the girl brought the garment, and I replaced my skirt with the trousers, content with the fit and pleased with my overall appearance. I gave Kitten a quick hug before hurrying toward the door into the corridor, clutching my cloak. As I grasped the latch, I realized that I had forgotten something and reentered my bedroom to kneel before the trunk that sat against the far wall, slowly lifting the heavy lid. The official crown of the

Queen rested before me atop a plush cushion, and I carefully picked it up, then went to the mirror and positioned it on my head for the first time since the coronation. Satisfied that I looked as a ruler should, I tore my eyes from my reflection and ventured into the corridor where Destari waited for me.

When my bodyguard and I reached the top of the Grand Staircase, I saw that upward of thirty men were gathered in the Grand Entry Hall, some wearing the uniform of the Elite Guards, others that of the Palace Guards. Steldor was standing near the eastern wall, arms crossed in a tense posture, with Galen at his side.

As I descended the stairs, Cannan emerged from the antechamber, followed closely by London. To my surprise, my father came next, frown in place and hands in motion to accentuate his displeasure. I did not shy away when he shook his head at sight of my clothing, for I was not about to let his potential judgments dispirit me.

Cannan acknowledged me with a short nod, and London came forward to speak with me. My father's frown intensified as he examined me further, then he scurried after the captain, who had left him behind to talk with Halias and some of the other men.

"You're just in time," London said, with a nod of acknowledgment to Destari. "We'll be moving out shortly." He smirked, then added, "I was about to send a servant to wake you."

Looking at the many soldiers milling in the hall, I asked what I had already deduced.

"They're all coming with us?"

"And cavalry troops, as well. If the negotiations turn sour, we don't want to be outnumbered."

For the first time, I fully appreciated the danger into which I would be walking, and tingles ran up and down my arms. Although I was frightened, I was also exhilarated about being involved in a political and military matter, for these were the things generally thought the province of men.

Cannan was drawing near, and Destari moved to his side. Halias had called the other soldiers to attention and was now directing them out the palace doors and down the long courtyard path.

"We are ready to depart, Your Highness," the captain informed me, and I understood that formalities would be strictly observed this day. He and his deputy captains then began to escort me to the double doors, forming a triangle around me. As we passed Steldor and Galen, Cannan, who was nearest to them, clapped his son on the shoulder. Steldor nonetheless kept his gaze trained on me. I was just about to step over the threshold when he called my name.

"Alera, wait." He walked to me, then reached up and removed my crown. "Not this time," he said, looking deep into my eyes. "No need to mark you more visibly as a target. I'll keep it for you until you return."

I nodded appreciatively, then proceeded out the door with my escorts. My lungs were burning with the unexpectedly crisp morning air by the time we neared the gates where fifty mounted cavalry soldiers, in well-ordered ranks, waited for us. Halias and his troops stood by with their mounts, as groomsmen, horses in hand, stepped forward to meet me and the three military commanders who would stay by my side throughout the day.

A horse had been specially prepared for my use with an intricate leather saddle befitting a queen over a rich blanket in Hytanica's colors of royal blue and gold. The horse itself was larger than any I had ridden before but stood quietly enough in the hands of its groom. I employed a little more bounce than usual to boost myself into the saddle, for many eyes were upon me and I did not want to appear even remotely inept.

Once everyone was mounted, we began our procession through the city, attracting many spectators, who lined up on either side of the wide thoroughfare to send us on our way. I rode toward the front, following Cannan and London, with Destari, Halias and other high-ranking Elite Guards protecting my back.

We passed through the city gates in grim silence, then picked up speed, and again I felt many of the men watching me as though waiting for me to tumble to the ground. I gripped the reins tighter, determined not to falter, yet having a superstitious feeling that the mere thought in their minds would cause it to happen. It wasn't long after we departed the city that Halias and the troops under his command broke off, heading to the east, and I knew they would have some part to play in a rescue attempt if Miranna were indeed brought to the meeting.

For nearly two hours we rode south toward the river at a steady pace, my cloak pulled close to ward off the cold. When the bridge at last came into view, my heart began to hammer from more than the mere exertion of traveling. The Cokyrians surveyed us from the opposite bank, perhaps one hundred yards back from the river. We came to a halt, and the rustling of trees in the wind increased my sense of foreboding, raising the specter of lurking danger. I squinted through the autumn sunlight, already trying to make out my sister among the enemy troops, who were just slightly less in number than were we.

Both contingents sized up their adversary across the significant expanse of the Recorah River, while Cannan deployed archers along our bank. The captain then motioned for us to advance, and we rode our horses slowly across the narrow bridge.

We halted opposite the wall of black-clothed Cokyrians, more of our troops fanning out behind us, and the man and woman at the forefront of the enemy rode forward with an accompaniment of ten guards. I recognized the High Priestess at once by her flaming hair, but the man was not immediately familiar to me, and my first horrible thought was that the Overlord had come with his sister. But the closer the small group came, the clearer became his face, and my heart began to beat as loudly as a drum. Narian was here after all.

The Cokyrians dismounted about halfway between their troops and ours, then one of the High Priestess's guards stepped forward to hail us.

"We come forward unarmed to talk peacefully with the Queen of Hytanica. Do us the honor of the same."

In the margins of my vision, I caught the glints of sunlight that reflected from Cannan's and London's swords, although in truth I was paying little attention to my companions anymore. We dismounted, along with the dozen guards who would accompany us to meet the enemy. Without a word passing among them, each man in our negotiating group handed his weapons to a counterpart on horseback. I glanced quizzically at London, aware that he had not relinquished the dagger he kept hidden in his boot, and I both marveled at and was grateful for his lack of faith in our foe. Then we all walked forward until about forty feet separated us from the Cokyrians.

The enemy's negotiators, four in number, including the High Priestess and Narian, broke from the group and came forward several paces, their red-lined black cloaks billowing behind them in the gusty wind. Cannan, London, Destari and I likewise advanced. As I neared the man whose features I had spent hours studying, through whose thick hair I had run my fingers, whom I had kissed more times than I could count, I was awestruck at how much he had changed in just six months. He had grown and filled out remarkably. He was no longer a boy, and his height and build were a close match for my husband's. I wondered what rigorous training he had undergone in the past half year to bring about such a dramatic transformation. Beneath it all, however, his piercing steel-blue eyes were the same. I searched for compassion in them to reflect the warm tones of his golden hair, but the love I had grown accustomed to seeing was absent, replaced by the cold guardedness reminiscent of our first encounters.

Narian's presence, although I had anticipated it, affected me profoundly, and I could not pull my eyes from him. I wondered if my tangled emotions were visible on my face, the near irrepressible urge to run to him coupled with the bitter knowledge that, as London had said, he was now the enemy, a notion fortified by the fact that he stood across from me, shoulder to shoulder with the people who had abducted my sister.

Seeing Narian among the Cokyrians made plausible Cannan's excruciating conclusion that he had been the one to reveal the existence of the tunnel. Devastating confusion besieged me. Could I love Narian when logic screamed that I should hate him? Could I hate him when even now I frantically searched for a way to prove his innocence in all of this? I forced my thoughts to return to the most important matter—my sister.

"Have you brought Princess Miranna?" London asked as we stopped twenty feet from the Cokyrians. I noticed that, even though she had requested me, the High Priestess's green eyes were locked upon my former bodyguard, her former prisoner.

With a flick of her hand, Nantilam brought one of her guards to her side.

"I am not a fool," Nantilam proclaimed, keeping her steady, accusatory gaze on London. "If you would reclaim your princess, she waits for you in Cokyri. But I have brought proof of her well-being."

The weightiness of dashed hope pushed down on me, for there would be no rescue this day. I struggled to maintain my composure, the High Priestess's promise of evidence the only thing preventing my collapse, while the intensity of Narian's eyes upon me joined in the effort to defeat me.

"What proof?" London demanded, and I could tell by the tautness in the postures of every Hytanican around me that even this early, the meeting was not going in our favor.

"My lieutenant bears a letter from Princess Miranna to your Queen. The princess was instructed to let her sister know how she fares. I assure you the letter is written by her hand, and it contains details that will show it was written yesterday."

Nantilam's lieutenant took a few steps toward us, carrying a small scroll of parchment. There was silence as London stared distrustfully at the High Priestess, who waited expectantly for a Hytanican to likewise come forward.

"I admire your caution," Nantilam stated, when none among us made a move. "All of you. But you will remain in the dark until you see what this parchment contains. If you are not to be the one who claims it, London, perhaps your friend will be." Her eyes flicked briefly to Destari, who stood near London, before they shifted to Cannan. "Or maybe your captain?" At last, she focused on me. "Perchance your Queen will come forward, if cowardice is all you men can muster."

The tension following her challenge was intolerable, for I was the only person in the Hytanican party who had not been dealt an insult. Cannan and London, however, appeared impervious to her slight, for which I was thankful, and a glance between them resolved the issue.

Cannan stepped ahead, as Destari was assigned to me, and London, like the High Priestess, was fulfilling the role of negotiator. Every one of the captain's strides seemed to take longer than it should have, and stories of the enemy's cunning whirled through my mind, raising the specter that all was not as it seemed. But Cannan would not walk defenseless into an unstable situation—unless he had determined there was no other option. I examined the Cokyrians' faces, wondering if behind those inscrutable expressions there was deceit, trying to convince myself there was not. But when I came to Narian and thought of the tenderness and compassion I had discovered beneath his cold and detached manner, I knew this enemy could disguise anything.

The captain stopped about ten feet in front of us, waiting for the enemy soldier to close the gap. When she neared, he stretched out his hand to accept the scroll.

"Cannan, move!" London shouted, and the captain immediately stepped back, looking at him in alarm.

The Elite Guard leapt forward and hurled the dagger from his boot at the High Priestess's lieutenant. The dagger struck the hollow of her throat, and blood sprayed across Cannan's jerkin and face. She gasped, gurgled and clawed vainly at her neck before hunching forward and collapsing against him. Then something thudded to the ground at his feet—a dagger, brought for an assassination.

Cannan thrust the dying lieutenant away from him as

all hell broke loose. Destari, who was already at my side, dragged me away, everything happening so quickly that I didn't even have time to feel afraid. The Cokyrians charged, extracting weapons that had been concealed in every fold of clothing, and London and several others ran to meet them, though all the Hytanicans were presumably unarmed. Just before Destari shoved me in the direction of the horses, I saw Cannan pull a dagger from a sheath strapped to his forearm, and I could only assume the others had likewise kept weapons.

Destari literally threw me onto his horse then jumped up behind, shouting for guards to come to the aid of the Queen. I glanced back toward the fray and saw Cannan break free along with several others, returning to their mounts with haste. Our men rode for the bridge while arrows from our archers rained down on the enemy. The High Priestess and Narian retreated behind shields while I searched frantically for London, one of the few missing. I knew from Destari's hesitation that he was doing the same.

"Destari!" Cannan bellowed in reminder to the deputy captain.

Just as my bodyguard made the decision to flee, the knot of Cokyrians unraveled, and we could see enemy soldiers gripping a struggling London, dragging him back, ultimately, to the Overlord's empire. With an arm wrapped tightly about my waist, Destari gave our horse one swift kick, and we rode at a gallop in the opposite direction.

I stumbled through the palace doors, hair and clothing in disarray, much to the shock of the guards stationed in the Grand Entry Hall, with Destari not far behind. Others in our party followed, talking frenetically to one another, trying to determine exactly what had happened and what should now be done.

Just as Steldor, Galen and several of the King's guards burst from the antechamber, lured by the commotion, Cannan pushed his way to the front of the troops, and his bloodied clothing drew the startled eyes of those who had stayed behind. Before Steldor could speak, Destari stepped up to confront his captain, his black eyes strangely crazed.

"We left London," he growled. "We let the Cokyrians take him, after he saved your life!"

"What happened?" Steldor interjected, coming to his father's side.

"It was not my intention to lose London—" Cannan vehemently returned.

"Then why didn't you send men back for him?" Destari shouted.

Steldor frowned, frustrated at being in the dark. "Would somebody just tell me what—?"

"The Cokyrians attempted to assassinate the captain," Destari informed the King, then he began to pace in a manner not in keeping with his character.

"I retrieved the scroll," Cannan stated, ignoring Steldor's pallid complexion and bringing Destari to a standstill. I took a step forward, my mind shutting out the hum of conversation in the hall, as he took the parchment from the inside pocket of his military jerkin.

"Open it," Destari prompted, earning a scowl from Cannan.

Though Steldor was confused, he did not speak as his father untied the leather band the enemy had fastened around the scroll and unrolled it. Without a word, the captain crushed the parchment in his hand.

"What?" Steldor demanded while Destari grimaced in understanding.

"Blank," Cannan said simply, and the chatter of those who had been listening increased dramatically in volume as everyone began to argue and debate, frustration pulsing beneath the surface of each word.

The temperature of the crowded hall soared, and removing my cloak did nothing to alleviate the problem. In addition, my body and mind longed for silence so that I could rethink what had happened. The negotiation meeting had been nothing more than a ploy to allow for the attempt on Cannan's life, or perhaps on others among us as well, and possibly the recapture of London, the two military men most vital to our defense. The kidnapping itself might have been part of that ploy. It was entirely possible my sister had been killed the day she was snatched from us, since she had played no role in the Cokyrians' scheme save that of bait.

Suddenly overwhelmed by the heat, the noise and the smell of sweat and blood, I broke from the furor and hurried up the Grand Staircase, to no one's notice. I ran down the corridors to my quarters in a wholly unladylike manner, trying to hold back tears, for I did not want to deteriorate into a weeping mess until I had reached the safety of my bedroom.

I never quite made it to my sanctuary. After sending the parlor door flying open, I stumbled to the center of the room and sank to my knees on the woolen tapestry that covered the floor, tears dropping on my hands as I began to sob. I had thought this meeting would bring my sister home, I had thought I would see her and draw her to me, warm and very much alive. Instead my whole body was quivering, for it seemed ever more likely that she was gone from me forever.

While I struggled to check my emotions, I heard the creak of the door closing and knew I was no longer alone. Thinking that Destari, or perhaps even Steldor, had come to check on me, I took a shuddering breath, then rose slowly to my feet and turned around. I froze as I took in the face of the man who stood before me for, although I had long dreamt of being with him, I could not help but be afraid.

"Alera," he said, taking a step toward me. Although he had been dressed all in black at the negotiation, he now wore the royal-blue tunic of the Palace Guards, and I wondered from whom he had taken it and in what condition he had left the man.

I backed away without conscious thought, knowing that if he continued to come toward me, I would not be able to run, would not be able to scream, for I was finding it difficult to breathe. He stopped, and his mesmerizing blue eyes somehow steadied me.

"You can listen to me, or you can call for your guards," he stated calmly. "It is your decision."

"Narian," I whispered. "What are you doing here?"

"I don't have much time. Someone will soon look for you. But we need to talk."

"Now?" I said, struggling to focus, hastily wiping the evidence that I had been crying from my face.

"No. Tomorrow night, at Koranis's country estate. Come alone."

I stared at him, no longer certain who he was, excruciatingly aware he had aligned himself with the enemy.

"Trust me once more, just as I trust you. Please, Alera." His eyes captured mine, and there was only one answer I could give.

"I'll come," I promised, not knowing how I would accomplish this, only that I must.

Without shifting his gaze, he approached, pushing up his left shirtsleeve to reveal a dagger strapped to his forearm. I did not give ground, perhaps foolishly, for I recalled all too well the weapons he carried on his person. He stopped before me and unstrapped the sheath.

"I want you to take this. There may come a time when you will need it." His voice and demeanor were composed, as if he offered me a mere trinket.

I pondered the weapon, remembering how Steldor had rebuffed me when I had requested one from him. Narian knew better than anyone what danger was coming to Hytanica, what peril could befall me and my countrymen, for he would be the one executing it on the Overlord's behalf. Yet here he was, arming me for my own protection, and though there were still many things regarding his actions that I did not understand, I knew without doubt that his heart in all this time had not wavered.

He reached out to take my left arm, and I shook as a strong desire to touch him, to be in his embrace, to pretend nothing had changed between us, surged within me. I did not move, however, when he brushed my white blouse out of the way and strapped the dagger in place. After dropping my sleeve to conceal the weapon, he raised his eyes once more to mine.

"Wear this at all times," he instructed, then he reached out to touch my hair, and without thought I moved forward to rest my head upon his chest.

"Miranna," I choked as he folded his arms around me.

"She's alive."

Relief flowed through me, and for the first time since this nightmare had begun, I felt a measure of peace. After a moment, Narian gently grasped my arms to move me away from him, and an agonizing sense of shame and remorse took control of my tongue.

"I'm married now," I blurted, even though it was clear he already knew the truth.

"Tomorrow, after nightfall," he said as if I had not spoken. "Alone."

"Yes, I will be there," I repeated, not bothering to consider the danger in which I would be placing myself, for no matter how blind or unwise, I had complete faith in him.

Before he released me, he bent to softly touch his lips to mine. Turning, he strode toward the door, then glanced back at me, not quite able to stay his emotions. I took a step forward, irrationally wanting him to remain with me, but he cracked open the door to glance into the corridor, then slipped out to disappear from view.

I had given no thought to how he had entered the palace and did not worry now as to how he would make his escape. He possessed the ingenuity to come and go at his desire, for he had on several occasions during the winter months climbed across the roof to my balcony to sneak me away from the palace.

My eyes remained glued to the spot where he had last stood, and an aching weariness seeped into my bones at the renewed sorrow of being without the man I loved. Even though I felt some relief that I would soon learn more about how my sister and perhaps London were faring, the trauma of the day propelled me to my bedroom. I undressed without waiting for my maid, drew the heavy drapes over the fading light of early evening and crawled under the covers.

I heard Steldor come into the parlor minutes later and realized that had he been just a little earlier, he and Narian would have come face-to-face. My heart thudded with fear at the thought of what that encounter would have wrought.

Hearing my husband's approaching footsteps, I closed my eyes in feigned sleep, although my body felt bowstring taut. He rapped gently on my bedroom door, then opened it to step inside, and I could feel his eyes upon me.

"Alera," he softly called.

I lay still, desperately hoping he would make no further attempt to wake me, for I was certain he would see in my eyes that I had dealt him another betrayal. After a moment, he departed, apparently satisfied that I was fine. Only I knew how far from fine I was.

CHAPTER 15

HONOR IN WAR

THE NEXT MORNING, I WAS FACED WITH A problem. I needed to meet with Narian that night, to ask him about my sister, about London, about why he had disappeared the previous spring without a word to anyone, and why he had agreed to fight for the Cokyrians. I craved answers to these questions, and Narian was offering me the chance to know the truth. But in order to reach Koranis's estate at the appointed time, I would have to leave the palace grounds at dusk, on horseback, and with the ability to pass unchallenged through the city gates, all of which promised to be impossible given the high state of security in which I lived.

Afternoon arrived, and as the sun continued to slip from its position in the sky, I reluctantly admitted that there was only one solution. Gathering my resolve, I opened my parlor door and beckoned to Destari to come inside. He followed me toward the bay window where I sank into one of the armchairs my mother had always favored. I invited him to sit, but he refused, preferring to stand as was most proper.

I could see in his eyes that he was fatigued, though it did not show in his stance. I could not imagine what he was feeling. He had been in the military seventeen years ago when London had made his escape after spending ten harrowing months in the enemy's dungeon, and had no doubt played an integral part in his friend's recovery. Now we were all faced with the prospect that, even if London were to miraculously survive this second time in Cokyrian hands, he might not come back as even a semblance of himself. That thought was enough to close my throat, but I swallowed hard and met my bodyguard's gaze.

"Destari, I need your help."

"Of course, Your Highness. What can I do?" His reply was automatic, although a flicker of concern showed in his eyes.

"I will share what is on my mind only if you promise to take it in strictest confidence. This must remain between the two of us."

Wary now, Destari at last took a seat in the chair I had proffered.

"Alera, if this is something I will be required by duty to disclose, it might be best if you do not tell me."

I stared down at my hands while I chose my next words. I did not like what I was about to do but could conceive of no other option.

"Duty will not require you to reveal what I am about to say," I informed him, and his understated but visible relief caused me a twinge of guilt. "Your loyalty belongs to me before it does to your captain, so duty will in fact require you to stay silent according to my bidding."

I was not worried Destari would go to Steldor with the information I was about to divulge. My concern was that he would relay it to Cannan. If abusing my status were the only way to ensure that he would keep my secret, so be it.

I had expected him to look at me as would a man betrayed, since I was in truth trapping him into a corner. Instead, his dark eyes were curious.

"What is it, Alera? Something is obviously upsetting you."

"Narian was here, in the palace."

"What?" he exclaimed, and I gestured for him to keep his voice down. In a near whisper, he added, "When?"

"Last night, when everyone was arguing in the Grand Entry. He wants to meet me tonight at his father's country estate, alone, but I need a horse in order to get there. You must help me to acquire a mount—and to leave the palace and the city without challenge. After that, I'll ride on alone."

"I won't let you go by yourself," he declared, his expression conveying his belief that I had gone mad.

"But I must. Narian will have information about both Miranna and London, information I need, *we* need. And he was adamant. I'm not to bring anyone."

"Nor was Miranna, according to *Temerson's* note."

Despite his brashness, I had to recognize the truth in his statement. Destari had never fully trusted Narian, and I could not expect him to do so now, nor to understand why I still did when the young man had stood with the High Priestess at the negotiation. I should have known that he would never leave me unguarded with someone he viewed as a threat, whether or not he reported it to his captain.

"Very well, then. You can come with me if you wish."

While it seemed best to let Destari come along, worry nipped at me. I did not know whether Narian would be willing to speak openly in the presence of one of the men who had been most suspicious of him during his time in Hytanica.

Destari nodded, rising to his feet. "Wait for me here. I'll

secure the horses, then use Casimir to occupy Steldor elsewhere in the palace so that I can come for you."

"Thank you," I said, and he bowed and departed.

The time had come, and I threw a black cloak over the breeches and blouse into which I had changed, then went to answer Destari's knock, wrapping my plaited hair into a bun at the nape of my neck as I walked. I opened the door, and my bodyguard took me out of the palace through the servants' entrance so that we emerged just to the west of the garden wall. I did not spend much time pondering how Destari had cleared this area of Palace Guards but assumed that a deputy captain would have his ways.

"We can't be seen," he offered, by way of explanation. "Or questions might be raised."

The steadily setting sun cast hues of pink and orange across the horizon as Destari led me west from the palace and into the small apple orchard that stood between our estate and the Military Complex. Two horses, hidden by the trees, patiently awaited riders. We climbed upon our respective mounts, then rode south at an inconspicuous pace toward the Market District, and I understood that Destari intended to keep us off the main thoroughfare that divided the city in half for as long as possible.

Most of the shops along the streets we traveled were devoid of customers at this late hour, but I veiled my face with the hood of my cloak, not wanting to be recognized. For his part, Destari nodded genially to the few preoccupied people we passed.

Eventually, the route we traveled led us onto the still-crowded thoroughfare, but we stayed to the side and moved at a brisk trot until we reached the entrance to the city. The gates of the city had been dropped, and only those citizens bearing a pass with the King's seal had the right to enter or depart this late in the day.

"We were dispatched by the Captain of the Guard," Destari said crisply to the sentries who stood on either side of the barrier. To my great relief, they signaled their counterparts in the towers to raise the spiked iron bars, not daring to question a deputy captain or his companion, and I was suddenly thankful that Destari had refused to let me travel by myself. I was not certain the guards would have so readily obeyed their Queen. I was quite certain, at any rate, that they would have reported my activity to Cannan.

We traversed the countryside in the soft gray light of early evening, the chill of the air increasing with our speed, and I tugged my cloak tighter about me, nestling within my hood, trusting to the steady hoofbeats of Destari's horse for guidance. By the time we arrived at Koranis's estate, it was almost too dark to distinguish our surroundings. Apprehension stole over me for I did not see another horse on the property. Had we arrived before Narian? Or was he waiting beyond the line of trees to see if I had kept my promise to come alone? And if that were the case, was he even now on his way back to the Cokyrian encampment, disappointed by my inability to keep that promise? This last thought was enough to make me want to call out for him, but I stifled the urge and dismounted to walk to the house with Destari.

The front door was unlocked, and memories of London's actions when he had found me here a few months ago came rushing back. I almost smiled as I pictured the indignation that Koranis would display if he were to learn of his ostentatious home's vulnerability. My mood was quickly sobered by Destari, who had stepped ahead of me over the threshold with his sword drawn, wary of an attack. When none was forthcoming, some of the tension left his body.

"I expected someone to accompany you."

Destari jumped slightly as Narian's voice cut through the dark interior, then he thrust out an arm to prevent me from advancing.

Narian's form was almost indiscernible until fire came to the lantern in his hand. He was dressed in black, with a hood pulled over his blond hair, enabling him to hide among the shadows. Without speaking further, he beckoned us through an archway leading to the home's dining room. I made to go forward, but my bodyguard again detained me with a hand upon my shoulder, quite unwilling to show the enemy our backs.

Narian gave a minute shrug and went ahead of us, demonstrative of his innocent intentions. He placed the lantern on top of the polished wood surface of the table, then sat down on the far side, Destari and I taking up seats across from him.

"I'm sure you have questions for me," he said, pushing the hood back onto his shoulders.

"Miranna?" The name burst from me immediately.

"She's well," he answered, with a subtle downward glance.

I let go of the last vestiges of fear that had clung to me, even in the wake of his assurance that my sister was alive, feeling as though I could at last release the breath I had been holding ever since she had disappeared. Then I saw the ache in Narian's eyes, and I knew there was more to be made known.

"What is it? What's wrong, where is she?"

"You need not fear for her safety. She is being housed in the Temple of the High Priestess and is treated in much the way I was during my time as a prisoner here in Hytanica."

"But that doesn't make sense," I responded, furrowing my

brow to recall what I knew of the enemy's tactics. "Why keep her so well? What purpose is she yet to serve?"

"She is already serving her purpose. It is because of me that she is receiving such good care."

I frowned in confusion, becoming even more troubled when I looked to Destari and saw pained understanding on his face. Sensing that I was lost, Narian elaborated.

"I have agreed to do the Overlord's bidding in order to ensure that Miranna is not harmed. He will kill her if I don't obey him."

My energy depleted as a sinking feeling pervaded my stomach. The Overlord would kill her. And the only way for Narian to save me the sorrow of losing a sister was to attack and destroy my kingdom. I was thankful Narian was not asking me what I wanted him to do—what answer could I have given? It would have been selfish and unreasonable to request that he spare Miranna at the cost of Hytanica, yet the thought of sacrificing her for any cause was intolerable.

Tears welled in my eyes, for there was nothing that could be done. Miranna would be kept alive as long as Narian obeyed orders. Yet ironically, were she returned to us at the end of it all, to what would she be returning? A fallen kingdom, a despoiled homeland; she would travel from the enemy's clutches to the enemy's clutches.

"Why did you leave us?" I lamented, though I knew it no longer mattered. "If you had stayed in Hytanica, both you and Miranna would be safe."

"There was never any guarantee of my safety, anywhere," Narian replied, his tone resigned as though he had accepted this fact long ago. "I left Hytanica because I thought the captain, knowing of the legend, would have me killed before he'd run the risk of my return to Cokyri. He understood better than I that the Overlord would never stop searching for me, that his reclamation of me was inevitable. But I thought at the time that I could escape my fate. So I fled into the mountains and hid there until the Cokyrians forced me back. I tried to placate them with information initially—Hytanica would be well able to defend itself as long as I kept my distance—but I did not know they already had someone inside the palace to make use of my discoveries. Now I know that there is no escape—I will never be free until I fulfill my purpose."

You always have a choice, Narian had once said to me, and he had made his choice—to protect my sister.

Seemingly still on high alert, Destari had not moved or spoken during my entire dialogue with Narian.

"And London," I said, my voice subdued. "Is he now in your *master's* care?"

"No," Narian said, showing no reaction to the inflection in my voice. I studied him, but his attention had shifted to Destari, who, as far as I could tell, had not even adjusted position. "London was taken by the High Priestess to her temple. The Overlord does not know of his presence in Cokyri."

"Why?"

"I do not know. It was the High Priestess's orders that the Overlord be kept ignorant."

Narian's steely eyes again flitted to Destari, prompting me to once more examine the deputy captain. In the strained silence that followed, a noise from outside, a rustle of branches, the crack of a twig, made me jump, and I scanned my surroundings, though there were no windows in the room in which we sat.

My breathing calmed, and I settled back into my chair, but Narian's and Destari's bodies had grown taut. The two men were staring at each other, Narian calculating, Destari obscure, and I realized something was not right.

"How many did you bring with you?" Narian's controlled and knowing voice slashed the tension like a knife.

Destari did not answer, but his right hand tightened around the hilt of his dagger. In desperation, I responded for him, refusing to acknowledge the message in his body language.

"No one came with us," I said, shooting a significant look at my bodyguard, urging him to confirm my words. Neither he nor Narian paid attention.

"We're alone," I insisted. "Just as I promised we—"

But another small sound from outside, which could easily have been the snort of a horse, stemmed my words.

"Destari?" I asked in disbelief.

"If you come willingly, they may not hurt you," the Elite Guard said bluntly to Narian, whose soft exhale might have been a sigh or a laugh. "The house is surrounded. If you try to run, the captain has given the men leave to stop you in whatever way necessary."

"No!" I shouted, jumping to my feet and rounding on my bodyguard. "You swore fealty to me! You promised not to tell Cannan or anyone else, you were under orders from me to—"

"I never swore to anything. And your orders? You weren't thinking straight, Alera—"

"Do not address me informally! I am your Queen, and you are my betrayer."

Destari's only response was to come to his feet, and though I felt justified in my anger, I could not meet the burning indignation in his eyes.

"It would be best for your men if you let me go peacefully."

This time Destari glowered at Narian rather than at me, unamused by his assertion.

"You're outnumbered, Narian. You'll never make it out of here alive if you attempt anything rash."

"The blood of Hytanicans will be shed," Narian warned. "If not now, then in the future. It is your choice whether it flow at my hands or the Overlord's. He will enjoy it, prolong it, kill as many as he can. And not only soldiers, but anyone in his path. If I'm in command of the troops, I'll do everything in my power to keep the deaths to a minimum."

"Surrender your weapons to me and I'll take you outside," Destari said, ignoring the younger man's words.

After a moment, Narian shrugged and came to his feet, raising his hands.

"Disarm me then."

"Lay your weapons down," Destari instructed, drawing his sword and pointing it, sharp and glistening in the lantern light, at his enemy.

Narian did as he was told, removing both sword and dagger from their sheaths and laying them on the table.

"Now your belt."

Again, Narian obeyed, unfastening his belt and likewise placing it on the wooden surface, thereby surrendering the poisoned darts disguised as stitching and the pouch full of explosive powder. He watched Destari, who had not lowered his weapon.

"And your boots," the deputy captain grumbled impatiently.

"With respect, I won't walk back to Hytanica without my boots, sir."

"The boots or the blades," Destari shot back.

With a sigh that could very well have been accompanied by a roll of his eyes, Narian pulled two thin, jagged-edged daggers from the hidden sheaths in the heels and soles of his boots and dropped them among those already on the table. At a flick of Destari's sword, he followed with a dagger that had been secured within one of his boot shafts.

"Now push up your shirtsleeves."

Again Narian complied, revealing a sheathed dagger strapped to his right forearm. Destari seemed satisfied after the young man had removed it, for he held his sword down, motioning his captive toward the doorway with his left hand.

"I'll warn you again," Narian stated as he came around the table. "Your men are in danger if you try to detain me."

"Don't talk," Destari snapped. "Alera—*Your Highness*—go before us and open the front door slowly, then stand back and keep out of the line of fire."

I nodded, but my brain was working fast. I couldn't let my stupidity be the cause of Narian's death—and he would be killed, of that I was certain. And allowing Narian to leave was the only way to ensure Miranna's well-being. Had Destari forgotten that?

I pulled open the door but deliberately stepped out first into the garish light of a half-dozen torches. As my eyes took in the scene, I saw thirty or forty men on horseback with bows and arrows aimed at me. I was not their intended target, but nonetheless the sight gave me chills, knowing that those sharpened points were meant to pierce Narian's flesh if he so much as twitched.

"Please," I choked out, focusing on Cannan at the forefront. The captain had no bow in his hands but was, regardless, an imposing figure upon his large and mighty steed, his face stern, one hand raised to keep his men from shooting.

"Stand down," he shouted when he saw me, for I had

placed myself in a very dangerous position, and his men complied.

"Please," I repeated. "Let him go."

"Your Majesty, over here," Cannan directed, as Destari and Narian appeared, my bodyguard standing on my right, his hand firmly gripping Narian's left arm, but I stubbornly shook my head. While I did not know what my action would accomplish, I had a feeble hope that Cannan would hesitate to override the Queen, or that the consternation I was causing would provide Narian with an opportunity to escape.

"He's unarmed," Destari called.

Cannan nodded once. "Alera, you need to walk to me."

When I did not move, he motioned to Halias, who sat upon his horse across from where I stood. Halias dismounted, intent on collecting me, but I ducked behind Destari, moving to stand next to Narian and taking a firm grip on his right arm.

"There are things you don't know," I called to Cannan, the pitch of my voice rising along with my distress. I looked at Destari for assistance, but he emphatically shook his head.

"Alera, stop."

It was Narian's steady voice that finally penetrated my obstinacy, and I stilled, wanting to hear him. He gazed calmly at me, disentangling my arm from his. As he pulled back, I felt him slide the dagger strapped to my left forearm from its sheath and, in one fluid motion, tuck it into the waistband of his breeches.

"Cannan's right," he continued matter-of-factly, his voice low, for he intended his words only for my ears. "You must go with Halias."

I stared at him and saw Destari, the only other person close enough to hear, cast him a grateful glance.

"I won't forget anything that's happened between us, Alera, but you need to forget it. Don't defend me, don't try to help me. I'm not who I used to be. I'm your enemy now."

Horror no doubt registered on my face, then blackness closed in on me. My eyes saw nothing, my ears heard nothing. I could not catch my breath, finding no air for my lungs. I felt utterly alone and stranded. When Halias reached me and put an arm around my waist, I did not resist him. He led me back toward Cannan, who swam before my eyes as he raised his arm, the signal for his men to once more raise their bows. As my dizzy spell passed, the house came back into focus, and I saw Destari shove Narian on the shoulder to urge him forward, but he did not budge. I could feel the men on either side of me tense, itching to loose their arrows.

The captain, however, did not give them leave to shoot, instead posing a basic question to the seventeen-year-old who stood defiantly before him.

"Will you surrender willingly into my custody, boy?"

"Will you release me, Captain, for the sake of your troops?"

Cannan examined Narian, then gave the answer everyone knew would be forthcoming.

"You will not be released."

"I'm sorry for that."

"Come forward of your own accord—"

"And I'm sorry for this."

Flames exploded out of nowhere, roaring ten feet high as they rapidly formed a wide barricade, blocking the house from view and separating us from Destari and Narian. Horses shrieked and bolted, taking their riders with them and, in some cases, leaving them behind. Halias pulled me back to avoid the fire as Cannan's mount reared in alarm, ultimately obeying its master, circling but staying on the premises. Men were yelling, removing their cloaks to beat at the flames, and I buried my head against Halias's chest to block out the din.

"Where is he?" Cannan, fierce and terrifying, demanded of the milling soldiers. "Find him! Search the woods, he can't have gotten far."

The men hurried to comply, and I lifted my head to see that the wall of fire was gone, replaced by grayed darkness and the smell of smoke. But as Cannan scanned the front of the house, I saw a different emotion play upon his face—concern. Where was Destari?

Cannan dismounted and grabbed a torch from one of his men, then strode toward the front door of Koranis's home in search of his deputy captain. I broke away from Halias to pursue him, likewise worried, my exasperated escort having no choice but to follow.

It did not take the captain long to spot Destari where he lay crumpled on the ground a few feet away, his back against the wall of the house. From a distance, he looked like a puppet propped into a sitting position, but I shook the notion from my head and went to my bodyguard's side.

Cannan was already kneeling next to him, and Destari had peeled his blood-covered hand away from his stomach. Even in the dim light I could see the dark stain that was spreading across his jerkin.

"How badly are you injured?" the captain asked.

"Could be worse," Destari replied, wincing. He tipped his head back against the wall, his face pale and coated with sweat, and again applied pressure to his wound with his hand. "I tried to keep him from getting away. I thought he was...but he always has a weapon."

My heart thudded because I knew whose weapon Narian had used, and I struggled to suppress the guilt that urged me to speak, for despite Destari's injury, I was glad Narian had escaped.

"I'll have one of the men tend to you."

"Sir—how did he do it? Did you see?"

Grimly Cannan shook his head. "We searched the perimeter before we approached. There was nothing. No reason for a fire to ignite."

Cannan stood and motioned to a nearby soldier. When the man approached, the captain sent him to bring the medical supplies before again focusing on Destari.

"Can you ride?"

"I can make it to the city."

"Good."

"To give Narian credit, sir, he could have killed me."

Cannan contemplated his Elite Guard for a moment but gave no response. Instead, he went to his horse to remount. He called out orders to a few soldiers, directing them to ride to the bridge and alert the border patrols to keep their eyes open for Narian, though there was not much optimism behind his commands.

Halias and I stayed with Destari until someone brought the medical supplies, then we followed after Cannan, and I was close enough to hear the words of the soldier who approached to report.

"Sir, there isn't a trace of him. We searched the woods to the best of our ability, but we can't pick up a trail in the darkness. We might be able to track him if we return in the morning—"

"Morning will be too late," the captain said shortly. "Round up the others. Tell them we're returning to the city."

As soon as Destari was bandaged for the journey and had been helped into his saddle, we set off. I rode in front of

Halias on his horse without raising an argument. I was exhausted, and my head ached from trying to process all that had happened. But the ache in my heart from the wound Narian had inflicted with his final words to me was much worse.

CHAPTER 16

TO HELL WITH DISCRETION

THE CITY WAS PEACEFUL AS WE PASSED UNDER the spiked iron gates that secured its entrance, and the thoroughfare was deserted. Just before we reached the palace, Cannan dismissed his troops so they could return to the military base, issuing an order to one of the men to take Destari to the infirmary. Two other Elite Guards continued on with us, and it seemed to me that the captain wanted to avoid drawing attention. For the first time since leaving the palace that evening, I thought of Steldor and realized that he likely knew nothing of this military action. Destari certainly would not have told him, knowing the position in which he would have been placing me, and I assumed the same was true of Cannan. Trouble would certainly brew if Steldor found out.

Unfortunately, trouble was well under way, for Steldor, Galen, Casimir and two Palace Guards were in the entrance hall at the time of our return. Steldor's eyes fixed on me the moment the doors opened, within them a combination of annoyance and worry. I recognized the guards as among those who frequently stood sentry at the palace entrances and deduced that Cannan must have called them from their posts so Destari could take me out undetected. With the five men together, it was easy to guess what they had been discussing and potentially unraveling.

Steldor, trailed by Galen, advanced on his father, his worry now banished.

"What the hell is going on?" he demanded.

The Elite Guards who had started toward their quarters in the East Wing slowed their steps.

"This isn't the place," Cannan replied curtly. "In my office."

Steldor glowered, showing no willingness to comply, but Galen clapped a hand on his upper arm to give him a subtle shove in the right direction. Before Cannan followed, he issued an order to Halias.

"Take Alera to her quarters."

Steldor stopped in his tracks and turned on his father. "No, take her to the office."

Cannan met his son's seething eyes with a solid, stern expression, but Steldor was adamant.

"She's obviously involved in whatever this is, so if we're going to talk, *everyone* is coming."

After a tense moment, Cannan nodded to Halias and motioned Steldor and Galen forward, though I noted with some trepidation that he indicated to Casimir and the departing pair of Elite Guards to come, as well.

Once we all were in the office, the captain moved behind his desk but remained on his feet. Steldor stood across from him, and the rest of us drew back against the perimeter of the room, yielding a radius to father and son.

"Well?" Steldor inquired.

"We had an opportunity to ambush Narian. Obviously, it did not go as planned."

"Because Narian wasn't caught? Or because I found out about it?"

The captain let out his breath in what seemed like resignation. "You won't understand or accept this, but it was important that you—"

"Oh, I understand it well enough. It would be essential to keep from the King that you're going to use the Queen as bait. That was her role in this, wasn't it?"

For the first time since I'd known him, Cannan vacillated over an answer, caught between lying outright to his son or telling the truth and condemning me. His split second of indecision was enough to alert Steldor. He stared at his father, and I prayed that he would not put the pieces together.

Steldor remained fixated on Cannan as the seconds passed.

"She was going to meet him," he finally declared, voice flat. "She was going to meet him of her own accord, and you took advantage of her idiocy."

I could only hope that Steldor's attention would stay focused on Cannan, on the fact that his father had kept things from him. My mouth was dry, and I tried not to breathe, wanting to fade into the wall. My only security was that Halias was at my side, sturdy and reassuring, able to shield me from harm if my husband lost control.

Steldor closed his eyes in an actual attempt to keep his temper in check. He put his hands palms down on the captain's desk and bowed his head, although his body was rigid. The silence was dense, but breakable, fragile, terrifying.

"How?" he asked at length. "How was the meeting arranged? When did you talk to him—at the negotiation?"

Only at the word "you" did I realize he was speaking to me. I was too frightened to answer, lest I fracture his resolve; still, with every second that passed, his anger grew.

"N-Narian…" I took a deep breath, wanting to eliminate

the shake in my voice, and in my hesitation, Cannan spoke in my place.

"Narian somehow gained entry to the palace in the aftermath of the negotiation while the rest of us were arguing in the Grand Entry. He and Alera spoke in your quarters."

Cannan's answer startled me, for I would not have expected him to be so frank in light of his son's state of mind.

Steldor did not look up or change his posture, but his body was practically shaking. He was dangerously close to the breaking point, and I feared what would lie beyond.

"In *my* quarters. He was in my quarters, and she didn't raise the alarm. He was here, *in the palace,* and she didn't call for a guard, didn't so much as make a sound."

Steldor seemed to be addressing no one in particular, simply trying to come to grips with what he had learned. He let out a snarl of laughter that contained no mirth, then at last turned to me. I inched closer to Halias, finding the malevolence in his dark eyes more than a little unsettling.

"Did you kiss him?" he demanded, any trace of laughter gone.

I stuttered out a few sounds, not knowing what conclusions he would draw if I left this query open.

"Did you kiss him?" he thundered, and I cringed.

There was something missing from his gaze, the something that told me deep down he remembered that he cared for me, and I abruptly understood why Cannan had brought so many guards with him. I knew that I was endangering myself further by not speaking, but also that Steldor would be able to detect a lie. I prayed that Halias and the others would be able to restrain him if it came to that.

"No...and yes. That is, he kissed me," I said, no longer able to suppress the quaver in my voice.

"And you fought him off, did you?"

"Well, no, I mean…I—I…" My voice trailed off as my cheeks turned scarlet. "Steldor, it doesn't matter anymore—"

"It'll matter every day until you go to hell for being an adulteress, you—"

"Steldor!" Cannan barked, catching his son before his mouth got away from him completely.

But Steldor wasn't listening. With a sweep of his arm, he knocked the few things atop the captain's desk to the floor, then grabbed the nearest of the wooden chairs and smashed it against the stone beneath our feet with such strength that the wood splintered and flew apart. Picking up part of a broken leg, he hurled it at one of the cases protecting his father's weapons, shattering the glass. I gasped and cowered against the wall, Halias shielding me with his body, Casimir and the other Elite Guards on full alert. Cannan, however, merely crossed his arms and took a step back, stoically watching his son demolish his office. I doubted Steldor was even aware of what he was doing as he crashed the bookshelves to the floor, sending a few books flying to again strike glass, finally kicking what remained of the weapons cases to shards.

The tumult ended, and the room throbbed with silence. I peered out from my hiding place to see Steldor standing before Cannan's desk. He was breathing heavily, wildness still evident in his posture, as though the only reason he had stopped was that he had run out of things to destroy. The captain scrutinized him, hardly ruffled and definitely not afraid.

"Are you finished?" he asked, still in charge of the situation despite the havoc that had just ensued. "If not, *your* study awaits."

Father and son locked eyes, and though Steldor was still tense, physical and emotional exhaustion was setting in. To my great relief, the exertion seemed to have taken some of the fight out of him, although I wasn't confident it was safe for me to be around him.

Very subtly, Cannan motioned with his head for Halias to take me out of the office. Without a word, the Elite Guard grabbed my upper arm and tugged me through the door, and I let him guide me up the stairs and to my quarters. As soon as he left me, I hurried into my room to sit on the edge of the bed, trying to make sense of everything that had happened.

I was petrified by the side of my husband I had just seen. What was to prevent a similar explosion the next time I saw him? He had not hurt me in Cannan's office, but if we were alone? What then might he do? Despite my weariness, I could not lie down, too agitated and afraid to attempt to sleep.

And what of Narian? How had the fire at Koranis's estate erupted? Had Narian *conjured* it? As ludicrous as the idea seemed, it was the only explanation I could fathom. Pushing my sluggish brain to work harder, I began to weave together an alternative. Perhaps he had used the explosive powder, marked a line of it on the ground before we'd arrived, in anticipation of a need to make an escape. But this was almost more implausible. Who anticipated needing to make a wall of flame? If anyone, it would be Narian, but that didn't solve the question of how he had caused it to light at the correct moment, and so my theory floundered. Then I recalled my first conversation with London concerning Cokyri, in which he had said our soldiers believed the Overlord could kill people with a wave of his hand. Was it possible that Narian had similar powers? If so, why hadn't he ever told me?

My head swam with all the information I was trying to process. Narian was saving my sister's life with every order he obeyed; his failure to follow his master's commands would result in her death, but not prevent an assault on Hytanica. He had implied that the Overlord would attack with or without his aid, and that the fighting would be brutal. He had appeared to believe that it would be best for us if he led the offensive against our kingdom; that he could best protect the Hytanican people by becoming our conqueror. In some twisted way, it made sense—that is, if we were willing to concede defeat before the war had even begun.

Nothing had gone right this evening. Destari had betrayed me; Narian had told me to forget all that had happened between us and to live as though we'd never met; and the man to whom I was married was ready to throttle me.

I heard the parlor door open, and the subsequent slam left no question that it was Steldor who had entered. I hardly dared breathe, afraid he might come after me or call for me, but he did neither. Instead, the next sound I heard was the aggressive closing of his bedroom door. I exhaled, finally allowing myself to sink into my pillows.

The weather the next day was bent on contradicting my mood. Bright sunlight filtered through my bedroom window, and I could hear birds chirping in the most idyllic manner from just beyond the pane. Following on the heels of the night's events, such cheeriness was grating. I was still tired as I dragged myself from bed to dress with Sadhienne's assistance, and my mind was sluggish, not yet having digested everything.

What I wanted most was for all of this to be *over.* I wanted Miranna and London back, along with the peace that had existed but two scarce years ago. I wanted to be unmarried and thereby rid of Steldor's jealousy and anger, and I wanted Narian to… There the thought halted, for I knew not how to finish it. To make things simple, I could wish that I had never met him, as seemed to be his desire. But when I thought of him, I could not wish that, could not wish anything but that we could be together in the absence of all the troubles that had descended on us like a plague. I wanted to run from this devastating life, but I had no choice but to endure, with the meager hope that somehow all would turn out well.

I went into the parlor and sat on the sofa, waving Sahdienne on her way. The absolute quiet from behind Steldor's closed bedroom door meant that he had already departed, a situation with which I was pleased. I sank onto the sofa, not wanting to leave and worried about what this day might bring, only to be disturbed by a knock on the door.

"Come in," I called, thinking Sahdienne had forgotten something. I rose stiffly, for my muscles ached from yesterday's activity, and sleep had provided no real respite.

I was taken aback when Cannan crossed the threshold. He gave me a scant bow, then his eyes flicked around the parlor.

"Is Steldor in his room?" he inquired.

"I thought he'd left, although I suppose he could be. If he's here, he hasn't made a sound."

I could not meet Cannan's eyes, certain that I would find condemnation there. A few months ago, when he had first learned of my relationship with Narian, I had been besieged by worry as to what his opinion of me might be; now I didn't think I could bear it.

Cannan went to his son's door and loudly rapped his knuckles against it three times.

"Steldor!" he called, to no reply.

"I assumed he'd be in the Throne Room, or with you."

The captain glanced at me, then opened the door and stepped inside to stop dead in his tracks.

"What's wrong?" I asked, suddenly frightened.

Without acknowledging me, Cannan turned on his heel and marched back across the parlor.

"Halias, Casimir!" he shouted, summoning the two guards who were posted in the corridor.

The door swung open, and I read alarm on the faces of both men.

"The window is open," Cannan said, pinching the bridge of his nose and closing his eyes for an instant. "He's gone."

"Signs of a struggle, Captain?" Casimir inquired. "Surely the Queen or the Palace Guards on patrol would have heard—"

"There was no struggle," Cannan replied wearily. "The room is in order except that some of his weapons are gone. He left of his own accord. What did he do after we talked in my office last night?"

"He went directly to his quarters, sir," Casimir replied, for he would have been with the King.

"That puts him eight hours ahead of us, easily, if he's left the city," Halias calculated.

"He's beyond the city," Cannan confirmed.

Halias and Casimir exchanged a glance, their eyebrows rising as they wondered how their captain could have determined this.

"Sir?" they asked in unison.

"A horse was missing from the stable at my city estate this morning. I supposed a thief, but Steldor would have been smart enough not to take his own mount. Anyone would have recognized it. And he wouldn't have taken a horse unless he intended to leave the city."

Cannan sidestepped his guards and marched out the door and down the corridor. Casimir followed, Halias unable to do likewise, for he was assigned to protect me. I wasted no time in pursuing the men, however, and my bodyguard did not object to my nosiness. I hurried down the hall, fighting guilt and worry. How angry had I made him? Was I the reason he had taken off, or had something else transpired last night?

Cannan had already disappeared around the corner, heading for the Grand Staircase. I quickened my pace, but by the time I reached the landing, he was on the first floor, calling for Galen. The Sergeant at Arms emerged from his office just in time to see Cannan's retreating back, and he and Casimir hastened after their superior officer. Cursing my inability to eavesdrop, I decided to wait for them to reappear from the captain's office, in the hope that I would be able to catch snippets of conversation. I sat down on the top step in an undignified fashion to do just that, Halias taking up position behind me with his back against the wall.

What I eventually gathered was this: Steldor, a hooded cloak pulled low, had left the city unrecognized, riding one of the captain's horses and presenting a pass with the King's seal, something he naturally had no difficulty obtaining. This gave him a considerable advantage. Cannan had decided that Galen and Casimir would head a discreet search party into the mountains, with Galen leading the way to all the places he and Steldor had frequented in their youth. The sergeant had been insistent that his best friend would not have gone to any such locations, since he did not want to be found, but Cannan was resolute that this was the most logical way to begin.

After the search party had gone on its way, I went to my drawing room, where I would be able to hear the return of the men from down the hall. Cannan came after me just long enough to make certain that I would follow my usual daily schedule; he did not trust that our city was free of Cokyrian spies, and he feared that if the information broke that the King was unaccounted for, the search would turn into a race. He also reminded Halias that he was to stay with me, able to see as easily as could I that the Elite Guard craved involvement in the effort.

Hours passed without word, and I began to feel desperate for news of any sort. I opted to walk past the Throne Room under the guise of needing to retrieve a shawl from my bedroom, hoping I would encounter my father-in-law. I meandered through the entrance hall, finding it strangely quiet, then climbed the stairs at an impossibly slow pace. I even pretended at the top that my shoe had slipped off my heel, and I spent a good minute readjusting it, hoping something of importance would take place while I lingered.

Halias, who hadn't yet said a word, finally broke his silence, his tone dry. "I don't think your shawl will be found here, Your Highness."

I sighed and turned away from him with a frown, for he had surmised what my true intentions were. Giving up the pretense, I leaned upon the railing. The hour was growing late, and I wondered if the search party would return at all this day. But surely someone would come to update Cannan, even if some of the troops stayed in the mountains.

At that moment, a soldier stumbled through the double front doors of the palace and limped into the Grand Entry, face smeared with dirt and sweat, calling for the captain. The Palace Guards at the entrance maintained their posts, while I went rigid. Halias came to my side, all of us waiting for Cannan.

"Report," the captain ordered as he strode through the antechamber, taking in the battered soldier, who, despite his obvious exhaustion, came to attention.

"Sir, the Cokyrians are at the river. We need reinforcements."

The Palace Guards broke into hushed mutterings at these words, and my stomach gave a sickening lurch. The war had begun anew. I felt as though a death march had commenced, with the only questions being who would die and when.

"They will be sent," Cannan curtly responded, but then he placed a steadying hand on the man's shoulder. "Stand at ease and tell me how things were when you left."

"We did not expect their attack, sir," the soldier admitted without shame. "We were disorganized—" the slight scowl on the captain's face made it clear that he had not left things that way "—and the Cokyrians could probably have overcome us, had they employed their full might. But at the time I rode for reinforcements, our troops were beating them back. In truth, I think they were testing us, sir. Their second attack will be far worse."

"Doubtless. Was there any sign of the boy?"

"No, sir."

There was some relief for the captain in this statement, as I knew he and his men had yet to explain the fiery barrier that had impeded them in their attempt to capture Narian.

"Then you are dismissed. Report to the infirmary and have your leg examined."

"But sir, I should return—"

"You have your orders," Cannan said sharply, the strain of the day at last beginning to show. "You'll be of no use fatigued and injured." A beat passed, and he regained his unflappable demeanor. "I will send additional men. Go."

"Yes, sir."

Noticeably cowed, the soldier hobbled through the front doors once more, on his way to the military base.

★ ★ ★

The men Cannan sent to offer aid at the river proved to be unnecessary, for the soldier who had brought news of Cokyri's assault had been correct about the enemy's intent—they were testing us, toying with us, their attack halfhearted. The servants and guards even jested that our troops alternated between fighting and napping on the battlefield. Through it all, I had to wonder if it were Narian who was trying to belittle and badger us with this technique.

There was still no news of Steldor, and it was becoming harder to keep up the appearance that nothing was wrong. When Galen returned early the next afternoon without the King and without any idea of where he might be, it began to penetrate my brain that Steldor was truly *missing.* Everyone had assumed he would be back by now, and despite the discreet search parties Cannan had dispatched in every direction, no evidence of his whereabouts had been discovered. It was possible, Galen pointed out, that Steldor, a trained military man, had covered his tracks and would not be found until he chose to be. Cannan, however, instructed his men to search again and again, arguing that every person, no matter how well trained, leaves a trail. I could tell the captain hadn't so much as closed his eyes since his son's disappearance.

Late that afternoon, I paced, alone in my parlor, feeling a surprising desire to have my husband join me. Despite our disagreements, I desperately wanted him to walk through the door and be safe. When I could pace no more, I visited the Royal Chapel, the first time I had done so since Miranna's abduction. Although it was painful for me to cross the threshold, I sought the peace I had always found within its walls. The altar had been repaired, and no sign of the tragedy remained, other than the fact that a new priest now served our family. I sat in one of the pews, letting my fears wash over me as I thought of Steldor alone somewhere for a second dark night, possibly injured, certainly in danger. *Come home,* I breathed, closing my eyes. *Be all right. Please be all right and come home.*

When I left the chapel to return to my quarters, Destari waited for me in the corridor, having returned to duty as my bodyguard.

"Your Highness," he greeted me, not referring to me by name, which suited me perfectly. "The captain feels I am sufficiently healed to return to your service. I will seek reassignment, however, if this is not to your liking."

"I have never questioned your ability as a bodyguard," I coolly responded, relieved that his wound had not been more serious. "It is your suitability as a friend that I question."

He grimaced, and I stalked past him, my resentment over his deceit on the night I had met with Narian warring with my guilt over how he'd been injured. Could I truly fault him for what he'd done? I knew that the men were right to consider Narian our adversary. Would I begrudge Destari his deed had that adversary been the High Priestess or the Overlord? No. But yet I could not pardon him, simply because to do so would require me to abandon hope that Narian was still the young man who had promised he would never hurt me. And that I was not ready to do.

I rose early the next morning and went to the first floor, my jittery mind and nerves having kept me from a restful slumber. Needing to know if there had been word, I knocked on the captain's office door.

"Enter," he called.

The office had been restored since it had been subjected

to Steldor's wrath, the glass weapons cases replaced, the bookshelves put back in order. Another chair had even been brought in to take the place of the one Steldor had smashed. The captain, anchored behind his desk, gestured for me to sit.

"Nothing," he said, rubbing his unusually shadowed jaw, and I took my place on the wooden chair he was indicating.

"Will we find him?" I asked tentatively, for I did not want to hear the answer unless it was the one I craved.

"Yes."

"You're certain?"

"I have to be."

I didn't know what to make of this statement, so I waited in discomfited silence. Just as I began to wonder if that had been my cue to depart, Cannan elaborated, leaning back in his chair.

"Growing up, Steldor was, at times, difficult, and he took off like this on more than one occasion. He knows the land and is a well-trained soldier, so from that standpoint, I don't worry about him. What he fails to see is the difference between being a boy who needs to get away and being the King of Hytanica. There is greater risk to him, and to us, because of his status. If no enemy discovers him, we'll either find him or he'll return of his own accord. If he is or has already been discovered…" Cannan shrugged in what would have seemed a callous gesture had I not been aware of the sleep he had been losing. "Well, then I cannot say." He paused before finishing. "It is easier to keep going if I believe the former."

A commotion from the entryway thwarted my reply, and Cannan came to his feet. Our eyes met, then he walked through the guardroom to investigate while I took the liberty of following him. Galen and several others were gathered, all struggling for breath, as though they had been riding hard.

"What is it?" Cannan demanded, striding toward the Sergeant at Arms.

"It's a diversion, sir," Galen panted, wiping sweat from his brow, desolate and worn-out.

"What is?"

The captain waited for the sergeant to recover, running a hand through his hair in an uncharacteristic gesture.

"At the bridge, where the Cokyrians are attacking. They're just diverting our attention. We followed the river high up into the mountains searching for Steldor and stumbled upon Cokyrian troops crossing into our lands. They're gathering forces, preparing to descend the mountain and assault us under cover of the forest."

"Send for my battalion commanders. We need to put up defenses to the north." Glancing around at the exhausted soldiers, Cannan added, "And get your men some rest."

"Attention," Galen called, drawing the weary soldiers upright. "Return to your quarters. You've got six hours."

Galen then stepped into the guardroom to instruct others under his authority to summon the battalion commanders. I stared at Cannan, knowing it was no longer such a remote possibility that our King might fall prey to the Cokyrians.

The soldiers departed, some heading toward the barracks at the military base, some going to their rooms in the East Wing, a few following Galen's specific instructions. When the hall had emptied, Cannan turned once more to his sergeant.

"To hell with discretion," he said, and the simple fact that he had sworn spoke volumes about the level of danger he now believed to exist. "Steldor has to be found, *now.* It's time for a major troop deployment."

"Your Highness!"

I heard the call and looked around but could not determine who desired my attention. But when the palace doors swung wide, I realized the shout had come from outside, and had not been directed at me.

Steldor strode in and proceeded to walk past us to the Grand Staircase, offering a mere nod of his head in response to our incredulous stares. His arrival was so unreal I half expected that I was the only one who could see him, and that Cannan and Galen would resume their discussion about how to find him as soon as he had disappeared up the steps.

I stood frozen, expecting Cannan to stop his son, but to my astonishment, it was not the captain who marched forward and addressed Steldor. It was Galen.

"Where the *hell* are you going?"

Galen waited a few feet from the base of the staircase, glaring up at his best friend. Steldor turned and slowly made his way back down, and I thought Cannan would intervene to prevent the sergeant from lambasting the King. He did not seem inclined to do so.

"Wherever the hell I please," Steldor replied, noticeably testy and worn-out.

"Don't talk to me like that." Galen clenched his fists and jaw in barely subdued fury. "I don't give a damn how you talk to anybody else, but not like that to me, not after what you've put us through."

"Oh, sorry," Steldor rejoined, a complete lack of sincerity in his voice. "How's this? You're dismissed."

The words, once said, could not be taken back. Whether or not Steldor regretted them was unclear, for his stance remained belligerent, despite the fact that Galen had gone so rigid he appeared to be driving his fingernails into the flesh of his palms. When the tension in the Grand Entry

Hall had become so dense it threatened to crack the walls, Galen exploded.

"You *bastard!*" he yelled, and then, seemingly of its own accord, one of his balled-up fists smashed into Steldor's jaw, knocking the King to the floor.

I sucked in my breath, frantically looking to Cannan, who was surveying the scene with no more than a raised eyebrow. Galen stood over his friend, panting from the effort to control the anger raging within him, while Steldor rubbed his jaw in disbelief, too shocked to formulate a comeback.

"You can't think of anyone but yourself, can you?" Galen stormed, and to my surprise, Steldor stayed down, gaping silently up at him. "You run off when things get a little more complicated than you'd like, and leave us to cover your tracks so the whole *valley* doesn't find out that Hytanica bloody lost its *King*—meanwhile, the Cokyrians are infiltrating our lands to the north, so it becomes entirely possible that you've walked right into their camp. We have men out there still searching for you, men who should be helping to barricade the northern border—to make sure that in a week you still *have* a kingdom to rule. And you have the gall to strut in here and be an ass! I swear, Steldor, if we didn't need someone to sit on that throne, I'd dispatch you with my own hands!"

The two erstwhile companions stared at each other, Galen challenging Steldor to respond, and Steldor too staggered to do so. Eventually, the sergeant threw his hands in the air and marched into his office, slamming the door behind him.

In the silence that followed Galen's departure, I came to appreciate the true meaning of the word *awkward*. Steldor did not rise to his feet, and his eyes were glazed. I felt unneeded, but there was no way for me to make a polished exit. The Palace Guards, bound by duty to remain, searched the walls, the floor, the ceiling, for anything plausible in which to show an interest, not wanting to be caught gawking at their King. Cannan at last stepped forward to extend a hand to his son, hoisting him to his feet, but Steldor forestalled any intention the captain might have had to speak.

"I'm going to change clothes," Steldor said, sounding genuinely contrite. "I'll meet you in the Throne Room in half an hour."

Cannan nodded in approval of his son's change in attitude. Steldor's eyes flashed to me, but he said nothing, simply heading up the stairs. I decided not to follow, instead walking toward the Queen's Drawing Room, certain I was the last person with whom he would be willing to talk.

CHAPTER 17

WAR AND TEA

IN THE AFTERMATH OF THE KING'S RETURN and in light of what we now knew to be the enemy's military strategy, activity around the palace increased drastically. Soldiers came with frequent reports from the field, scouts brought reconnaissance information, and Cannan's battalion commanders became familiar faces. Marcail, the Master at Arms in charge of the City Guard, also came and went more often, for he had been given the task of stockpiling food and supplies in anticipation of a siege.

The location of my drawing room in the East Wing just down the corridor from the Grand Entry turned out to be quite beneficial, as the entryway, due to its proximity to the Throne Room, the Captain of the Guard's office and the Sergeant at Arms' office, had become the hub of all activity. If I left my door open, I could hear when anyone of importance came to deliver information. While Cannan or Galen would usher military personnel into their offices or through the antechamber to meet with Steldor, I was able to catch enough bits and pieces of conversation to have an idea of what was happening. From this I knew that the attacks at the river were intermittent rather than brutal, designed to keep us engaged while the Cokyrians prepared to launch a full-scale assault from the north. It was ironic that the King's disappearance had alerted us to the enemy's plans, giving us much-needed time to prepare a defense.

Destari, thus far, remained my bodyguard, although I was certain he thought he could be put to better use elsewhere. I suspected Cannan felt the same and that it was Steldor who had insisted the deputy captain remain in this position. I did not know whether to interpret this as a positive sign from my husband, for he certainly knew I felt safer with Destari than with any guard other than London, or as a sign of distrust, for Destari was also one of the guards who knew me well and could, therefore, keep me in line. Regardless of the King's reasoning, I was content with the arrangement, for the deputy captain had long ago given up the notion that the affairs of the kingdom were none of my business, and he willingly kept me abreast of our military campaign.

It was from Destari that I learned of the defenses Cannan had our troops putting in place along our northern border, beginning at the west bank of the Recorah River and extending along the line of the forest. The captain believed the Cokyrians, who did not realize they had lost the element of surprise, would descend the mountain through the river gorge, for that approach would provide the easiest and surest footing. Our best scouts were monitoring the enemy, and when word came that the Cokyrians were on the move, our archers would be deployed along the gorge to slow their advance as much as possible. In addition, Cannan was taking advantage of the fact that our men knew this part of the forest better than anyone, and traps were being rigged along the natural pathways through the trees. While these tactics would weaken the enemy, their real purpose was to buy time to put in place our primary line of defense. Hytanican soldiers and villagers were felling trees to create a blockade in the area where the enemy would emerge from the gorge. The plan was to contain the Cokyrian troops, and therefore the fighting, to a specific location, pinning them down and preventing them from overrunning our lands. For how long we could hold them in this manner was unclear.

When I asked Destari about the fighting at the river, he explained that our military positions to the east and south had been reinforced, and that nature made these borders easier to defend. The rapidly flowing Recorah River threatened a watery grave, while the primarily open land on the enemy's side provided little cover. The terrain to the east, in particular, was inhospitable, giving way to the Cokyrian Desert, which stretched into the foothills of the mountain range. To the south, the number of troops protecting the only bridge that spanned the Recorah had been substantially increased, and barriers to prevent the Cokyrians from storming it had been put in place. Our men had strapped logs together, with sharpened points aimed at the enemy, and placed them at intervals along the bridge's expanse. Destari also assured me that Cannan would burn the bridge if he felt it was going to fall. When I smelled smoke on the wind one day, the Elite Guard explained that the captain had ordered our archers to set fire to the trees that grew on the far side of the river so that there would be no wood with which the enemy could build rafts.

I was thankful to know of the measures Cannan was taking, but not naïve enough to believe they would ensure our victory. If there were truth in the legend, then Hytanica would crumble under an attack led by Narian; and Narian would lead the attack as long as the enemy had Miranna. It thus appeared to me that the way to save Hytanica was not by building defenses but by rescuing my sister. Destari was more than a little surprised when I tentatively brought this theory to him. After telling me I had a good head for military strategy, he explained that Cannan, Steldor and the Commander of the Reconnaissance Unit were already trying to formulate a rescue plan, but they were greatly hampered by London's absence, for he was the only Hytanican who had ever been in Cokyri long enough to learn the layout of the city—and live to bring the information home.

It was three days later that the fighting stepped up at the river and the attack commenced from the north. Destari was again my source of information, and he assured me that Cannan's strategy on the new front was working, for the Cokyrians were having difficulty moving through the gorge. He also proudly relayed that our archers were highly effective along the borders we had in common with the river, shooting down at the enemy from wooden platforms that had been constructed in the trees along our banks, as well as showering them with arrows from the ground, where our men used shallow trenches and earthen mounds for protection from return fire. For the first time, I appreciated the ingenuity of those who were planning our defense, and understood the reason that Cannan, then the newly appointed twenty-four-year-old Captain of the Guard, had been credited with beating back the Cokyrians during the last war. Meetings were frequently held in the strategy room involving the captain, the King, the deputy captains, the Sergeant at Arms, the Master at Arms, the Reconnaissance Officer and various battalion commanders.

Steldor and I had not spoken since his return, so in addition to the anxieties of the war, the fact that I had gone to meet with Narian remained unaddressed. While I felt foolhardy and remorseful, I was scared to broach the subject with him. I also wondered if putting the matter to rest weren't more important to me than it was to him, for he was dealing with other, more pressing issues—among them righting his relationship with Galen.

I had briefly experienced life in a kingdom at war when Cokyri had made its initial attempts to reclaim Narian almost a year ago, but though I had suffered under the circumstances along with everyone else, that had been but a taste of what was now at hand. Rarely did any of the men smile these days, more and more women lost husbands, brothers and sons, and I realized, though no one told me, that the battles were becoming much more brutal. The populace did not know, however, what those of us in the palace, in the inner circle, knew. Though none wanted to acknowledge it, rife was the belief that the legend might be true—that this might be the beginning of the end for Hytanica.

It was in the midst of the mounting stress that my mother came to me with a suggestion. She approached me in the drawing room that was now my office but had for thirty years been hers. I sat beside her on the sofa in front of the bay window, uncertain as to what she might want, sadly aware that her honey-blond hair had lost its satiny sheen, and that her blue eyes no longer had the same sparkle.

"It's good to see you, Mother," I offered, but she stared past me into the East Courtyard, and I wondered if she were seeing something other than the overcast skies, barren trees and withered flowers.

"It has always been within the role of the Queen to bring together the young noblewomen in the kingdom," my mother said, turning to face me. "The last such event occurred prior to your wedding, so perhaps it is time to consider hosting such a function yourself. I was thinking a tea party would be appropriate."

My mother had often hosted social functions on the grounds at which she had been gazing, the stateliest of the three courtyards. Its central area, paved with multicolored stones that formed concentric circles around a large two-tiered fountain, had been designed for this purpose and had seen many garden parties, betrothal celebrations, picnics and holiday galas. Nonetheless, the incongruity of a tea party during a time of war did not escape me, and I couldn't help but wonder if her grief had touched her mind. Or perhaps the slight relief engendered by the news of Miranna's humane treatment in Cokyri had lifted her mood to the point where such a normal activity seemed appropriate. As if reading my thoughts, she offered an explanation.

"There is nothing we women can do with respect to the defense of our lands, but we can offer solace in other ways. At a time like this, everyone feels the need to gather friends and loved ones closer."

In truth, I had not seen any of my friends since before my sister's abduction, and the timing of such an event seemed right, as many of them were now betrothed, a surge that had come only after Steldor's bachelorhood had ended.

"I will consider it, Mother," I assured her.

She sat for a moment longer, then stood to depart.

"Not all battles are fought with weapons, my dear," she finished, the melodic lilt that had too long been absent once more in her voice.

I gave my mother's suggestion further thought, realizing that such a gathering would permit me to efficiently deal with the problem of my growing stack of correspondence. Acquaintance after acquaintance had written to me in the aftermath of my sister's disappearance with concern etched behind every word, and yet I had refused face-to-face contact with any of them. As I still had limited desire for social interaction, a tea party seemed like an appropriate way to handle the situation.

The time felt right for another reason, as well. In the past, during the month of October, the kingdom would have been abuzz over the annual Harvest Festival and Tournament. With the advent of the war, however, no such celebration would take place, making this the first fall I had seen without the popular event.

I arranged invitations to the tea party, writing out a brief apology for my silence and instructing the scribe to add it to the end of each sheet of parchment. I allowed one week's preparation, during which time I tried to convince myself that this social activity would be good for me and everyone else in attendance, for it offered both a welcome distraction and a chance to commiserate.

When the date and time were upon me, I met my guests in the tea room in the western wing, which had been prepared with several small tables draped in white linen tablecloths. The day was sunny but cool, and a fire blazed in the hearth about which most of the guests had congregated. It seemed strange to attend such an event without my sister and to be the hostess in place of my mother. Lanek announced my arrival, and the girls—or women, as I supposed we all were now—curtsied generously to me upon my entrance. I took in their eager faces, marveling at how different they all appeared to me. Of my close friends, Kalem and Reveina were present, both brunettes who had grown slightly taller and had shed the extra weight of their youth. Reveina, in particular, had evolved into a striking beauty, though I noticed some discoloration about her jaw and left eye that resembled bruising. She had married three months ago, while Kalem bore a betrothal ring, though to whom she was promised I did not know.

Tiersia, betrothed to Galen; her younger sister Fiara, married to Steldor's cousin Warrick and quite pregnant; and several other engaged or recently wed young noblewomen were present, as well. I couldn't help but glance at Fiara's swelling belly, trying to envision what it might be like to be with child. I knew the entire kingdom was anticipating the day Steldor and I would announce that there was another heir on the way. Indeed, I supposed, beyond that, everyone would be keen for a glimpse of Steldor's offspring. They would be hoping for a son, to be just like his father and grandfather. My stomach twisted with nervousness, feeling the invisible pressure of the populace's eyes upon me, all the while recalling Steldor's words from our wedding night: *willing or not, you have an obligation as a wife and a queen to bear an heir.* I exiled these troubling thoughts at once, determined to take my life one day at a time, wondering if there would be a point in the future when I would not be so averse to letting Steldor bed me, or would have no choice but to let him do so.

I greeted each of my guests in turn, finally moving to my place at one of the tables. The other young women did likewise, seating themselves only after I had taken up position in the ornate chair that had been provided for me. I had chosen to place Reveina, Kalem and Tiersia at the Queen's table, and as we politely sipped our tea and nibbled on biscuits, I found the former two quite changed since my wedding.

Vivacious Kalem, who had always babbled nonstop about every available—and sometimes unavailable—man in the kingdom, now spoke only of the one she was bound to marry. Once I learned his identity, I could do little to curtail the amused smile that kept appearing on my face for I could not understand how anyone could be so infatuated with Tadark.

Reveina, on the other hand, was bizarrely quiet. She had always been the boldest among our group, leading the conversation and sometimes taking it in directions the rest of us would not have dared. She had been the one who somehow made it acceptable to speak on scandalous topics, and I had fully expected her to offer up an inappropriate retelling of her wedding night experience. But she was silent and submissive, and again I wondered about the purplish-green blemishes that marked her face.

"Yes, and Tadark has so many sweet things planned for our married life," Kalem was saying, her cheeks pink and her light gray eyes misty. "He's in the Elite Guard, you know, and well-off financially, and he's chosen this beautiful house for us, for our family. He wants to have as many children as we can, you see. He's accustomed to a large family—eight older brothers, he has, can you imagine?"

"I wish you the best of luck keeping them straight." Tiersia laughed. "And I hope for your sake none of them are twins! I'm afraid I'll never be able to tell Galen's sisters apart—he's always correcting me, and I feel such a fool!"

"And how are you finding married life, Reveina?" I asked, taking the initiative since my friend was behaving so oddly.

"Oh, it's fine, really, thank you."

"And what is your husband's work?"

"Lord Marcail is a military man."

"Marcail? The Master at Arms?"

"Yes, he works in the city and is home most evenings. It is very fortunate."

Though Reveina's responses were polite enough, her tone was somewhat contrived, and she rarely met my eyes. Given her obvious reluctance to discuss her marriage, I did not pursue the topic further, but I also did not believe for a moment the pretense of happiness she was attempting to put forth. How could a man have reduced the audacious, charmingly self-important girl with whom I had grown up to this timorous shadow of a woman?

The conversation continued, and I learned that a date in November had been set for Galen and Tiersia's wedding. The green-eyed brunette spoke fondly of the arrangements that had been made, of how Steldor would be Galen's best man just as Galen had been his. Her manner showed no awareness of a rift between the two friends, and I wondered if she knew of their recent dispute, or if they had repaired their relationship so quickly that any tension between them had passed her notice. I couldn't picture them staying mad at each other for long, and indeed, I still heard Steldor leave our quarters most evenings to relax elsewhere. It appeared all that was left was for the King and Queen to begin speaking to one another again.

"You must be in bliss, Alera," Kalem said, then quickly corrected the way in which she had addressed me. "My apologies! Your Highness. You must be so happy, *Your Highness. Your Royal Majesty.* You're the Queen now! And Lord Steldor is, no doubt, quite a king."

There was a suggestive sparkle in her eye, suffused by silliness, which was enough to keep me from being uncomfortable.

"What happens between me and His Grace stays between me and His Grace," I replied, playing along. I found it strangely enjoyable to pretend for a few minutes that I had a normal marriage, and my answer seemed to make her giddy.

"It's hardly fair of you to have him all to yourself and not share a few secrets," she replied.

I smiled at her daring in saying such things, feeling again like a young girl of fresh courting age.

"Very well, one secret," I said, leaning forward and dropping my volume. "We all know His Highness is exceedingly talkative and charming, but only I know *exactly* how to close that lovely mouth."

Kalem gasped, delighted that I would say something so outrageous. I silently assured myself that I wasn't lying—Steldor often ended up storming out of the room when we were together, then would refuse to talk to me for days. If that didn't qualify as closing his mouth, what did?

Tiersia, ever proper, seemed slightly ill at ease with the direction our conversation had taken, but the corners of her lips turned up nonetheless. Even Reveina emitted a hesitant laugh. Enjoying our new game, Kalem demanded a secret from our other tablemates in exchange for hers, which she swore would be well worth the price. Reveina appeared quite distressed at the idea, but Tiersia was intrigued enough to participate.

"If I share some information, you must never repeat it to a living soul," she murmured, and we all nodded. "All right, then, Galen is dreadfully ticklish."

She said "dreadfully," but I could tell by her deepening color that she found this attribute endearing. We chuckled and teased her before turning to Reveina, who instantly rebuffed us.

"Oh, I shouldn't, I couldn't. My lord would not like it if I spoke of him."

There was an awkward hush, during which Reveina glanced around the table, then cast her troubled brown eyes on the linen tablecloth.

"Very well," Kalem said brightly, trying to restore the atmosphere. "On to my secret." She grinned and motioned us all closer. "Tadark has a tattoo, on his left shoulder blade," she imparted, knowing the fact that she had seen his back bared would, in and of itself, raise eyebrows. "But that's not the very best part. Guess who convinced him to get it?" She waited, building the suspense, then exclaimed in a whisper, "The King and the Sergeant at Arms!"

I frowned, perplexed, wondering when Steldor and Galen had made time to spend with Tadark, then enlightenment came as to how Steldor had always seemed to know so much about my activities during the time of our courtship. My sometime bodyguard obviously had been spilling information, probably desperate to be on good terms with the two most admired young men in Hytanica.

"They went to the pubs together one night," Kalem went on, shamelessly enjoying how masculine her betrothed sounded in that sentence. "And eventually, Steldor and Galen got to talking about *their* tattoos. They persuaded Tadark to get an identical one—same design, same location, everything."

Tiersia shot me a questioning glance, and I knew that she, too, was not aware of any tattoos borne by her man. It was possible, of course, that Galen had such a mark unbeknownst to her, for it was not likely she had seen his bare back. But I was not ignorant of Steldor's physique, despite the fact that we had yet to share a bed, for I had seen him without his shirt many times. I had never noticed a blemish, let alone a tattoo, upon his torso. I cringed, guessing Tadark had not seen the tattoos, and hoping the men with whom Tiersia and I were involved, men who were known to be occasionally unruly, had not taken advantage of their naïve companion. Even though I found Tadark intolerable, he did not deserve to be victimized by Steldor and Galen.

The true irony was that at the time of the incident Kalem was describing, Tadark would have outranked them both.

"And what is the tattoo?" Tiersia hesitantly asked.

"It's a Latin word—*virgo.*"

I could say with certainty that neither Steldor nor Galen would have had *that* word tattooed anywhere on their bodies. Tadark had not grown up a nobleman and, therefore, had probably never been taught even basic Latin, while Kalem had always been too fanciful to pay much attention to her lessons. It was unlikely that she would recognize what her beloved had been coerced into slapping on his back.

"I think it means man, or manly," Kalem finished proudly.

Though Reveina remained withdrawn, Tiersia and I covered our mouths to hide our amusement. Kalem's mistake was an easy and unfortunate one. *Viro* meant man; *virgo* meant virgin. Steldor and Galen would have known this full well, just as Tiersia and I did.

"How wonderful," Tiersia said, the first of us to recover her poise, clearly feeling it was not her place to correct Kalem's misconception. I likewise held my tongue.

I rose to my feet and, in so doing, freed my guests from the tables to move about the room. As they conversed, I wove among them, extending congratulations on marriages and betrothals, and gathering news about their families. When fatigue set in, I indicated to Destari that I wished to bring the event to a close. He summoned Lanek, who stepped into the room to inform the guests of my impending departure.

"Noble ladies, Her Majesty Queen Alera takes her leave with a prayer for your continued well-being."

The women curtsied and I withdrew, dawdling in the corridor to give an instruction to Destari before proceeding to my drawing room in the East Wing. It was perhaps ten minutes later when Reveina appeared at my door.

"You wished to speak with me, Your Majesty?" she hesitantly inquired.

"Yes, I thought we could visit more privately."

I came around my desk, motioning toward the seating area in front of the bay window, and we sat down next to each other on the sofa.

"You've changed," I commented, uncertain how best to proceed.

"My apologies, Your Highness, if my disposition was not pleasing to you," she replied, eyes on her folded hands where they rested in her lap.

"Don't apologize," I said, worried about her. "There's no need for that. I just wish I understood the reason."

"I'm married now," she said, as though that fact explained everything. "It was time to stop being a little girl."

"Of course, but being married doesn't mean you have to be unhappy."

She was startled by my simple statement, and her eyes for a moment flitted to the courtyard that was visible through the window, betraying a desire to escape.

"What would make you think me unhappy?" she finally stuttered.

"Am I wrong?"

She began to pluck at the fabric of her skirt, a sign of distress with which I was familiar. Sadness filled me, for I could hardly detect in her a trace of the girl I had known but a few months ago.

"I—I am married," she said again, and I had the impression this was now a rote response to any inquiries into her well-being. "This is who I am now."

"Is it your husband?" I pressed, taking her hands in mine.

At my touch, her breathing quickened, and she struggled to control her emotions. I put my arms around her, and she lost the battle she was waging, breaking into tears. She covered her face with her hands, and I stroked her hair as I waited for her to quiet. When she had calmed, I tried again, knowing that what I was asking was intrusive.

"Does your husband mistreat you?"

"He disciplines me," she managed, sitting up and taking a rattling breath. "I try to—to be obedient, but there are more rules than I can remember. It's too much—I can't do it. I can never do it. Alera…I'm sorry."

"You're *sorry?*"

I was scared and infuriated. How could a nobleman, a military man or, for that matter, any man, treat his wife so poorly? I was suddenly filled with appreciation for my spouse, toward whom I sometimes failed to show the proper respect but who had not laid a hand on me.

"Reveina, don't say you're sorry. That isn't discipline. It's cruelty."

"I don't know how to please him. I'm terrified when he comes home, when I should be happily welcoming him. He's not a bad man—he's well respected within the military, and he's a good provider. I know if I were a better wife, he would not deal with me so."

Her words made my stomach turn, for the idea that she thought she might somehow deserve such treatment was revolting. She looked at me desolately, and I wanted so badly to keep her from him, to keep her safe.

"Beg pardon, Your Majesty, but I really should go. I must be home before Lord Marcail returns at the end of the day."

I nodded, not wanting to cause her further problems. I came to my feet, prompting her to rise, as well.

"I don't know what I can do, but I will try to find a way to help you, Reveina. You shouldn't have to live like that."

"Oh, please do not," she implored, catching my arm tightly as I made to walk toward the door. "He will only learn that I complained of him."

I gently pried her fingers loose. "I swear I will not endanger you."

I stayed in the Queen's Drawing Room for a long time after Reveina's departure, reflecting on her ghastly revelations. I had said I would do what I could for her, but what exactly was within my means? To offer her a shoulder upon which to cry? An occasional safe haven? Such assistance was feeble at best and did not change the fact that she could not leave her husband; her reputation would be ruined. I hated that I had made a seemingly empty promise.

I tried to think of anyone who could help me. Whom had I consulted in the past? London? But he was gone, locked away in Cokyri, a sickening thought despite Narian's assurances. My mother? But she had not been herself since Miranna's kidnapping and would have little ability to assist in this matter in any case. My father? We were still not on the best of terms, and his views of women were such that he would side with the man by default in any quarrel. Then it came to me, and I hurried into the corridor.

I went through the antechamber into the Hall of Kings, then turned right to knock on the captain's door and was greatly relieved when he bade me enter. He sat behind his desk, quill in hand, scratching out words on the parchment before him, and I knew how fortunate I was to have caught him alone. He glanced up at me fleetingly.

"Is there something I can do for you, Your Highness?" He set his quill down and leaned back in his chair, eyeing me.

"Yes," I said, crossing to stand in front of the desk. "I seek some advice...perhaps some assistance."

"Of course." He rose, beckoning me to a chair, and I sat while he resettled himself behind the desk.

"The Master at Arms, Lord Marcail," I began, wasting no time with pleasantries, fully aware of the rarity of gaining the Captain of the Guard's full attention during such a trying time for the kingdom. "He is a severe man."

"He is a good military man. Do you have a quarrel with him?"

"No," I said automatically, then doubled back. "Well, yes. Not personally, but...yes."

I looked down at my hands, uncertain how to proceed. As Cannan had implied, Marcail was a valued component of his military force. I did not want to offend the captain with what I had to say, but there was no way to guarantee I would not. Still, I had reason to hope that he would identify with Reveina's situation; after all, Baelic had told me that their father had "employed the method too liberally."

The captain did not prompt me; he waited for me to gather my thoughts, even though he probably had other things he would have preferred doing.

"Lord Marcail took a wife early this summer, my friend Lady Reveina," I said, for he would appreciate the direct approach. "I have concerns regarding his treatment of her. I believe he is too hard on her."

"I see. In what way?"

"I saw her just an hour ago. She was bruised about the face, and when I asked after her well-being, she became quite distraught. She did not wish to speak poorly of her husband, but she told me he frightens her and that she dreads his return home at the end of the day. He strikes her more than he should, I know it. I want to help her, but am not certain how." I paused, then took the plunge. "Could you—"

"I appreciate the position in which she finds herself," Cannan said, leaning forward to rest an elbow on the surface of his desk, averting my request. "But I cannot interfere with how another man runs his household."

His answer pierced me like an arrow, and I fought down tears as I searched for a way to convey to him the urgency of the situation, the absolute necessity of coming to Reveina's aid.

"She is already not herself—he's well on his way to destroying her. I can do nothing on my own, yet she has no one else to whom she can turn. Surely there is something you can do."

Cannan gave a minute shake of his head, his dark eyes never leaving my face.

"I'm sorry, but they are married. It is his family, and it is his business how things are conducted in his home. It's not my place, or yours, to get involved."

"I know it is his family and his home, but it is *her* home, as well. Why should she have to live in fear? She will feel his fist every day, and suffer, *every day,* while we sit and say we cannot interfere. Lord Marcail *is* the master of the house, he *is* entitled to punish his wife. But when she is perfect and obedient, and still he beats her, what then? I'm not asking you to arrest him or remove him from his position. All I am asking is that you contemplate any means you might have to alleviate her circumstances. Please. I beg of you."

I waited in silence after my heartfelt speech for some reaction from him and thought I detected sympathy in his visage, although it was impossible to determine whether it was for me or for Reveina.

"Alera," he said, and the softness of his tone gave away his intention. "I don't approve of the treatment you're describing, but you're overestimating my power in this matter. I can do nothing."

I wanted to argue. I wanted to tell him that he was the Captain of the Guard and therefore Marcail's superior officer, and that he was not helpless in this or any situation. But his manner told me he considered our discussion concluded, and I had no choice but to accept it. I stood and walked through the door, heart laden with defeat, railing in my head against the unfairness of a world that would place my lovely friend in the hands of such a man.

CHAPTER 18

A MARRIAGE OF CONVENIENCE

I SWIPED AT MY EYES AS I LEFT THE CAPTAIN'S office, forbidding myself to cry. Tears would serve no purpose, and they undermined my ability to be taken seriously. Although Destari looked at me questioningly, he did not ask about my business with Cannan, merely stepping forward to close the door behind me.

I glanced about the Throne Room, surprised to find it devoid of activity, although I supposed the war had altered everyone's routines. Deciding to consider my options in the peace and privacy of the library, I moved toward the King's Drawing Room, thinking I would pass through it and take the spiral staircase to the second floor. When I neared the dais, I heard a door open, and Steldor emerged from his study, Casimir at his heels. He took note of me at the same moment and waved his bodyguard away. Though Casimir regarded the King with a certain amount of skepticism, he went on to the captain's office. Steldor then dismissed Destari, who walked through the drawing room to wait in the corridor, leaving me alone with my husband.

Steldor came forward to lean against the edge of the dais, adjusting the leather bracers on his forearms while I waited self-consciously to see if he would speak. I was already upset and had no desire to feel worse, so was less than enthused about talking with him. I began to count my heartbeats in my head, planning to dash when I hit ten if he hadn't addressed me before then.

Seven…eight…nine…ten. I gave him a slight curtsey and hurried toward the door.

"You can stop behaving like a frightened rabbit, you know," he said, forcing me to halt and turn toward him. "I won't hurt you."

I didn't know what to make of this statement or how to respond, and so continued to inch toward the exit.

"I mean it," he stressed, and I knew it bothered him that I was still positioned to flee.

"Thank you, my lord," I murmured. "I'm sure I will sleep easier."

He looked away from me to the ceiling, then down toward Cannan's office, then back to his bracers to adjust what no longer needed to be adjusted. Something about my comment had hit a nerve, when I had intended it to pacify him.

"I need to talk to you," he said, focusing the commanding dark eyes he had in common with his father on me. "And I need you to be honest."

"Aren't you supposed to be meeting with the captain?" I asked, not liking the sound of his words and presuming that Casimir had continued on to their intended destination.

"He can wait."

I nodded, succumbing to the inevitable, and walked back toward him.

Once more he cast his eyes away from me, then pulled a dagger from his boot, turning it over in his hands as though he had just discovered some interesting new aspect, desiring to focus elsewhere in order to discuss what was troubling him.

"You went to him," he said bluntly, meaning Narian, of course.

"Yes."

My voice surprised me with its near inaudibility—saying that one word in this context had been more difficult than I would have imagined. He grimaced, and I knew this conversation would be equally painful for both of us, despite how necessary it was that we have it. We needed to make peace.

"Why?" he pressed.

There were multiple answers to this question, and he had probably guessed them all. Fidgeting with the folds of my skirt, I chose the one least likely to brew conflict.

"Narian had knowledge of Miranna that I could have gained in no other way. I needed to know if she was safe."

"Had Miranna not been at risk, would you still have gone to him?"

I bit my lip, wary of his possible reaction, but then answered truthfully.

"Yes. I would have wanted to see who he had become."

"And if he called for you *today,* would you still go to him?"

My failure to speak immediately provided his answer, but his temper did not flare. Rather, he watched me as if fully aware of my struggle, with an emotion deep in his brown eyes that broke my heart.

"I won't be angry with you," he promised. "Just say it."

I took a deep breath to summon my will, then met his gaze.

"Yes, I would go to him. I can't say that I would not. I—I love him. I'm sorry."

"You can't be sorry for loving someone," he said brusquely, flipping his dagger over in his hand before resheathing it, and I thought he was going to leave the room. He paced past me, then turned to walk back again, stopping a few feet in front of me. "You can't help it, even when it isn't good for you anymore. I should know."

The comment stung, though he hadn't meant it to offend me, and I shifted, wishing for this conversation to end. He sighed, then moved to sit on the edge of the dais.

"I can't do this anymore, Alera. I can't continue to fool myself into thinking you will let go of your feelings for him and devote yourself to me, and I can't continue to hope you will come willingly to my bed."

He stood once more, the subject too sensitive for him to be idle while discussing it. I had never tried to view things from his perspective, but now that he was forcing me to do so, I realized that I was not the only one whose wedded life was not what they'd wanted or expected.

"From now on," he resumed, his voice thick with controlled emotion, "I will treat ours as a marriage of convenience, merely in place so that I can be King. I won't pressure you for companionship or expect you to meet my needs. I will leave it up to you to decide if and when our relationship should advance. All I will ask is that you play the part of wife and Queen at public functions." He examined me carefully, then added, "I think we'll both be happier this way."

My eyes widened in astonishment, stunned by the proposal, by the sacrifice I knew he was making. If he were true to his word, I would be as free as possible under these unalterable circumstances. But my sense of relief was quickly overcome by guilt, for I could hardly bear his expression:

distant and collected, it nonetheless told me that inside, he was aching.

"Thank you," I said softly, wondering if my heart would always sorrow, for no resolution seemed to be without cost.

"Don't," he objected, but not in anger. "Don't thank me."

He tore his gaze from my face and strode across the hall, then through the antechamber doors, leaving without a word to his father, with whom he was supposed to be meeting, or to collect his bodyguard. He was clearly not in the mood to face anyone else.

•

Over the next few days, my relationship with Steldor improved. The tension was gone between us, for we had at least resolved our relationship, even though it was not in the manner he would have wanted. Nonetheless, we were more civil and relaxed with each other than had been the case in a long time.

While the stress in my personal life had eased, the pressure of the war had not. The Cokyrians had not yet attempted to breach the Recorah, but they had enough troops deployed in the area that we could not ignore the possibility; given the length of the river that needed to be monitored, we had to devote far more troops to that front than did the enemy, for we could not afford to guess wrong about where they might cross. Our forces thus remained divided.

To the north, our troops had the upper hand, although the enemy had sent soldiers of their own to try to outflank our archers. If the Cokyrians could clear our men from the gorge, their own troops would no longer be pinned down in the narrow valley. Cannan's scouts had again done their job, however, and we knew of the enemy's movements almost before they had begun. Foot soldiers and cavalry men engaged the enemy in the woods, and the traps that our men had rigged—deep trenches covered with branches and mulch into which the enemy would plummet, trip wires that could break a leg or snap a neck, and small boulders and weighted spears that would rain down from above—were wreaking havoc, as well. These latter measures would be effective only until all had been sprung or disabled, however, so eventually our men would have to rely on hand-to-hand skills to protect our archers. Knowing how well trained the Cokyrian warriors were and the unusual and lethal types of weapons they carried, I knew it was only a matter of time before the enemy's troops would again be advancing through the gorge.

While part of our success was credited to Narian's inexperience in engineering a war campaign, everyone realized that this advantage would be short-lived. Cannan had already begrudgingly admitted that the Cokyrian strategy at the river was brilliant, for a small number of their troops were able to occupy a large number of ours. It was beginning to feel as if there were little we could do to affect the ultimate outcome of the war, as if we were fighting fate itself.

There was another aspect to the war that I had not anticipated, but this one was bittersweet and beautiful. Weddings were occurring in Hytanica at an almost alarming rate, for young women feared the loss of their men in battle, and young men wanted to marry and potentially sire an heir before they met their untimely deaths. Among the many couples who would make the walk up the aisle were Galen and Tiersia, whose upcoming November wedding likewise had a sense of urgency about it. The ceremony would take place in one of Hytanica's churches, with the reception in the Royal Ballroom, an honor bestowed on few, but Galen was the Sergeant at Arms, an unofficial second son to the

Captain of the Guard and the King's best friend. Given the state of siege that prevailed, however, and the rationing that had been instituted, the palace would not host a wedding feast; simple refreshments would be offered in the ballroom.

The afternoon of the much-anticipated wedding was blustery and cold, and the overcast skies threatened rain. My concern that this would put a damper on the celebration was unfounded, however; I had never seen a happier couple. Tiersia, in an ivory gown, was escorted down the aisle by her parents just as mine had escorted me, but she had no reluctance to take the arm of her groom. Galen, in a gold-embroidered black dress coat and black breeches, awaited her with his mother and Cannan, the man who had been a father to him since the age of three. Despite the sergeant's efforts to appear collected and dignified, as was befitting a military man, he continued to break into unabashed grins. Steldor, his best man, was magnificent in rich red and black, although there was an air of melancholy about him, as though he were remembering our wedding and the less than idyllic marriage it had wrought.

When the couple had answered all of the preliminary questions posed by the priest, they came before the altar, and Fiara, looking ready to give birth at any moment, moved to Tiersia's side. It wasn't long before Fiara's husband ignored protocol and brought her a chair, for it seemed she might not be able to stay on her feet. Warrick had just returned from a military mission on which he had embarked but four days after they had wed, and the glances that passed between the freshly reunited couple left no doubt that they, too, were in love.

It was when the priest began the exchange of vows that I felt a shift in the atmosphere of the ceremony, as though the solemnity of the occasion, as well as its joy, had descended upon the wedding guests. From my vantage point at the front of the church, I watched as the elderly clergyman joined Tiersia's right hand with Galen's, then the couple turned to face one another, blissfully oblivious to everyone in attendance.

"Do you take this woman as your wife?" the priest asked Galen.

"I receive you as mine, so that you become my wife and I your husband," Galen said, with barely managed emotion. "And I commit to you the fidelity of my body, and I will keep you in health and sickness, nor for better or worse will I change toward you until..."

His voice suddenly trailed off, as though the very real possibility that his life would be cut short had been brought home to him. For one horrible moment, I thought he would be unable to finish, but Steldor stepped forward and gripped his shoulder, enabling him to complete the vow.

"Nor for better or worse will I change toward you until the end."

It was Galen's unexpected struggle that brought the reality of the war and its true ramifications into sharp focus for me, likely having the same effect on many others in the church.

The priest then turned to Tiersia. "Do you take this man as your husband?"

"I receive you as mine," she began with a pretty blush, "so that you become my husband and I your wife. And I commit to you the fidelity of my body, and I will keep you in health and sickness, nor for..."

Like Galen, she trailed off, but it was clear from the widening of her eyes that she had simply forgotten the words. As her blush spread, I heard Galen lean toward her and tenderly advise, "Just promise to love me."

"And I will love you until the day I die," Tiersia finished, and everyone forgave the slight modification she had made to the last of the traditional vows.

Next came the rings. Removing his right hand from Tiersia's, Galen raised her left, palm downward, then flashed an endearing smile.

"With this ring, I thee wed," he said, sliding the ring partway onto her thumb. "This gold I thee give—" moving the ring to her index finger "—with my body I thee worship—" sliding the ring onto her middle finger "—and with all my worldly goods I thee endow—" finally bringing the ring to rest on her third finger.

After the couple had shared their first communion as husband and wife, the wedding ceremony came to a close, and Galen drew his bride into his arms for a long and shameless kiss while the guests cheered. The newlyweds then quickly walked down the aisle, followed by Fiara, escorted by Warrick, and Steldor and me. I could feel a slight stiffness in my husband's otherwise cordial manner, as though being so close to me were tearing at his heart.

From the church, we proceeded to the palace, the members of the royal family riding in the royal carriages, Elite Guards and Palace Guards in full accompaniment. We traveled down the main thoroughfare, and a strange sensation of peace washed over me. For the first time in a long time, I was looking forward to a palace gala, for there would be little pressure on me. The tension between my husband and me had dissipated, and I was but a guest at the party.

Steldor and I entered the Royal Ballroom onto a small stage by way of the adjacent Dignitary's Room. Lanek made the usual announcement, and the guests displayed the usual respect. I parted from Steldor immediately after and began to mingle with the crowd. I saw Tiersia chatting with her ladies-in-waiting and some other young women and decided to join them, in large part because Reveina was among them. Amid many excited congratulatory words for the bride and a lot of giggling, I managed to drop a simple question to Marcail's unlucky wife.

"How have you been?"

I expected an evasive answer, but to my surprise, she sounded genuinely happy.

"Better. My husband and I have had good fortune."

"I'm relieved for you," I replied, quite baffled as to how her living conditions might have changed. "How so?"

"My lord was promoted to Battalion Commander. It's not an increase in rank, but it does provide higher pay, and he was quite pleased by the Captain of the Guard's confidence in him." She turned scarlet before confiding, "I'm afraid I may be happy for the wrong reasons, for his new position keeps him away from home for weeks on end."

Our conversation ended there, and she joined in with the chittering of the others, but her words stayed in my mind. After extending warm congratulations to Tiersia, I excused myself and scanned the room for the captain, whom I spotted thirty-some feet away with Baelic. I walked in their direction but not necessarily to speak with my father-in-law; the sight of him alone might be enough to confirm my intuition. Cannan thought Marcail well suited to being Master at Arms, yet he had without apparent need shifted him to a position that would permit the man little leisure time. Perhaps he had not turned a blind eye to what I had told him after all.

Lost as I was in studying Cannan, I didn't realize that Baelic had noticed my stare, and a flush crept up my face. Nonetheless, I gave him a dignified nod, thinking he would simply return the greeting and continue his conversation with his brother. But my uncle instead clapped a parting hand on Cannan's shoulder and walked toward me.

"You know, my dear," he said as he arrived at my side, "it's impolite to stare at the infirm."

"Which is why I was not staring at you," I replied with a smile, by now accustomed to his brand of humor.

He laughed, then escorted me toward one of the refreshment tables.

"I wanted to apologize, Your Highness. I've been neglecting my promise to take you riding."

"Don't be ridiculous. You've been a bit preoccupied with more important things—the war, for example."

"Ah, my good Queen, never should anything take precedence over spending time with a beautiful lady—even be it single-handedly saving the kingdom."

Now it was my turn to laugh, and a half smirk curved his lips as he picked up two glasses of wine from the table before us, handing one to me.

"You, sir, are an incorrigible flirt," I teased, with a slight nod of my head as I accepted the goblet. "But I do believe I see your wife up ahead, and she appears to be looking for you."

"Does she seem annoyed?" He placed a hand on my forearm and leaned toward me. "If not, she is probably looking for someone else. Perhaps my wayward daughter—I'm afraid Shaselle and her mother have been at odds in my absence. But in any case, I should go to her."

He took my hand, giving it a kiss as he bowed.

"Until we meet again, Your Majesty."

With a boyish grin, he walked off to seek out Lania.

Finding myself alone, I glanced in the direction of the balcony where Tiersia stood just inside the double doors with our two husbands. Steldor and Galen were joking with each other, Galen happier than I had ever seen him. Tiersia stood nearby, an occasional blush warming her cheeks, and I couldn't resist joining them. Steldor's demeanor did not change when I arrived; rather, he greeted me as though nothing were going on between us, which, I supposed, was for once the case. With a smirk, he took the almost full glass of wine from my hand.

"I believe wine is not to your liking, my dear. It seems a shame to waste such succulence on an ungrateful palate." He swirled the liquid around in the goblet, then finished it in one draught, handing the empty chalice to a passing servant.

We talked pleasantly, although Steldor and Galen could have more accurately been described as bantering, given their upbeat moods and the wine they had been consuming. Tiersia and I played along until Warrick, Steldor's cousin and the husband of Tiersia's younger sister, came over to us. I expected him to talk to Steldor, but instead he made a request of me, casting my husband and Galen a disdainful look. I had the feeling that these young men, although related, had not been friends growing up.

"Your Highness," Warrick said, "I wonder if there might be a private place where my wife could lie down. She is feeling unwell."

"Of course, I'll see to it at once. Shall I also send for the physician?"

"Thank you, Your Majesty, but no need for that. She is just overtired."

I motioned to Destari to approach and instructed him to escort Lady Fiara, who was seated by one of the refreshment tables looking quite pallid, to the Queen's Drawing Room. He went to assist her, and I hoped Warrick was correct in assuming her ailment was nothing more than overtiredness.

"Perhaps I should go with her," Tiersia said to Warrick, her brow creased with worry, but her brother-in-law shook his head.

"You should enjoy your wedding." He gave her hand a squeeze, and I had the impression he was going to accompany his wife himself.

It was at that moment that Galen and Steldor exchanged a cunning look, and a warning flashed through my mind.

"Congratulations on your wife's pregnancy," Steldor said. "You're about to become a proud father."

Warrick gave him a quick nod, accompanied by a scowl, as though he resented receiving the King's good wishes. Still, he was intent on departing, at least until Galen entered the conversation.

"How many months is she now?" he asked, apparently unable to recall when his wife's sister had married.

"Five," Warrick said, somewhat warily. "As you know, the wedding was in June."

"Only five?" Galen not-so-innocently inquired.

There had been gossip, of course—Lady Fiara was far larger than she should have been considering the date of her wedding—but no member of the nobility would publicly make such an inappropriate observation. Except, it seemed, for the wine-emboldened scoundrels before us.

"Either she is expecting twins or you have your dates confused, cousin," my husband remarked.

"I don't know what you mean to imply—"

"Oh, I don't mean to imply anything. But originally you were to have a fall wedding, am I not correct? So I can't help but wonder which came first, the marriage or the pregnancy?"

Tiersia and I froze, caught between embarrassment and

fascination. Warrick laughed in disbelief at Steldor's audacity, ultimately waving off the question with a snide remark.

"Come now, I know what this is about. You're bitter because I serviced my wife in a matter of days and you've been married, what now—six months? Need a little help?"

The temper sparked to life so quickly no one saw it coming, least of all Warrick. But he felt it, for Steldor cocked his fist and struck him hard across the jaw, knocking him off his feet. Tiersia gasped, and I took a step backward in light of the manic glint in the King's eyes as he repaid his cousin's insolence in exactly the same manner the Sergeant at Arms had repaid his not long ago. Galen hastily separated the two men, inhibiting Steldor with an arm across the chest.

"Let it go," Galen muttered. "Just let it go, he's not worth it."

Steldor was not struggling, but neither did he respond to Galen. Casimir, who stood nearby, had tensed, ready to intervene. Thankfully, we were somewhat removed from the throng of guests, and only a few heads had turned. I hoped my husband would glower and have done with it so that the celebration would not be ruined. At last, as Warrick recovered from the blow and came to his feet, Steldor shrugged Galen off and started to move toward me, earning a pat on the back from his best friend. But at Warrick's sneer, I knew this was not over.

"Struck a nerve, eh?" the father-to-be taunted, capturing Steldor's attention once more like a glutton for punishment. Warrick wiped blood from the corner of his mouth with the back of his hand but stood his ground. I swallowed tightly, knowing a storm was about to break. "What is it then—are you inept, or have you not yet dropped the royal drawers?"

I stood in stunned silence, my hands clasped over my heart, for I had never been subjected to such an insult in my life. Warrick had only meant to provoke Steldor, but I was nonetheless appalled and offended, and for once wished that my hot-blooded husband would do something rash. Steldor did not disappoint me, but when he leapt at his cousin, Galen grabbed him and yanked him back. To my astonishment, the Sergeant at Arms had not done so to prevent a fight, but rather to get the King out of his own way. Galen shoved his friend behind him and jumped on Warrick with fist raised, and in no time at all, the groom and his new brother-in-law were brawling on the ballroom floor.

It was hard to say whether or not Steldor would have joined the fray, but Casimir pulled him aside and reinforcements arrived in the form of Cannan, Baelic and Destari, who had returned from escorting Lady Fiara. Other guards swarmed the area as well, keeping gawking guests at bay, but despite all the attention, the two young men showed no sign of letting up. Galen had taken a few good hits, but was once again on top and appeared to be gaining the upper hand, when Cannan and my bodyguard grasped his upper arms and hauled him to his feet. He struggled ferociously against them and even managed to land one more swift kick to his opponent's side before Baelic and the Baron Rapheth, Tiersia's father, dragged Warrick back, breaking up the quarrel.

Warrick was panting, blood running from a cut above his eye that had been caused by the betrothal ring Galen wore on his right hand, and he seemed battered and bruised enough to let the fight be over. But the young Sergeant at Arms was not so easily deterred.

"Get off me!" he yelled, still trying to break free of Cannan and Destari. "I wasn't done killing him!"

"Stand down, Sergeant!" The captain's stern command reverberated through the room, seeming to pass through the ears of every shocked spectator before finally penetrating Galen's senses. "You won't be killing him today."

Galen stopped straining against the hands that held him, though he maintained a fearsome glower, while guards continued to shuffle about, creating a commotion of their own. Cannan was at last able to release him and take up position between the two clashing soldiers, his livid but controlled expression enough to make me tremble where I stood on the sidelines. Destari kept his grip on Galen's arm, not quite trusting that he had sufficiently calmed.

"Now you had better explain to me," Cannan said dangerously, addressing Galen, "why my Sergeant at Arms is starting fistfights—and this had better be good."

Galen's eyes flicked to Warrick before resting belligerently on the captain.

"With all due respect, sir, he deserved it. Just ask him what he said."

"I have no doubt it should not be repeated, but I am not interested in his conduct. I am interested in yours."

Behind the captain, Warrick snickered, prompting both Galen and Steldor to lurch for him. Casimir and another guard restrained Steldor, who relented with a scowl and began to pace in annoyance beyond the barrier they presented. Destari wrapped an arm around Galen's chest in a bear hug of sorts, a tactic that worked only because of the Elite Guard's fortuitous size.

Cannan turned his glare on Warrick, who had fared the worst in the fight, then motioned for Baelic to remove him. After Baelic had taken their nephew into the corridor, the captain again focused on Galen.

"You have placed yourself in a poor position, son," he said, his voice low and tight, making it hard for the gathered onlookers to overhear. "That's twice now in six months you've dishonored yourself and the rank you hold. I cannot have an undisciplined Sergeant at Arms, Galen, and that means your behavior must be above reproach at all times, in all contexts, so that you can sustain the respect of your men and of the people. If you are unable to handle that expectation, then perhaps you are not yet the right man for the post."

Galen's jaw tightened, but he did not argue.

"Your wedding is not the appropriate place for me to deal with this, so for now you are free to go. But you will report to my office tomorrow afternoon."

Cannan turned and strode out the ballroom doors, probably to deal with Warrick, who did not have the excuse of being a groom to temporarily save him. Destari released Galen, who was rubbing his bruised and bleeding knuckles, and Steldor pushed past Casimir to come to his best friend's side. Taking in Galen's blood-smeared shirt, Steldor led him through the crowd toward the stage and the Dignitary's Room, from whence they could access the King's and Queen's quarters for a change of clothes.

The excitement over, I noticed Tiersia standing next to the wall, her soft eyes wide and her hand covering her mouth, freezing the moment when the fight had begun.

"Do you need to sit down?" I asked, for her upbringing had been sheltered, and I doubted she had ever seen conduct of this sort before.

"Oh—oh, no," she stammered. "I'm fine. It's just..." She gave a short, strained laugh.

"Yes?"

"I—I already married him."

She looked at me, then began to laugh in earnest out of shock and relief. I laughed along with her, for her statement summed up all of my feelings, as well.

CHAPTER 19

THE END AT LAST

IT WAS TWO WEEKS LATER THAT I AGAIN smelled smoke on the wind, and when night fell, the glass in my bedroom window glowed red. Flames ripped across the countryside to the northeast, like the jaws of hell coming to devour us. The barricade built by our soldiers that extended west from the river, then turned north, had been set on fire. Cannan's orders had been for our troops to drench the wood with pitch and light it from behind the enemy, trapping as many of them as possible, if the fighting went sour. Most of the Cokyrians would burn; others would drown; a few would escape. The thought of the fates of the enemy soldiers turned my stomach, and I was glad I could hear no screams above the whiplike cracking of the fire.

The conflagration burned itself out in the night, aided in part by cold drizzle, and our troops formed ranks beyond the charred ground, waiting for the inevitable next wave of Cokyrians. In order to concentrate our troops, Cannan had also burned the bridge to the south and pulled our men back—archers to the city, cavalry and foot soldiers to the northeast. At some point, all troops would retreat behind the stone walls where our final stand would be made.

Cannan did not want to provide aid or comfort to the Cokyrian soldiers in any way, and crops that we had not been able to harvest were burned, wells in the villages were poisoned and animals were slaughtered. The land beyond our city walls looked like death itself—all was barren; all was stagnant.

The city, in contrast, throbbed with activity in the first few weeks of December. Churches, meeting halls, livery stables, schools—any defensible structures—were made ready to shield citizens should the Cokyrians bring down the walls. The palace's first-floor windows and balcony doors were boarded over so there would be no easy access to its interior, whether by arrows or soldiers. Glass in upper windows would be knocked out when the time came, to give our archers a vantage point from which to shoot. Weapons, medical supplies, firewood and food stocks were being doled out to each potential stronghold.

The first sign of our troops' imminent withdrawal into the city was a noticeable increase in the number of wounded. Widows with children would show up at the palace in staggering numbers, begging for assistance and shelter from the King. Steldor had asked that I attend him in the Throne Room in the afternoons when such petitions were heard, and I came to a new understanding of how stressful his life had become, for there were no words of consolation that could be offered, only a willing ear and a few coins. I once again felt as though I were seeing my husband through new eyes, for the compassion and patience he showed were astounding. And then, just before Christmas, I was told that our citizens would no longer be permitted entry into the palace.

Steldor was in the Throne Room when I sought an explanation from him, for even Destari declined to tell me what was happening. Cannan, Galen and Casimir were with him, along with the usual arc of Elite Guards, but they did not react to my entrance, almost as though they were expecting me. Steldor stood and came down the steps of the dais to meet me, taking my hands in his, which was enough to tell me something was terribly wrong.

"Alera," he said, with a glance toward his father, "we've pulled our men back into the city and are preparing to defend the walls. Unlike last winter, Cokyri will not attempt to starve us out. Our surrender has already been demanded, and a full-scale assault will soon commence."

"Have we given thought to surrender?" I asked, my blood thudding in my temples. It was the captain who answered.

"No. Frankly, we would rather die fighting than risk death by execution. If the time comes for surrender, we will negotiate the best terms for our people, knowing that the Overlord will not be merciful and that the best they will be able to hope for is a life of slavery."

Seeing the horror upon my face, Steldor led me onto the dais, and I slowly took my place on the Queen's throne, but he did not sit, continuing to stand beside me.

"And the closing of the palace?" I asked.

"Certain factions within our own people may pose a danger to us now. One of the buildings at the Military Academy has been set up to handle distraught citizens so they do not feel deserted by their rulers, but I can no longer allow access to the King." Weariness lurked at the edges of Cannan's composed tone.

"For the same reason, you must stay within the palace at all times," Steldor stressed. "Do not even go into the garden or the courtyard. And you should know that my mother and

Tiersia have been granted refuge within these walls. They are now housed on the third floor."

I took in Galen's ashen face, realizing that only his wife had been given this privilege, leaving his mother and sisters to fend for themselves.

"What about Lania?" I whispered, and the distress on Steldor's face would have been answer enough, but Cannan addressed my question nonetheless.

"I talked with Baelic, but we feel it is best not to make such a move at this time. We fear panic—we fear that our own people will storm the palace if they become aware that we are taking such measures. I have guards watching out for my brother's family, however, and when Cokyri breaks through the walls of the city, they will be brought here."

"When?" My voice was almost inaudible, the finality in that one word chilling beyond anything else.

"Yes," the captain said, his eyes sympathetic, and Steldor put his hands on my shoulders. "It is only a matter of time. I tell you this because I believe you have the fortitude to handle it and because you have the right to know the truth. As long as Narian leads their troops, our defeat is at hand. Cokyri's weapons and resources have long outmatched ours, and he will blow the wall to pieces with exploding powder. I also expect he will set most of the city on fire—he seems to have that ability, with or without flaming arrows."

He paused, shaking his head out of either an effort to understand or explain.

"He has tremendous power, Alera—sorcery. We've long known of the pain and destruction the Overlord can cause, but Narian's power is unlike anything we've ever seen. You are not privy to what happens on the battlefield, but you were there when he conjured the fire at Koranis's estate—the nature and reach of his power is beyond what we expected, and we do not know how to defend against it."

"So the legend is true after all?"

"It might well be."

Everyone in the room fell silent, and I stiffly rose, shaking off Steldor's hands. To my surprise, I did not feel like crying; instead, I felt a firm resolve to face fate in the manner of our brave men.

"Thank you," I said, my voice steady. "I will see to Tiersia and offer what assistance I can. And I will ask my mother to take charge of Faramay. The least I can do is prevent her from assailing you, as well."

While I did not intend the statement to be humorous, everyone smiled, needing a break from the mounting tension, no matter how short-lived it might be.

The Cokyrian troops that were poised just outside our city were prepared to attack, and yet the assault did not begin. Instead, a surprising tranquility reigned. At first, this made no sense; then with a rush of gratitude, I understood. Narian would not attack on Christmas. Despite the fact that he did not celebrate the holiday, he knew we did and was granting us this stay of execution out of respect. Although I did not leave the palace, I could see men and women in the city coming out onto the main thoroughfare to greet each other in the spirit of the season. I knew they would likewise be filling the churches and chapels to honor the day, although I couldn't help but question the value of prayer. Still, the momentary reprieve from the noise and stress of the war felt like a heaven-sent gift, and I relished it, for it might be the last peace we would experience in a very long time.

The attack on the city began on the first day of the new

year. Under cover of darkness, the Cokyrians began to tunnel under our walls at several points simultaneously, presumably with the intent of using explosive powder to crumble the stone and make an entry point for their soldiers. Cannan had ordered the placement of pots of water in each of the towers, and those with rippling surfaces gave us an idea of where the tunneling was taking place so that countermeasures could be launched. The Cokyrians were bombarded with arrows, scalding water and stones, and as morning approached, the diggers retreated. Our soldiers did their best to collapse the tunnels, knowing that each succeeding night the enemy would get a little farther until they inevitably brought down our walls.

To the north, enemy soldiers were felling trees in the forest and using the trunks as battering rams; to the east, they were bombarding us with newly constructed catapults, using boulders hauled from the foothills and the river. The ongoing barrage sounded like rhythmic thunder.

The Cokyrians also shot flaming arrows over our walls, simply to keep men occupied dousing fires. Our archers, from their higher and better protected vantage points, did their best to interfere with the enemy's efforts, but we were thinly spread at best.

The explosions that brought down sections of the walls finally came in mid-January and were sufficient to make the floor vibrate and the chandeliers shake. Tiersia was with me in my parlor, and the terror I felt was reflected in her eyes. Destari stepped into the room to tell us what had happened, but the worry in his voice prevented him from allaying my fear. I scooped Kitten into my lap while tears ran down Tiersia's tense and colorless face. We leaned toward each other, linking arms, then sat in silence for a time, for I had no words to soothe her.

"I don't want to lose him," she rasped, voice thick with emotion.

"I know. But it is out of our hands."

We continued to sit quietly together, lost in our individual misery. My mind went to Steldor, for I did not want harm to befall him, either. But I knew he would sacrifice everything to protect those he loved, including me. The reality that Galen, Steldor and so many other young men, lives barely begun, might not see another day, sickened me. I shuddered, pushing such thoughts away, forcing myself to trust in Narian's promise that he would restrain his soldiers.

With the crumbling of portions of the walls, the war moved to the streets. Our indefatigable soldiers struggled to keep the Cokyrians from reaching the palace, and day and night I could hear shouts amid the clanking of swords and armor. The Hytanican people had begun to retreat to the churches, livery stables and schools that had been prepared as fortresses. Many had chosen to flee to the palace, the sturdiest and best-defended safe haven. Its thick walls and the determination of our men had thus far kept the Cokyrians from breaching it, though the crafty warriors of the mountains were also attempting to scale the forty-foot back wall that protected the garden. Blood had been spilled, and men had lost their lives within my precious retreat.

Never had I seen so many people filling the halls of my home. It seemed half the city had squeezed inside and were crawling over each other, frantic for security, their numbers swelling daily. The noise was unbearable, parents straining to keep hold of their children, men calling for friends and relatives who had been lost in the confusion, babies crying and officers shouting commands, trying to reassure everyone and find order.

I knew when Cannan stepped in, for suddenly Elite Guards were laboring much harder for organization, herding women and children into the Royal Ballroom and the King's Dining Hall on the second floor, calling all capable, unarmed men to the Throne Room to be fitted with weapons from the armory and taking the injured and infirm to the Meeting Hall next to the office of the Royal Physician, where any and all healers had also been summoned.

I made my way through the second-floor corridors, not really knowing where I was going, feeling more and more overwhelmed as I advanced. The palace was bursting at the seams, and there was so much need, so much despair. I struggled through the crush of people to stand at the top of the Grand Staircase, covering my ears to shut out the noise that made my head ache, trying to avoid being jostled about by those who had climbed up the stairs to make room for new additions. I couldn't think; there was no sense beyond all this madness; there was no hope in anyone's eyes.

Hytanica would fall. Today, or tomorrow, or the next week, or however long we could stave them off, but eventually, inevitably, Hytanica would fall. What would happen to me, to the people I loved, to all those within the city and to those who swarmed like flies about me? At yells from the entrance hall, I looked to see guards using the butts of their swords to clear the doorway. I was certain the Cokyrians had broken through our final barricades until I focused my gaze and understood we were fighting off citizens we could no longer protect and for whom we had no room. In their panic, our own people had become an enemy. When at last the men had forced the door closed, dropping the wooden bar to lock it tight, cries were heard from the other side. No one answered, instead piling up furniture and anything else that could be found against the entrance.

I pressed myself against the banister to make way for the scurrying, bustling civilians, feeling light-headed—I would have sunk to the floor, but space constraints wouldn't allow it. The heat from hundreds of bodies packed together was sweltering.

I moaned, though no one could hear me, wondering how I had gotten separated from Destari and if he were trying to locate me or had instead become involved in some other aspect of the crisis. Squeezing my eyes shut, I raised my hand to wipe perspiration from my forehead, but someone's fingers twined with mine.

I opened my eyes to see Steldor standing next to me, ready to lead me out of the crush of people. I stumbled after him, clinging to his hand, letting him clear a path down the steps to the first floor using his height and intimidating build, for no one gave a care to status anymore.

Together, we pushed our way toward the Throne Room, which was now being used for the improvised training and arming of new soldiers. Even as we walked, I saw a woman heavy with child collapse and a man, his respect for the law forgotten, snatch one of my home's precious possessions and stuff it in his pocket.

A second man fell into Steldor, who without thought grabbed his collar and threw him aside, but never once did my husband's hand relinquish mine. At last we entered the Hall of Kings, hurrying on to Cannan's office, where the captain and his high-ranking Elite Guards had congregated.

"I have her," Steldor announced, slamming the door behind us and muffling the ceaseless noise.

"Good," Cannan said from behind his desk, motioning for us to take seats. "Galen?"

"I didn't see him. He's here somewhere, though. He'll find us."

Right on cue, the Sergeant at Arms hurtled through the door, Steldor drawing me out of the way just in time to avoid a crash, and I sank gratefully into a chair. Galen was panting and sweaty, a state that was prevalent in most of the men around me.

"It's mad out there, sir. They're killing each other—we don't even need the Cokyrians for that."

"We're doing our best to keep order," Cannan replied without elaboration. "In the meantime, now that both the King and Queen are here, we have some decisions to make."

"Is there anything more to be done in our defense, sir?" It was Casimir who had spoken, one of the six deputy captains in the room.

Cannan stood and answered bluntly. "We're trapped, men. The enemy has the city, and before long they'll have the palace, as well—"

"They've broken onto the grounds." My bodyguard, the only deputy captain who had been absent, had somehow stepped unnoticed into the room. Everyone took in his somber demeanor without comment. "They're inside the Central Courtyard. The soldiers that were defending the walls are either dead or have given up arms. It's over."

Cannan's jaw tightened almost imperceptibly, but he showed no other reaction. "Are they trying to breach the doors?"

"No, sir," Destari answered, then rubbed the back of his neck as if it were stiff. "They're celebrating. They're waiting."

Understanding came easily to Cannan, but he spoke his conclusion aloud regardless. "He's coming."

Destari nodded, and a stoic expression formed on every face in the room except for mine, which was fraught with terror. Steldor moved to stand next to my chair, and I took his hand, clutching it as though it alone would keep me sane.

"Narian has departed for Cokyri," Destari said, sounding like a man who has had no choice but to accept fate. "The siege is over, and the Overlord wants to see the very moment of our defeat with his own eyes. Narian will tell him it is time."

So this was it: the end at last.

There was a welcome lull that night. The people had not been told what was happening, which seemed kinder and prevented panic from shattering the fragile order Cannan had established. I stayed in the captain's office while men came and went, including the captain himself, for it was the only place I could be without constant fear for my safety. Steldor showed me the small room located off the back of his father's office, encouraging me to use the bunk so I could get some sleep. The room was dark and uncluttered, and somehow peaceful, for the noise from elsewhere in the palace was muted here and so steady it might have been silence.

I dozed in a strange, dreamlike state, voices in my ears, snippets of conversation from the office that I did not want to understand, until finally it penetrated my brain that there was talk of taking the King and Queen from the palace. There was one escape tunnel that could still be used, the one that led north, outside the city. I lay in my borrowed bed, staring at the pitch-black ceiling, straining to hear.

"We're facing a mere matter of hours," Cannan said, his tone low, but not soft enough for me to miss. "Keeping the two of you here is no longer an option."

"There was fighting in the forest beyond the northern wall, sir." I recognized Casimir's voice and knew that he, and perhaps a few others, were present in the room with the captain and Steldor. "Do you think it's safe to take the royal family out where Cokyrian troops may still be positioned?"

"Arrange for scouts to sweep the area," Cannan replied. "We need an idea of what we'll be facing. But ultimately, we'll have no choice but to take whatever risks are presented."

I heard a door open and close, and assumed Casimir had gone.

"Sir, our plans to destroy—" I heard Destari's voice, though it was quickly interrupted by my husband.

"I'm not leaving," Steldor said abruptly.

"The kingdom has fallen, Steldor," Cannan countered "The only thing we may still be able to do is protect you and Alera."

"Take Alera, take the former King and Queen, but I'm not leaving."

A chair scraped, and I knew the captain had come to his feet.

"When the Overlord arrives, he will kill you. Do you understand that? And it will not be a quick or dignified death."

"What is dignified about running away?" Steldor's voice had grown louder, reflecting the passion in his speech. "You say I am King and that you need to protect me, but even if I go, of what will I be King? There will be no kingdom to come back to." There was a pause, and I could picture father and son staring at each other. Then Steldor, equally determined, made his judgment known. "I die with my people."

Another silence ensued, then Cannan dropped the issue. "We'll discuss it when the scouts return. Destari, your report?"

I recalled that the Elite Guard had been speaking at the time Steldor had begun to argue with his father.

"Sir, I was considering our crisis strategy. If there is a way for a few men to reach the targets, now would be the time."

"You're right," Cannan said, and I heard him retake his seat. "However, it would be a gamble sending men out the door at this point. The palace is surrounded, and the city is swarming with enemy soldiers. As much as I would like to take some of the sweetness out of the Cokyrians' victory, I need to devote my men and my deputy captains to other matters. I cannot send soldiers on such a dangerous mission when it is not absolutely necessary."

"Yes, sir."

There was a slight commotion in the hallway, and the sound of the door opening and closing a second time told me that the brawny guard had gone to check on its cause.

No one spoke, leading me to believe that only Steldor and his father remained. When the silence continued, I rose from bed and padded on bare feet to the door, pushing it open the tiniest bit so I could peek into the office.

Steldor had moved to the padded armchair in the far corner, his head resting against its back, his eyes still open despite his obvious need for sleep. Cannan was, as I had guessed, seated behind his desk, but his gaze was on his son. I could not decipher what he was thinking, what anyone responsible for the safety of so many would be thinking.

"You should sleep," the captain finally said, but Steldor did not respond. Cannan did not address him again but waited patiently for him to share what was on his mind. When Steldor finally did speak, his voice was strained.

"Father, what will happen to us?"

Cannan took a moment, and I could see his jaw clench; then he answered.

"When the Overlord comes, he will demand our surrender, and his terms will not be compassionate. He will torture and kill Hytanica's leaders—you, if you remain, Alera, if she is here. He may take Adrik and Elissia, to make an example. Beyond that…I do not know."

My pulse raced at Cannan's words, and I thought the terror coursing through me might cause my heart to explode, granting me a kinder and less painful death than would torture. Steldor's chest rose and fell heavily several times while he considered his father's words, then he rolled his head to the side, so neither Cannan nor I could clearly see his face.

"You?"

The rest of the question was unspoken, but Cannan understood. He waited for his son to look at him, and the instant Steldor did, I knew that, for this moment, Hytanica's young King was done being brave.

"Yes."

The word hit me almost as hard as it hit Steldor, and I stole back to lie once more on the bed, a strange ringing in my ears. How many would suffer a slow and agonizing death? Cannan had told me I had fortitude, but I did not have the fortitude to nobly face such an end. And how could my parents? In truth, how could anyone? At last I understood the reason for the myths surrounding the Overlord; at last I understood the reason for the fear and panic generated by the mere mention of his name.

CHAPTER 20

ONLY ONE MAN

THE FOLLOWING MORNING, FINDING MYSELF alone in the office, I ventured one last time out into the palace. While fear no longer permeated the air, it had been replaced by something worse—despair. Children begged to go home, while parents couldn't even assure them their homes were still standing. Families held each other close, spending what they viewed as their last hours in the arms of their loved ones.

I had not seen Steldor since I'd dozed back to sleep after his conversation with his father—he had vanished into the crowd, probably desperate for time alone to think. I doubted he would find it.

The scouts Cannan had sent to investigate our escape route had not, to my knowledge, returned. I wondered if—when—they did, my husband would indeed refuse to evacuate. I thought of all the people I would be leaving behind, family and friends whom I loved. Could I abandon them? The coward in me said yes, with certainty. Could I bear life without them? That was a harder question to answer.

I climbed the Grand Staircase to the second floor, which

was still bustling with activity, then stole through the door into my old quarters, where memories of my childhood and of Narian lurked. Nostalgia over years past, coupled with the knowledge that I might never walk the corridors of my home or set foot in this room again, would have brought unstoppable tears if I had allowed my mind that freedom to wander. And thoughts of Narian, the strong, brave, tender young man with whom I had fallen in love, juxtaposed against the dark entity I envisioned overtaking my homeland, would have shredded my sanity.

The suite of rooms, which had not been looted by the encroaching throng of people in light of the more readily accessible and spacious King's Dining Hall, was exactly as it had been before I'd moved to the King's and Queen's quarters. I walked through the parlor and into my old bedroom, noting that the personal things I had neglected to take with me—writing paper, childhood toys, books, an old hairbrush—were untouched, and I was filled with the urge to lay on the bare bed and pretend I was a little girl and that all was right with the world.

But I ignored these feelings, going toward the boarded-over balcony doors, then peering out the window to their right side and down into the West Courtyard. The trees and foliage were dead from the change of seasons, but I stared in horrified fascination at the assemblage of lively enemy soldiers, both men and women, moving about, laughing, drinking, feasting on food that had probably come from our stores in the city's main warehouse. Destari had been truthful when he'd said the Cokyrians were celebrating.

In more peaceful times, I would have been able to see past the city walls and into the fields beyond. But now a haze of smoke and dirt hung in the air, for which I was somewhat thankful, as I did not want to see the damage our own troops had been forced to inflict on our lands in order to confound the enemy.

I pulled back when I realized that, had I come but a few hours earlier, I might have seen the bodies of some of our soldiers. Fighting had taken place in the courtyard, but by now it appeared the enemy had disposed of those who had fallen. Their bodies would never be claimed by grieving families, and many would never know for certain the fates of their loved ones. I sighed and gave in to the longing to lie down upon the bed, closing my eyes as though to close out the knowledge that I was a prisoner in my own home.

I awoke disoriented, my head nestled against someone's shoulder, and gradually became aware that I was being carried through the somewhat less hectic but still overcrowded corridors. Without even looking up, I knew in whose arms I was cradled, for his rich, musky scent and the manner of his walk were familiar. As Steldor maneuvered his way down the Grand Staircase, he noticed I had roused.

"I would be angry with you for disappearing on us," he chided, "but I'm too happy to have found you unharmed."

I nodded, not wanting to abandon the lethargic cocoon into which I had escaped. Without another word, he carried me into the captain's office, walking past the others who had gathered, to deposit me on the bunk Cannan had been permitting me to use. He left me to join the other men, and I rested for another moment. But when my sleep-induced stupor fell away, so did my desire to be alone, and I slipped into the office to sit on the floor against the near wall, drawing my knees to my chest.

Although there were no windows in Cannan's office, I knew from having passed through the Grand Entry that the sun had set, and that a second night in limbo stretched out before us. Activity around the palace had slowed as there came to be less and less to do, yet the people were anxious and restive, eager to learn of our final plan, the secret way in which we would emerge triumphant from this tragic chaos, not knowing such a plan did not exist.

When the scouts returned that evening, after a much longer absence than Cannan had expected, their news was not reassuring. Despite being highly trained reconnaissance men, and even with the cover provided by the forest, they had encountered difficulty moving about on the other side of the city's northern wall. The enemy was everywhere and saw everything. Taking a woman, maybe two, through the forest and into the foothills would be near impossible, bordering on suicidal, and probably more risky than having my mother and me remain within the palace, adopting disguises to try to fit in with the populace.

"Damn it," Cannan muttered in response. "You don't suppose they—"

"The tunnel's entrance wasn't specifically guarded, so I don't think it's been compromised, sir," one of the scouts said. "And we did nothing to alert the Cokyrians to its existence."

I couldn't help but wonder, knowing London had been a scout, if it were a common trait among them to interrupt their superior officers. At any rate, Cannan did not take offense, merely waving the three men out of his office, giving one of them an order to send his deputy captains to him.

"Will someone be taking them soon?" Steldor asked distantly, assuming his father's plan had not changed and sounding as though he were so exhausted he could scarcely concentrate. He moved to take up position in the padded armchair in the corner, once more leaning his head back.

"Yes. The exit may not look good, but we have no choice.

As soon as my deputy captains arrive, I'll arrange departure for all those who *should* go."

I knew this pointed phrasing would not be lost on Steldor, but he did not react to it. He rubbed his eyes in an attempt to stay awake, but when he moved his hand, his lids stayed shut, and his head tipped to the side, body shutting down against the mind's resistance. Cannan watched him for a long time, and I imagined he was storing up memories, not knowing how much longer he would have with his son.

The deputy captains trailed in one after another, in the order the scout had located them, until there were six in total. Steldor did not awaken, and Cannan made no attempt to bring him round before addressing his most trusted men.

"Two of you will be escorting the Queen to the safe place as soon as possible. Davan, you will go with her—I want at least one Elite Guard who was formerly a scout to protect and guide her. Gather whatever supplies you may need. Where is Destari?"

"He has not yet been located, sir," Halias replied.

"He should also accompany Queen Alera. If he is not found timely enough, you, Halias, will go in his stead."

"Yes, sir."

Cannan glanced at Steldor, still asleep in the chair.

"I'll try again to convince him to leave willingly. But if he will not, we'll take him by force—knock him out, if we have to."

The deputy captains accepted this, undoubtedly having anticipated it.

"Davan, report back to my office when you are prepared. There's no time to waste. And if anyone sees Destari, send him—"

A great rumble overtook the palace, shaking its very foundation, stopping Cannan's words and jolting Steldor awake. The quake lasted only a few seconds, but there were shouts and screams from beyond the office doors long afterward.

"What was that?" the captain demanded, but he did not dismiss the men in the office to find out, knowing someone would come to inform him.

No more than a heartbeat later, a scout came bursting through the guardroom door.

"The armory, sir. At the Military Complex. It's…it's been demolished!"

"What?"

The captain was for once stunned. Steldor had gotten to his feet and everyone else had broken into harried discussion. I stayed on the floor, trying not to draw attention, for I wanted to know what was happening. Sudden realization came to Cannan.

"Find Destari," he ordered, then his eyes connected with Steldor's. "The crisis strategy. He's the only one not among us who knew the plan."

But at that moment, the supposed rogue guard walked through the door.

"You decided to go ahead with the plan after all, sir?" Destari asked, then he frowned as he took in the startled expressions of his fellow deputy captains. "Sir, what's going on?"

A second rumble, less fierce but still noticeable, shook the floor beneath us. Cannan grabbed the scout who had brought news of the armory by the collar and flung him toward the door.

"See if that was the infirmary. Go!"

The man hastily exited, and the captain turned back to the rest.

"I gave no orders for this strategy to be carried out. And

we alone should have been privy to its details. Did one of you coordinate this without my knowledge?"

"No, sir," came the collective reply.

"Captain, the power of the explosions we're feeling—only the Cokyrians have the means to cause this type of destruction," Halias said. "Although it makes no sense for them to take such action."

"There are people at the Military Complex, Baelic, for one," Steldor reminded everyone. "Intelligent men who might independently decide that such resources should not be turned over to the enemy. And they could have gotten access to the Cokyrians' explosive powder from a dead enemy soldier."

"Both the armory and the infirmary, if that's what we felt, are at the Military Complex, so men there could have reached those targets," Destari agreed, sounding a bit dubious. "But if the King's theory is correct, none of the other targets will be hit. It would be impossible."

"We wait," Cannan decisively replied.

The minutes passed in stony silence, then the scout rushed in to confirm that the infirmary had, indeed, been destroyed. Before anyone could respond, the largest tremor we had yet experienced tore through the palace, knocking objects to the floor and causing the men in the room to stumble in an effort to maintain their footing. Screams of true terror now echoed in the corridors.

"What the hell is going on?" Cannan shouted as he stormed from the office, and I jumped to my feet to follow him to the Grand Entry Hall, Steldor at my side. Destari also came, but the other guards stayed in the office, probably a little unsure of their commander at the moment.

As Cannan prepared to harass his soldiers for an explanation, a man from the floor above, where the windows provided a view, called to us.

"The mill and the main warehouse! Gone in one blow! The enemy is frantic!"

I could tell Destari's mind was working furiously, and evidently so could Cannan.

"Who?" he asked, and his dark eyes scrutinized the clouded visage of his deputy captain.

"Only one person who knew the plan is not with us. That same person would know how to use Cokyrian powder and might be able to move amongst the enemy undetected. I would say…it's London, sir."

The captain scowled, caught between knowing this was impossible and realizing that the pieces fit.

"How can that be?" I said in a near whisper, not quite believing Destari's words, but desperately hoping he was correct, for the thought of London's return gave me irrational hope. No one answered me.

"Go to the stables," Cannan at last directed. "If you're right, we need to bring London into the palace, and I suspect he's on his way to the final target."

Destari nodded and set off. Cannan glanced at me, then took me by the arm to lead me back into his office, Steldor following.

Once the other deputy captains had been brought up to date, an irrepressible buzz filled the room while the men debated. As some pointed out, it was possible we would never know what was happening. Destari might leave and find no one; and it was all too easy to forget he might be going to his death. Danger abounded outside the mighty stone fortress that was our palace.

It was unspoken that those of us headed for the safety of the predetermined hiding place would await Destari's return. If London were with him, he might have important information. If London were with him, everyone wanted to know how he had escaped a second time from Cokyri.

Then we felt it—the fourth explosion rippling the ground. I dropped my eyes to silently bid goodbye to the Royal Stables, praying no horses had been trapped inside but knowing it made sense to destroy the carriages and tack. I also said goodbye to my bittersweet memories, for it was in the stables that Narian had first spoken freely to me; and it was there I had told him of the tunnel, inadvertently paving the way for my sister's abduction.

With greater force even than the explosions, fear shook me as I let my mind touch on what the Overlord would do with Miranna now that everything was over. My heavy heart told me I would never see her again, that she could already be dead. I envisioned an even worse fate were she alive, for now that she had served her purpose, the Overlord might view her as part of his spoils of war and subject her to his whims.

Thirty minutes was all it took for Destari to reenter the captain's office, for the enemy was greatly distracted in the aftermath of the explosions. Miraculously, London came behind him through the door, Destari's cloak thrown over the Cokyrian uniform that he wore. He stepped to the side, guiding a young woman who tightly gripped his hand across the threshold. She wore black pants and a dark cloak in the manner of a Cokyrian woman, but there was no mistaking her identity.

"Miranna," I breathed, faint with relief, then I rushed forward, all else forgotten, to pull her into my arms. She did not respond or hug me back, but still I held her close. When at last I drew away, she gazed at me with vacant blue eyes. Physically, she seemed well—she bore no scars that I could see and moved without sign of pain; she was not starved; even her curly strawberry blond hair seemed healthy. It was trauma of another kind that caused her to look so unlike herself.

"She's in shock," London said to me as he closed the door. "She has been through much."

I nodded, my eyes pooling with tears. Without thought to status or appropriateness, or for London's undemonstrative nature, I threw my arms around him, and he momentarily returned my embrace.

"Thank you," I choked. "Thank you for bringing her home."

I returned to my sister, guiding her into a chair, hugging her once more, wanting never to let her go. Halias stared at us from across the room. As Miranna did not seem to be aware of his presence, I guessed he was resisting the urge to go to her as I had, not wanting to make this harder on himself. At least she was alive.

"London," Cannan said and, in his signature style, summed up every possible question into one word. "Report."

"We have about eight hours until the Overlord arrives."

This blunt statement seemed to ricochet around the room, and the moment it hit each man could be determined by the expression upon his face. Cannan, however, remained as stoic as ever.

"We knew he would come," he stated.

"Narian released me," London went on, "so that I could return here and take Alera out the remaining tunnel. He will pull troops from the area to the best of his ability without arousing suspicion—he is under close watch."

"He knows about the second tunnel?" A note of unease

registered in Cannan's voice, and the muttering that had already begun at the mention of Narian's name increased.

"Yes, but he has told no one and will tell no one, I swear it." Looking into Cannan's eyes, he added, "I trust him, Captain."

Whether it was the conviction in London's voice or his rare show of respect for authority, I knew not, but everyone seemed to accept London's opinion, waiting only for the captain's response. Finally Cannan nodded.

"And Miranna?" It was Halias who spoke, still unable to tear his eyes from his charge. "How did she come to be with you?"

"I took her, after Narian let me go," London answered, urgency punctuating each of his words. "I could not leave her behind. But I had to travel more slowly with her and so have arrived later than I intended. And on that note, we need to get moving."

The captain stepped around his desk, ready for business.

"We were already preparing to take the royal family out through the tunnel," he informed London. "Our plan was to move in two groups, ten minutes apart, following different routes to the hideaway. You, with Alera, Miranna and Davan, can go first—both you and he were trained as scouts, so Destari and Halias will stay to assist with matters here. Galen and I will follow with Steldor, and when we've gotten beyond the enemy's reach, I'll return."

"Sir—" began Destari, ready to argue about Cannan's intention to double back.

"I will not desert my troops," he said, shutting down all argument.

"You don't have to go anywhere. I told you, I won't leave." Steldor's gaze was determined, and his posture was tense, ready for a fight.

"Listen to me, boy," Cannan said, striding over to his son, and there was something in his voice very near to desperation. He put a firm hand on the back of Steldor's head, enmeshing his fingers in his dark hair. "As long as there is a king, there is a Hytanica. As long as you are alive, there is the hope that someday we will be restored."

"A dead king is of no use to anyone. A live king is dangerous, and your survival will rob the Overlord of some of his victory," London added. "But we have little time to convince you—just trust those with the experience to make the judgment."

Steldor stared at his father, resolve failing. Cannan squeezed the back of his son's neck, knowing the decision had been made.

Steldor and I were taken to our quarters to change clothes. My husband gave me a brown shirt and a dark green cloak, which I put on along with the trousers I had worn to the negotiation meeting, tying my hair into a tight bun. When I reentered the parlor, Kitten came skittering out of hiding, and I picked him up, snuggling him close. Sadly I set him on the sofa as Steldor, likewise dressed in dark colors, came from his room, knowing I could not take a pet with me. To my surprise, my husband carried a small dagger which he offered to me. To his surprise, I slid it into the sheath that Narian had strapped on my left forearm, for I had continued to wear it despite its uselessness. Neither of us spoke, however. We left our quarters, in all probability never to return, and I left the door open, giving Kitten, who had grown considerably in the past few months, freedom to find his way however he could.

We reconvened in the captain's office, where our guards awaited us, Galen among them. Everyone was now dressed in brown leather jerkins in the manner of the scouts, with black cloaks for warmth. Cannan directed that we go out in pairs so as to draw as little attention as possible, for the last thing we needed was for every terrified, stranded citizen to learn there was a tunnel leading outside the city; the ensuing chaos would exceed belief. I went first with Davan, pressing through the crowd gathered in the Hall of Kings until we reached the door to the dungeon, slipping through it onto the landing of the steep, narrow steps. An Elite Guard waited within, ready to bar the door behind us if necessary. He handed Davan a torch, and we waited in tense silence until London and Miranna joined us, knowing that the others would in due course follow.

The staircase was dimly lit, cold, suffocating and sinister. We were going underground, to a place where people were sent for punishment, torture and death. As we started downward, the incessant noise of the palace diminished, but I could not escape the feeling that we were descending into a tomb. When Davan and I reached the bottom, I was glad to see that the stairwell opened into a large room, the place where the dungeon guards normally congregated. Torches had been lit along the walls, but no men were on duty, no doubt at Cannan's decree. I turned to London as he and Miranna emerged from the stairwell, then quickly went to my sister, who was hanging on to the Elite Guard, burying her head against his chest. The reality that she had been in the Overlord's dungeon hit full force, and my heart ached for her and for the fact that, although she was back among us, she was far from safe. I took her into my arms, freeing London, who walked toward one of several heavy wooden doors that opened onto a row of prison cells.

As the second party emerged from the stairwell, Cannan took a torch from its bracket on the wall and joined London. After a brief exchange of words, the two men beckoned us into the corridor that lay beyond the door. The cells that lined the sides of this aisle looked as though they had not been used in ages, but still my skin crawled as Cannan led us inside one of them. London walked to the center and began to kick away layers of dirt on the floor to reveal a trapdoor, and it was clear why this particular cell had not been put into use. The chance could not be taken that a prisoner would discover the secret.

London pulled up the wooden door, then dropped his torch into the hole so we could see the bottom. Davan jumped down, disappearing from view as he confirmed that the tunnel had not been blocked or discovered.

"All clear," he called a few minutes later.

"Alera, give me your hands," London said.

With a sinking feeling, I accepted that I would be going in next. London would lower first me and then my sister, as Miranna needed to be constantly with someone she knew, especially under such conditions. She had to be kept calm, no matter what, for she could alert the enemy to our presence if she became hysterical. As I sat on the edge of the opening, feet dangling in the air, I silently cursed whoever had constructed the entrance of this tunnel for not making access easier. Then I let London take my hands.

He lowered me in carefully, giving me a moment to taste the stale air before my feet touched ground. It was freezing, colder than the dungeon had been, and every breath burned my nose and throat and made me want to gag. I moved down the tight corridor to make room for Miranna, hoping the tunnel would not be this small for its entire stretch, for if it were, we would be traversing single file.

"No," I heard from above, and I recognized my sister's voice. "Not down there, don't make me go down there."

"Mira," I called, stepping back to where she could see me. "It's safe. We're just going into hiding."

"Alera," she said, a crack in her voice, then her pale face peered down at me. "I'm—I'm scared. I don't want to..."

"I know," I replied, and I truly did. I was afraid of leaving behind everything I knew; I was afraid of what we would encounter when we exited the tunnel, for Cannan's scouts had thought there was a good chance we would all be killed. I was afraid of surviving, for I did not know how long we would need to hide, living in shadows; and I was afraid for my future, for I did not know where we would end up, only that there would be no Hytanica to welcome us home.

"I'm going to stay right here," I said, subduing my own unease. "Just keep looking at me, and you will be beside me in a moment."

She at last consented, and London dropped her to the ground. I hugged her, then Davan called, urging us to follow him, and I led Miranna forward, listening to the thuds as the rest of the men dropped down behind us.

The tunnel did widen after a bit, so we could walk in pairs, and the ceilings were high enough to allow even Cannan, the tallest of the men, to stand without crouching. London had joined Davan to lead the way, and I was directly behind them with Miranna, whose head was buried in my shoulder. Then came Steldor and Galen, with the captain bringing up the rear.

It remained difficult to breathe as we took step after step, and though Davan carried a torch before us and Cannan one behind, the way was shadowy and dank, and seemingly never-ending. My anxiety was growing, along with my need for fresh air and for the knowledge that the world above us still existed. Though my mind told me I could not stand another taste of the murkiness of the tunnel, I gulped the air more quickly with every passing moment.

"London, when will we—" I started, but he shushed me, pointing to the ceiling.

"They're above us," he whispered. "We're almost to the end."

I listened closely and could indeed hear the distant, muffled pounding of what were probably hoofbeats over our heads.

At last, the light from London's torch fell upon an earthen wall, and I knew it was time to ascend, potentially to our deaths. I took a look around at the men with whom I traveled, realizing that every one of them would be willing to sacrifice himself to protect Miranna and me. If this were to be our demise, I would be dying among Hytanica's best and bravest, a thought that lifted my spirits and fueled my determination.

CHAPTER 21

CAPABLE MEN

WHEN THE TUNNEL HAD ORIGINALLY BEEN constructed, a wooden ladder had been left to aid escape. Through the years, the rungs had decayed, and they currently looked none too sturdy. London adjusted the angle of the ladder, then tested the first rung, which gave way before he had even put his full weight upon it.

"This will be interesting," he murmured, turning back to us with a wry smile. "Someone steady it."

Davan stepped forward and did as London asked, while the nimble former scout climbed upward, putting as little weight on each of the rungs as possible by moving quickly and keeping his feet on the outer edges. Fortunately, the rung on which he eventually had to balance to press upon the wooden escape hatch was sturdier than the first had been. Unfortunately, the hatch would not budge. No matter where London shoved, there was no give.

"Earth, grass, perhaps even roots must be interfering," London muttered as he jumped to the floor. He spoke briefly to the captain, then once more scaled the ladder. Davan and Steldor hoisted Galen up so that both he and

London could apply pressure to the wood, but still it would not yield.

"We're going to have to blow it," London said, voice low. "There's no turning back now."

"Even if Narian has pulled his troops, the noise will lure the enemy, so we had best move quickly," Cannan agreed. He then addressed Miranna and me. "Move back into the tunnel until we have it open. But stay in front of the others so we can quickly lift you up and out."

As Steldor, Galen and Davan moved into the tunnel to stand behind us, London removed a pouch from his pack, climbing yet again. Using two fingers, he removed some explosive powder and packed it carefully around the edges of the wood. He again jumped to the ground, then ducked down low, touching the torch to the ceiling. I covered my ears, but still the sound was deafening in the narrow tunnel. Wood and earth rained down on top of the deputy captain, extinguishing his torch and almost burying him in rubble. When the dust had settled, he straightened, staring at the haze until moonlight filtered through. He glanced at Cannan, who smothered our other torch, then London scrambled up the ladder to hoist himself out the opening.

"Hurry," he said urgently, peering down at us. "Lift Miranna."

Cannan put his hands on my sister's waist and boosted her as easily as if she were a doll. London grasped her arms and pulled her above ground.

"Now Alera," my former bodyguard prompted.

Steldor took my hand and stepped forward, but when he gripped my waist and lifted me high enough for London to reach me, he seemed reluctant to let go.

"I'll see you soon," I felt the need to say before London hauled me out.

Davan climbed out next, and London spoke one last time to Cannan.

"I hear riders. I suggest you move now."

He and Davan herded us into the cover of the forest, and we began our dangerous trek to safety.

Two hours later, I was exhausted, but we pressed on, through the thick trees and the undergrowth that continually caused me to stumble, going always uphill. At times it was so dark I could hardly see my companions; at other times, the moonlight filtering through the skeletal trees reflected off patches of snow to cast an eerie glow. My cloak was thick, but not thick enough to keep the frigid winter air from numbing my fingers and toes, and my very bones seemed to throb. Miranna was not faring any better than I.

I didn't have any idea where we were going, but London seemed sure of himself, while Davan brought up the rear. We traveled slowly out of necessity, and London left us more than once in the oppressive and terrifying shadow-land to scout out the area ahead.

Several times, our guards tugged us to the forest floor when voices, Cokyrian accents distinct, reached our ears, often accompanied by the tramping of horses' hooves. Every time, my fear was indescribable, and I pictured sharp swords coming down on us, unable to imagine what it must feel like to be run through with a blade—if it would be quick, if I would be aware when the weapon was withdrawn from my flesh. The prospect of a bloody death, which had been almost inconceivable, was now so very real.

When the enemy had passed us by, the Elite Guards would pull Miranna and me to our feet, but I would glance behind us and wonder if the same Cokyrians would pass the King and if our second party would be as lucky. From

London's parting words to Cannan, it seemed they would likely face even greater danger.

When the first rays of the sun glowed on the horizon and dull gray light appeared between the branches of the barren trees, London at last told us to rest. Miranna and I collapsed to the cold ground in the small clearing in which we stood, and he tossed us a pack containing bread and jerky, along with a water flask so we might quench our thirst.

"Eat and sleep while you can," he said, still standing, scanning our surroundings. "We won't stop for more than an hour. I don't like moving during the day, but in this case, the farther west we travel, the farther we are from harm."

Davan, whom I was rapidly learning preferred listening to talking, did not comment, but took up position at the edge of our makeshift camp to stand watch.

"Won't the others catch us?" I asked, stuffing food into my mouth and drinking readily. Miranna was eating very little, a fact that troubled me, for I did not think her stamina could last much longer. Still, she drank as thirstily as did I.

"No," London replied, not giving me his full attention even though Davan was on guard. "They are taking a different route. We won't see them until we reach our destination."

"What exactly is the safe—"

"You'll know soon enough," he said, cutting me off, not out of annoyance, but likely because his instincts as a soldier told him to keep us quiet. "We'll be far from any lands the Cokyrians might search. Take the time you have to sleep."

I nodded, then ripped off one more chunk of the bread before returning the loaf to the pack. Hoping to stop my sister's quivering by sharing my body heat, I curled up close to her and began to doze.

* * *

"Alera, wake up."

London's voice was hushed and urgent, and he clamped a hand over my mouth as I forced my eyelids apart. Miranna beside me sat up in confused alarm, only to be likewise dealt with by Davan. He hoisted her to her feet, pulling her into the undergrowth and out of the clearing.

"Go with them," London ordered. "Now. We have company."

I scrambled to my feet, heart pounding, as boisterous voices reached me from farther up the forested hill. As they neared, I could hear the sound of horses' hooves rustling through dried leaves. The riders were Cokyrian, but judging from the volume of their voices, they had spent a good part of the night reveling in their victory. I hurried into the trees after my sister, unable to see where Davan had taken her, and was abruptly tugged to the ground by his hand about my ankle. My fall would probably have gone unnoticed by the enemy, but my small cry of surprise caught their attention.

"Silence," a woman ordered. "Did you hear that?"

"Hear what?" A few chuckles from her male companions drifted down to us. "I think you had too much ale."

"Hush, you mooncalf, there's someone here," the woman insisted, but the man who had spoken remained unperturbed.

"So we aren't the only ones who stayed behind to celebrate," he said dismissively. "Are you surprised? The kid just doesn't recognize that this war is *finished*. He's got no business trying to give us a different assignment when we've already won. The only thing that might be left is to kill a few Hytanican stragglers as they try to run away."

"Exactly."

The point having penetrated their brains, the men grew

serious to the best of their abilities in their semi-inebriated states. They dismounted to creep erratically down the hill on foot, and the moment they came into view, I heard Davan slide his long knives from their sheaths.

But where was London? I couldn't see him from where I was hiding and had not noted where he'd gone when I'd fled the clearing. The Cokyrians were close now, too close. One, a large, burly man, was leaning over the place Miranna and I had slept, examining the imprints our bodies had made. The second, slightly smaller than the first, lumbered over as well, his eyes following the tracks I had left.

"Looking for me?"

London had snuck partway up the hill and now stepped out from behind a tree, gripping the Cokyrian woman by her hair, a dagger pressed against her throat. The men turned away from us, fists clenched at their sides, disgruntled with their compromised position.

"Keep your heads down," Davan muttered to Miranna and me as he carefully stood, and we promptly buried our faces in our arms.

Davan moved away, and I cautiously lifted my head, my good sense defeated by my desire to know what was happening. As the Elite Guard approached the two men from behind, I realized that the Cokyrian woman could not see her comrades due to the slope of the land and the angle at which London held her head.

"Let her go," one of the enemy soldiers growled, but it was the last sentence he would utter. Davan plunged one of his long knives into each man's neck, jerking both blades outward. Their backs were to me, but blood showered the ground in front of them, a spray of thick, dark red. The men coughed and choked, and sank to the earth just before I heard the nauseating snap that could only have been London breaking the woman's neck, granting her a much cleaner death.

My former bodyguard thrust the Cokyrian's body to the side, where it fell among the trees, and he swiftly descended the slope to the clearing. I scrambled to my feet, fighting the urge to retch, as Davan wiped his blades upon the ground and proceeded, with London's assistance, to heave the bodies of the men out of sight. Miranna still hugged the ground, which meant she had seen nothing, but she was trembling, not totally oblivious to the actions of our guards. London gently coaxed her to her feet, then his manner stiffened.

"We need to leave here, now," he said.

Davan motioned for us to follow, and I walked after him, arm around Miranna, ignoring my fatigue. London had once more disappeared, only to come into view after a few minutes, leading the mounts of the felled Cokyrians, and I felt extremely fortunate to be in his capable hands.

Davan lifted Miranna into the saddle of the horse he would ride, while London permitted me to take my own. I had never ridden through such rocky terrain, but I said nothing, content to be viewed as competent.

London had been right in his prediction that the farther we went, the fewer Cokyrians we would encounter. When we came into the foothills to the northwest, our going became rougher but less eventful. The Cokyrians had no need to be this far from our kingdom or their own empire.

We were leaving behind the trees that had dropped their leaves, instead coming into pines, and the heretofore rocky ground was now strewn with boulders and patchy with snow. I was grateful the bulky nature of the evergreens was sufficient to block much of the wind that had been picking up during our continual climb.

The land was so steep now that we wound our way back

and forth, traveling many miles to gain a few hundred feet in height. It was late afternoon when we breached the top of a steep incline that had been hard even on the horses, only to find ourselves on a narrow ledge before a red-streaked rock face so immense it cast a shadow over much of the land below. London dismounted, and I felt certain we had lost our direction somewhere along the way. When Davan likewise dismounted, lifting Miranna to the ground, I dubiously did the same.

Massive pine trees, like giant sentinels, guarded the sheer rock in several places, their branches overgrown and sweeping. London passed between two of them, reemerging a few minutes later.

"It's safe to enter," he said.

He and Davan pulled aside the trees' laden arms to reveal a large vertical fissure in the rock face. It began halfway up the mountainous wall, then ran toward the ground, ever widening in its descent.

Without a word, the two men waved us forward, and I ducked through the trees, Miranna's hand clasped in mine. Brushing against the rough rock, I slipped through the crevice, pulling my sister along behind me. I stopped, waiting for my eyes to adjust, for the only illumination was provided by slim shafts of fading daylight at the far end. My sluggish brain also detected a trickling sound that could be made only by water.

I was jostled by London as he came in behind us, but I dared not move forward until he brought a torch to life with his flint and steel. He walked around, shining the light against the rock walls of a cave, easily thirty feet in depth and twenty feet in width, with a ceiling rising to three times my height. It was considerably warmer in the cavern than it was outside, due to both the lack of wind and the insulating quality of the earth. Surprisingly, the air was not as dank as had been the air in the tunnel, and I could feel a slight draft flowing through the interior. When Davan joined us, having hidden the horses, London touched the head of another torch to the burning one he held, then passed it to Davan. With a flick of the wrist to indicate we should follow, my former bodyguard led us to the back end of what would be our hiding place, and the flame caught a small cascade of water that tumbled down the right-side wall to form a pool.

"Welcome to your new home," London said sardonically. Once more he shone his torch around the area, and my eyes took in barrels of grain and alcohol, bundles of dried herbs and fruits, stacks of animal skins and furs, a variety of quilts and various other foodstuffs and supplies along the right side. In a hollow to the left, there were stores of weapons, and a little farther away, a virtual wall of firewood. It was obvious this shelter had been stocked for us, probably gradually over the past six months.

"I won't make a fire tonight," London said in an unassailable tone, "so you should grab several hides and some quilts to make yourselves a place to lie down. We'll eat the bread and some of the jerky. As you can see, we have plenty of fresh water. Other than that, I suggest sleep. There will be much to do in the morning."

He stuck his torch into a bracket on the wall and opened his pack, tossing the items he had mentioned to me. I grabbed an armful of furs, spreading a few on the ground along the right side of the cave for warmth and cushioning. I returned for quilts to drape around my sister and me, then tugged her down beside me on the makeshift beds, offering her some of the food. London moved to speak to Davan.

"I'll take the first turn on guard," he offered. "You should eat and sleep, as well."

Passing me, London grabbed a handful of jerky and disappeared through the sheltered cave opening. Davan stopped to offer us some water, then prepared a bed for himself on the other side of the cave near the stacked firewood, granting us some semblance of privacy. I lay down next to my sister to fall into an exhausted slumber.

I awoke to the sound of voices and sat up, hoping that Steldor and Galen had arrived. Cannan would be on his way back to Hytanica by now—he could even be there already. My stomach tightened as I recalled what the captain had said to his son about his own probable death and an example being made of my parents. My father and I had never fully repaired our relationship, and neither of my parents had been told that Miranna was alive. Maybe it was too late now for either of those things to happen.

I looked around in the dim torchlight through still-tired eyes to see it was only London, who had come to switch watch with Davan. As he made a bed for himself toward the cave opening, I forced myself to think rationally. We had left ahead of the others, after all; their different route might take them longer; and we had ridden horses a good part of the way. I suppressed my pessimistic thoughts and lay down again, for London was already dozing peacefully, a sure sign that there was nothing about which to worry. It did not take long for sleep to again seduce me.

Morning broke, bright sunlight spiking down through the shafts in the cave's arched ceiling, illuminating narrow areas of the interior while leaving the rest in shadow. Despite how stiff and sore I was, I felt refreshed and curious about my surroundings. My sister was still sleeping, and neither London nor Davan were in the cave, so I began to poke around.

It would take some doing to make the cave comfortable for living, but the necessary supplies were here—in addition to the firewood, animal furs and foodstuffs I had noticed the night before, there were medical supplies, including bandages, needles, cotton thread and sinew for stitching; some nondescript clothing, including breeches, shirts, a couple of skirts and cloaks; and barrels of wine and ale. I was pleased to see that the cave had a fire pit, almost a natural fireplace, at the rear that vented through the ceiling, hoping the small blaze that had been kindled was an indication that a hot breakfast would be prepared.

I gazed at my still-sleeping sister, who seemed unlikely to awaken anytime soon, then hurried outside and through the pine trees, onto the ledge overlooking the steep hill we had climbed the previous day.

I spotted Davan and London at once, the former on horseback, the latter giving him instructions. Davan glanced up at my approach, and London swiveled to check his back, frowning when he saw me.

"Has there been news?" I asked, shivering in the cold morning air, knowing one of our guards would not be riding off unless there was a problem.

"Steldor and Galen have not come," London told me outright. "They may just have had slower going, but twelve hours is long enough to wait. Davan is going to backtrack, see if he can spot them."

"Do you think something's happened to them?"

My mind was racing, remembering the dangers we had narrowly avoided on our journey. But surely Steldor and Galen were just as proficient as London and Davan, and they would have been given an extra advantage while Cannan had been with them. The captain had intended to see them out of harm's way before heading back.

"They're capable men," London said with certainty, reading my mind. "They may turn up of their own accord." Then his voice lost some of its optimism. "But they're not invincible."

"I'll see what I can find out," Davan promised.

London slapped the horse on the haunches, and the animal set foot on the precarious decline, then the deputy captain and I reentered our hideaway.

Miranna awoke shortly after we came back inside, but she did not rise; instead, she sat upon the animal furs, her knees drawn to her chest. After a little while, London showed me where we could wash and prepare for the day, and I helped my sister to do so.

I was correct about the fire representing a warm breakfast, but not the scrambled eggs to which I was accustomed. Instead, London showed me how to make gruel from the oats we had in plenty. All it took was to add water and cook the mixture over the heat; using milk would have been better, but we would be seeing none of that for a while. London also showed me how to tend the fire, wanting to keep it low to minimize smoke during the day when it might be detectable. I understood from his manner that I would be in charge of the kitchen, as it was one of the few ways in which I could be of help.

We spent the day in the cave, barely speaking. I took some time to move supplies away from the back right corner so that I would be able to lay out Miranna's bedding in the cozier space, thinking it would make her feel more secure, then moved the hides, furs and quilts upon which we had slept into place.

Miranna did, indeed, seem to feel comfortable in the corner, for she dozed on and off all afternoon upon her bed. London kept watch, occasionally checking on us, but never venturing far from the ledge. I saw him glance a couple of times toward his hunting bow, for we had no meat stores, but he could not leave us on our own. Instead, we feasted on gruel, soldier's tack and dried fruit.

I wanted very much for Miranna to talk to me about her experiences in Cokyri, but she was almost unresponsive to any topic I tested. Narian had told me she'd been living in the High Priestess's temple, and it was from there that London had taken her, but despite this civilized treatment, she was nothing like herself. Of course, the kidnapping alone would have traumatized her, regardless of her other experiences. Her continued silence made me dread what had happened between the time she had first arrived in Cokyri and the time Narian had struck his bargain with the Overlord to protect her. How had she been treated then? Unless she spoke with me, I would never know what she had been through and was at a loss as to how to help her. While I would love her no matter what, I doubted my naïve and exuberant sister would ever truly reappear, and that thought filled me with infinite sadness.

When night fell, I was too anxious to sleep, while Miranna seemed to want to do little else. London, too, was uneasy. My former bodyguard paced, occasionally stoking the fire to keep the cold at bay. When he needed a break from pacing, he would cross his arms tensely upon his chest and lean against one of the walls. It had been too long. London had suspected something might be wrong after twelve hours—at over twenty-four, it was a certainty. Steldor and Galen were in trouble.

Lying wide-awake next to my sister, I wanted to pummel London with pointless questions. Were they dead? Had they been captured by the Cokyrians? Would Davan find any trace of them? I held my tongue, knowing London would neither be receptive to my queries nor be able to give me answers.

I closed my eyes to try to join my sister in oblivion, but the sleep that came to me was restless, and I woke almost every hour. My dreams were haunted by images of death and injury: London horribly wounded, Cokyrian soldiers with gaping throats, a blood-spattered Cannan. And woven among them all was the face of the husband I had never loved.

CHAPTER 22

ESCAPES

DAWN BROKE AND SUNLIGHT DABBLED ITS WAY into our cave, and I realized that London was gone, probably on lookout once more. I stretched to relieve the stiffness in my back, then scrambled from my bed at the sound of voices, my twinges forgotten. I hurried toward our sliver of an entrance.

"The enemy descended on us as we were concealing the entrance to the tunnel. We managed to flee, but we were tracked for miles by the blood trail, until Davan found us and diverted the Cokyrians with a false one. I think he was successful—at any rate, no one overtook us."

I pushed past the sheltering tree branches and stumbled into blinding daylight, knowing it was the captain who had spoken.

As my eyes adjusted, I saw Galen, ragged and worn-out, hanging on to the reins of a dark bay gelding. Behind him, London and Cannan stood on either side of the animal, untying someone's legs from the stirrups, and even before I saw his face, I knew it was Steldor. No longer restrained, he slumped toward his father, who caught him under the arms from behind while London crossed to take his feet.

"Galen, get rid of that horse," Cannan commanded, and when the shaken-looking Sergeant at Arms complied, I saw the dark, crusty stain on the animal's withers, trailing down its right shoulder and foreleg to the ground.

London and Cannan came toward me, carrying Steldor, who was barely conscious, and I pulled aside some of the branches so they could more easily pass. They carried him into our refuge, to the far end where the light was best, and I followed. As they were about to lay him down, I grabbed a couple of animal hides to place underneath him, then glanced over at Miranna, thankful to see she was still asleep.

"We tried to stop the bleeding," the captain said, kneeling on one side of Steldor, London kneeling on the other. They pulled open the two cloaks Steldor was wearing, one of which belonged to him, the other to his father. "But we had to keep moving. I don't know how much he's lost."

London unsheathed a dagger and cut through what remained of Steldor's now crimson shirt to expose the blood-soaked bandaging the captain and Galen had tied around his midriff. The injury was on his right side, but that hadn't stopped the rich red from spreading across his torso, onto his breeches, and into the thick cloaks. Then I remembered the blood that had flowed onto the horse and couldn't believe he was still alive.

I stood a few feet behind London as he sliced through the bandages with one quick motion. Although I averted my eyes, I could tell from the tensing of London's body that it was bad.

"We had no choice but to pack it, to try to check the bleeding. We couldn't stop long enough to clean or stitch it,"

Cannan said almost angrily, capturing my attention. "They were too close behind."

I understood from his words that in order to apply pressure to the wound, he and Galen had stuffed it with wads of cloth. Without comment, London began to extract the packing. Steldor inhaled but did not cry out, and I was unsure if I should offer comfort or leave him be. The two men leaning over him blocked my view of the injury, but the agony on Steldor's face and his labored breathing told me that London was determined to remove every last strand.

"The blade hit his lower ribs, then must have slid down and under," the Elite Guard muttered. "The stab wound is deep. And the edge of the knife was serrated, otherwise it wouldn't have torn like this when it was withdrawn." His examination finished, London gazed steadily at the captain. "We have to stop this bleeding."

Cannan stood and looked around, his eyes coming to rest on the embers of the fire.

"We could cauterize with a heated blade."

London shook his head. "We'd have trouble laying it flat against the bleeders, and there'd be too much danger of puncture. But I know what will work."

His tone gave me pause, as though he himself did not like what had come into his mind. He got to his feet and gave the just-returned Galen orders.

"Get everything we have for treating injuries. We'll need alcohol—lots of it—bandages and goods for stitching, water and more alcohol."

Galen nodded, his eyes darting around the cave in confusion. I beckoned to him to follow as I walked toward our supplies, and London went to rinse his bloodied hands.

"Get him drinking," London said, tossing a wine flask to Cannan.

The captain sat on his heels and touched Steldor's shoulder, looking down into his son's tormented face.

"I have to prop you up so you can swallow."

Steldor nodded, wincing as Cannan slid his hands beneath his arms and pulled him carefully upward to lean against his father's chest. The captain helped his fading son to drink while Galen and I gathered the supplies, setting them near Steldor on the gravelly floor.

"We'll wait twenty minutes for that wine to take effect," London said as he joined us. "Plus I'll need the time to experiment. This will have to be done very precisely."

He went across the cave to where he had stored his pack, and returned with the pouch that we all knew contained exploding powder. He did not come where Steldor could see him but cleared a space on the floor in front of the fire pit several feet behind the captain. He opened the pouch and scooped a small amount of gray powder with his fingers, cautiously placing it on a flat rock in front of him. When he caught me staring, he offered a brief explanation.

"This is all I have left, but it's more than enough to cauterize that wound. I only have to figure out the amount to use. I need enough to sear the wound, but not enough to blow him apart."

Cannan twisted round at his words. Filled with sudden understanding, he tipped the flask of wine a touch more so that it flooded Steldor's mouth.

I was no longer focused on my husband, too entranced by what London was doing. Galen, who had finished organizing the medical supplies, stood and walked over for a better view, then paled as he, too, realized what the deputy captain had in mind.

London took a small piece of glowing wood from the fire and touched it to the sprinkling of powder on the rock.

The powder popped and sizzled, consuming itself almost immediately, so the next time, he used more of the highly volatile substance, and so on and so forth until he was fairly certain the amount would serve its purpose without causing much additional damage. Then he went to Steldor's side.

"I'll need you to hold him," he said to the captain, who eased away from his son, laying him down once more.

"Alcohol," London said to Galen, stretching out a hand. "I need to disinfect this before I begin."

The sergeant handed over another flask, and the Elite Guard poured clear liquid into the gash, causing Steldor to stiffen and moan in pain. I remembered small cuts and scrapes I'd acquired as a child that had been cleaned in this manner, and I shuddered, knowing how much even a skinned knee could sting with alcohol applied.

London picked up a cloth, dipped it into the bucket of water Galen had brought and wiped away blood, dried and fresh, so he would be better able to see what he was doing. When he had finished, he handed the reddened rag back to Galen and picked up his pouch.

"I'm going to do this carefully," London assured Steldor at the quickening of the young King's breathing. "And I won't light it yet. I'm just going to place it."

Steldor grimaced as London packed the powder into his slashed abdomen. At last he stood and walked to the fire, retrieving a splinter of wood with a smoldering end. He again knelt beside the injured man, then nodded to Cannan and Galen.

"Hold him."

My earlier reservations about whether I should try to comfort Steldor left me, and I sank down next to him, lifting his head to place it in my lap. With Cannan on Steldor's left and Galen at his feet, I ran my hands through my husband's hair. The captain removed his own leather belt, folding it to place between his son's teeth, then leaned over to pin Steldor's upper arms to the floor, while Galen likewise held his legs.

"Get it over with," Steldor growled. With this encouragement, the Elite Guard touched the glowing stick to the powder, which flared brightly with a whiplike crack before dissipating into smoke and sizzle.

There was nothing Steldor could have done to keep himself from crying out. As the revolting smell of burning flesh reached my nostrils, my husband fought his father and Galen insanely, his screams so intense that I thought it plausible Cokyrians somewhere might hear him and find us. In a way, it was fortunate that Steldor had lost so much blood—if he had not been weakened, it would have taken more than two men to pin him down.

Cannan looked to be in almost as much agony as his son, and I felt tears dampening my hands where they touched the sides of Steldor's face. Then the King's cries died out, and he slipped into welcome unconsciousness.

Neither the captain nor the sergeant moved, even though Steldor had gone limp, until the powder had burned out. London waited for many minutes after the fire had run its course, examining the wound for signs of continued bleeding. When there were none, he again demanded the alcohol to disinfect the now-cauterized gash.

I still had not closely examined Steldor's wound, too afraid of how I would react. London seemed to sense this.

"Alera, he's not aware of us anymore. Miranna is more in need of you right now than is he."

After an uncertain glance at Cannan, who gave a small nod, I relented, laying Steldor's head on his bed of animal skins. As I did so, my eyes fell on the wolf's head talisman that he always wore. It lay slightly off-center on his chest, spattered with blood. Knowing how much it meant to him, I felt a sudden desire to keep it safe.

"May I have this?" I said to Cannan, fingering the chain.

"He is your husband, so it is yours to take."

I nodded, then removed the talisman. With one last look at Steldor's handsome face, I rose to my feet and went to clean it before hanging it around my neck.

Miranna had awakened while we were ministering to Steldor, and sat with her hands over her ears, despite the cessation of screaming. I went to her and tended to her as well as I could, for she still had no interest in talking, while London stitched the wound closed. Galen rose to retrieve a clean shirt and bedding, while the other two men cleansed Steldor of blood and filth to the best of their ability, trying to make him more comfortable. When they had bandaged his midriff again, they gingerly lifted the still-unconscious King, moving him onto fresh animal skins to the left side of the fire pit and covering him with a quilt.

As London, Cannan and Galen washed and changed out of their blood- and grime-covered clothing, I made some gruel. They gathered round to receive a bowl filled with the unappetizing mixture, wolfing it down where they stood without a word. To my surprise, Galen swayed on his feet, and I wondered if my cooking skills were so poor that I had made him ill.

"Get some sleep, Sergeant," Cannan ordered, catching the young man's arm to steady him, making it clear that the malady from which he suffered was fatigue.

Galen nodded, then forced himself to stay awake long enough to lay out quilts and animal skins along the left cave wall, near where Davan had once bedded down, but ten feet from Steldor. He was literally asleep before he had lain fully down, and I knew he would be out for a very long time.

Peace having descended, London motioned to Cannan to accompany him toward the entrance. I glanced at my sister, who had returned to sit on her bed with a bowl of gruel, and then followed them. The men were aware of my approach, but neither attempted to send me away. London leaned back against the wall of the cave, crossing his arms over his chest, as he asked the question that had been burning inside of me.

"What happened?"

"We had barely covered the tunnel's entrance when the Cokyrians attacked. They outnumbered us three to one, but Steldor and Galen fought with the strength of twenty. When the last Cokyrian had been slain, Galen caught three of their horses so we could escape before the enemy launched a pursuit. It was then we discovered that Steldor had been grievously wounded."

Cannan looked away for a moment, shaking his head in amazement.

"I don't know how the boy continued to fight after sustaining that injury, but none of us would have survived had he not done so. I packed and wrapped the wound, then we rode on, intending to stop and tend to it when we had put some distance between us and the enemy. But our trail was picked up almost immediately."

I stared in stupefaction at the captain, who so matter-of-factly spoke about their ordeal as though it had been a training exercise rather than a life-or-death situation. Inside, his emotions had to be in turmoil, yet none of it showed in his manner. What was manifest, however, was that Steldor had pulled them through. I prayed that London and Cannan could do the same for him.

"Galen and I took turns doubling back to try to throw

off the Cokyrians, but they are well-trained trackers. They came after us unrelentingly, gaining a little more every hour. We dared not come directly here as a result and were about to split up when Davan found us. We took a gamble and gave him two of our horses, as the Cokyrians were tracking three; he cut open his own arm and stayed behind to confuse the blood trail and lead the enemy astray." The captain paused for a long moment before finishing. "As Davan has not joined us, I worry he worked his plan a little too well. He may have saved our lives only to forfeit his own."

A weighty silence fell at the conclusion of the tale, for the losses we had suffered, might still suffer, were agonizing. Cannan looked back at his son for a moment, then returned his attention to London.

"And how did you make your return to Hytanica?" he asked in his inimitable fashion.

"Narian released me—he made it possible for me to escape. I was being detained in the Temple of the High Priestess, for she seemed to think the way to secure my cooperation was through kindness. At least, she knew from prior experience that torture would not work. She must have kept my presence concealed from the Overlord, or he would certainly have killed me. He and I did not part on the best of terms seventeen years ago."

The mention of Narian's name and his action in freeing London reaffirmed what I had never truly doubted—that Narian's love was steadfast and his loyalties were with me, despite the battle he was waging for the Overlord. I closed my eyes, taking a steadying breath, realizing as I did so that this was the most I had ever heard the deputy captain say about his time in captivity during the last war.

"I had already seen Miranna and knew where she was being housed," London continued. "Leaving without her wasn't an option, so I handled her guards and brought her with me. Once we were outside the walls of the temple, I stole a horse, and we rode double, virtually nonstop, back to Hytanica."

I took advantage of the silence that ensued to raise a question of my own.

"What do you think happened to her in Cokyri?"

London studied me, and I had the impression he was trying to judge how much I could handle. Then he pushed away from the wall to stand before me.

"Let me tell you what I observed. Miranna was in the High Priestess's hands, and Nantilam provided her with a decent room, decent food and decent care. She was not harmed in any way within the walls of the temple."

"That's what you observed. But what do you believe?" My heart thudded painfully against my rib cage as I waited for London's answer.

London sighed heavily before continuing.

"All right, let me tell you what I have surmised. When I went to get her, it was night and I was wearing a black cloak, and she was terrified of me. She spoke very little on our journey to Hytanica and slept even less and was quite afraid of the dark. All of this leads me to the certainty that she had, probably in the first instance, been brought before the Overlord. I believe she was in his custody up until the time she was used to pressure Narian, in which case she spent time in his dungeon. Beyond that, I will not guess."

I struggled to breathe, for my lungs did not want to expand.

"She will recover, in time," he promised, and he was the only person I would have believed.

The two men continued to talk while I retreated to the

back of the cave to check on my sister. Before long, London went to get his pack, and Cannan joined me.

"If Steldor rouses, he needs to eat. Wake Galen for assistance. I'm going out to stand watch."

The captain said this normally enough, but his eyes flicked uneasily to his son's still form. I knew he had to be just as tired as the Sergeant at Arms, who had barely been able to stand, and I wondered what it was that kept him going.

I nodded my assent, and Cannan and London exited together, London carrying his daggers, hunting bow and quiver. It took me a moment to realize that, with all the men absent, occupied or incapacitated, I was, for the time being, in charge.

I gladly shouldered this responsibility, pleased to be of use. I had never been in charge of anything except the household staff, and I was experiencing an entirely new feeling—that of empowerment.

The firewood was still stacked against the wall, but almost everything else had been tossed about haphazardly. I organized the medical supplies that had been scattered during the rush to treat Steldor, even going to retrieve those that lay on the floor where London had tended to the wound. I rerolled bandages, corked flasks of alcohol and untangled the needle and thread that had been used for stitching. When these items had been stored away, I gathered the bloodied cloths and tossed them into the fire. I did not know if the cloaks could be washed, so I set those aside for the time being. The animal hides were stained as well but could probably be salvaged, so I left them by the cloaks. While I worked, I chatted to my sister, chronicling my actions, hoping she would at some point be drawn into a conversation.

"Are you hungry?" I asked, knowing she had not eaten

much when she had first awakened. "I should make more gruel in case Steldor wakes up."

I looked to where my husband lay by the fire, doubting he was anywhere near the surface of consciousness.

"No," Miranna murmured, bowing her head. "I'm not hungry."

I considered her and saw a tear splash against the rocky floor.

"Mira, what is it?" I coaxed, hoping she would say more.

She sniffled once or twice, and it was so strange to see my perpetually bouncy sister crying that I couldn't think of any words of solace to offer. I knelt beside her and brushed my fingers through her snarled curls.

"I'm so confused, Alera. I—I don't know where we are or why we're here. I don't even know…I can't even remember what happened."

"We are north of the city, in a hidden cave." I explained, heartened by the fact that she had at least uttered complete sentences. "We had to come here to be safe. Our home… Hytanica fell, to the Cokyrians."

"Father and Mother?"

My throat constricted, and I bit my lip, then I put my arms around her shoulders, not certain how to answer the question, not even certain that I could make myself give an answer. After a moment, she repeated her question, even more apprehensively.

"Mama and Papa?"

"They had to stay behind," I choked out, struggling to maintain control, not wanting to frighten her.

"And what…what happened to me?" she said, huddling in my arms like a small child. "Everything is so jumbled. I remember going to the chapel. I thought…I thought Temerson would be there. But everything was dark…and someone grabbed me…and I was choking." She trembled and tears flowed. "I was so scared. I don't remember much after that, except that I was eventually taken to the High Priestess. And then London came."

Hysteria was now creeping into her voice, and I hugged her tighter, wanting so badly to cry along with her. I held back, instead pouring my emotions into our embrace. When she quieted, I tried to reassure her.

"It's early February, and spring will be here soon. I know it doesn't make sense right now, and maybe it never will. But it's over, and you're safe. And I'm here to help you."

She didn't reply, but I stayed with her until her breathing slowed and she fell asleep. I wished I could stop worrying about her, but she was always tired, and she ate very little.

I was now the only wakeful person in the cave. Galen had not so much as shifted since he'd collapsed on his bedding, lying half on his side, half on his stomach, with his mouth open, and Steldor would have appeared cadaverous if not for his steadily rising and falling chest.

I eased my sister out of my lap and onto the ground, then hurried to retrieve a couple of animal furs, lifting her gently so I could provide some cushioning between her and the hard cave floor. Then I took a cooking pot and filled it with water to boil for the gruel. I went to our supplies to scoop some oats, stopping to examine the dried fruits in the hope of adding some flavor to the bland mixture. Raisins caught my eye, so I took a goodly portion of those.

I cooked enough for Miranna and me, plus some extra in case Steldor came to consciousness, then poured a little of the thin mixture into a bowl, sprinkling a few raisins on top. I ate in silence, deciding the gruel would be a bit more palatable at a thicker consistency and that the fruit wrought a definite improvement. Eventually, I moved to lean against the rough side wall opposite Galen, positioned to keep an eye on both Miranna and Steldor, and trying to make myself believe the things I had told my sister.

CHAPTER 23

PRACTICAL DECISION

AT LAST, SOMEONE STIRRED. I HEARD A MOAN and sat bolt upright, my eyes falling upon my injured husband. As I observed him, he tried to shift position but gave a small cry, and I hurried over, wanting to see how he was before I attempted to wake Galen. If it seemed I could handle Steldor myself, I would leave the sergeant to his slumber.

I called Steldor's name softly, trying to bring him to full awareness, and when his eyes opened to gaze blearily at me, I put my hand to his forehead, checking for a fever. I knew from when London had been injured that one of the main risks from such a wound was infection.

"How do you feel?" I asked, relieved that he was not overly warm.

He did not immediately answer, staring at me in confusion. Finally his eyes cleared, and my question seemed to make sense.

"I feel…" He faltered, speech itself difficult. Then he took a slow, deep breath and managed, "I feel like my gut was sliced open and lit on fire."

I smiled despite the gravity of the situation, relieved that, unlike Miranna, he was still himself. My smile faded, however, as he clenched his fists at his sides in a spasm of pain. He turned his face from me, but his breathing was suddenly rougher. I wanted to touch him, to comfort him, but knew just from the fact that I was looking at the back of his head that he didn't want me to see his plight.

"I need something," he pronounced after a time, his voice strained. "For the pain. Bring me something, anything."

I looked toward the storage area I had just arranged, thinking of the various herbs that had been provided to us. Then I recalled Cannan's instruction that Steldor should eat. The captain hadn't said anything about painkillers, and I didn't want to harm the King by giving him the wrong thing. I suddenly felt less confident that I could handle the situation.

"Your father said it was important for you to eat." I glanced at Galen, thinking I should wake him, but he was out cold. I hated to cheat the young man out of much-needed rest, so decided against disturbing him. "I really think it would be best if I brought you some gruel."

Steldor sighed miserably, his dark brown eyes beseeching. "Alera, trust me. I won't be able to eat unless—" He inhaled sharply, and his neck and jaw flexed in an effort to suppress a groan. "Just get me whatever we have, *now*."

His expression banished my indecision, and I hurried to our supplies to gather every plant and herb in sight.

"What do you need?" I asked, sitting beside him and fumbling through the mishmash in my lap. "How about this?"

I examined a container and read the label.

"Will belladonna do?"

"That's a poison, dear. I'd prefer if you didn't give me that." Even with his ghastly injury, his dry humor survived.

I quickly put the belladonna aside, not wanting to handle it further.

"This says crushed oak," I continued, reading the label attached to a small pouch.

Steldor held up a finger to tell me I'd found something useful.

"Well, what do I do with it?"

I pushed the other containers, pouches and bundles of herbs off my lap as I awaited his directive. He seemed to find my complete ignorance amusing but did not laugh, aware of what that would cost him.

"Mix it with wine and bring it to me."

"How much?"

"Plenty."

"But I don't want to give you too much—"

"Alera, I'll take the risk."

His eyes closed again, and I stood, not wanting him to pass out from pain before he had eaten.

I grabbed a flask of wine and added what I thought to be a generous measure of the brown substance, then corked and shook the container to blend its contents. I was about to hand it to him when something else occurred to me.

"Will this put you to sleep?"

He growled and tugged at his hair with his left hand, evidencing his frustration.

"It might. Seems to me that would be a good thing."

"Your father said if you woke, you should eat. I can't let you go back to sleep until you do."

"Damn it," he muttered, and I knew this was not so much in opposition to food as it was to the agony I was prolonging. "Where is my father?"

"On guard duty. He's outside somewhere."

He dropped his hand and breathed.

"Just give me the drink, and I'll eat afterward. It won't knock me out immediately."

This seemed reasonable, so I pressed the flask into his hand, waiting to see if he would ask for help, not wanting to insult him by suggesting that he needed it. He did not speak.

"I'll get the gruel, then," I said, leaving him to manage on his own.

I had left the pot simmering over the fire, and put several spoonfuls into a wooden bowl to bring to him, sprinkling raisins on top just as I had for myself. When I turned around, he was propped on his left elbow, guzzling the wine, no doubt having swallowed a considerable amount of pain along with it. He drank until the flask was empty, then tossed it aside, motioning impatiently to me, not wanting to lie back down until he had eaten, as well. I could see the strain he was placing on his body and would have preferred he not try to brace himself in such a manner; however, I could think of no way to assist him without offending his pride.

He looked askance at the fare I presented to him but did not complain as he put away a few bites. I tried not to watch him eat, moving to stoke the fire, but I heard when he settled back down, and looked to see that he had abandoned the bowl after consuming only half of its contents. While I could hardly blame him for his lack of appetite, given his condition, I wasn't sure Cannan would think it sufficient. On the other hand, there was at least *something* in his stomach other than wine.

Within fifteen minutes, the alcohol and crushed oak had taken effect, and Steldor fell once more into a heavy slumber. Again, I was on my own, this time with little to occupy me. I returned to the fire, stirring the gruel and adding more water so it would not become too thick. Thankfully, it was not long—half an hour at most—before Cannan returned to the cave. He stopped next to Galen and put a booted foot to the Sergeant at Arms' shoulder, shaking him awake.

"Enough beauty sleep," Cannan said when Galen groggily opened his eyes. "Time to take a turn on guard duty."

Galen struggled to his feet, nowhere near ready to rise of his own accord, while the captain walked toward me, casting a glance at his injured son.

"Steldor?" His voice was weary, gruff and worried.

"He woke. I talked to him and he ate some. Not very much, but some."

"He seemed coherent?"

"Yes. Tired and hurting, and not exactly pleased with me, so definitely coherent."

I suddenly remembered the painkiller I had given him and snatched up the pouch to show the captain.

"He asked for this, crushed oak, so I mixed it in some wine. It seemed to help, and he fell back asleep. I hope that's all right."

Cannan was nodding before I finished speaking. "Good. I assume you managed without Galen, then."

The sergeant was across the room next to the small waterfall, tossing cold water on his face, and appeared not to have heard a word.

"I don't think I could have roused him," I said, with a touch of affection. "He was about as gone as were you."

The captain went to Steldor, dropping to one knee and touching the back of his hand against his son's cheek, feeling for a fever. I scanned his face for signs of a problem, but there were none; he merely brushed a hand over Steldor's hair before leaving the younger man to his rest.

"Are you hungry?" I asked him, but he shook his head.

Galen was now approaching the fire, staring at the cooking kettle, and I knew I would not have to ask if he were in the mood to eat.

"He's good, so far," Cannan commented as he passed the sergeant on his way to lay out a bed for himself near the cave entrance.

I ladled gruel into a bowl for Galen, adding the fruit, and he gobbled it down.

"Best slop ever," he said with a slight smirk, wiping the back of his hand across his face. "Thanks."

He headed outside to take up guard, passing the captain, who was already lying down in preparation for a long-delayed and much-needed break.

"Wake me if Steldor stirs," Cannan called before allowing himself some rest.

The captain's words meant that I was, once more, expected to stay alert on my own within our damp and dim refuge. I was thankful for the shafts of natural light that came from above, but they illuminated only the floor where they fell, and they shifted with the position of the sun. Our torches and the fire did not reach far either, and there were dark patches along the walls and in the corners. The silence within the earth was also of a different quality, more complete, for there were no bird sounds, no wind or rustle of branches, or even footsteps. Ours would be a chilly and dreary existence.

I had little to do as time marched onward. Seconds passed, turning into minutes, followed by more seconds and more minutes. My longing for something to occupy me increased, for my unfocused mind wandered in unpleasant directions. I did not like having this opportunity to reflect, for I could not help wondering if my kingdom still existed, could not help thinking of my parents, my friends, my people, couldn't help thinking of Narian, who had saved London and my sister, but probably lacked the power to shield others, perhaps even himself, from the Overlord.

Then I remembered Galen's marriage of only a few months—he hadn't let a thing show, but inside he had to be aching. And back in the city, if Tiersia were still alive, she would have no idea where Galen was and would probably assume him dead. She would cause herself so much unnecessary grief. But was it unnecessary? Trapped out here, were we not as good as dead? We would never be going back. And that reality was more than I could stand to consider.

I came to my feet, determined to find something to do to ward off despair. Deciding I might feel better if I cleaned up a bit, I heated some water. If nothing else, my hair desperately needed to be washed. I ran a hand over my head, my fingers snagging on snarled locks that had escaped the bun I had fashioned before we'd left. I tried to release the remaining coils of hair, but had to tug repeatedly to get them to come loose. Some of my hair pulled out in the effort, and I let it fall into the fire.

My mane, as it could truly be called, presented a significant dilemma. Now that it was down, it made me cringe to feel it against my shoulders and back. It was beyond dirty, for it contained bits of twigs and leaves and was impossibly tangled in places. If I were going to attempt this, I would need to cut off the matted pieces. I pulled the dagger Steldor had given me from the sheath on my forearm, recognizing the incongruity in using the weapon he had unenthusiastically provided to shear some of the tresses with which he loved to play.

I carried the pot of hot water with me to the pool at the base of the waterfall, adding some cold so it would be the proper temperature, trying to decide the best way to approach this task. I had nothing with which to brush my hair and nothing other than warm water with which to clean it. In frustration, I snatched up the dagger and hacked off one of my front tresses at the shoulder, letting it fall in a clump at my feet. I picked up the dark brown lock that was lifeless and devoid of sheen and came to a practical decision.

Tossing the lock aside, I gripped another handful of hair, likewise slicing it off. I continued, cutting it all, piece by piece, to the length of the first. After examining my reflection in the water, I took up the blade again, shortening my hair from shoulders to chin, the length at which the High Priestess wore hers. A gasp from behind startled me, and I swiveled to see that Miranna had awakened and was walking toward me.

"Alera, what are you doing? Your hair!"

I put a finger to my lips to remind her to keep her voice down.

"I had to do it, Mira. Come see, it's not so bad."

She fell to her knees beside me and picked up a lock from the cave floor.

"But short hair..." she tremulously began.

"It will grow back."

Miranna had been going to remind me of the associations there were with short-haired women in our kingdom. Shearing the hair above the shoulder was a common punishment for prostitution and other misconduct, identifying women who should be jeered and shunned. Although I began to feel nervous about what the others would think, I knew that I had done the right thing, the necessary thing. After a few weeks of living like this, my hair would have been unsalvageable anyway, and besides—what society did I have to judge me now?

"Mira, I think…to be sensible…"

I reached out and tried to detangle some of her untidy tresses, but she snatched the hair back, knowing what I was proposing.

"No," she snapped.

"It's only hair," I said gently. "And you'll be much more comfortable once it's shorter. You can braid and keep what I cut off."

Water was pooling in her eyes, and I understood the reason—Miranna had always loved her hair. It was bouncy and beautiful, styled or otherwise, and she played with it constantly, twirling it around her fingers. Boys watched it swish as she walked, her friends adored fashioning it and it had been a source of regular praise from our own mother, whom Miranna was smart enough to realize we might never see again. Nevertheless, as I gazed at her, she nodded and turned her back to me, tears streaming down her face, and bottom lip stuck out like a little girl's.

I again took up the blade and began to cut, not making my sister's hair as short as mine. Shoulder length would be manageable, and yet leave her with some of the exquisite tresses she cherished. She cried silently while I trimmed strand after strand, until finally it was done. I raked my hands through the curls that remained, then tied them back using the ribbon that had held my bun in place. I wouldn't be in need of it anytime soon.

"There," I pronounced. "That will be much easier to care for, and it isn't even terribly short."

She reached around and felt what I had done, still sniffling, simultaneously examining her reflection in the water. I waited for an opinion that did not come. Instead, she picked up the strawberry blond hair I had bunched together for her and retreated to her bed in the corner, where she curled up, still clutching her precious locks, and lay still.

I monitored her for a time, feeling both regretful and sympathetic, then rinsed my head with the warm water. After combing through my hair with my fingers, I rumpled it agreeably. Though my neck felt exposed, the look was fresh and exciting, at least as much as anything could be in our current state. I felt as though cutting my tresses had freed me to be a different person from the pampered princess, then Queen, I'd been in Hytanica. Out here I could be capable, respected.

I sorted through the pieces of my hair, braiding and tying the least tangled before tucking them into the pocket of my breeches so I would not lose them. I was certain Miranna would do the same when she had recovered from her shock.

After a little while, I went to sit by my sister and managed to entice her into a conversation. We spoke only of happy times, for I was not confident what her mental state would allow, and because sad times were not worth remembering.

My attention was pulled from my sister by the sound of Steldor stirring, and I saw that he was turning his head restlessly from side to side. I went to him at once, reaching out a hand to touch his brow, but his eyes opened and he pulled slightly away.

I wasn't sure what to do, for he seemed more discontented than he had the last time he'd awakened. He was pushing at the quilts that covered him with his left arm, trying weakly to remove them.

"Steldor?" I said, checking for alertness.

"What?" There was a snap to his voice that assured me there was no issue with his mind. "Are you all right?"

"I'm too warm."

He shifted to the extent his wounds would allow, unable

to find a comfortable position, and I worried that he had developed a fever.

"Let me get your father," I said, then realized Cannan was already getting to his feet. He came over, taking up position on Steldor's other side and pressing the back of his hand to his son's brow.

"I'm too warm," Steldor repeated, this time for Cannan's ears.

"You're perhaps too close to the fire," the captain reasoned, doing away with the coverings Steldor no longer wanted. "But I can't move you on my own."

"Where's Galen?"

As Steldor asked the question, I examined him, noting that he was not sweating; perhaps Cannan was right that he was simply too near the heat.

"Galen's fine," Cannan answered, and Steldor's expression revealed that his question had not been posed because of his discomfort, but out of concern. "Just on guard duty."

Steldor swallowed and nodded. "Everyone else?"

"The others made it here safely, but Davan doubled back to find us. He led the Cokyrians who were tracking us on a false trail." Cannan paused, then finished, an edge to his voice. "He hasn't returned."

Steldor nodded but did not speak further. The captain turned his attention to me, a quizzical expression crossing his face at sight of my sheared hair.

"Alera, bring some water for him to drink," Cannan said, offering no comment on my appearance.

I hurried to the pool, snatching a cup on the way, relieved to have the captain in charge. As I filled it, he spoke again to his son.

"You didn't eat much before. Food is necessary for your recovery."

"I know," Steldor answered, sounding unusually vulnerable. "I'm just not..."

He trailed off, hurting and too tired to bother with excuses.

"Understandable," Cannan acknowledged. "Still." His tone indicated that Steldor was expected to get something of substance into his stomach.

"Do we have anything other than gruel?"

"Not a lot of choices. London has gone hunting, but until he returns, it's bread, gruel, a few dried fruits and hard tack. Take your pick."

In addition to the cup, I filled a bucket with water, bringing both back to Cannan. For the second time, he hooked his son beneath the arms and lifted him toward a semi-sitting position, but Steldor cried out in pain and his breathing grew rough.

"Easy, boy," Cannan said, right arm around his son's chest to steady him, left hand upon his forehead, disheveling his dark hair. "Easy now. You're all right."

Steldor calmed at his father's reassuring tone, though his breathing remained uneven. I handed the cup to Cannan, and he assisted his overheated son to down all the water, then passed it back to me so I could fill it again from the bucket. After asking me to bring some dried fruit, gruel and a rag, he again helped Steldor to drink. When I returned, he dipped the cloth in the bucket and sponged the cold water onto his son's face and neck. Having better positioned Steldor, he coaxed him to eat, achieving greater success than had I. When he was satisfied with the amount consumed, the captain eased him back onto the animal hides so that he could drift into sleep once more.

"Do you think he's all right?" I asked, wondering if Cannan would share his true thoughts now that Steldor would not overhear.

"He cooled off faster than he should have if he were ill," the captain replied, again checking for a fever. I averted my eyes as he pulled Steldor's shirt up to check how the injury was healing. "The wound itself may be mildly irritated, but there's no cause for alarm yet."

I didn't comment on the captain's use of the word *yet* as he repositioned both the bandages and his son's clothing. He then nodded toward my sister where she sat on her bedding, staring into space.

"How is she?"

"She's…different. Changed."

"She's dependent on you then?"

I made a noise of confirmation, at the same time confused by his somewhat odd question.

"I'm just trying to determine who could manage in a crisis without assistance," he explained, reading my reaction, and my skin prickled.

"Do you expect a crisis?"

"Yes. It's the only way to be prepared for one. But no, I don't believe we'll be discovered here."

Before I could respond, he stood and moved toward the bed he had made for himself.

"Steldor will sleep for quite a while. I'm going to try to do the same." He considered me for a moment, and a smile played most unusually upon his features. "And, Alera, short hair is clearly not always a mark of shame."

CHAPTER 24

DYING FOR THEIR KINGDOM

WHEN LONDON RETURNED HOURS LATER, HE was not alone. Galen had descended from his watch post to bring the meat—venison—into the cave, but when my former bodyguard stepped through the crevice, he had Lord Temerson in tow. The boy was exhausted and filthy, and the shredded remnants of his clothing hung on his body, covered halfheartedly with a dark cloak.

"I found him wandering the forest a ways off," London told us, tugging him farther into our sanctuary. "He's not quite right," the Elite Guard added, with a vague but significant gesture toward his own head.

Indeed, Temerson seemed as dazed as Miranna, but when his eyes fell upon her, his demeanor changed. He jerked free of London to stumble toward me and my sister, who had come to her feet and taken a couple of steps in his direction.

"Mira," he murmured as he stopped in front of her, surprising me by his use of the nickname I had adopted for her. He bowed his head, cinnamon-brown bangs tumbling forward, but Miranna reached out her hand to brush them back, drawing his eyes to hers. He looked near tears, and I could not conceive of what he had endured before London had stumbled upon him.

The men were spread throughout the cave—London at the center, Galen by the food stores and the captain, having awoken when the men entered, standing near his bed—and all were staring at the new arrival, trying to comprehend Temerson's presence. Steldor was asleep, more content now that he was no longer as heavily covered, and I surmised Cannan would make no effort to move him.

Miranna and Temerson stayed exactly as they were, not speaking, she touching his hair, he gazing into her eyes. I felt as though I were imposing, but there was no way in our present living conditions to give them privacy. After a few minutes, Miranna retreated into the corner with the young man who had been courting her, and Cannan approached London.

"What happened to him?" he muttered.

"I don't know. He never has been particularly talkative, and recent events have not persuaded him to be otherwise. I haven't tried to question him. I wanted to get him to safety first."

"All we have is time right now," Cannan replied. "We can afford to give him a little."

"And Steldor?"

"He woke a couple of hours ago, complaining he was too warm."

London's eyes met Cannan's, understanding the potential significance of this seemingly casual statement.

"He ate a little bit, not enough," Cannan continued, "but he's resting peacefully now. Time will tell with him, too."

"Shall I take the next turn on guard?"

"No, I will. It'll do me good to get out of the cave for a while. Just..."

"I know. I'll watch him."

Cannan nodded, and London strode toward Galen to offer assistance in preparing the venison. I followed, needing something to do and wanting to give Temerson and Miranna some time alone. As I drew close, both men glanced at me with raised eyebrows, having noted the new length of my hair.

"Breeches, horseback riding, short hair...what next?" London asked, a tease in his voice.

"I hope the ability to cook more than gruel," Galen responded.

The three of us laughed, greatly in need of a way to relieve stress. I looked at London, wondering what his true opinion might be, and he gave me an approving nod.

"Let's face it, Galen," he said more seriously. "We can use all the warriors we can get. Now let's get some food in everyone's stomachs."

Meat was like a miracle—I hadn't realized until it was in my mouth how much better it tasted than gruel and dried, hard foods. We congregated near the fire pit, using stones the men had gathered as stools, enjoying our feast. Cannan had forsaken his guard post to join us, his eyes sweeping occasionally toward his son's still form, but he did not wake him. Steldor could always eat later.

Miranna and Temerson sat close together like two broken-winged birds sharing the same perch, bolstering each other without sound. He had washed and changed clothes, improving his appearance, but not his mental state.

As we finished the meal, Temerson's eyes darted between the three fit men, knowing they would soon start asking things of him. He seemed resigned to this, however, entwining his fingers with Miranna's for security and courage.

"Do you want to tell us how you came to be lost in the woods?" Cannan asked, his voice free of expectation and pressure. Scaring the boy was not the way to proceed.

Temerson sat motionless for a long time, staring only at Miranna's hand in his, and no one tried to spur him. Finally, he raised his head, his countenance unexpectedly hard.

"I ran away," he told the captain, his trademark stutter oddly absent. "The Overlord—he came to Hytanica, just as everyone said he would."

At our dreaded enemy's name, Miranna gave a small whimper, and Temerson clasped her hand tighter. My blood pounded in my temples, for I was eager and yet terrified to hear Temerson's story.

"Narian was at his side as he demanded that the King and Queen come before him to negotiate our surrender. King Adrik and Lady Elissia came to the Grand Entry to speak for us when the Overlord's soldiers forced the door.

"He was horrifying, like the devil. Tall, broad, dressed all in black. Anyone who got in his way he knocked aside with some invisible power from his hands. King Adrik tried to speak with him, but the Overlord was furious. He said that he had been 'looking forward to breaking our boy-King' and that His Majesty's absence, his cowardice, did not invite his compassion. Then he asked King Adrik how much we would be brave enough to sacrifice. The King told him anything would be given for the sparing of innocent lives.

"The Overlord for some reason looked at Narian before he answered the King. 'I have already sworn to protect the innocent,' he said. Then he told the King to call forth every officer in our military. He said their lives were forfeit, or he would not be so merciful with our troops."

Everyone in the cave seemed to have stopped breathing. The rank of officer included every Elite Guard, every battalion commander, every soldier no less than a lieutenant. While the Overlord's pledge to protect the innocent had no doubt been extracted by Narian, he had probably not anticipated how his master would treat the soldiers who had surrendered.

Temerson's posture had gone tense, and something like anger was building within him.

"We were completely at his mercy. King Adrik had no choice but to send for all the officers in the palace and at the Military Complex, and each one of them came. The Overlord allowed the King to meet privately with the men. As he did so, the rest of us who had taken refuge in the palace were called into the courtyard. When the officers filed out of the Throne Room, they were resolute, reconciled. My father caught me and told me..."

He faltered, but his expression betrayed no weakness. He was determined to continue without giving in to his feelings.

"He told me to know that King Adrik had given permission for any man among them to escape if he could, that they would not be cowards for it. My father said for me to remember, even if no one else did, that not one of them chose to flee. They chose instead to die for their kingdom, to protect the people and their men.

"The officers were marched to the military training field and we were herded along behind. The training field was overflowing with Hytanican citizens who had been forced to assemble. The Overlord charged the officers to stand side by side in an execution line at the top of the hill overlooking the field, where all could see. We were made to watch—

wives, children, sisters, brothers, parents. *I* watched. My father was the seventeenth to die."

Speech was impossible; the horror was too great. The Overlord's cruelty was legend, but never had any of us imagined that he would be so heartless after his victory was complete, when we could no longer put up a fight. And the way Temerson spoke of his father's murder, which he had witnessed, so matter-of-factly—it was haunting, inexpressible. Clearing his throat, the young man pressed on.

"Before he started, he searched for you—all of you. He knew the King and Queen were gone, but he wanted the captain, the Sergeant at Arms, London, to torture especially. When none of you were there, he realized you must be with the royal family. So he called for the royal family's bodyguards to come forward, those who would know the location of your hideaway, or he would kill everyone as slowly and painfully as possible.

"After he'd slowly tormented the first two officers to death, Halias, Destari and Casimir gave themselves up for interrogation, in exchange for the quick deaths of their comrades. They were taken away, back to the palace."

In the midst of this gruesome tale, I recognized that the deputy captains had handed themselves over when Narian could easily have identified at least two of them. He had told me he would save as many lives as he could, extend what mercy he could, and I tried to convince myself he was being true to his word, despite the welling anger that insisted he should have tried harder to stop his master from performing these atrocities.

"He went down the line then," Temerson said, "making each man scream and fall to his knees, slaughtering them with no visible weapon. He was fast with most. They died within seconds, merely part of the demonstration. The only one he…"

Temerson's brown eyes briefly met the captain's, and behind his implacable deportment, Cannan knew what the boy would say.

"He recognized your brother, sir. He thought for a moment Lord Baelic was you. Narian corrected him, said he was mistaken, but the relation was obvious, and…"

"And he took his time," Cannan finished, his face stony. His eyes, however, were strange, blazing with a fury unlike any I had seen. His brother had been viciously punished because of an unlucky family resemblance, because of the position Cannan held, because Cannan had not been there himself to accept retribution. Rage was first and foremost in the captain's gaze, but guilt burned there also, and grief, betrayed in no other way. How did he manage such control?

My hand was over my mouth, and tears trickled down my cheeks as I grappled with this horrible truth.

"Not Baelic," I choked out. "It's wrong, not Baelic, he can't…he can't be…"

My uncle of only a few months could not be dead. Envisioning his lifeless body was absurd; surely nothing could have taken away that perpetual grin, his love for his family, his hopeless affection for the horses Lania scarcely tolerated. What would Lania and the children do without him? Someone so needed could not pass away. But the Overlord had given it no thought, none at all. He didn't give a care for the family he had destroyed, for the wonderful man whose life he had unjustly taken.

Galen, whom Baelic had treated as a nephew right along with Steldor, had blanched, and his jaw was tight. He looked to Cannan, struggling to match the incredible fortitude of the captain. I could tell it was his instinct to back out of our circle, to find solitude, but he resisted, drawing from Cannan's example and fighting back his emotions.

"I—I ran, once it was done," Temerson said, glancing to the back of the cavern, wanting to be dismissed. "The Overlord saw me but laughed and told his soldiers to let me go, I was only a boy. The next I remember, London found me."

Finished with his tale, Temerson stood, and when no one tried to stop him, he led Miranna by the hand, and the two of them stumbled toward the corner of the cave.

"Get him some bedding," Cannan said huskily to Galen, shrugging in Temerson's direction. Somehow I knew this was done to remind the Sergeant at Arms of our circumstances, of the necessity of discipline; it was a strange sort of comfort.

Galen seized the excuse to escape, but I was afraid to be alone. Faces were flashing through my mind, each and every person now gone, making this nightmare all too real: Baelic, of course; Baron Rapheth, Tiersia's father; Temerson's father, Lieutenant Garrek; Tadark and all the other Elite Guards. And the three who had surrendered themselves for interrogation—Halias, carefree and devoted; Destari, stoic and trustworthy, London's best friend; and Casimir, undyingly loyal, even with a difficult charge. All were suffering for naught; none of them would betray our location. And perhaps the most terrible aspect of it all was that several days had already passed since the Overlord's day of execution, several days in which families would have endured unspeakable sorrow, and countless other horrors could have been perpetrated, including the deaths of the men who had escaped the execution line to be dealt a worse fate.

I needed comfort. I needed someone to make me believe that Temerson's tale was only the invention of a confused and frightened boy. I longed for my parents, who, if I had interpreted Temerson correctly, were still alive. More than for my mother and father, however, I yearned to crawl around the fire and sink into London's secure arms. He was safety, he always had been. He could make all of this disappear. But London's hand had fallen on the shoulder of his captain, for despite the power struggle in which the men often engaged, he was extending Cannan his support, sympathy and admiration.

I scanned the room in the aftermath of Temerson's revelations, bleary-eyed and lost, but my skin went cold when I studied Steldor for the first time since we'd sat down to eat. Peaceful sleep eluded him; he tossed and turned to the extent he could, never lying still. Even from a slight distance, I could make out his flushed skin tone and see his frustration at having no blankets to discard and thereby dispel the heat that had set upon his body.

"No," I murmured, pulled from my grief-stricken trance. I staggered toward him, repeating that one word, while Cannan and London reacted just as quickly.

Waking Steldor was the captain's first objective. He lightly but urgently slapped his son's cheeks, calling his name again and again, each time a little louder. At last Steldor made a soft noise, and his eyes flickered opened.

"Father," he mumbled, recognizing the man hovering above him.

London and I looked on, while Galen hung in the background, equally worried, but giving father and son space. Steldor shifted uncomfortably, his shirt sticking to the light sheen of sweat on his skin.

"Father," he said again, but this time he had squeezed his eyes shut and was asking Cannan to *do* something, to help him, to take away the pain.

“Steldor, stay awake,” the Captain ordered.

He slapped his lethargic son’s cheek once more, startling him back to consciousness, and Cannan and London wasted no time in removing the King’s shirt. The bucket and cloth that the captain had earlier used had not been moved, and he once more dampened his son’s neck and chest, attempting to curb the fever before it became life-threatening. Meanwhile, London removed the bandages to examine the wound. I backed away, and in my place Galen came forward, grimacing at sight of the injury.

“What should I get you?” he asked London.

“Yarrow, to fight the infection. Also fresh bandages—we’ll need to lance the wound.”

I did not watch the men as they worked on Steldor, retreating to sit by the fire, but I knew well enough what they were doing. Lancing meant reopening. They would cut through parts of their own stitching in order to drain as much of the infection as they could.

Cannan stayed with his son long after London had finished, trying to prevent him from shifting too much, as it was Steldor’s impulse to try to escape his discomfort. Keeping him cool aided in this endeavor, so the captain continued with the wet rag, running it over his son’s hot flesh, talking to him. Although the King too easily succumbed to sleep, he would rouse with encouragement and was still able to communicate.

London came and went, frequently checking Steldor as he attended to other matters. He and Cannan attempted at one point to feed Steldor some thin broth, made with venison, but my husband turned his head and would not open his mouth, and nothing could convince him to withdraw his refusal.

Eventually, London knelt down opposite Cannan, Steldor

sleeping between them. They had moved his bedding farther from the fire, and though the captain's periodic checks of his temperature revealed only a slight drop, he seemed to be resting more comfortably. I knew this deterioration in his health was exactly what Cannan and London had expended serious effort to prevent, and that his recovery was no longer a certainty.

"I want to act," Cannan said flatly to London, casting a brief glance toward me. I stared at the burning embers in the fire pit, not wanting him to know I was listening. Night had fallen, and Miranna and Temerson slept in the back right corner of the cave beside each other—normally this would have been improper, but as things were, their only intentions were to lend each other solace and warmth. Galen had long since returned to guard duty outside, seeming to want nothing more than to be alone, and I wondered how he was coping.

"I want to cripple him," Cannan continued, accepting my bowed head as proof of my lack of attention.

"I feel the same," London replied. "But we're the crippled ones right now. Even if there were some way to embitter the Overlord's victory, we don't have enough men. We can't leave the women and Temerson without sufficient protection, and Steldor needs care."

The captain seemed to seethe over their uselessness but was forced to acknowledge it all the same.

"Our chance will come," London ground out, his voice barely audible. "And then he'll regret all this. We'll make him regret all this."

Cannan did not respond, instead feeling his son's forehead for the thousandth time and allowing a lengthy pause to ensue. London regarded his captain, a question poised on his tongue.

"Will you tell him about Baelic?" he finally asked.

"No. He doesn't need to know. Knowing will tear him apart, and the Cokyrians have already done a fair job of that."

London nodded, respecting Cannan's decision, and both men fell silent. After a time, I found myself struggling to keep my eyes open and, despite the terrible dreams I feared I would have, made my way to bed.

I managed only a few hours' sleep; then Steldor was too agitated for me to ignore, and I went to where he lay. Cannan and London were still next to him, attempting to cool him but having very little success. He was delirious with fever, thrashing, not wanting their hands on him when they had no choice but to restrain him so that he would not aggravate his injury. Talking to him was pointless, though Cannan did so anyway—Steldor didn't seem to hear and certainly could not comprehend. The sounds that came from his parched lips were nonsensical. At one point, morbid curiosity compelling me, I reached out to touch him but stopped within a few inches of contact, able already to feel the dry heat radiating from his skin.

"If this doesn't let up soon, it will affect his mind permanently," London said, the stress putting him on edge.

"I know that," Cannan grumbled. "Don't you think I know that?"

Without warning, London got to his feet.

"Where are you going?" the captain demanded, as Steldor gave a long, heart-wrenching whimper, a sound I would never have believed could come from him.

"Snow," London replied, snatching the near-empty bucket from Cannan's side and rushing out the door of the cave.

I stood helplessly by, thinking I should perhaps return

to my seat by the fire, but too worried about Steldor to do so. Cannan glanced at me but did not comment, giving me silent permission to stay, and I moved toward the wall so as to be out of the way.

Within ten minutes, London returned with a full pail of the white ice that sparingly covered the ground outside. Cannan nodded his appreciation of London's resourcefulness, taking a handful to run over his son's neck and bare chest. It melted instantly, giving further evidence of Steldor's body temperature. Before long, the bucket was empty, and London headed toward the cave entrance to replenish it, tossing a comment over his shoulder.

"I'll send Galen in."

The Sergeant at Arms had been on watch this entire time, and there was concern for him in the expressions of both men. Contrary to what the young officer obviously wanted, it was not best to let him withdraw, and he would surely need sleep by now. I pondered this logic, wondering when Cannan and London would allow themselves to give in to their exhaustion—when they would stop sacrificing their own needs for ours.

Galen returned in London's place, full bucket in hand, and went to join Cannan, falling to his knees beside his surrogate father, staring in dismay at his best friend. Cannan again used the snow, knowing London would have already brought Galen up to date on Steldor's condition.

"What can I do?" the sergeant asked, trembling with exhaustion and sorrow, but his words contained the hope that Cannan still believed there was something *to be* done.

"Go to bed," Cannan answered, not looking up.

The reply was immediate. "I can't."

"You must. You need to take care of yourself before you can take care of others."

Galen gazed desperately at Cannan. I knew he didn't want to be idle, not while his friend's life was in danger just paces away.

"Perhaps you should take your own advice," he retorted.

"Galen, don't. Just do as I say."

The captain was hanging on to self-control by a thread, his posture rigid, still not glancing the younger man's way. He was so close to the breaking point that perhaps eye contact might have been too much—we all were playing this delicate game, avoiding the small things that would inevitably break us while we tried to deal with the bigger ones.

Galen lurched to his feet, then turned his back on Steldor's moaning and agonized writhing and stumbled to where he had laid out some animal skins and quilts. I moved to again sit by the fire, knowing I should also try to get more sleep. I did not want to do so, on some level feeling I should keep company with Cannan. At last I identified my emotion—it was guilt that I was not as good a wife as the captain was a father.

CHAPTER 25

TIME TO STRIKE BACK

AT SOME POINT I FELL ASLEEP AGAINST MY WILL. Perhaps I closed my heavy eyelids for a moment, just to stop my eyes from stinging as I stared into nothingness, then failed to reopen them. I awoke sprawled uncomfortably by the cold fire pit, late-morning light coming through the shafts in the ceiling of the cavern. Someone had tossed a quilt over me, but still I shivered as I sat up, appreciating for the first time how much of a difference the fire made.

Cannan was asleep, on the far side of the cave from me, but London was still not to be seen. My eyes went to Steldor, plagued by fever even after all this time. He was not muttering, however, which I very much wanted to believe was a sign of improvement. Galen sat beside him, back against the wall, head upon his drawn-up knees. The bucket stood empty nearby—had they given up?

As I studied the two young men, Steldor took a sharp breath, and his dark eyes flew open, flicking around in alarm. Galen jerked his head up and then dropped a restraining and reassuring hand on his friend's shoulder.

"Steldor?" he said, sounding fearful. His eyes darted to the captain's sleeping form, then fell on me, and some of the anxiety left him as he realized I was awake and could rouse Cannan if need be. That proved unnecessary, however, as Steldor's disoriented state gradually transformed into one of recognition.

"Galen?" he asked hoarsely.

"That's right," the sergeant confirmed, shifting closer. He squeezed Steldor's arm, wearing a small smile that shone weakly through his despondency. It was this sorrow that dashed my hope; the fever was temporarily reduced, but it hadn't broken.

I did not want Steldor to die; I could never have *wanted* him to die. A few months ago, I might have more easily accepted death's inevitability, grieving less once it was over. Now, my heart ached for him to stay alive, the same way it had ached for Narian to return to Hytanica in the days before the war. He *couldn't* die. The idea was even more unbearable and inconceivable than that of Baelic's absence from the world. Steldor was young; he was vital; he was full of himself. Though he had the ability to aggravate me with distressing frequency, he was also brave, loyal and, at heart, a good man, with the potential to do so much. I had always treated being his wife with contempt, but though I would never be in love with him the way I was in love with Narian, I believed now that those feelings could change—if he lived.

"I'm hot…and thirsty," Steldor groaned, sweat dampening his brow.

At Galen's glance, I went for water, leaving without pause to do so a second time, for Steldor gulped the first cupful down. He likewise drained the second, but Galen motioned to me to leave the mug empty. The sergeant was trying to pace him—he was obviously parched, and a rush to his system could have a negative effect—but Steldor's eagerness for the drink was making it difficult.

There was a silence, and I gave the two men space, going to retrieve some wood in preparation for restarting the fire, but still I heard Steldor's scratchy voice when next he spoke.

"It's not good, is it?"

Galen's reply was convincingly nonchalant. "I've seen worse."

"Yes—on a dead man."

Galen averted his eyes for a moment before giving reply. "Don't talk like that."

"Sorry."

"Don't apologize, either."

Steldor gave a wry laugh. "Would you mind telling me what I am allowed to do?"

Galen couldn't suppress a smirk, though it was laced with sadness, as he recognized the beginning of one of their classic bickering contests.

"Sure—you can shut your trap."

Steldor was smirking, too, then he grimaced, arching his back as unexpected pain shot through him, and new drops of sweat materialized on his forehead.

"Steldor—" Galen started, humor lost, reaching toward him with undetermined intent. Steldor smacked his hand away with as much vigor as he could muster.

"No," he growled, gritting his teeth. "Ignore it. I don't want to think about it."

Galen nodded, though he looked uneasy. "Just tell me what to do," he said in a small voice.

"Tell me to shut my trap again."

Understanding his friend's desire for normalcy, Galen did as he was told, and eventually the lighter, nostalgic atmosphere was restored. I listened as they traded stories, much as Miranna and I had done not long ago, except that for my sister and me, there was still the opportunity to create new ones. The moment his fever spiked again, Steldor would be lost to us, and it was no secret he might not return. These two young men, bonded like brothers, were remembering now, so Galen would not forget when they were separated permanently.

"Steldor?" Galen said urgently, and my eyes flew to the two of them. The sergeant was on his knees, leaning over Steldor, clutching a handful of his friend's hair and shaking his head none too gently. Tripping over myself to reach them, I realized Steldor had slipped into unconsciousness, almost without warning. In response to Galen's efforts, the King came awake once more, but he was mumbling, his words failing to flow together in a comprehensible fashion.

"Steldor!" Galen yelled, and I stood helplessly by as my husband struggled to focus, only to push at his friend, rejecting his nearness as the infection once more fed his fever.

Galen's shout roused the captain, and he came to his feet as the sergeant's chin dropped to his chest in anguished defeat. As Cannan drew near, Galen jumped up. He pivoted, slamming his open hand against the rock wall with a choking scream that comprised so many emotions I could only guess at them all—anger, helplessness, despair, fear, sorrow.

Cannan was there to catch him when Galen slid to the floor, going down to his knees to pull the sobbing young man against his chest in a fierce embrace. My throat tightened, and I could feel hot tears on my cheeks, but somehow Cannan did not let go of his feelings, did not succumb to the agony that was surely tearing him to pieces. Stoic as ever, he simply held Galen; even when the younger man's crying had at long last died away, he stayed in place, not saying a word, continuing to console his second son within his strong arms. Feeling like an intruder, I went to fill a pail with water for use in cooking, trying to give Galen and Cannan as much privacy as I could in our cramped living space.

I returned to the fire pit, and Miranna came to assist me in preparing food. Not exactly certain of what I was doing, I began to concoct a venison stew, believing that it would at least be better than gruel. As I added ingredients, subdued voices reached my ears. Galen was sitting up, his face still tearstained, and the two men were talking by Steldor's side. I didn't try to listen. By the time I was finished, they had come to their feet, and Cannan was giving Galen one final pat on the back as the sergeant left to replace London on watch.

The day dragged on, and with it raged Steldor's fever. I tended the fire and kept food ready, as the men would eat at odd times depending on when they came and went on guard duty. Temerson continued to care for Miranna, the two seeming content just to be with each other.

London and Cannan were once more dousing Steldor with cold water from gathered snow, drenching his hair and every inch of his exposed flesh, but still the fever would not abate. I was sure London would have taken him outside into the perpetual cold if it had been safe to move him, but the risk was too great that he would be reinjured in the process—if, I thought morosely, such a thing were even worth worrying about now.

London and Cannan tried frequently to make Steldor drink through his delirium, but success did not come often. Still, their efforts were essential; at the rate he was sweating, the more water they could force him to consume, the better. Night arrived a heavy burden, and I did not welcome the sleep that threatened to crush me.

★ ★ ★

"Someone's coming!"

Galen was breathless as he hurtled through the cave entrance, jolting me awake with his words. Darkness was still upon us, and as I looked around in the glow from the fire, I saw that Temerson, like me, had sat bolt upright. London had jumped to his feet and was strapping on his weapons, and Cannan had left Steldor's side to go to the sergeant. Miranna stirred, but Temerson laid a hand on her shoulder, soothing her back into her dreams.

"Cokyrian?" Cannan demanded, as I also scrambled to my feet.

"I couldn't tell," Galen replied. "It's too dark. I barely saw him moving."

"You weren't seen?" It was London this time who spoke.

Galen shook his head. "But whoever it is, he's headed this way, like he knows exactly where he's going."

"Stay here, both of you," London instructed, accepting Galen's assertion without comment. "If someone is coming, you'll want to give him a healthy reception."

London was on his way to retrieve additional weapons from near his pack, and for once, Cannan did not bristle at his commanding air. Then I saw that the captain's eyes were on Steldor's restive form and understood the reason he had no objection to his Elite Guard's decision to be the one to leave.

"I'll find out what I can," London finished, walking back toward the other men with his bow in hand, slinging a quiver of arrows across his back.

He went out to find this potential enemy, dousing the torch near the cave entrance, leaving us with the light of the flickering fire and the torch that burned near Steldor to provide some comfort. I frantically tried to think how we would manage if we had to flee. Steldor would have to be carried, for which we would need two men, and Miranna and Temerson would have to be shepherded, likely by me. And what if London didn't return? Who would be left to protect us as we moved? And to where could we move?

I understood from Cannan's and Galen's conduct that if we found it necessary to run, we would leave almost everything behind. They were readying nothing for travel and were talking in hushed voices to one another, though I did hear Galen assert several times that he had only seen one person. Overcoming just one person would not be difficult, nor would it compromise our position. Then again, there was always the risk that the person could be a scout for a larger group.

Despite all this, I could not afford to panic as Cannan came to urge Temerson to his feet, placing a sword in his hand just as Miranna came fully awake. He motioned to me, telling me to keep my sister quiet. The captain then went to the cave mouth to keep watch, leaving Galen to monitor Steldor.

Not a word was spoken as we waited, the only sounds the trickling of the stream into the pool, our ragged breathing and an occasional moan from my husband, which I suspected Galen was prepared to stifle with his hand if necessary. Miranna had buried herself under my arm, whimpering every so often, and each time she did, Galen's eyes would flash a warning in my direction, though there was little I could do to stop her.

Minutes crawled by, then a call reached our ears, like a bird but louder, but not the call of any bird with which I was familiar. Cannan stepped back into sight to shoot a puzzled look at Galen, whose return shrug confirmed that something strange was happening.

Galen stood and approached Cannan, and I wondered what they knew that I did not. What was it they suspected? A creature? Cokyrians signaling each other? Had the call perhaps come from London, and they were deciding whether or not to answer it? But no measures were taken. They continued to listen, until the call repeated itself, slightly different this time.

"That's London," Cannan muttered with certainty. "Wait," he said sharply as Galen opened his mouth to reply.

I had the impression the captain was counting the seconds as they slipped by, then the original call sounded again, apparently precisely when he'd expected it.

"It's one of our men," he pronounced.

"It can't be!" Galen exclaimed. "Temerson said they all died except for—"

"It's one of our men. I don't know who, but he's one of us."

Galen seemed to want a better answer. He did not have long to wait. Noises from outside a mere ten minutes later announced London's return, and he and another stepped into the shadows of the entrance. The light that dimly illuminated our end of the cave eerily fell on London as they came toward us, then Halias stepped up beside him, looking as though he'd been through hell.

Jaws dropped as much at the state of him as at his unexpected coming, for he was gaunt and his blue eyes were strangely vacant. His clothing was a mess, rumpled and torn and dirty, and the left shoulder of his shirt was soaked with blood. The long blond hair he had always pulled back and casually tied at the base of his neck had been cut, hanging at irregular lengths along his jawline. I wondered if he had done it himself with the same mind-set that had possessed me, or if the Cokyrians had for some reason hacked it off.

It didn't really matter—what mattered was the glaring truth that a few meager days in the Overlord's hands could so transform a person.

Miranna was shaking but had not raised her head. It was just as well, as I doubted she would have recognized her bodyguard in his present condition. I tried not to move or give her any indication that it was safe to emerge from my embrace, but then Temerson made eye contact with me, kneeling to take my place and pulling her into his arms instead.

"I'm fine," Halias muttered, in response to our stupefied stares. "Did everyone else make it here safely?"

"Davan fell," Cannan answered, avoiding any uncertainty on the issue, though his tone did contain the proper respect for the dead. "Steldor is wounded, but the rest of us made it unscathed."

I had moved in front of the fire pit, close enough to see Halias's forehead crease with concern as his gaze fell upon the King. He was experienced enough to know from a glance that Steldor's injury was not minor.

"Will he recover?"

Cannan took a moment, his jaw tightening as he looked away.

"I don't think so," he said, candidly enough, though his voice was rough with emotion.

Halias nodded, his eyes meeting the captain's, then the men moved to congregate around the fire, sitting on the rocks we were using as stools. I went to stir the venison stew that we had kept warm, for our new arrival was obviously in need of a lot of things, including food. Halias motioned to London, indicating his shoulder as he pulled off his shirt to reveal an ugly gash. London went for medical supplies, setting to work the moment he returned, cleansing the wound with alcohol in preparation for stitching. Trying my best not to pay attention to what London was doing, I ladled some stew into a bowl and brought it to Halias, who ate hungrily. Then the inevitable questioning began.

"We found Temerson in the forest," Cannan began, his voice as hard and cold as steel. "He told us what happened in Hytanica, how the Overlord took you, Destari and Casimir, killing the rest of our officers. How did you escape?"

"I'll explain," Halias said, his voice tight and his eyes downcast, and I sat near London, needing to know, yet afraid of what I might hear.

"He tortured us individually at first," Halias said, raising his head and breaking the eerie silence with a statement devoid of cushioning. "I don't know for how long. I could hear the others when he…" He cleared his throat. "He wanted to know where the royal family was, but his chosen method wasn't delivering, so he brought us all together. He picked Casimir to torment in front of Destari and me."

Halias was trembling, fury and horror clear on his face, and London's hands froze over the wound he was supposed to be closing, pinching the needle much tighter than was necessary. Cannan watched Halias, silently commanding him to continue, and I wondered if he was fighting back the same sick feeling that twisted my stomach.

"We didn't tell him anything," Halias resumed, wincing as London remembered what he was doing and pushed the needle through. "And neither did Casimir. He would not have wanted us to give you up to save his life. We all swore an oath to die in defense of the King and Queen, and Casimir…he fulfilled that oath." His eyes found Cannan's as he added, "You would have been proud of him, sir."

With a heavy breath, he pressed on. "The Overlord reverted to his first approach, but my cell door was not closed properly when I was returned to the dungeon, and I was able to break out. He thought I would not realize he had allowed me to escape, and that I would run to this hiding place. I took the bait, but not unwittingly, and led his trackers in circles until I could double back and kill them. There were only two—it was not hard. Only then did I come here."

"Destari?" London asked, apprehension in his tone.

Halias shrugged, apologetic and somber, grimacing as the movement irritated his shoulder.

"There was no way for me to get him out—the Overlord made sure of that. He could still be imprisoned, undergoing torture. If there is a kind God, he is dead. No matter what, he has not revealed this location."

The silence was dense. London had finished his work, and now his hands were white-knuckled fists at his sides. The fire was back in Cannan's dark eyes, and Galen, fidgeting, finally stood, muttering that he would take guard, although I suspected his willingness to volunteer was motivated by the same desire to be alone that he had earlier exhibited.

"Galen, wait." It was London who spoke, his jaw set. "Get anything you'll need. We're leaving, now."

"What?" Galen said, stopping in his tracks. "What are you talking about?"

Everyone stared in confusion at the silver-haired deputy captain as he turned to Cannan.

"One good thing has come of this—Halias is in our midst, giving us another man. We're not as crippled as we were."

"What are you thinking?" the captain asked, brow furrowed.

"It occurred to me last night, but I knew we did not have enough men to act," London explained, rising to his feet as his fervor grew. "The Overlord and Narian are in Hytanica, along with countless Cokyrian troops, leaving their home city less well guarded than is usually the case—more susceptible to infiltration than I gamble they realize."

"You're not suggesting we attempt a conquest, are you?" Galen interjected, his heavy sarcasm earning a scowl from my former bodyguard.

"Of course not. I'm suggesting—" London paused, his eyebrow arching "—we attempt an abduction."

Cannan caught up before the rest of us.

"The High Priestess."

It was brilliant, really. Halias and Cannan could protect us, while Galen and London journeyed to Cokyri. Halias seemed certain that the High Priestess had not been present in our homeland, and we had London's knowledge of the Cokyrian city. He also knew something about the layout of the High Priestess's temple from his time as a prisoner there.

As London was insistent that no time be wasted, he and Galen readied themselves for departure. This made me uncomfortable. Wouldn't it be better to allow Halias at least one night to recover? Wouldn't it be better and easier to travel in daylight? But I couldn't imagine these things had not occurred to London. Perhaps he had some vain hope that, if he moved fast enough, he could secure Destari's release by the ransom we would pose to the Overlord.

Cannan took guard duty, appreciating Halias's need for rest and probably also aware on some level that the time would come when he would no longer want to leave his son's side. I caught Halias staring at Steldor, no doubt having the same thoughts, then London stepped up beside him, extending a clean shirt.

"I need to talk to you for a moment."

He was already prepared for the journey, a lightweight pack slung over his back and multiple weapons tucked on his person. Halias stood, pulling on the shirt, and the two of them stepped farther away from Galen, which out of necessity brought them closer to me. Very few words passed between them, but each one hit me like a heavy blow.

"When Steldor dies, we're going to lose the captain."

Halias did not respond, his silence acknowledgment enough.

"I will try to be back before that time, but if I am not... You'll have to watch him. I don't trust he'll remember the value of his own life."

"Can I make use of the boy?" Halias asked, nodding toward Temerson.

"I think so," London said, trying to shrug off some of the weight of his last statement. "He's been coming around. I think he's stronger than he appears. And Alera can be used for certain things. She's more capable than you'd expect."

My heart warmed at London's statement; they had come to believe as I had that I wasn't just someone who needed to be protected, that I could be helpful, that I could be counted on in a crisis. Galen and London left shortly thereafter, and it was easy to forget the danger they would face amidst the anticipation and in light of the leverage success would bring us. In reality, there were very few certainties in connection with this plan. We might be triumphant, or Galen and London might die. Panic pumped through me at that thought, but this mission had to be attempted regardless of the risks, for we were tired of hiding. It was time to strike back.

CHAPTER 26

STRENGTH OF THE KINGDOM

STELDOR WOKE ONE LAST TIME. IT WAS IN THE morning, and the air was stale, cold. I had gone to fetch more wood for the fire, wanting to bring back the blaze for warmth as well as to prepare some food.

He came to consciousness more calmly than he had with Galen, perhaps because of his father's nearness. Despite my desire to give them time alone, I could not seem to focus my attention anywhere else. Cannan sat beside him, Halias now on guard duty, and he laid a hand on his son's arm the instant Steldor's eyes opened, bleary and confused. They didn't speak for a long time, although Steldor's breathing became steadier as he gazed at his father, who was as strong as ever, the ache only visible in his eyes. But Steldor saw it.

"Am I going to die?" he asked.

"I'm doing everything I can to prevent it," Cannan answered, taking his son's hand, then he hesitated, struggling to be honest. "But probably."

Steldor nodded as if he had expected this but broke eye contact nonetheless, no doubt trying to come to terms with the ending of his life. I wondered if he was scared, in denial, angry that his time would be cut short, but none of those feelings came out. Instead, he gazed once more at Cannan.

"Papa…don't leave me."

Somehow the captain's iron will reined in his emotions, but he leaned closer to touch his son's forehead with his other hand, brushing his damp hair away.

"I won't."

"What will you tell Mother?"

There was no way to know if Cannan would ever see his wife again, a fact that escaped neither man, but as long as the possibility existed, the captain would bear a message for her.

"What would you like me to tell her?"

"That I…that I made it out alive."

Steldor—lying minutes, hours, days from death—wanted to protect the mother he resented, for he knew the truth would destroy her. Tears filled my eyes as I stood by the fire pit, and I held my breath as I tried not to give in to sorrow.

"Is Alera here?" Steldor asked next. His eyes were glazed with fever and it took great effort to push out every word, but he seemed unwilling to let it conquer him just yet. "I need to talk to her."

Cannan nodded, then looked at me, and my face grew hot, not from the fire but because he had caught me staring. He did not comment, but came to his feet, gesturing for me to come to Steldor's side. I complied, hastily wiping away my tears, and he took a step back so I could kneel in his place, but he did not leave, honoring his promise.

"Alera, I…I think…I'm going to die," Steldor said, flinching, though whether from his injury or from his thoughts I could not know.

My hand flicked toward him, but in the end I let it fall into my lap.

"Steldor, you don't have to—" I started, struggling to speak as tears again trickled from the corners of my eyes, but he cut me off.

"Don't tell me to stop," he growled, chest heaving. "I don't have much time and I want to say this."

I nodded, railing inside at the unfairness of it all. Couldn't fate grant him some peace during these last few, lucid minutes?

"I know I've hurt you, more than once," he said through gritted teeth, and I could not disagree, though I had without question reciprocated. "I wish I could say I never meant to, but…I can't." He shook his head to try to keep the predatory illness at bay for just a short while longer.

"What I'm trying to tell you is…"

He was having trouble focusing. His eyes closed, and I knew he was fast fading away. Then they reopened, dark and passionate, within them willpower I would not have expected. "You saw me at my best and at my worst, Alera, but even at my worst, I always…"

He trailed off, his unremitting pride forcing him to leave the sentence unfinished. "I just want you to know," he tried again, "I…I regret it now. I could have—*should have*—been better to you."

My stomach was twisting with remorse and sadness, my mind flitting through trite responses. None would suffice; I could no more lie and say he was wrong than I could explain the burning in my throat at the thought of his death, the absolute denial that raged inside me. I felt weak, pathetic, as salty tears rolled without restraint down my cheeks, but he bore none to match, despite the intensity of his feelings. Then I knew what to do. I leaned down and pressed my lips to his, kissing him tenderly, closing my eyes to let forgiveness and gratitude and even love flow from my heart into his, and for a time his lips responded. Then he yielded to his unrelenting fever.

Every succeeding hour saw him further from us. Cannan, keeping his promise, would no longer leave his side, refusing meals, accepting only water which he would occasionally sprinkle between Steldor's dry lips. It was thus necessary for Temerson, shaky and uncertain but with military training, to take a few hours on guard duty to give Halias a break. I wondered if London's vague words about "losing" Cannan were rebounding as agonizingly in the Elite Guard's head as they were in mine.

I stayed with Miranna throughout the next day, no longer trying to approach father and son, for Cannan, resting Steldor's head and shoulders in his lap, would cast me a dark glare if I tried, as though anyone who came near meant to harm his defenseless boy. It was terrifying in a way, that expression, as if he didn't recognize me, but his fierce instinct to protect his son also made me glad…glad that his arms would be the ones in which Steldor would die.

By evening, thoughts that I did not want had begun to torment me. What would we do with my husband's body? We couldn't bury it; the ground was too rocky in places and frozen in all others. Could we burn it? Or would a funeral pyre alert the enemy to our location? It grieved me to know that he should be buried in Hytanica's Tomb of Kings, but that we could not give him that honor. He had been crowned Hytanica's youngest King, and now he would also die its youngest ruler, having just reached his twenty-second birthday in this heartlessly cold month of February.

The hate that rose within me for Cokyri was so intense, I

could hardly contain it—a Cokyrian blade had caused Steldor this injury; Cokyrian soldiers had prevented him from receiving medical care; and it was Cokyri's rulers who had forced us to flee our home in the first place. And what right had they to take that home? My kingdom, my city, my land, my people. They had caused the destruction of so much, and I would never stop hating them for it. Never stop hating *him*. I wanted to bring about his death, wanted to destroy him, wanted to drag down the great Overlord of Cokyri before his very people, just as he had made our soldiers fall before those they loved.

But nothing, none of those things, would bring Steldor back.

His breathing was almost undetectable now, and every passing second jarred my heart, for I knew his chest would, at some point, fail to rise.

London and Galen returned late that night, just over two days since they'd left. They had taken the horses that we had originally used to reach the cave, but even with mounts, they had run hard.

London was the first to step into the torchlight at the front of the cave, a rope in hand that I soon saw was attached to the left wrist of Nantilam, the High Priestess of Cokyri, sister to the feared Overlord. Behind her entered Galen, gripping the rope attached to her other wrist. She was blindfolded, and her flaming red hair was dirty and mussed, as was her black clothing, giving evidence of a rough journey. Still she held herself with a level of arrogance that would have earned a Hytanican woman a beating. As London removed the cloth covering her green eyes, she shot him a haughty glare, then her gaze swept the cave, examining us and our hideaway. I swallowed and came to my feet where

I'd been sitting by the fire, intimidated by her even in her current state. Her attention fell on me, and though I was sure she could see my disquiet, I refused to look away. Our eye contact lasted what seemed an eternity, until London's voice broke the silence.

"Is he still alive?" he asked Halias, glancing at Cannan and Steldor, and I could hardly believe his insensitivity.

"Yes, barely," Halias answered.

I guessed Miranna's bodyguard had planned to say more, to inquire after the successful mission, but London didn't give him the chance, snatching the rope from Galen's hands and jerking the High Priestess toward our dying King. She resisted, but he was too strong for her, and in the end stumbled along behind. Galen and Halias likewise took a step forward, looking unnerved by London's action, while I stood frozen, none of us understanding his conduct. As he drew Nantilam to him, he placed a hand on her shoulder, pressuring her to her knees just paces from Steldor.

In an instant, Cannan had shifted position and drawn a dagger, but London stood, perhaps inadvertently, between the captain and the Cokyrian, his mind clearly not on his commanding officer.

"Heal him," London growled, his eyes locked on the belligerent High Priestess.

Halias had moved behind Cannan and I had stepped nearer, while Galen stood back and Miranna cowered in the shadows, perhaps recognizing the latest addition to our group from her time in captivity. Temerson was posted on guard outside; but while my sister probably needed comforting, I was too intrigued by what was happening to go to her.

Although Halias was positioned to restrain his captain if need be, the Elite Guard's bewildered gaze was upon London. His eyes flicked to mine, trying to assess my reaction to the bizarre statement that still reverberated in the air. Had London's mind been affected during the journey? But there was no confusion in Nantilam's return glare.

"This is your renowned boy-King?" she asked, and Cannan's knuckles went white around the handle of the dagger.

"Yes, this is our King. You will heal him."

The High Priestess did not answer for several moments, her manner lofty as she and London continued to stare at each other.

"He will die."

London grabbed the front of her shirt to pull her upright and then threw her hard against the cavern wall, where she crumpled to the floor. She did not rise but glowered up at the deputy captain as he stood over her with his arms crossed, simmering with fury.

"You will heal him," London repeated, every word punctuated with anger. Then his tone changed, becoming less hostile and more self-assured. "It will serve you, as well as us, if you do as I direct. If things do not go as we would like, and your brother finds us, what better gift could you extend than the King, alive and well, to torture to his satisfaction? On the other hand, if events favor us, you will be in need of my mercy."

Nantilam did not break eye contact with London, nor did her countenance change, but she also did not respond, seemingly considering her options. The tension in the room continued to heighten, making it hard to draw air, although none of us understood what was transpiring between the deputy captain and the High Priestess. I could not conceive of what Nantilam could do to help Steldor, but if she had some ability, London's logic seemed infallible. She apparently also reached this conclusion, for she came to her feet, her proud gaze fixed on her captor, then nodded and turned to approach my husband. To my surprise and hers, London's hand fell upon her shoulder, momentarily stopping her.

"Cannan," London said, and I understood his concern. "Let the High Priestess come near. She won't harm him."

"You're damn right she won't."

The captain's voice was low and gravelly, and though I could see very little of the Cannan I knew in this ferocious man's eyes, I was nonetheless inclined to take his side. London wasn't making sense—Steldor deserved the dignity of dying in his own time amongst his own countrymen. But London came forward, kneeling at Steldor's side so he was across from Cannan, extending an open palm to take the blade.

"Listen to me," he implored. "There isn't much time. If you don't trust me, Steldor will die, but if you do, she may be able to save him. Your son can live if you just listen. Now, give me the dagger."

London's ardent expression, coupled with something in his voice, connected with Cannan's rationality long enough for the captain to relinquish his weapon, and London motioned for Nantilam to approach. She joined the men on the floor and pulled open the bandages around Steldor's middle, showing no reaction to the swollen, damaged flesh that nauseated me. She laid her hands upon the wound, causing Cannan to tense, and then closed her eyes.

Nothing seemed to be happening, but as the minutes reached a half hour, I could see the strain on her face. All her concentration and energy seemed to be focused on her hands, and I wondered if her palms would be hot to the touch. At last she swayed to the side, catching herself with her forearms as she collapsed upon the floor.

"That's all I can do, for now," she said, exhaustion lacing

her words. “I can only sustain the power for so long. I need to rest.”

“Will he live?” London demanded.

She scowled at him, resentful of his dubious tone. “I have done what you asked, London. He is no longer in imminent danger. But it will take much more than this to save his life, and I cannot continue without rest.”

London looked at Galen, who took his cue to retrieve bedding for her, the sergeant’s frown expressing his opinion that some ruse was being played out by our captive. Soon after, the High Priestess was lying down, her hands tied behind her back, London hovering stiffly near her to make sure she did not cause any problems, while Halias went outside to check on Temerson. I examined my former bodyguard curiously, until he finally noticed my stare. Throwing caution aside, I asked my question.

“What did she do to him?”

Cannan, still with Steldor, raised his head to listen, as well.

“She healed him,” London replied brusquely. “Not completely, not yet, but she will. I can’t explain how it works.”

“She has powers, then,” I said, unease and awe sending a shiver through me as questions chased round and round in my mind. I hesitated, then asked the one that had come to the forefront. “But…how did you know?”

“Just accept it, Alera.”

There was suddenly a sharper edge to London’s words, and I wondered if I were delving into those pieces of his life he himself had not explored for years—those pieces about which he had never spoken. I dropped the subject and went to join Miranna. Taking advantage of the lull, I lay down at her side to get some sleep, my eyes on the High Priestess’s still form, aware that the Cokyrian ruler possessed knowledge of London's past that I never would.

When I woke the next morning, London and Halias were in serious discussion near the fire pit; Temerson was back inside the cave, lying down a few feet from Miranna; Galen, nowhere to be seen, was apparently on watch; and Cannan, still at Steldor's side, was monitoring the High Priestess as she once more laid hands upon his son. I did not know how she felt about the captain, but had I been in her position, I would have found his mistrustful dark eyes highly unsettling.

I began to fuss with breakfast, all the while listening to the exchange between the two Elite Guards.

"One of us will have to find a Cokyrian soldier and send her back to the Overlord with our message," London was saying.

"And what exactly will the message say?" Halias asked.

"I think it should be written, to avoid any miscommunication. We tell him we have his sister and are willing to negotiate terms of her release. We designate a meeting spot far from here, and make it clear that if there is any foul play, if any of our men are attacked, tracked or even sneered at, the High Priestess will be executed."

"And what do you think we'll be able to get in exchange for her?"

"I don't think we can expect the return of our lands, but I believe we can secure the release of our people. Their only worth to him is as slaves. I think he will trade their freedom for the safe return of his sister." Halias gave a short nod, then brought up the next issue.

"If the note is delivered as we desire, who will meet him?"

"I will," London said without hesitation. "I know what to expect."

Halias's brows had pulled together. "You can't go alone."

There was a pause as Halias waited for London's response, but my former bodyguard's eyes flashed to mine before he continued.

"With so many to protect, the necessity of guard duty and now the High Priestess to watch, I can only afford to bring one of you with me. Galen's skill with a bow makes him the logical choice—he can scout from above. You need the remaining numbers here."

"You'll be walking to the slaughter."

"Only if he's willing to sacrifice his kingdom's true ruler. Without Nantilam, Cokyri falls into disarray and their clean takeover is lost. He's their weapon, she's their ruler. He needs her. I don't think I'll be in danger—nor would Alera—if she would decide to come."

The goblet of water I had been holding clattered to the floor as I reeled in shock.

"You don't have to, of course. But it would be better to have you with me to impress upon him our seriousness, and to prove to him that we still have a sovereign. It won't matter to him that you're the Queen and not the King."

I sat, slack-jawed, considering London's request. My first instinct was to be terrified. Could I face this person, this monster, who had done so much evil? Who had ordered the kidnapping of my sister, coerced the man I loved to destroy my home, murdered the soldiers who had struggled so hard to defend us, tortured Casimir, and possibly Destari, to death? Could I stand before him and not cower? But now that I had the option of seeing for myself this warlord whom I hated, passionately, unconditionally, how could I refuse?

"Alera?" London prompted, reminding me that I had not responded.

"I'll go," I said, coming to my feet, images of how the Overlord would look, how he would speak, what could happen, spinning in my head.

"It is not a necessity," London repeated, aware of my unfocused expression.

"I'm not afraid." My voice was more emphatic than I expected it to be, but I knew the rush of anger and anticipation inside me was feeding my confidence. "I want him to know that."

A gasp from across the cave interrupted us, and our heads snapped to Steldor at an exclamation from Cannan.

"Steldor, it's all right! Steldor!"

The gasp had not come from the young King in question, but from the High Priestess, around whose throat Steldor's fingers had closed. She was clawing at his wrist, tugging in vain against his grip, and it wasn't until Cannan reached out to pry his fingers away that Steldor relaxed his stranglehold.

"Steldor, stop, she's not hurting you," the captain repeated.

London, Halias and I drew near, stunned but relieved that Steldor was actually awake. Cannan extended a hand, advising us to give them some space, while the High Priestess coughed and rubbed her throat. She was staring incredulously at our King, who, despite his weakened body and disoriented mind, had been aware enough to recognize her as an enemy. Pride rose within me as Cannan tried to bring his son out of his agitated state. It was as though Steldor had been under water for days and was just coming up for air. He seemed lost and confused, and the rush to his senses was overwhelming. I could not imagine what it would be like to have accepted death, to have sunk into its embrace, then to awaken yet in this world.

It was not long before Steldor slipped again into unconsciousness, but Cannan and London shared a look of understated triumph.

"He's coming back." London smirked.

It was Halias who bore the message to the Cokyrians. London had composed it and entrusted it to his fellow deputy captain after allowing the other men, and me, to read and approve of its contents. The High Priestess had dryly offered to give her input as well, but London had only glowered in her direction.

I was worried, of course, that something would go wrong, but Halias returned four hours later, having doubled back to conceal his trail. Skipping the details, he assured us that he had convinced a lone, wandering Cokyrian soldier to deliver the note. It was easy, for the most part, to fight down anxiety over the role I would play, for London and I would not set off until the following morning. But every time I let my mind drift to the foggy image of the Overlord it had conjured—a petrifying, hulking figure—dread unhinged me. Half of me harbored the same murderous thoughts I'd had earlier, and the same desire to show him he could not conquer me; and the other half wanted to hide, to let him think I was dead so he could never come after me. I didn't know which half was dominant.

The night grew late, but sleep would not come, and I rose from my bed to sit by the fire. To my surprise, Cannan left Steldor for the first time in days to sit beside me, his expression telling me he had something on his mind. The High Priestess was once more bound and lay a fair distance from his son, giving the captain cause for some respite, but still I knew he would not want to risk Steldor waking alone and disoriented. Whatever he had come to say had to be important.

"I knew your uncle," he revealed, voice hushed as if he did not want to disturb the sleep of the others who lay around us, though I suspected he would have viewed this as a private conversation regardless. "Andrius was my best friend, Hytanica's Crown Prince. He was treasured, and would have been a great king, one history would never have forgotten. Strong, stubborn, intelligent and not afraid to challenge anyone, not even his own father." He smiled, remembering tales I would never be told. "He was compassionate, Alera, and bold—traits that ultimately led to his death on the battlefield, but without which he would have been half the man he was."

As he pondered the flames, I began to wonder why he was telling me this, then his eyes found mine and he spoke once more.

"I see him in you, Alera. You have his spirit, which your own father, for all his goodness, lacks. But that is why I know you can do this. You won't cower before the Overlord—you'll show him the strength that lies in our kingdom, in the blood of our royal family. You'll cause him that second of uncertainty that will open the door to our victory."

His eyes held mine a moment longer, then he rose and returned to Steldor's side. The doubts that had been plaguing me dissipated, and I knew I would face the Overlord with dignity at the meeting in the morning. For the second time I had been compared with this distant man of strength and valor, whose death had left a kingdom in mourning. Whoever he was, I would not let him down. And I would not let down my courageous comrades.

★ ★ ★

Cannan's words and his confidence were with me when London and I left at dawn for a clearing in the woods just west of the Hytanican city. London had chosen the location carefully, wanting it to be close enough for ease of travel, yet far enough to prevent the discovery of our cave. He also wanted there to be a vantage point from which we could monitor the clearing, not trusting the Overlord in the least. Galen, known for his prowess with a bow, was even now taking up position to give us added protection.

The negotiation had been set for noon, and London was certain of two things: that the Overlord would attend, and that it would be unwise to be late. Like London, I wore breeches and a leather jerkin, with a cloak covering all; with my short hair and oversized clothing, I probably looked more like a boy than a queen.

We traveled on horseback about half the distance, hiking the remainder, London not even wanting our mode of transportation to give clues as to the whereabouts of our hiding place. The Elite Guard scanned the clearing where we would meet, which was about a hundred feet across, leaf-strewn and patchy with snow. It was surrounded by thick trees, mostly oak and elm, with relatively few pines, and the undergrowth was so dense it was grueling to push through. Then we settled in to wait, the clearing within view but our position difficult to detect.

We waited about an hour, with the hoods of our cloaks over our heads, slowly becoming stiff with the cold, before the sound of horses' hooves moving through the brush became distinct. My heart threatened to explode, but I tried to breathe steadily. I was determined to show the Overlord the strength of our kingdom.

Though I could not yet see our adversaries, I knew more than one mount had broken through the underbrush.

"I thought he would come alone!" I seethed.

London pressed a finger to his lips, silencing me as a forceful voice echoed through the trees.

"You conceal yourself from me like a coward! Step out where I can see you, London. I know this is your game."

I swallowed back the bile rising in my throat as London rose from his crouch to saunter into the open. I wanted to cling to the ground like the frost beneath my feet, but I followed his example to the best of my ability, pulling back my hood at the same time he did his.

Across from us, two Cokyrians, cloaked and dressed in black, were dismounting. My heart beat erratically as I realized one was Narian. The other was a tall man wearing a black tunic over silver chain mail with metallic bracers on his forearms, his shoulders broad enough to block out the sun. He was not hulking as I'd pictured him; his movements were fluid, eerily graceful, as he stood by his thickly built black warhorse. His hair was red like his sister's, but longer, pulled back at the nape of his neck. His green eyes were also identical to hers, though they were made striking not by their depth but by their harshness and cruelty. The foliage itself seemed to quake in fear as he walked, and the cold that came from him was different from that of the weather—it was a cold that weakened everything it touched. He was the first person I had ever met who felt utterly devoid of humanity.

Narian had likewise dismounted from his slightly smaller dark bay horse and was trailing his master by a few steps. Given his growth and increased bulk, he had a powerful look about him as well, but was not as imposing in stature or demeanor as the Overlord. There was something about the warlord that made everything around him shrink and tremble.

"It is you," the Overlord sneered, scowling at my companion.

"Yes," London replied, voice steely. "And that is why you can rest assured none of this is a bluff."

The warlord snarled and abruptly thrust his arm out toward London. At once, the deputy captain screamed, collapsing to his hands and knees, but I stood rooted in place, too horrified to react or go to him. He fell to his side, writhing in agony, and only then did our enemy relent.

"I should have killed you long ago," he spat as his victim panted, unmoving in the aftermath of the attack.

I had a strong desire to run, to save myself, not even caring if I left London behind, and probably would have if I had not caught the flicker of emotion that played in Narian's blue eyes. Whether it was pride or love or admiration, I did not know, but it was enough to root me in place. I gazed at him, absorbing some of his spirit, and I felt my confidence return.

The Overlord began to pace, stalking back and forth in front of us, but he did not come closer, and this small detail told me we still held the upper hand. The warlord was furious, but he would not risk his sister any more than he already had.

I stepped in front of London to address our foe, suddenly defiant.

"And who are you, little one?" he asked.

"I am Queen of Hytanica," I responded, voice firm, head high. "The High Priestess's life is in my hands. Will you negotiate to save her?"

He stopped pacing, scanning me perhaps for signs of

weakness, but I made sure that all he could read was my antagonism.

"Be careful what you demand. Only so far will I negotiate."

He was trying to intimidate me, and thereby maintain control of the situation. But I could see the boast in his statement, and I did not vacillate over my next words.

"My kingdom has fallen, but thousands of my people still live. Let them walk free of the city, every last one of them, and I will spare your sister."

His lip curled and he gave a low growl.

"You wanted Hytanica's land, not her citizens," I insisted. "My request is reasonable."

I waited, feeling almost light-headed from my audacity, while he deliberated, still wearing that fearsome scowl. London stepped up beside me, having struggled to his feet, and his presence reinforced my demand.

"Tomorrow," the Overlord said at last. "I will give answer then."

I nodded. "Very well."

London and I stayed in place as the Overlord and Narian returned to their horses and mounted. Just before he disappeared into the trees at his back, the warlord trained his vicious and unforgiving eyes on me.

"I will not forget your face, Alera of Hytanica," he promised, and I felt for a moment as if I could not breathe.

We departed shortly after our enemy had. London, regardless of the clear instructions in the message we had sent the Overlord, and despite Galen's ability to survey us, did not trust that we would not be followed, so he took us on a very roundabout route back to the horses and ultimately back to the cave, always checking behind. There was no trouble, however, which meant that the Overlord had taken us seriously.

I began to shake as my bravery drained away, and the full extent of the evil I had met registered. Nonetheless, I dared to believe we might succeed. When we arrived at the cave, the men gathered around the fire pit as London explained what had happened, leaving out the details of the Overlord's attack on him, but still giving me credit for the negotiations.

"I was unexpectedly indisposed," was as close as he came to the truth. I wondered if Galen might later provide the others with a more honest account of the meeting.

As we began to disperse, any lingering doubt I felt as to whether I had conducted myself correctly was alleviated when London for the first time in weeks cracked a genuine smile, nearly positive that all would go according to plan.

CHAPTER 27

NO CHANCE FOR GOODBYES

LONDON JOURNEYED BACK IN THE EARLY hours of morning, before the sun had risen, to await the Overlord, not believing it would be necessary for me to come a second time. Now that I knew of what the warlord was capable, I did not like the idea of the deputy captain going alone, but he promised everything would be all right and that he would return with word by evening, if not sooner.

For most of that day, the High Priestess continued healing Steldor. I sat at a fair distance from them, distrustful but enthralled, and unable to deny her abilities. Steldor's fever had broken, the infection was leaving and he was rousing much more often. Cannan encouraged him now and then to eat and drink, and had tried explaining what Nantilam was doing, but Steldor was mostly unresponsive, likely still grappling with the fact that he was alive.

Halias had been assigned to guard the High Priestess and so rarely took watch anymore. Galen and Temerson were quite willing to shoulder this assignment, Temerson surprising everyone with his resiliency. The things he had seen, the cruelties he had firsthand experienced, had made him tougher and given him the desire to help in any way he could. It was odd to see him so changed; even his shy stutter was gone, an indication that he was no longer intimidated by life.

Miranna, unlike the boy she loved, was making very little progress. She remained quiet, skittish and altogether uncertain of the world and who she was. She needed a stable environment in which to mend, and right now she had the furthest thing from it. She had shyly acknowledged Halias at last, but it was only to Temerson that she spoke. I was thankful to have her suitor among us, for he was content to stay with her for hours on end.

Galen, between shifts on watch, was keeping busy sharpening and resharpening the multitude of weapons we had brought with us, along with the ones that had been stocked in the cave. He had not, to my knowledge, spent time with Steldor since his friend had begun his recovery, but with Cannan and the High Priestess always at the young King's side, I didn't know when he would have had the chance. At any rate, I knew Steldor's steady return to health was lifting Galen's mood tremendously. Considering our dire circumstances, things were going well.

When London returned, the sky was darkening, and I was cooking stew for our evening meal, Miranna sitting nearby. Temerson was on guard outside, and Galen was in charge of the High Priestess, enabling Cannan and Halias to talk, for they had begun to consider whether there had been a problem. An expectant hush descended as London entered the cave seemingly unharmed, only the grim set of his mouth giving us pause. All eyes went to him as he stopped in the middle of our hideout, running a hand distractedly through his unruly silver hair.

"Negotiations have changed," he said curtly.

I got to my feet, his strange, aggravated manner staying all of our tongues.

"London, what is it?" I asked, clearing my throat as I realized how hoarse I sounded. "What happened?"

"Something we did not anticipate." His hands formed fists at his sides, and he closed his eyes, taking a heaving breath. "I should have known the Overlord would not so easily accept our terms."

Even the High Priestess was engrossed, her forehead creased, as Cannan and Halias stepped toward London, and Galen came to his feet.

"What happened?" Cannan repeated my question, his tone bracing, for he knew the news would be bad.

"King Adrik and Lady Elissia—they are alive. The Overlord offers their lives for that of the High Priestess."

The blood drained from my face, and I stumbled a few steps toward London, emitting a small cry of distress that did not sound as if it had come from me.

"He'll kill them?" I choked out, and London nodded.

"We can't let him do that!"

I scanned the faces of the men standing solemnly around me, and their demeanors were anything but soothing.

"We have to rescue them!" I said shrilly.

"He'll have taken them back to the palace by now," Halias sadly told me. "They're most likely in the dungeon—there is no way to get to them."

"The only way to secure their release is to give up the High Priestess, and even that is without guarantee," London reiterated. "The Overlord is heartless, and now that we've angered him, he will not be interested in a fair trade."

"Regardless of our desire to save the former King and Queen, we cannot give up the High Priestess for their lives alone. We need a better bargain," Cannan argued, and even I knew from a military standpoint that this was true.

"You can't just let them die!"

While those exact words had been on the tip of my tongue, it was not from my throat that they had sprung. I turned and looked at my sister, who was on her feet, eyes wide as she stared at us in horror. She was almost hysterical, but I did not go to her, hoping her outburst would make the others see sense.

"After everyone else we've lost," she shrieked, "you can't let them die, as well!"

Cannan and his two deputy captains looked at her guiltily and compassionately, but did not answer. Instead, Halias turned to me.

"We have no choice, Alera. I'm sorry, I truly am, but I agree with the captain. We can't give up the High Priestess. She's all we have." His tone was pained, and it was plain that everyone's nerves were strung taut.

"The Overlord is clever enough to know that we won't kill his sister lightly," Cannan added. "He's going to torment us to the extent he can. He enjoys playing these games."

"But they're my *parents!*" I cried, the inside of my throat feeling as though it were torn and bleeding. "London, please!"

I turned to the man who had been my bodyguard for years, who understood the love I had for the people whose lives were in question, and pled my case with him.

"The Overlord's wrath should not fall on them—they're no longer even Hytanica's rulers! We need to save them. *I* need to save them. This is the Overlord's way of making me pay for standing up to him. I beg you, don't let this happen!"

"We can save them," London resignedly declared, and lost in the instantaneous rush of relief, I did not notice the strange blankness of his expression until Halias said his name. He looked up at his fellow Elite Guard as if he'd forgotten the rest of us were present, and the thanks that had been on my lips died away.

"How?" I asked, wary.

"We make an exchange, but not with the High Priestess," London explained, complexion as pale as the patches of snow outside.

My head was swirling. "Then what do we give him?"

He crossed his arms upon his chest, hesitating for a moment before he answered.

"Years ago, the Overlord and I forged a bond, born of mutual hatred. If I were offered to him, he would release your parents. He would derive much greater pleasure from having me in his hands."

"No," I said at once, and the word was echoed by a few others.

"You can't do that," Halias ardently asserted. "You're the reason we've come this far. I can't let you make that sacrifice."

"My brother would make the trade," said the High Priestess unexpectedly, her gaze revealing awe and a deep-rooted respect as she examined London. "Have no doubt."

London nodded his head her way, appreciating her endorsement, though his eyes contained no warmth. Then he turned again to Halias.

"You can and you will let me do this. It's one life in place of two."

"But...but he'll kill you." I was stating the obvious, merely repeating what he had already made clear. "You'll die."

"Eventually."

"No," I whimpered, stepping closer to him. "No, I don't want you to die, please. There must be some other way."

"I'm not giving you a choice, Alera. I've protected the royal family my entire life. This sacrifice is one I have long been willing to make."

It was London's life or my parents' lives. I knew this, but I didn't want to accept it. How could I say goodbye to him? As my tears flowed, I walked forward into his arms, tucking my head against his shoulder. I clung to him, struggling to come to terms with the fact that this would be one of the last times I would feel his warmth, take in his familiar scent and be comforted by his strength. I loved him, fiercely. He had never in all the time I'd known him been one for displays of affection, but he returned my embrace, holding me as I wept like a child.

When my sobs subsided, he led me over to Miranna, leaving me for once in her care, and she and I went to sit together on our beds. He returned to talk to Cannan for a few minutes, and Halias came to check on the stew.

Eventually we all ate, then Galen took guard duty, sending Temerson inside to eat, as well. After that we dispersed, Halias to watch the High Priestess, Cannan to check on Steldor, the rest to find respite in sleep. For the second night in a row, I was not to be granted such release, afraid that if I closed my eyes I would wake to find that my last hours with London had disappeared.

I dozed off at some point, only to jolt to awareness after a short while, haunted by nightmares. I got up to find that everyone else still slumbered, with the exception of Halias, who was seated not far from Nantilam with his back against the wall. I did not say anything to him, though I could feel his eyes upon me. Instead, I walked closer to where London had laid out his bed, but he was not there. He had wanted me to sleep, yet he himself apparently could not. I scanned the rest of the cave, but there was no sign of the deputy captain. Alarm twisted my gut for an instant. He had promised he would not leave until morning, so where had he gone?

"He's outside," Halias informed me, as if reading my mind.

I nodded, then slipped through the crevice and into the cold night, wishing immediately that I had grabbed a cloak. But as my eyes fell on London, I abandoned all notions of going back for one. He was sitting against the rock face to my left, head hung desolately forward, and even when I sank down beside him, he did not acknowledge my presence.

"London?"

He lifted his head to glance in my direction, then turned away, but not quickly enough to prevent me from seeing the tracks that only tears could have made. I was taken aback to have caught him crying, for it was his nature, like Cannan's, to quietly endure. But the stress under which we lived was enough to wear down even the most resilient—Cannan himself had come close to losing his mind.

"I'm sorry," I murmured, not sure for what I was apologizing but knowing that I meant it.

"It's not what you think," he replied, still hidden in shadow, voice strange.

"Then what is it?"

I wanted him to talk to me, for once to tell someone what was wrong. He couldn't go to his death tomorrow with the world bottled up inside him. He was silent for a long time, but I knew he wasn't ignoring me.

"Alera, I didn't tell you everything," he finally said.

I let his words resonate, uncertain as to his meaning.

"Do you want to tell me now?"

"Don't," he said, but again I was uncertain as to his meaning. He began sentences without knowing where they would end. "It's... You don't... You can't... It was my fault. If I'd known, I could have..."

"What are you talking about?" I asked when I could stand it no more, still trying to be delicate though the pain in his voice was making my chest tighten. I wanted to help him but did not know how to do so, for he was making no sense.

"I told you, I kept things...things that happened today, with your parents."

I felt myself pulling back from the conversation, though my mouth formed the words I wasn't sure I wanted to utter.

"What things?"

"I never spoke to the Overlord. I went to our vantage point above the clearing, where Galen waited yesterday, and I saw him arrive, bringing your parents, but...not just your parents. He knew I would be there, that I'd be watching, so he seized the opportunity to make a demonstration, to express his intention of killing your parents if we didn't cooperate."

The agony behind his words was scaring me; I had never seen him like this before.

"He...he tortured and murdered Destari, in front of me, and I didn't do a thing to stop him. I'd thought Destari was already dead. If I'd known he was still alive...I should have done something, anything. I should have saved him, long before the Overlord had the chance to do this. All that time, he was suffering, and I know what it means to suffer at the Overlord's hands."

"London," I breathed, unsure what else to say, shocked and sorrowed myself by Destari's death. How could he have harbored this knowledge alone, even for these few hours? Destari had been one of my trusted bodyguards, but he had been London's best friend since before their graduation from military school—they had climbed the ranks side by side. To have witnessed him die in such a horrible manner…I couldn't comprehend it. The thought made me sick, and without thinking, I reached out to touch him, yearning to comfort him, but he brushed my hand away.

"I protect everyone," he stated simply. "It's what I do, what I have always done. But I failed him."

"You didn't kill Destari," I said, incredulity fighting its way into my speech. How could he hold himself accountable? "It was better you didn't know he yet lived, because you could not have gone back for him. He knew that, London. Destari knew it when you parted ways at the palace—he knew it when he surrendered himself to the enemy for interrogation. You didn't fail him or betray him, and don't you dare take responsibility for what the Overlord has done. It was *his* hand that ended Destari's life, not yours. His brutality is the reason for all of this, and your compassion would compel you to shoulder the blame that is his. Where is the justice in that?"

I wanted so much for him to recognize the truth in my words, to find some relief from his torment. Once more, hatred for the Overlord overwhelmed me—he was tearing all of us apart. Soon, I would never see London again, and the Overlord was even preventing us from finding peace in our final hours together.

"He left the body behind," London said after a time. "I buried it after he departed."

It didn't matter that London had already rejected my touch; I lifted his arm and crawled beneath it, knowing he needed me near, perhaps as much as I needed to be near him.

Early the next morning, we left to meet the Overlord. I accompanied London, both because I was Hytanica's Queen and because I did not wish to lose a second with him. I wanted him to know I loved him, and that I admired and appreciated his courage. Cannan left his son in Galen's capable hands to travel with us, another gesture of respect for the man who was voluntarily giving up his life in the name of our cause.

When we arrived, after again taking a circuitous route, we stepped into the clearing, relying on London's knowledge of how the enemy would act. The deputy captain was certain that the Cokyrians would have the clearing under observation. He also was confident that no one would try to harm us, that the Overlord would let us walk freely until his sister was safe.

"Tell your master to bring the former King and Queen," London loudly called to the invisible Cokyrian soldiers who surrounded us. "We have come to secure their release."

There was no response, but none had been expected, and we waited in silence for about an hour, cold and wary. Then we heard our enemy's approach. He had brought others with him, but only he came into the open, on foot, to address us. I scanned the trees behind him for Narian, anticipating his appearance, but he did not emerge.

"What is this?" the Overlord demanded as he took in the three of us, realizing that we had not brought his sister.

"Have you brought King Adrik and Lady Elissia?" London asked, ignoring the Overlord's question.

The warlord looked behind him, motioning to someone in the trees, and two Cokyrians, a man and a woman, pushed my parents before them into the clearing.

"Alera!" my father blubbered as he caught sight of me, then he stilled as a knife was pressed against his throat, drawing a small amount of blood. My mother did not speak, and I was not certain she could, for her head hung forward, her hair dirty and matted, obscuring her face.

I wanted so much to rush to them, to pull them away from the Cokyrians, but I did not move, knowing that in order for authority to be retained, emotions had to be held in check. I kept my gaze on the Overlord as London moved forward, indigo eyes icy. Our adversary spoke first, voice low and dangerous.

"Be careful what you say, London, for if your words are not what I want to hear, I will kill them both where they stand."

"You will entrust the former King and Queen to my companions and take me in their place," London replied.

Silence ensued as the two men stared at each other, the Overlord searching for weakness, indecision, and London daring him to find it.

"You always were the martyr, weren't you?" The Overlord snickered, and I closed my eyes briefly, relieved and devastated that he was accepting the trade. "So loyal, so brave, so foolishly self-sacrificing. I will see you regret it all before you die."

"You failed the last time you tried," London shot back. "I'm quite eager to see if you've improved."

The warlord's lips twitched at this cavalier statement, then he raised his voice to address Cannan and me.

"And you! You would allow your greatest asset to simply walk away? How will you live with yourselves, knowing the torment he will be enduring? And the torment will be great, I assure you. More important—how will you manage without him? The genius behind your plot, this perpetual thorn in my side."

He had stepped forward to grasp London's jaw, making his powerful size all the more apparent. London's build was that of a scout, muscular but lean, ideal for quick movement and passing unnoticed in the shadows, but the Overlord was pure warrior. He easily had four inches on the deputy captain, and the gloved hand with which he gripped his prey seemed larger than it should have been. Still, London did not blanch or break eye contact.

I looked to Cannan and understood that there was no point in responding to the Overlord's taunts. It would change nothing, and our nemesis was merely enjoying the game, what he viewed as a small victory.

"Hand them over," the warlord said to his soldiers, who shared a glance before obeying. They clearly had loyalty to the High Priestess and appeared dubious about this decision, but they did not dare question it. The Cokyrians pulled my parents forward and thrust them in our direction, my mother stumbling toward the captain and my father into my arms.

"Alera," he said again, taking me in a swift hug. "Thank God you're all right."

Over my father's shoulder I could see enemy soldiers tying London's hands behind his back. The moment he was bound, the Cokyrians hauled him out of sight without a chance for goodbyes. Casting a nasty smile my way, the Overlord likewise disappeared into the dense trees.

In the couple of hours Miranna had been in the palace following her escape with London, no one had told our parents she was alive. Around the lump in my throat, I tried to talk reassuringly with them as we returned to the cave on horseback, Cannan leading the way, supporting my mother in the saddle in front of him. When I mentioned how it would help Miranna to see them again, my mother looked at me in shock, for the first time allowing a glimpse of her heavily bruised face.

"Mother..." I exclaimed, aghast at what she must have endured. My father seemed free of injury, but apparently she had not been so fortunate. I could only suppose that her perfect, unblemished features had been too much temptation for the Overlord to resist.

"Miranna is with us?" she asked, swollen lip trembling as she cut off any remark I might have uttered about her condition.

"Yes, she's safe. London..." I trailed off, unable to continue. I closed my eyes for a moment, gathering my resolve, then tried again. "London brought her with him when he escaped from Cokyri."

"At least there's one reason to thank God," she whispered.

The reunion of my parents and their youngest child was long overdue, and after my father had embraced her, Miranna spent most of that day and evening in my mother's arms. As time passed, she motioned me over as well, and I curled up on her other side by the fire, feeling some measure of peace, even though my thoughts continually drifted to London. I tried not to dwell on what he might be going through, whether he was even still alive or if he might be better off dead.

Cannan talked with my father, explaining how the High Priestess had come to be in our custody, as well as our plan to use her to secure the release of our people. As they conferred, I examined the two of them, noticing that my father's hair was grayer and his face more lined, etched by worry rather than laughter. He had also lost weight, which made him look almost insignificant standing next to the tall, broad-shouldered, powerfully built Captain of the Guard.

My father and Cannan crossed to the left side of the cave, and the woman about whom they had been speaking rose to her feet to give the King she had twice confronted a cold glare. My father was equally inhospitable in greeting her, but his real attention was captured by Steldor, who was sleeping peacefully, though obviously still weak. Galen had dozed off as well, slumped sideways while still propped against the wall near his friend, but Cannan did not rouse him.

"What is wrong with Steldor?" my father asked, probably thinking illness since a shirt now covered his torso, concealing the last of his bandages.

"He was wounded," Cannan said, leaving out any hint of the strife we had experienced. "He's on the mend now." He cast a glance toward Nantilam, who still stood stiffly in the background, hands bound, Halias on alert next to her. "We have the High Priestess to thank for that."

"Not that she would have assisted willingly," Halias muttered, but she bowed her head toward the captain in appreciation of his acknowledgment.

Sleep that night came more easily than I would have anticipated, likely because I was so deprived of rest by this point that my body craved it. But with sleep came dreams—dreams filled with tortured screams, and visions of pain reflected in a pair of familiar indigo eyes, which always blurred into cold emerald green. When I snapped awake, it was morning, and shafts of sunlight chased away some of the gloom in the chilly cave—still the screams continued.

Only Temerson, my mother and my sister remained asleep, and it wasn't until I staggered to my feet that I realized the cries were real. They were a mere echo, so faint I had thought them to be inside my head, but as I took in the grim expressions and sympathetic eyes that had fallen on me, I bolted for the opening.

I moved too quickly for anyone to stop me, but Cannan followed, taking me by the arm to try to lead me back inside. It was too late. The screams were louder once I was free of the cavern's enclosed walls, the suffering within them magnifying their effect.

"What is that?" I asked, even though I was certain of the answer.

I stared at Cannan, my eyes watering, waiting for him to say the words, to confirm what I already knew. He was as frank as ever.

"We sent Galen earlier this morning to investigate. It is London. The Overlord has brought him higher into the mountains so the sound will reach us wherever we are. Go back inside, Alera, it's better if you try to ignore it."

"Ignore it?" I shrieked, not caring about my volume. I jerked away from him, feeling as though I might go mad. "How can you say that? How can you s…? How can you…?"

I was gasping for air, my sentences lost between sobs. Cannan again took my arm to lead me inside, but I planted my feet.

"After everything he's done for us, he doesn't deserve this. He doesn't deserve this, it isn't *fair.*"

Another scream rent the air, encircling us, but this time I acquiesced to Cannan, letting him take me back into the cave.

"It's a time of war, Alera," he said, putting an arm around my shoulders, guiding me toward the others who had gathered around the fire pit. "Nothing is fair, and nothing is right, and it isn't easy to understand or accept. But we haven't lost yet. London made sure of that."

CHAPTER 28
MY NAME IS LONDON

FOR DAYS IT WENT ON, BEGINNING EVERY morning when we awoke, and lasting until London presumably could stand the agony no more and fell unconscious, usually after a few hours. It was unbearable, but impossible to block out, affecting everyone, even the High Priestess. With a rescue attempt sure to fail and likely to endanger our people within the city, Temerson finally voiced his dark thoughts.

He set down his bowl of gruel none too gently at breakfast, letting it clatter, and pressed both palms against his temples, fingers in his overgrown cinnamon-brown hair, rocking back and forth. Galen was out on guard duty, and Temerson would soon be replacing him.

"Can't we just end it—just take his life? This has gone on long enough, I can't stand it anymore."

"Who among us could do it?" Halias asked from where he stood near Nantilam. "Call it a mercy killing, and a mercy killing it would be—I still couldn't aim an arrow at London's heart."

Cannan interjected before any more pointed words could be spoken.

"We need to divert the Overlord's attention. It's time we act again, repeat our original demands. We have to show him we are not playing."

"What do you suggest?" My father, like Temerson, had lost his appetite and was pacing in front of the fire pit, wringing his hands.

"He doesn't believe we'll do it."

The voice was quiet, scratchy, but unmistakable. Steldor had awoken and was propped up on his elbows to join the conversation. His eyes were still shadowed by circles, but he was fast growing restless, although with health this time instead of fever.

"Take it easy," Cannan told him, moving closer, but Steldor shook his head.

"He doesn't believe we'll kill her. He's having his fun, torturing London, without even considering what consequences might result for his sister. He thinks we're soft." Steldor's jaw clenched as he locked eyes with his father, angry and determined. "Take a hand for him. See how soft he finds us then."

I caught the arch of the High Priestess's eyebrows and my father's sharp intake of breath as my stomach clenched. The captain's eyes narrowed but in consideration rather than outrage, and Halias rubbed the back of his neck. Could they actually be deliberating this? I could never permit them to *cut off her hand.*

Steldor grimaced, and his father cautioned, "You should lie back down. You don't have your strength back yet."

"Not his strength, but his brain," Halias pronounced, while Steldor dropped back with the tiniest bit of exasperation for the state of his body. I stared at the blond-haired deputy captain, who had been Miranna's bodyguard since birth, whose blue eyes were generally kind, who was known for both his competence and his generous, easygoing nature, and wondered what had brought him to the point where he would endorse such a suggestion. Was the Overlord managing to change us all, to remake us in his own image?

"I did save your King's life, if you recall," Nantilam interjected, making a good point. "I have thus far been cooperative—try to take my hand, and you will see how that changes."

"If it came to it, we would not need your cooperation," the captain replied, eyes flashing.

Though she spoke the truth, she was still our prisoner and a Cokyrian, not one of us.

"Please, no," I mumbled, taking a deep breath to dispel my queasiness. "You can't do that. You can't cut off her hand. We may be at war, but we can still be humane."

"The Overlord scoffs at humane, Alera." Steldor, though he had taken his father's advice, was not interested in keeping his opinions to himself. "If we want his attention, we have to respond in kind."

"Perhaps you're tired," the High Priestess said sharply, and I could feel ire rising inside me, both because of the cruelty of his suggestion and because his argument, though I did not want to admit it, made sense.

"So we have to become like him in order to fight him," I harshly concluded. "We have to be malicious and heartless and sink to this sort of violence in order to stop it. Is that what you're saying?"

"That's exactly what I'm saying." Steldor had pushed himself up on his elbows again to scowl at me. "Think of it like a language, Alera. He won't understand unless we speak his."

I wrung my hands, floundering, but Cannan interrupted the two of us.

"I believe I told you to lie down," he said to his son before turning to me. "Alera, try not to get emotional. No decisions have been made." Then he walked toward the cave entrance. "Halias, I need to speak to you alone."

Halias nodded curtly, casting his eyes over Temerson, my father and the High Priestess. Probably deciding she was more capable militarily than any of those who would be left to watch her, he stooped to tie Nantilam's hands in front of her.

"Keep your eyes on the prisoner," he instructed, glancing around at us. "We'll be right outside if she tries anything." This last sentence was meant as a warning for our captive. With one last check of her bindings, Halias followed his captain, and I suspected they had gone to continue the conversation without our input.

Still annoyed with Steldor, I turned toward the fire, spotting a plate of food that Cannan had readied for him. I picked up the goblet of water beside it and surreptitiously dumped out its contents, refilling it with wine to which I knew crushed oak had been added. It was probably wrong, but a little herb-induced sleep certainly wouldn't hurt him.

I carried the goblet to him and pushed it into his hand, intending to walk back to retrieve the generously filled plate, but he grasped my wrist.

"Your hair…" he slowly said, brow furrowed. "It's…"

"Short," I finished, reaching up self-consciously to rake my fingers through it.

"It looks fine," he said, and I knew, for him, that was quite a compliment, for he had always loved to play with my long locks.

"Drink," I suggested, and he obliged, unsuspecting. I

waited a few minutes, then retrieved the plate of food, handing the dish to the High Priestess instead, who, like Steldor, had not yet eaten. She glanced at my husband, for whom she knew the food had been intended, slightly puzzled. As she registered his increasingly drowsy state, she nodded to me, deducing what I'd done.

London's screaming had died off, but as I scrutinized Nantilam, I could still hear its echoes in my mind. It was obvious she could, too, for her somber expression was a reflection of my own.

"I do not commend my brother's actions, Hytanican Queen," she said, letting her spoon drop on the plate she was balancing on her knees as she finished the meal. I took the plate from her, wondering if she would say more.

"But by taking me captive, you both gave yourselves leverage and freed him of my control. There remains no one who can inhibit him."

The air left my lungs at her words, taking with it the coldness I felt toward her.

"You don't believe he desires you back." Panic was slowly rising, for if he did not want her back, we had no negotiating position.

"Admittedly, a part of him does not. But the dominant part remembers how he needs me, and that he is not the rightful ruler of Cokyri. He also has affection for me, if you would believe him capable of it."

The notion was hard to entertain, but I did not have time to consider it.

"There is a story that should be told, to you alone," Nantilam went on. "You will come to need it most. Sit, if you would hear it."

I stole a look at the others—Steldor, sleeping; my father on his feet, frowning at us from across the cave, not liking my proximity to the High Priestess; my mother and my sister huddled close together by the fire; Temerson near them staring at the crackling wood.

"Talk," I acquiesced, sitting down across from her, heart pounding, though I had no inkling of what to expect.

Nantilam nodded, wasting no time in beginning, for our chance to converse would end as soon as Halias and Cannan returned.

"My mother was the leader of Cokyri, its proud and strict Empress," she said, her voice that of a storyteller. "She alone had been gifted with the divine right to command and punish, and to bless and reward—this magic, of both the dark and light sides, had been passed only from mother to daughter for generations, creating a natural assumption among the Cokyrian people that women were fit to rule while men were not.

"When the time came for my mother to give birth to an heir, something unexpected happened. She gave life to not one child, but two—a boy and a girl. The magic which had been meant for me was split, half going to me and half going to my brother. As we grew and were taught to handle our powers, it became evident that the magic had divided evenly, so that I had no power akin to his and he had no power akin to mine. We were Chaos and Creation, Life and Death. He was Warlord and I was merciful Empress. But an Empress I could not truly be, for I did not on my own possess the full power necessary to govern Cokyri. It was, therefore, determined by my mother that my brother would rule beside me. I was destined to become the High Priestess Nantilam, greatly admired and respected for my political actions and dealings with the affairs of the people, while my brother would become the Overlord Trimion, protecting our lands and leading us to war and victory using the ultimate weapon—his gift for death.

"Ten years after our birth, while my mother was Empress still, a man came to Cokyri, introducing himself as Prince Rélorin of Hytanica, an ambassador sent by his father, the King, to propose a trade treaty between Hytanica and Cokyri. He was no more than a child and a fool, and when he was brought before my mother, his bigotry overcame his reason. He refused to discuss the matter with a woman and his disrespect left my mother with no choice but to end his life and thereby reject the treaty.

"Naturally, the Hytanican King was not pleased at word of his son's death, and viewed my mother's actions as ruthless murder. But our forces were strong, and when the Hytanicans attacked, we drove them back.

"By the time my brother and I were fifteen, we had assumed our positions as Overlord and High Priestess. My brother grew increasingly frustrated as the years passed, and your people would not be defeated. There was no logical explanation for the way triumph eluded us, but we continued to fight this violent war for nearly one hundred years, finding ourselves incapable of victory. My powers of life and healing kept both of us vibrant and able, so though we were almost a century old, we appeared the same as we had in our youth."

The beautiful woman before me, her skin tanned and flawless, her hair red as cherrywood, had been alive since before the beginning of the Cokyrian War. I knew by the Overlord's cruel demonstrations that his powers were great, but the High Priestess had been born with a blessing…the ability to give and keep life. Her regality was overwhelming, her gift leaving no question as to why she had the love and respect of her people. For whatever it signified, Hytanica had never had a ruler like her.

Nantilam fell silent for a moment, lost in her memory, and I sensed she was about to segue into a significant element of her tale.

"Many years later, a large battle took place in which the Cokyrians greatly outnumbered the Hytanicans. Your people retreated, leaving behind their dead. As our soldiers collected the bodies of their fellow warriors, my brother walked his horse to the place where he had seen a particular Hytanican fall, a soldier of high rank, the one who had ordered the retreat. The way this Hytanican man had waited bravely until the last had reawakened questions within Trimion's mind that had for years been dormant. What was the secret to the Hytanicans' strength? Why could he not defeat them when the odds were in his favor?"

My mind was spinning, recalling the history that I had been taught concerning Hytanica's conception. According to ancient lore, Hytanica's first King, seeking to protect his foundling home, had been advised by his priests that a sacrifice of blood both royal and innocent would hallow the ground and make his kingdom invincible. The King had then taken the life of his own infant son, placing drops of the boy's blood at each corner of the land in order to shield the people he loved. But was this more than lore? Had some long-forgotten blood magic made our forces strong?

"My brother found the soldier lying on his side, blood flowing steadily from the gash across his abdomen, his silver hair falling over his blank, pale face. My brother saw the man grimace in pain, and when his warriors informed him that the bodies had been collected and that they would depart at his word, my brother lifted the wounded man, determining to take him to Cokyri."

She was reciting this as though it were a mere story, reinventing every moment for effect. But in her voice I could hear shreds of regret, of questioning, the proof that this was no work of fiction. It came to me along with the realization of the young soldier's identity that this was an encounter to which she had given much thought.

"He was strong," the High Priestess resumed. "I healed him as soon as my brother brought him to me, and by the next day, Trimion had begun to question him, beginning by demanding his name.

"The young officer's hands were tied before him, and he knelt on the stone floor of my brother's hall. When he refused to speak, my brother extended his arm to encourage him with pain. As Trimoin's power struck him, he fell forward, catching himself with his forearms, his body convulsing. Amidst his screams, a whisper escaped his lips. 'London,' he gasped. 'My name is London.'"

The High Priestess met my eyes, which were wide with sorrow and anger. I was terrified of the dark places her next words might explore. All the things London had never revealed to anyone, not even Destari, all his experiences in Cokyri, were within the mind of this woman and upon her lips. Could I withstand hearing what horrors had befallen my bodyguard and friend? *You will come to need it most,* Nantilam had said about this telling, and, bracing myself, I swore I would not risk that she was right.

"That was the first I knew of him," she divulged. "When my brother laughed at his quick answer, saying that he clearly did not hold much close to his heart, London swore he would not betray his kingdom. Trimion was delighted. It was a game to him and, the more defiant the prisoner, the more enjoyable it would be to see him fall. And my brother had made so many fall.

"Yet through weeks of merciless torture, London proved resistant. The only thing he would tell us was what we had learned upon his first questioning—his name. Every night, I would visit his cell in the dungeon and heal him enough to prepare him for more punishment, but as time passed, even I could not fully restore him. The Overlord's power pulsed inside of him, unable to dispel as long as more entered to block its escape. His body became a battleground for our magic, my healing force fighting Trimion's powers of destruction.

"'He is useless,' my brother announced to me after nearly five months. 'Then let him die,' I advised, hoping he would agree, for London had borne far more than had any other prisoner. Trimion's eyes were devoid of sympathy as he vowed, 'Not until I break him.'

"For two months following, the vile pattern continued. My brother would torment him for hours, and I would heal him so he could not escape into death. I stood aside and observed, day after day, as Trimion growled, 'Ask for death, London, and I will give it to you. Beg me to kill you, and it will all be over.' Despite his ordeal, London managed audacity again and again. 'It appears that you are the one who is begging,' he would mutter. And my brother would make London scream more loudly and more terribly than ever I had heard animal or human scream before.

"After eight weeks of this, Trimion reached a decision that shocked me. 'Never before has anyone resisted me in such a manner,' he seethed, though beneath his fury resided a measure of respect. 'I know not what to do with him, except to end his life.'

"'What if I were to heal him once more?' I ventured, for another use for London had occurred to me. 'A man with such impressive will is seldom seen, and it seems a shame to waste his life.'

"My brother was curious and suspicious. 'You lust after the boy,' he jeered, but I met his mocking gaze coldly. 'His spirit is remarkable. I do not desire him for any other purpose than to have his blood run in the veins of my child—for his fortitude to be passed to *our* heir.'

"Trimion contemplated me for a time, then assented, unable to deny that London had impressed him. I ordered our prisoner brought to my temple, where he was given quarters on the second floor, with a wide window overlooking the city. It would be a long time before he would become aware of the view, but I hoped sunlight in the wake of those dark months he'd spent in the dungeon would help him recover. I began to heal him, several times a day at first, for the serenity I could provide was easily eclipsed by the flood of dark magic that hid within him.

"Had he been anyone else, anyone weaker, he would have died, but though he did not wake for weeks, he clung to life with incredible determination. Often, he screamed and wept, the pain reaching him even in sleep, and I feared that, although I had thus far managed to save his body, there might be no way to rescue his mind.

"It was during this time that my brother's frustration reached its peak, for he had thought London would provide answers to his questions about the Hytanicans' invulnerability. He set his scribes to work searching for anything that might enlighten him, and they spent innumerable hours poring through obscure and ancient texts. Then a legend was discovered—"

"The Legend of the Bleeding Moon," I interrupted, wanting her to know she did not have to detail it for me, and she nodded her head.

"Had but a few more days passed, the prophecy would have been useless. The bleeding moon was predicted for the end of that very season. But my brother rejoiced at our fortunate timing and acted upon the information, kidnapping your newborns in search of the right one. And as usual, when he went out into the fields of battle, he entrusted his ring to me, the twin to which I wear."

Her hand flicked upward to show the royal ring she bore on her first finger.

"I strung it on a necklace and gave it not another thought until..."

She shook her head, recognizing that she was getting ahead of herself.

"London started improving, after a while. A single dose of my healing force would sustain him for longer periods of time, and along with this progression came consciousness. He was exhausted, still delirious to some extent, but he had grown to recognize my presence, and, I believed, to associate it with relief. When I came, the pain stopped—when I left, it was only a matter of time before it resumed.

"I wanted him to appreciate what I'd done, perhaps be in my debt. I stayed with him more than I needed to and did more for him than was necessary—my attendants would have kept him company and provided for him in my stead had I desired to be elsewhere. But he was fascinating to me, so unlike the Cokyrian men I knew."

Her obvious attraction to London was reminding me strangely of what had drawn me to Narian, with one exception: Narian had returned my affection. I knew from the looks London had aimed at the High Priestess here in the cave that there was no room in his heart for her.

"He spent ten months in Cokyri, and that time was coming to an end," the High Priestess continued. "He awoke one day and we spoke for the first time, though he was still to my knowledge not completely himself. In the end, I was so near to him I could not stop myself—I kissed him, and he momentarily responded—I did not even notice when he removed the necklace that bore my brother's ring. As he drifted off again, I turned and left.

"When next I came to see him, just a few hours later, he was gone. The window was open, a horse was stolen and he had disappeared. I had underestimated his cleverness, for he was further recovered than I or my attendants had suspected, and I had been careless in providing him with such a simple exit. He knew exactly how long he had before the pain would again incapacitate him, and it was just time enough to travel to Hytanica if he rode hard. He had escaped with much knowledge my brother and I never wanted revealed to your people."

"When he returned, he was…ill," I said, not sure if sickness was the best way to describe it. "Was that because of…?"

"Our conflicting forces were still at work within him. Your doctors would have been dumbfounded—the symptoms would have been unrecognizable. It was long before I heard word that London had survived. I had feared for him, but my magic must have been in greater quantity than my brother's when he'd made his departure. It is because of the remaining embers of my power that it is taking so long for him to die at Trimion's hand—he heals when he should not, fights forces for days that should kill him in minutes. He has not appeared to age over the last eighteen years because my magic preserves him. He will have a much extended life, if my brother does not kill him."

"How long does he have?" I asked, feeling as though scattered pieces I had gathered myself over the years were at last coming together into a coherent picture. The mystery of London was resolved, sadly just in time for him to die.

"Two days, maybe three. Then my power will have been depleted trying to contest the effects of my brother's."

"And..." I paused, knowing my next query was irrelevant but wanting to say it anyway. "And if we let you go, will he be spared?"

"My brother will have his revenge upon London," she told me softly. "No matter what. Your friend is no longer part of the bargain."

I rubbed my face with my hands, my mind overwhelmed by the abundance of information she had provided, but knowing the story was important for some reason. What could it be?

"Hytanican Queen," she said, and my gaze again found her beautiful countenance, those intense and intelligent green eyes. "You are different from most females of your culture and are underestimated even now—by everyone, I hope, except me."

This statement was maddening and puzzling, but I did not have time to respond. Cannan and Halias reentered the cave, the moderate volume of their speech seeming amplified as it jarred me out of my confused thoughts and drew my attention away from the woman with whom I sat.

"Temerson, take over for Galen," Cannan ordered, motioning the young man out the door to relieve the Sergeant at Arms of guard duty.

"And what did you decide?" my father asked, still on his feet, occasionally pacing.

The captain did not respond in words, but his significant glance in my direction was enough to confirm my fears. I rose to my feet, my skin clammy.

"Not now," Cannan said, his eyes still on me, and I understood that he meant there would be no severing of appendages at this precise moment.

No matter how much I detested the idea of cutting off the High Priestess's hand, I could not stand in Cannan and Halias's way. Perhaps, as the High Priestess had said, I was unlike other women from my kingdom, but it was to my kingdom that my loyalty belonged—I would not stand against my friends to protect my enemy.

CHAPTER 29

THE DEAD & THE DYING

NANTILAM HAD MEANT TO TELL ME SOMETHING beyond the obvious, but what? For hours, my battered brain floundered. In my mind I repeated all that she had told me, in as much detail as I could manage. That afternoon, as Galen sharpened the weapons, the sound was heavy with significance, and it grated upon my ears, distracting me. I lay back upon the furs that formed my bed, trying to block it out. *Empress, daughter born, magic passed, twins, Overlord embittered, London captured, tortured, healed again and again…London's escape, ageless, practically immortal…* Shaking my head, I began again, more slowly, considering the key words. *Empress, daughter born, magic passed, twins…*

At the negotiation meeting with the High Priestess before Hytanica's fall, London had been captured again and taken back to Cokyri, without the Overlord ever knowing. He had been hidden in the High Priestess's temple…now I knew why. But how did that help me?

Empress, daughter born, magic passed…

I sat up abruptly as a flame lit within my mind. I stumbled

to my feet and hurried to kneel at the High Priestess's side, ignoring Halias's alarmed expression.

"If you had a daughter, what would happen to your power and your brother's?"

"Alera, what are you—" the Elite Guard started, but I held up a hand for him to wait.

"No one knows," Nantilam answered, her green eyes intense, a sign that I was perhaps getting close. "There has never before been a case like ours. But however the magic will pass, it should belong to my daughter."

"You believe—your brother believes—that when you have a daughter, all the power from both of you will transfer to her," I finished, beginning to smile. I did not wait for a response, instead running to the back of the cave for parchment and a quill.

"Alera, what is going on?"

It was my father this time who put forth the question, sounding thoroughly appalled by my unladylike behavior.

"We must deliver another message to the Overlord," I announced, turning to meet each man's gaze individually—Galen still sitting with sharpened sword in hand; Cannan beside his son, who had once again struggled up on his elbows to gape at me; Halias monitoring the High Priestess; and my father offering a blanket to my chilled mother and sister. I explained my idea in further detail, leading up to my final conclusion.

"We will tell him his sister is pregnant, and that unless he releases the Hytanican people at once, including London, we will disappear with her."

"Will he believe it?" Halias asked.

"He doesn't have to believe it," I said, quill in hand, having opted to pen the message myself. "He just has to fear it."

★ ★ ★

When it came time to decide who would carry the message to the Overlord, Temerson surprised us all by volunteering.

"I want to help," he simply said.

I shifted awkwardly, as did the others. Temerson was not yet a man, his stability was still in question, and we unanimously doubted he would be able to approach the ruler who had murdered his father before his eyes. Yet no one wanted to tell him this.

"Boy, you are helping," Halias tried, speaking for us all.

"No." Temerson was unexpectedly strident. "I've seen too much to still be a boy. And I want to see the bastard's face when he reads what Queen Alera has to say."

This stunned us into silence, for prior to recent events, the idea of such a statement coming from Temerson's mouth would have made any of us laugh. Now, however, not so much as a chuckle was heard. Eventually, the captain spoke up, as usual the most decisive of us all.

"Galen will go with him." *Just in case,* rang through my head, but it was practical anyway, as the sergeant knew where the Overlord had been bringing London as a result of his scouting. "He'll wait while Temerson delivers the message."

The two young men left early the following morning, Temerson clasping the parchment I had signed. They wanted to be in place before the Overlord arrived, in the hope of saving London from the day's ordeal. We knew the mission had been successful even before they returned, for no screams echoed through the mountains. When Temerson and Galen were back among us, they confirmed that the message had indeed affected the Overlord—he had retreated at once to our city, taking London with him. All that remained was to wait.

★ ★ ★

And a long wait it became. Days passed, confidence waned, tempers flared and uncertainty was rife. Halias went to observe the city in case the Overlord acquiesced to our demands, but no word came from him. We all felt the possibility of defeat gnawing at us; if something did not happen soon, we would have no choice but to disappear as we had threatened.

"He is searching for some other way to secure my release," the High Priestess told us, the only person in the cave who seemed unperturbed. "There is no alternative, of course. He will do exactly what you want, in the end."

"Why are *you* offering reassurance?" Galen griped from where he was standing near Steldor, flipping his dagger over and over in his hand. He looked agitated, recently his constant frame of mind.

"I am ruthless in war," Nantilam informed him. "I do what I must to secure victory. But whether you would believe it or not, I understand mercy. Conquered, your people would have come to no harm at my hands. That is the Overlord's doing, for he thrives on pain. My greatest challenge when I am released will be controlling him."

Galen glowered at her, not appreciating her talk of his countrymen being conquered.

"You're right about one thing," he spat. "I don't believe you."

He then exited the cave with Steldor, who was weak but back on his feet. Restless by nature, my husband had taken to spending some time each day outside the cave, seeking fresh air and sunlight, but he always stayed close, for he did not yet have the stamina to handle weapons.

It was Galen and Steldor who announced Halias's return.

"He's back!" they exclaimed, slipping into the cave in

midmorning. Temerson was out on watch, Cannan was guarding the High Priestess, and the rest of us were gathered around the fire pit. "Halias is coming!"

We all stood, staring at the entrance, and it seemed as if no one took breath as we waited for the news Halias would bring. The moment had at last come when we would learn whether we had gained a small victory. It wasn't long before the deputy captain entered, panting from the haste he had made.

"He's opened the gates," Halias gasped, glancing around at us all. "He's done what we asked. Our people are walking free."

Jubilant shouts broke out, and relief swept through us like a gust of spring air. I shifted my gaze to the High Priestess, who wore a self-satisfied expression, then returned my attention to Halias, who was shaking his head incredulously as he tried to catch his breath, leaning forward with hands upon his knees. I could not imagine how it must have looked, thousands of people—most of our citizens—filing out the front gates to travel as one across the countryside.

"Miraculous!" my father exclaimed, amid the excited voices of the others, but the Elite Guard had more to share.

"The Overlord has men waiting for us at the clearing, and London is with them. They will summon their commander when we come with the High Priestess."

"Is London still alive?" I asked, my heartbeat thudding dully in my ears.

"I think so." Halias's eyes went to Cannan, expecting an opinion on his next statement. "We might be able to save him."

The captain gave the assertion due consideration, and I waited nervously for his decision.

"If he can last awhile longer, we may be able to do so," he

said. "But I think it would be best not to meet the Overlord until the majority of the people have left our lands." His keen eyes flicked to Nantilam as he added, "To prevent him from going back on his word."

Halias nodded, then Cannan sent Galen to oversee the evacuation and to designate leaders to take the civilians west. Steldor would have liked to have accompanied his best friend but did not need his father to tell him he was not yet ready for a cross-country trek.

Hours went by, not enough time to get everyone out of the Overlord's reach, but our unease was growing as we pictured London still within the ruthless warlord's clutches. When Cannan thought we had risked our enemy's patience as far as we dared, Halias tied the High Priestess's hands in front of her and blindfolded her. If things went wrong, the captain, always cautious, did not want Nantilam to be able to lead the way back to our hideout. Halias then held the reins of her horse as he, Cannan and I settled on our respective mounts, and we began the trek to take our captive to her brother. Steldor watched us go, recognizing not only his physical limitations, but also that I was the one who had started all of this and should therefore be the one to finish it. He and I had not talked much since his recovery, but his actions told me he viewed me with newfound respect.

This particular journey felt like the longest of them all, even longer than the night we had fled to the cave. Every step was weighted with fear and inevitable mistrust, for Cokyrians were, above all else, notorious for their deceit. There was faith and expectation as well, for though we were abandoning our homeland, our people would be free, leaving open the possibility of establishing a new Hytanica.

The Overlord had already arrived by the time we walked warily into the clearing. Although the snow was melting and

I could feel a warm breeze ruffling my hair, a sign of the approaching spring, the warlord's presence cast a pall over everything, draining hope from my very soul. I closed my eyes, trying to shake the feeling.

Narian was once more with his master and was supporting London under the arms. I studied the young man closely, the face I had worshipped, the neck I had kissed, searching for a sign that he was the same boy with whom I had fallen in love. When his keen blue eyes connected with mine, I had my answer, for they were not the cold eyes into which I had gazed at the bridge, and the concern within them was unmistakable. Whether Narian stood by Cannan or by the Overlord, he still stood with me.

London was limp, head falling forward onto his chest, and I wondered if we were swapping Nantilam for a corpse. Cannan pulled the High Priestess in front of him, using her as a shield against the warlord's power, and was pressing a knife to her throat. He was poised to kill her, if it came to that, and did not want to give her brother any possibility of preventing it.

"I have kept my part of the bargain," the Overlord stated frostily. "Return my sister to me."

"London first," I replied at once, my voice firm. "We have a longer history of honor than Cokyri can claim."

He stared at me disdainfully, then motioned to Narian to drag the deputy captain forward.

"Drop him," he commanded when Narian had crossed half the distance to us.

Although Narian probably would have waited for Halias to approach so he could make a gentler transfer, he obeyed his master without hesitation, letting London fall hard to the ground and taking several steps back. When Halias reached his fellow Elite Guard's still form, he lifted him under the arms, hauling him past us into the trees.

"Now, my sister," the Overlord demanded, and Cannan lifted away his knife. He cut through the ropes binding Nantilam's hands, then removed her blindfold and shoved her forward. She regained her balance quickly and strode, as dignified as ever, back to the side on which she belonged, Narian turning to walk slightly behind her.

"We're done here," the captain announced, wary now that the Overlord had no cause for reservations about harming us. He and I started backing away from the enemy toward the shelter of the trees, where Halias waited with London.

"Are we?" The Overlord clasped his hands behind his back, an unsettling smirk playing across his lips, his very expression an unspoken threat. "I had thought we would get to know each other better."

"Alera, go," Cannan ordered. "Now."

I could feel the captain tense beside me in anticipation of trouble. I glanced at Narian, whose posture had changed, telling me he also was on alert.

"Yes, Alera, go," the Overlord taunted. "Flee like a coward and leave your captain behind, just as he fled and left his brother behind. Or prove yourself a worthy queen and stay to face me."

Even though I knew I should listen to Cannan, I stayed in place, my body shaking with fear but my heart smoldering with rage. I thought of Baelic and Destari and our other felled soldiers. I thought of Miranna and my mother and their bruises, both of body and spirit. I looked into Narian's eyes, knowing the good soul that resided within, in spite of the Overlord's efforts to pervert him, and I recalled London's courage as he had confronted this evil shell of a man.

Then I straightened my back and met the Overlord's gaze, unwilling to run and tired of hiding.

"You have been bothersome to me," the Overlord said, his voice soft and dangerous. "I have had my fun with the others, punished them all. I destroyed your military and tortured your captain's brother. The deputy captain who accompanied you here today endured more at my hands than he will ever say. The boy who hides with you, I killed his father. And London has felt pain a hundred times more agonizing than you can ever imagine. But you…you have escaped me, thus far."

"I have felt the pain of every one of my people," I returned, anger masking my terror.

"Then your suffering must be intolerable. Death will be a welcome release."

I saw the alarm on Narian's face moments before infernal fire ripped through me, scorching me, blistering me. But it was beneath my skin where I could not see it or touch it or smother it. My vision went black, and all I knew was burning, burning…screams were futile but could not be withheld; still they seemed muted, far off, as though they came from someone other than myself. On some level, I believed that the ground had opened and I had plummeted into hell.

Then the pain stopped, leaving me trembling and weak. I lay on the cold earth, Cannan beside me, struggling to his knees, and I realized he had tried to protect me, only to bear the same fate as had I from the Overlord's wave of magic. Pushing myself into a sitting position, I strained my eyes to find our enemy, wanting to know the reason he had not killed me, or if he yet would, having granted a small stay of execution. But it was not the Overlord who captured my attention; it was Narian, for he was standing between his master and me, his body shaking as he intercepted the attack.

The Overlord let his hand fall. Narian was still on his feet, stronger than were we, the moments of torment he had endured not enough to send him crashing to the earth. He straightened his shoulders as he challenged his master, and I read disbelief in the Overlord's countenance, followed by ever increasing wrath.

"Move," the warlord ordered. Narian shook his head, fists clenching. Incensed, the Overlord stalked forward and seized his troop commander, tossing him aside with a terrifying snarl. Narian slammed into the ground, and Cannan shielded me with his body as our adversary prepared to once more make me scream.

It was not I who cried out, however, but the Overlord, for Narian had stretched out his hand and seemed to have turned the master's spell upon the master himself, proving that Cannan had been right about the young man's power and his training. It did not last long, for the Overlord threw aside the magic just as easily as he had thrown aside my protector, having cried out less from pain than from astonishment. Regardless, the young man who had once promised he would never hurt me had succeeded, for his master's menacing countenance was no longer fixed on me.

Narian had infuriated him—that much was clear, for the Overlord no longer desired to use magic but his own brute strength. He advanced on Narian, grabbing his shirt and hauling him to his feet. Scowling down at the young man whom he had trained, he viciously backhanded him across the face, sending him sprawling once more, and I could not stifle a small, terrified shriek.

"You are no longer necessary to me, Narian," the Overlord growled. "That is reason enough for me to kill you. If you interfere again, I will most certainly do so."

I caught sight of the blood smeared across Narian's cheek, courtesy of his master's ring, which I realized must have been reclaimed from London.

"Then you had better get on with it. I will not let you attack her."

Without a word, the warlord drew his sword.

"Trimion!"

The High Priestess's voice resonated with disbelief and fury, and her brother turned his head, giving the downed man the moment he needed to kick the sword away. It disappeared in the undergrowth, and Narian wasted no time jumping to his feet.

"I need no sword to end you, whelp," the Overlord mocked, his now empty hand curling into a fist. With a fearsome cry, he threw his invisible magic toward his troublesome charge, who leapt aside, rolling once more to the ground to avoid falling victim to his master's powers.

"You say you need no sword," Narian gasped, poised on one knee to move quickly, "yet you need to keep me at a distance with your magic."

Lips pressed together, eyes narrowing, the Overlord walked forward to prove he bore no such cowardice. Narian came to his feet once more, drawing his sword. To my surprise, he did not ready the blade for an attack, but rather stuck the tip into the ground before him, presumably relinquishing the weapon as his master had none to match. The Overlord, smirking at the advantage his troop commander was sacrificing, obviously assumed the same, for he was caught off guard and knocked flat on his back when Narian gripped the hilt with both hands and used it to swing himself upward, planting his feet upon his master's chest in a forceful kick.

Narian landed smoothly and pulled his sword from the ground, but the Overlord was already recovering from the blow, coming to his knees. Nonetheless, Narian struck downward at him with the blade. I could see in his determined movement, his absolute concentration, that he dreaded what would happen if he lost the upper hand, but I wasn't certain it was his to lose. The warlord caught the sword with the metal bracer on his left forearm, deflecting it with a growl, then punched Narian with his right fist, sending him sprawling on his stomach.

Now standing, the Overlord halted Narian's attempt to rise by placing one foot upon the young man's back.

"Let's see how you defy me with a broken back, boy," he snarled, savoring his quarry's struggles to liberate himself.

I was breathing at an unnatural rate, my hand over my mouth, trying not to scream. *Oh, God, no, not his back. Get up, Narian, get up, somehow, please…* The Overlord lifted his foot slightly, preparing to slam it down, but Narian threw his right hand back and hit his master with the magic the Legend of the Bleeding Moon had granted him. As the Overlord stumbled away, Narian rose to his feet, spitting blood and not bothering to stem the stream coming from his nose.

The Overlord was seething. Having taunted his master about cowardice, the young man had made a hypocrite of himself in his master's eyes by utilizing sorcery himself. As the warlord's lip curled, I knew Narian was in even deeper trouble than he had been before. Narian knew it, too, for he had tried tenaciously to steer this fight away from the use of magic.

No longer constrained, the Overlord thrust his hand forward, but Narian dove out of the way, somehow managing to avoid what was invisible. He was close to his master again and swept the ruthless ruler's legs out from under him; then he drew the dagger from the sheath strapped to his forearm, lunging forward to stab in any way he could. But the warlord, impressively fast for his size, caught his hand, and I heard the cry that accompanied the snap of Narian's wrist before the Overlord threw him aside.

Rolling, Narian stumbled to his feet, cradling his broken wrist. I wondered how long this could possibly go on, how much more of a beating the man I loved could take, but as the Overlord started once more toward his adversary, the High Priestess called out to her brother for the second time.

"Trimion—leave him. He cannot fight you, it is over."

"No!" The Overlord turned on his sister, and I thought for a heartbeat that he would do her harm. "It is over when he is dead." Then he again focused his fearsome glower on Narian. "He has challenged me for the last time. He has flaunted his necessity again and again, but no more. His Hytanican blood will run on the ground, where he can see it and know how poorly it has served him."

It tortured me to see Narian in such a helpless position, but he was not nearly as helpless as I, pathetically standing on the sidelines. Somewhere in my heart I knew that, even with a powerful man like the captain beside me, interfering would be futile. Despite his exhaustion and pain, the young man refused to give in. When the Overlord drew perilously near, Narian bent forward and moved sideways into his master, whereupon the warlord lost his balance and flipped over his troop commander's back, crashing once more to the ground. Narian staggered away with as much haste as he could, but the Overlord's temper was quicker.

Bounding to his feet, the fearsome warlord extended his arm toward his prey. I screamed, unable to restrain myself.

This time Narian was powerless to evade the magic. The Overlord caught him with it, unrelenting as his charge fell to the ground, screaming and thrashing. I had endured this same power for mere moments and had wished for death; I could not wish death for Narian, but neither could I bear to see him suffer. I would beg if I had to, if I could. Cannan was restraining me, although he had ceased trying to make me leave, too entranced himself by the unfolding battle. Once Narian was dead, we would feel like fools for having wasted our chance to flee, but it was impossible to do so now.

The Overlord approached his quarry, hand still outstretched, to stand directly over Narian, glaring at the young man who writhed in agony at his feet. I was sobbing, but I gave little thought to myself. As a plea for mercy rose in my throat, Cannan's hand clamped over my mouth, halting my thoughtless, pointless action.

Narian curled into a ball as his master dropped his hand.

"You should not have challenged me, boy," he said, rolling his dazed victim onto his back with the toe of one boot. Pulling a dagger, he bent down, drawing Narian upward by his hair. He glanced at me where I stood in Cannan's arms, then spoke one last time to Narian.

"Unfortunate that your death will prevent you from witnessing hers."

I braced myself for the plunge of the dagger into Narian's exposed neck, for I could not tear my eyes away, but the warlord seemed to have frozen. Something had happened, something was making him hesitate, but the combatants were too close together to discern what it might be. Then the Overlord's hold on Narian's hair slipped, and our greatest enemy sank to his knees, his hands gripping the hilt of the dagger Narian had thrust into his gut. The warlord had been careless.

Narian crumpled once more, then crawled away, attempting to put distance between himself and his master. He managed a few feet before collapsing. The Overlord did not go after him but pulled the knife from his stomach with a grunt of pain, warm blood soaking his clothing and spilling onto his hands.

"Sister," he called. "Heal me."

Nantilam walked resolutely to him, then took the bloody dagger that had inflicted his wound. As she placed a comforting hand on his shoulder, he closed his eyes, trusting that she would care for him. He did not see her move behind him.

"I will weep for you, brother," she said softly, but there was no apology in her voice. Then she reached around him with the dagger and swept it across his throat.

His eyes sprang open in shock as he clutched at his neck, blood seeping between his fingers. He tried to speak, but what sound emerged was a guttural cough; he was choking. Slowly, he slumped sideways and fell onto his back, his body giving way briefly to spasms before he lost consciousness. Blood continued to flow from his wounds, staining the ground around him and robbing him of life.

CHAPTER 30

ONCE A KING

CANNAN AND I STARED AT THE HIGH PRIESTESS, too staggered to react. She stood in the center of the clearing with her eyes closed, dagger still in hand, breathing deeply as she composed herself. Halias was behind us at the line of trees, kneeling next to London, a measure of shock equal to ours upon his face. She had killed her own brother. I tried to imagine taking Miranna's life, but the act was incomprehensible to me. I had already shown myself incapable of sacrificing my sister, even to preserve my kingdom. Yet somehow this brutal act had proven Nantilam to be a more benevolent ruler than the Overlord, and, perhaps, I could ever have been. He had accomplished his purpose, then had lost control. She had seen him for what he was, understood that he was capable only of hate and destruction and had ended his life, for there was no more evil that needed doing. The Overlord's attempt on Narian's life had convinced her of this; she had tried to stop him, but he had refused to acknowledge her authority.

"Narian," I gasped, struggling against Cannan's arms. "Narian!" My strangled cry prompted the captain to let me go, and I stumbled across the clearing to the young man who had just saved my life. By the time I reached him, the High Priestess was kneeling beside him, as well.

He was on his side, unmoving, his thick blond hair cascading across his forehead, looking as dead as his master. Nantilam took his head in her hands, trying to rouse him, but he would not wake. At last she closed her eyes, going still with concentration, and I knew what she was attempting to do. Minutes passed, but still he did not respond. She released him, then turned to me, her brilliant green eyes resolute.

"We must take him back to the city, London as well, if we want them to survive. They both barely cling to life, and it will take much time and energy to heal them." As I considered this, she continued, "I will keep the bargain my brother struck, better than would he, and will let you depart, with London, when the time comes. But he will die if you don't come with me."

I gazed pleadingly at the captain. "Cannan, help us."

He came forward, his face inscrutable as he studied the High Priestess, though I could tell there was no trust.

"There is no time to delay," Nantilam said, meeting Cannan's eyes. "My brother's men will have been given orders should we not return within a certain time. Be assured, your people are yet in danger."

Despite her words, he did not obey; rather, he seemed to be considering our options.

"Do you understand me, Captain?" she demanded, as though Cannan were the head of her military and not ours.

"Alera, we can walk away now, try to help London on our own," Cannan said, ignoring the High Priestess. "If we return to the city with her, we may not be permitted to leave."

"You will be safe as long as you are with me," the High

Priestess responded, then she touched Narian's brow. "This boy must live, and I would save London, as well. Help me, and I give you my word that I will let you walk free."

Though Cannan did not speak, he turned to Halias and motioned for him to bring London forward, then he went into the trees to get our horses. I could see how difficult this was for the captain, for it was not in his nature to put faith in anyone labeled Cokyrian. The enemy had deceived us too many times during our century-long war, and I did not fault him for his lack of faith in the enemy ruler. It was easier for me to trust her; she had shown me the way to obtaining our people's freedom and had ended the tyranny of the Overlord.

Cannan returned with our mounts, then talked with Halias, giving him his orders. He and the deputy captain lifted Narian into the saddle of the horse the High Priestess had mounted, positioning him in front of her. Cannan and I likewise settled onto our mounts, then Halias helped to position London in front of the captain. Halias would not be coming with us but would ride back to the cave to inform the others of what was happening.

We rode toward the city, to be quickly met and surrounded by Cokyrian troops as we broke free of the forest. The sight of the black-clothed enemy troops so close around me was terrifying, and I hoped we had not been wrong to trust the High Priestess. At her command, the soldiers fell in beside us and behind us as escorts, and we galloped toward the crumbling stone walls that had once protected my people. We cantered up the cobblestone thoroughfare, my heart aching with the destruction that I saw to my left and right, and I was filled with dread at the thought of the condition in which we would find the palace. When it finally came into view, it looked like a poor imitation of itself. Just as had been the case with the walls of the city, the courtyard walls were crumbling in places, and Cokyrian soldiers freely trampled its once beautiful grounds.

We rode to the palace doors, between the lilac hedges that were now in ruins. The white stone path upon which horses had seldom trod was smeared with dirt and blood, and the hooves of our mounts could do no damage that had not already been done. As the soldiers in the courtyard recognized their ruler, they abandoned their endeavors and bowed before her, daunted by her return. Then glances were exchanged as they noticed our presence as well as the Overlord's absence.

The palace itself bore evidence of the Cokyrians' celebrations: the boards we had put in place across the windows had been torn off carelessly, gleefully, and many of the panes were broken. The Grand Entry and the first floor appeared to have been rampaged, though this was to some extent due to the number of our own people who had sought refuge there. Tapestries had been torn from the walls, broken furniture was cast about, and blood stained the floors. Much of the damage had likely been wrought for the pure sake of demonstrating dominance and power. I closed my eyes, not wanting to think of the state in which I might find some of the rooms, especially the Throne Room.

I led the men carrying London and Narian up to the third floor, knowing that this area was likely to be the least damaged, the High Priestess and the captain following behind. I struggled to keep my emotions in check as we proceeded, for images of those who had died haunted these halls. I could not conceive of what Cannan had to be feeling, here in the heart of enemy territory, where the lives of so many of his officers had been taken, including that of his brother.

After directing that the injured men be laid upon beds in

separate guest rooms, Nantilam dismissed her soldiers. She then went into Narian's room, and I followed, knowing that she would attempt to heal him. Cannan did not object, apparently having decided I would be safe in her company. He did not join us, however, preferring to stay with his downed man.

"I have to divide my power between London and him," Nantilam told me, pulling a chair next to Narian's bed. She sat down, then pressed two fingers against his throat, checking for a pulse.

"He's still alive," she murmured, and the relief in her voice was plain. I didn't know the nature of her relationship to Narian, but it was obvious she had affection for him.

Without another word, she placed her hands, one over the other, on Narian's chest and recommenced what she had barely begun in the clearing. After fifteen minutes, she forced herself from his side, even though he showed no apparent improvement.

She and I walked down the corridor to enter the room in which Cannan guarded his near lifeless deputy captain. Just as she had in Narian's room, she pulled a chair to the injured man's bedside, then laid her healing hands upon him. Cannan did not speak but hovered nearby. His manner reminded me of the attitude he had adopted when Steldor had almost succumbed to his horrendous wound and bespoke of the tremendous respect he had for the Elite Guard who had risked everything to defend the kingdom and the people he loved.

I took up residence in a room on the third floor, but Cannan chose to bed down with blankets on the floor in London's room. Having endured many hours and days of torture under the Overlord's hand, London was struggling more than Narian, and his recovery was far from certain.

Despite the High Priestess's assurances that we would be safe, we did not venture into other areas of the palace, not seeing any reason to jeopardize our necks among the enemy.

The High Priestess posted guards outside the doors of the men she was working to heal and sent servants to see to their other physical needs. She also sent members of her guard to transport her brother's body back to Cokyri, offering no explanation to her troops as to the cause of his death. I doubted the true story would ever be told, and that he would be glorified as the man who had conquered Hytanica. Neither Cannan nor I knew what the future might bring now that Nantilam was the sole ruler of Cokyri, but we had little choice other than to trust her. We had put our lives in her hands the moment we had decided to come here with London.

During the following days, Nantilam and I went back and forth between the rooms, checking on the two men for whom we both felt affection. Cokyrian servants had bathed them and replaced their grimy clothing with clean nightshirts, and they lay lightly covered on fresh bed linens, at times looking almost angelic, at other times writhing in agony. London, in particular, suffered greatly, and my thoughts kept returning to the information my mother had shared about how ill he had been eighteen years ago after surviving similar torture. As always, his will to live was impressive, but I feared this time willpower alone would not be enough. It was heartrending for me to see the two men I cared about the most in such torment. I longed to see a tease in the indigo eyes I knew so well, and a flicker of love in those of steel-blue that had captured my heart.

Narian began to stir first, his pain easing and his sleep becoming more peaceful. London, however, showed no signs of coming to consciousness. It was as though he were trapped beneath ice, his still-beating heart pounding in vain against the unyielding surface.

Cannan was becoming edgier, worried about those we had left behind in the cave, as well as the Hytanican people who had been evacuated almost a week ago. He told me in subtler terms that he wished to leave, afraid the enemy would cease to be so hospitable, but would not go without me. Nor did he want to depart without London. The High Priestess was certainly also aware of his thoughts, but it was to me that she spoke. I was in Narian's room with her at the time she put forth her proposal.

"Hytanican Queen," she said to me unexpectedly as she lifted her hands from Narian's chest, repositioning his arm upon the bed. "I have given much thought as to how to govern this kingdom and would propose an agreement with you, an accord. Hytanica is Cokyrian territory now. The vengeance we sought on behalf of my mother has been taken, and we have what we have long desired—access to the riches of your land. But I cannot oversee this province from the mountains."

I waited, pulse racing, for her to elaborate.

"I would permit your people to return here, to their homeland, without threat of enslavement. Persecution of your people was my brother's ambition, not mine. My interest has always been in your land and not in your citizens. These are the options I see—I can place a Cokyrian in command here to govern and oversee the division of yearly produce between your people and mine, or I can give your people a ruler they know and trust."

"Me?" I choked as I grasped her meaning.

She nodded. "Thoughts of rebellion will be inevitable from the moment your citizens reinhabit this land. You, they will be inclined to follow. Cokyri will, of course, maintain a presence in Hytanica, but I believe that with one of their own as the leader of this province, they will more readily accept this change."

"They will not follow me," I insisted, not eager to consider myself in such a position. "Steldor is the King."

"Steldor is not the King," she informed me without a beat of hesitation. "I will leave this place with a woman in charge. If you refuse, I will put one of my own commanders in power, someone who will flatten your revolts with ease and run Hytanica with a firm hand. It is a matter of how you would like your people to come to terms with their circumstances."

While I knew my kingdom was now hers, the proposal she was making as to how it should be governed was new and surprising, and I could not fathom it. A woman in a position of authority in Hytanica would not be happily accepted, but Hytanica would not be permitted its King or any male ruler.

"Is there no one else?" I asked, feeling ill-equipped to undertake this task.

"I do not make this offer lightly. It is you whom I have tested. It is you who have proven yourself equal to the task. I thus put the choice of ruler to you—yourself or a Cokyrian emissary."

"I—I need time to think," I stammered, even though I already knew what answer I would give. I had to do what would be best for my people, despite how much it scared me.

The High Priestess stood and left the room to check on London, and I took her seat next to the bed, resting my head in my hands, trying to understand how we had come to this point.

"Alera?"

My thoughts were interrupted by a strained, but familiar, voice. I lifted my head at once to see Narian staring at me, obviously uncertain if his eyes were playing tricks on him.

"I'm here," I said, reaching out to brush back the thick golden hair from his forehead, my throat tight. Even though I was overjoyed to see him awake, everything that had occurred, and the responsibility that was being thrust upon me, had left me on the verge of tears.

"What happened?" he asked, and I recalled how much he had missed. "Where is the Overlord? Where…are we?"

"We're in the Palace of Hytanica," I said, answering the easy question first. "The High Priestess brought us here after she…" I took a breath, wondering how much information he could handle, then went on regardless. "After you stabbed him, the Overlord called for his sister to heal him, but she… instead, she took his life."

He seemed to lose focus as he struggled to grasp what I had said, and I feared he was once more fading away.

"Narian," I urgently said, wishing I hadn't overwhelmed him, but this time when I reached out to touch his hair, he took my hand, entwining his fingers with mine.

"I'm sorry," he whispered, eyes half-closed, voice anguished. "I'm so sorry, Alera. I would not blame you if you hated me, after everything I've done."

"Let me tell you what you've done," I said, fighting to subdue the quaver in my voice. "You saved my sister. You did what you could to protect my people. You freed London from the High Priestess's temple. You saved my life. You defied the Overlord, in the end. Those are the things you've done."

"You give me too much credit," he said with a weak laugh, intense blue eyes capturing me. "There are things I should have done, should have prevented, and didn't."

I couldn't respond, could no longer see him through the tears clouding my vision, for he was feeling another type of pain—pain of a sort even the High Priestess could not lessen. But when I at last blinked my tears away, he had slipped from me once more.

I signed the High Priestess's accord the following day. It had been drafted by a high-ranking Cokyrian officer at Nantilam's dictation, and both Cannan and I read it carefully, knowing the moment I put my name on the parchment, Hytanica would be in my hands. Then I scrawled my signature across the bottom.

The captain returned to the cave, for the rest of our party of refugees had been in the dark for long enough and it was now safe for them to come out of hiding. As I waited for their return, I walked into the Throne Room for the first time since I had come back to the palace, wanting to see the damage before anyone else did. I advanced to the middle of the hall, then sank to the floor, needing to grieve what we had lost before I could embrace the future.

The Cokyrians had dragged the thrones to the floor, removing most of the jewels that had been mounted into the wood. My family's coat of arms lay broken against the stone, having been pulled from the wall behind the dais. The banners that had hung upon the wall had been burned. But most wrenching of all, the portraits of the Kings that had lined the sides of this mighty hall had been damaged, some beyond recognition.

This was Hytanica's history, my history, so treasured by us and treated so lightly by the enemy. Could I repair the hearts and minds of my people? Could we ever live contentedly under Cokyrian rule? I knew that the terms the High Priestess had imposed permitted a far better outcome than we had the right to expect, for it granted us some autonomy, but still it would be challenging for those who had lost so much to see it as a positive step.

I did not hear Cannan come through the doorway, but he drew my attention by clearing his throat.

"Everyone is here, Alera. They're all waiting for you in the Meeting Hall."

I stood and walked toward him, and he gave me a slight bow as I drew near.

"Things can be restored," he said, eyes flicking around the room. "I will never forget the Overlord's brutality, can never forget it. I will live with its reminders for the rest of my days. But still I appreciate the chance the High Priestess has given us, and I believe you have made the right decision. We have lost much, Alera, and we will mourn much, but then we will rebuild. We will do so in honor of those who gave their lives."

That evening, after we had all dined together on fare provided by the High Priestess, it was Steldor to whom I needed to speak. I was happy to see that most of his energy had returned in the week since I'd last seen him and that there was once more a passion for life within his dark eyes. We walked together to the Queen's Drawing Room, a place that would afford us privacy and had not been as heavily damaged as the other rooms on the first floor, leaving our friends and family to their rejoicing.

Looking out into the East Courtyard, at the fountain that had miraculously remained intact despite the upturned soil and thousands of rough boot prints that surrounded it, I explained the High Priestess's contract to him, hoping he would not view me as usurping his power. He stood beside me at the window, listening carefully to my words, but displaying no reaction until several minutes after I had finished.

"I did not return here expecting to be King, Alera," he at long last said, and while he did not smile, there was no anger in him either.

"You'll always be a king," I reminded him, for that was Hytanican tradition. *Once a king, always a king.*

"Take my word—the crown fits you better than it ever fit me." At my confused and anxious expression, he went on. "I'm a military man, Alera. I was meant to be the protector, not the protected. I'm happier in that capacity."

His eyes delved into mine, suddenly tender, and I knew there was more he intended to say.

"Halias told us what happened in the clearing. I am sorry for what you had to bear—by rights, it should have been me. And Narian…while certain things will never be forgotten, I will thank him for what he did, at the end."

He reached out to twirl a strand of my shortened hair around his finger, an affectionate gesture he had employed many times before, then stopped, looking at his hand.

"I suppose I should give you this," he mused, removing the royal ring and extending it to me.

"And I have something of yours," I returned, taking the signet from him and removing the wolf's head talisman from around my neck.

"I wondered what had happened to it," he said, bemused. "Thank you."

He examined the pendant for a moment, then pulled the betrothal band off his left hand, pressing it into my palm. Startled, I tried to speak, but he placed a finger over my lips, halting my words.

"Ours was a marriage of convenience," he reminded me, although there was sadness in his voice. "It's not convenient anymore, is it?"

He brushed my cheek, savoring this moment, then turned and walked away.

"But…how?" I stammered, quite bewildered.

He was partway across the room and came about to face me one last time, his hand resting on the hilt of his sword.

"It's funny, actually. The one line I would not cross in our marriage, the one way in which I always showed you respect, is the key to its undoing. We never shared a bed, we never consummated our union. And consummation is one of the church's requirements for a valid marriage. I will see to its annulment as soon as the priest returns to the city."

A flood of emotions welled within me as I studied his handsome face—surprise, relief, elation, regret—and, underneath it all, gratitude. He didn't have to do this, didn't have to admit we had not coupled, could even yet take me if he wanted. But instead he was letting me go. He loved me—perhaps this was proof of that beyond all else—and he was letting me go. Before I could say a word, thank him, wish him well, he had disappeared into the corridor, closing the door softly behind him.

CHAPTER 31
THE DUST SETTLES

THE PEOPLE NEEDED TO BE BROUGHT BACK. The very next morning, Cannan and Steldor, as Captain of the Guard and the man the populace thought of as their King, set out on this task. No one had any objection, since they were the only ones who would be able to convince our citizens it was safe, and with Halias now in the palace, Cannan could use him to safeguard London.

During the time they were gone, Cokyrian soldiers, under the command of the High Priestess, began to clear the rubble from the city in preparation for restoring and rebuilding. It was mid-March, and just as spring sunshine worked to rejuvenate our lands after the harshness of winter, hope emerged from the desolation that had gripped everyone's hearts and minds.

Work had also begun in the palace, and I could see the character of our once beautiful home returning. My father, who had been treating me more deferentially, wanted to be involved, and I gladly offered his assistance to the High Priestess. She, in turn, soon had him working side by side with one of the women in charge of the effort. Seeing the graying, very traditional former King of Hytanica consulting with a young female Cokyrian military officer renewed my faith that the impossible could be achieved.

Temerson was also eager to help as he awaited the return of his family. He had seen his father die at the hands of the Overlord but had reason to believe his mother, Lady Tanda, as well as his brother and sisters, had survived. My father was quite willing to have his assistance, and so Temerson likewise became involved in the work of restoring the palace. The young man, of course, continued to spend many hours with Miranna, who was slowly recovering under the primary care of our mother. The two women seemed to have formed an even more special bond, born out of their experiences at the hands of the Overlord. Having had just one taste of what they had probably gone through, I was glad they could help each other deal with the memories and the aftermath.

It was at this time that I moved back into the quarters I had shared, in what had certainly been a different life, with Steldor. Although the Cokyrians had made their mark on these rooms just as they had with most of the other important areas of the palace, this section had been among the first to be repaired. It felt strange to be back within the living space that had been used by Hytanica's Kings and Queens for generations, knowing that the monarchy was no more. As with the Throne Room, the walls echoed with memories, and the air was thick with sadness.

The transition back to these rooms would have been much harder to bear had it not been for one thing. To my utter astonishment, I was joined the first evening by a lanky, gray-and-black tabby cat with a white stomach and paws. Although he kept his distance, watching me from across the room, his coloring and curious gray eyes confirmed that it was Kitten. With all the death and destruction, the survival of a cat was perhaps a small thing, but it felt like an extraordinary gift, helping to connect the past and the present. I sat motionless on the sofa for quite some time, deliberately ignoring my visitor, and the animal gradually moved closer. When Kitten jumped on the cushion next to me, I held as still as possible, barely breathing, letting him examine me and remember me. I could not, however, withhold a smile when he stepped onto my knees, finally settling into my lap. After a few minutes, I permitted myself to stroke his soft fur, and his answering purr was enormously comforting. I would not be living alone after all.

It took days, but slowly our citizens returned to their homes, or what was left of them. Galen, who had been sent by Cannan to oversee the evacuation, brought Tiersia back with him, both of them irrepressibly happy to be together. He had also found his mother and twin sisters, and took time resettling the four women back into their family home, upon which little damage had been inflicted. Cannan brought Faramay to live in the palace for the time being, probably concerned that the chaos that still existed in the city would shatter her mind. But it was Steldor who still searched for someone. Unbeknownst to Cannan, his son had been watching for a particular member of their family as they'd ridden the line of people.

"Have you seen Baelic?" he asked as he strode into the palace, encountering me in the Grand Entry.

I blanched, realizing he did not know about his uncle's death; with everything that had been happening, the terrible truth had not yet been revealed. Before I could form a reply, Cannan walked out of the antechamber, and Steldor redirected his question.

"I haven't been able to find Baelic," he repeated, a frown

creasing his brow. There was a trace of trepidation in his voice, for it was possible that anyone had died in the fighting, but there was no way he could have been prepared for what Cannan would tell him.

"Steldor, come with me for a moment," the captain said, reaching for his son's arm, but his tone was too gentle, too sympathetic, and Steldor, suddenly knowing, jerked away.

"What happened?" the younger man demanded, his breathing picking up. "Where is he? Tell me now!"

His temper was taking over for his fear and dread, but Cannan handled it calmly.

"Just come with me, and I'll explain everything." When his son did not look at him, he added, "Steldor, you have to hear this."

"Don't tell me he's dead," Steldor said, but it came out as a plea. "Don't tell me that, don't tell me he's dead."

Cannan didn't answer but put a hand on his son's back to guide him into his former office. I climbed the Grand Staircase, unable to stay in the entry, hating what Steldor was about to hear, remembering what it had felt like, knowing it would hurt him many times more than it had hurt me. I went all the way to the third floor and stepped into London's room, moving to sit at his bedside. Halias went into the corridor, thankful for a break.

Sitting with London was almost like being alone, but I could be near him and pretend he was there with me in more than body. The pain no longer tormented him, and he slept more or less peacefully, but still he would not rouse. The High Priestess visited him every day, but there was little more she could do for him. Physically, he seemed to have recovered, but his mind had, thus far, refused to come back. I tried to spend time with him every day as well, and would often read aloud, hoping the sound of my voice might draw him to consciousness.

It was several hours later that a knock on the door disturbed me. I did not answer, knowing that silence in this case was an invitation. I heard the door open, expecting to be joined at London's bedside, but when the visitor did not come all the way into the room, I turned and glanced behind. After everything I had learned from Destari, my mother and London himself, I perhaps should not have been surprised, but nonetheless I sprang to my feet, mouth open slightly but unable to form words.

"I…I heard he was unwell, Your Highness," Lady Tanda said, giving a curtsey.

When her eyes came back to mine, I saw in them the end of her thought: *I couldn't go to him the last time.* Her husband had died at the Overlord's hands, a tragedy to be sure, but in its wake she had been released, much as I would have been had Steldor died.

"Forgive me," she muttered, turning to leave, probably thinking I knew nothing of her history with London.

"Lady Tanda, wait, please." She stopped, and her soft brown eyes connected with mine. "You should stay with him. I've been here long enough—I really must go, and he should not be left alone."

"No," she replied, a touch of melancholy in her voice. "I just wanted to find out how he is doing." She glanced away from me, then finished, "He saved my son's life, and I cannot expect more of him. I don't think he would want me to stay."

"He is not awake." I stood and approached her, placing a hand upon her arm. "In all this time, he has not awoken. He needs someone, Tanda. Perhaps you are that someone."

She gazed at me with uncertainty and regret, but there

was love for London as well, even after all these years. She nodded, taking the chair at his bedside while I stole into the hall.

It was for her that he finally opened his eyes.

Narian was back on his feet, and the High Priestess appointed him as the official liaison between Cokyri and its new Province of Hytanica. This placed him in Hytanica indefinitely, with occasional trips to the land where he had been raised. In truth, he was ideally suited to the position, since he bore ties of loyalty to both countries, but I knew he had reservations because he had not had a chance to get my opinion on the matter. It would have been awkward for him to do so, however, as the High Priestess had not yet departed for Cokyri and did not know the full extent of his history with me.

I couldn't help but notice that Narian was rarely to be found within the palace. He had chosen to base himself out of the building formerly used by Marcail, the Master at Arms, another of the officers who had died at the hands of the Overlord. It was possible, of course, that his duties gave him little reason to be at the palace; more likely, he felt his presence at this point in time would be unwelcome.

The work of repairing and rebuilding our city had begun, and I was thankful to have Cannan at my side. With my thoughts and feelings in so much turmoil and a total lack of knowledge about how to run a province, I would otherwise have been a miserable failure. I was content to let him take over much of the work, though I knew he would gradually turn decisions over to me as he guided me toward becoming a leader.

By the end of the month, Narian had taken over command of the Cokyrian troops, paving the way for the High

Priestess's forthcoming departure. He had begun to move out some of the occupying soldiers and would eventually reduce their numbers until his force roughly equaled that of our disbanded City Guard and military. As each soldier left, I felt a tiny weight lift from my mind, as did for the captain, I believed. But while Cannan lauded the troop withdrawal, it remained difficult for him to work with Narian. I doubted that he would ever be able to look at the Cokyrian commander without seeing and remembering the younger brother he had dearly loved and whose life the captain on some level believed Narian should have saved.

London was also up and about. For the time being, he had a need to be outside and physically occupied, and Halias had thus stepped into the role of my bodyguard. Although London's customary wit had returned along with his energy, he still had a long road to emotional recovery. I would on occasion see him with Lady Tanda and knew she was the person who was doing the most to help him.

It was early April when genuinely good news came at last: Miranna and Temerson were betrothed. My father had wholeheartedly given permission for his seventeen-year-old daughter to marry the young man who had recently turned eighteen and was, therefore, of age to inherit his father's holdings and title.

It was heartening to see the change this event had on Miranna. With something on which to concentrate, she seemed to find herself once more, though she had been through too much to ever return to the naïve, bouncy girl she had been. Now her personality was more restrained, but if ever she came close to being her previous self, it was when she gazed into Temerson's eyes or held his hand. Planning for the wedding also gave my mother, Miranna and me a chance to reconnect. My life had become so busy that seeing friends and even family was increasingly problematic, so I rejoiced that we had this time together.

The High Priestess returned to Cokyri two weeks before Miranna's wedding. Just prior to her departure, she had a meeting with Narian and me in the palace to discuss the status of the province. I could tell from her manner that she suspected Narian's relationship with me had gone past mere friendship; I could tell from his that he did not want her to know to what extent it had.

In the course of our discussion, Nantilam informed me of my new title, Grand Provost Alera; she also dictated that the Palace of Hytanica be referred to as the Bastion. Finally, she decreed that London once more become my bodyguard, leaving Narian to make the reassignment as soon as feasible after my sister's wedding. I had the impression she felt this would provide London with the rest he still needed. I also had the impression she did not trust leaving him to his own devices. In any case, it would place him within Narian's purview.

Miranna and Temerson were married on a lovely May afternoon shortly after my nineteenth birthday, when the weather was still fresh and not overly hot. The event was held in the palace garden, which had been restored as much as possible, although it did not have near the splendor of its previous days. Still, just being in my once-treasured sanctuary was a boon to my spirits, as well as to those of everyone else in attendance.

My parents gave Miranna away, and I stood in as her lady-in-waiting. Lady Tanda and one of Temerson's uncles stood with the groom, and his younger brother served as best man. The ceremony was simple but beautiful and helped to reaffirm that life was moving forward.

After a dinner in the King's Dining Hall on the second floor of the palace, the blissfully wedded couple and their guests adjourned to the Royal Ballroom to continue the revelry. The party would go well into the evening, for entertainment was plentiful, wine was flowing and the dancing of the guests was more than congratulatory. This marked the first celebration since the Cokyrian siege, and though many lives were still in shambles, hope ran high with the knowledge that we had been given the opportunity to pick up the pieces.

As I walked around the ballroom, I saw Galen and Tiersia in each other's arms on the dance floor; my parents conversing with Baron Koranis and Baroness Alantonya, Narian's birth parents, with whom he hoped to forge some sort of relationship; Cannan and Faramay with Baelic's wife, Lania, and their oldest daughters; and a group of my friends that included Reveina and Kalem, both widowed by the war, and Galen's twin sisters, Niani and Nadeja. One person was noticeably absent, however, as London was not among the guests. While that seemed odd, I wondered if he had stayed away because he did not know if, or how, he fit into Temerson's family and wanted to avoid any awkwardness for Lady Tanda.

Almost by reflex, I cast about for Steldor, expecting to find him alone. I should have known he would be surrounded by fathers and their daughters, for word had spread fast after the annulment of our marriage, and he was once more the most sought after young man in the land. In previous years, he would have been flirting incorrigibly; now, however, I was surprised to find his eyes on me. He smirked and shook his head, and I laughed aloud, though the people around me could not have said what was funny. In many ways, life was returning to a state of welcome normalcy, but I still felt something was missing.

After a time, the room grew stuffy, and the open balcony doors beckoned, promising a welcome breeze. I crossed the ballroom and stepped out into the gathering twilight, not startled as I had once been to discover I was not alone. Narian was leaning back upon the railing, his hands resting on either side of him on the dark wood, his mesmerizing blue eyes fixed on me.

"Good evening, Lord Narian," I said politely, walking up beside him to look out over the city, my pulse rate quickening.

"Good evening, Grand Provost Alera," he replied with a slight smirk, inclining his head. He turned toward me, continuing to rest a forearm on the railing.

"Avoiding the crowds?" he asked, repeating the words of the first conversation we'd had on this very balcony.

"Perhaps," I responded with a smile, pleased that he remembered that night as clearly as did I. "And you?"

"I could not refuse your sister's invitation when I received it," he responded, his eyes seeming to burn right through me. "It was generous of her. But I do not think the Hytanican people are ready to embrace me. In truth, I cannot expect that."

"I cannot speak for the people," I lightly replied, my heart warming in anticipation of his reaction. "Only for myself."

The smirk once more fleetingly appeared, then he looked away from me toward the pinpricks of light cast by the lanterns in the city.

"I have been told your marriage has been annulled," he stated, his voice steady and unrevealing.

"Steldor was not the man I desired to marry," I murmured, willing him to understand how my heart had ached for him throughout everything that had happened.

He did not move but continued to stare into the darkness, his thoughts indeterminable. Releasing his breath, he finally returned his gaze to me.

"I am no longer that same man."

"And I am no longer the same woman."

"So where does that leave us?"

I reached out and put my hand upon his, twining our fingers, inviting the touch I knew he was not sure he ought to extend.

"Perhaps with a chance to start anew," I offered, fighting the tremor in my voice that evidenced my emotions.

"I would like that, Alera," he said, continuing to hold my hand despite the sadness and regret lurking behind his words. Then he straightened, coming to his full height as if preparing to leave. At my confused expression, he explained, "You should take time to make certain of what you want. I will be here, if and when you seek my company."

"I have long been certain of what I want," I almost breathlessly assured him.

He reached out to touch my cheek, and I searched his deep blue eyes, finding the love I had always known was there. Needing no further invitation, I moved forward into his embrace, nestling against his muscular chest, his earthy scent of leather and pine and cedar enveloping me. He held me close, then lifted my chin to kiss me, causing warmth to spread through me for the first time in months and confirming what I had long suspected: that in his arms, I was finally home.

★ ★ ★ ★ ★

To be continued and resolved in SACRIFICE,
book three of the LEGACY TRILOGY.

We hope you enjoy this excerpt from SACRIFICE,
the stunning conclusion to the LEGACY TRILOGY.

PROLOGUE

THE CAPTAIN OF THE GUARD INSTINCTIVELY glanced around, scanning the palace's third-floor corridor for enemies who might be monitoring him. In truth, there was no reason for anyone to fear subversive activity from the Hytanicans, not this soon after the takeover. But the Cokyrians were long on suspicion and short on trust. Thus, Cannan took careful note of the Cokyrian soldier at the end of the hall, one of the many fouling his kingdom, before pushing open the sickroom door.

As expected, the room had only one occupant. Having evaded death more times than could be counted, it was only fitting that London would be sitting up in bed a mere day after he had roused, pulling on his leather jerkin. The deputy captain had been unconscious for two and a half weeks following the torture he'd endured at the hands of the Overlord; only the High Priestess's strange healing abilities had kept him from death. Cannan's stomach tightened at that notion—if it was the last thing he did, he would see them out of her debt.

London reached for his boots, wincing as he pulled one on, and the captain strode toward him, letting the door shut.

"Is that wise?" Cannan asked, concerned.

"I'm done being idle." London pulled on his other boot, fastening the buckles, then his indigo eyes found his captain. "I assume you are, as well."

Cannan nodded. Through the window on the far wall, he could see the remains of his homeland—buildings crumbled, the city wall in ruins, streets upturned, Cokyrian flags flying high to lay claim to its newest province. And that was just the outer layer. Beneath, there were families in shreds, bleeding where the deaths of loved ones had left wounds so deep they would eternally fester. Cannan, his son and the family his murdered brother had left behind were bleeding. Hytanica had nothing left to give and, therefore, nothing else to lose.

For months, their kingdom had been under siege, their people living in terror. They had been overrun by the Cokyrians. The Overlord, in his brutality and malevolence, had slaughtered their military leaders like cattle before meeting his own end. They had struggled against hopelessness, hiding in the mountains to help their people, and at present had come to this, living under the enemy's rule. Here, now—this was not the time for the fight to end. Now was when the fight would begin. This was the time to regain what had been lost.

Bringing his attention back to the present, the captain said, "I have thoughts."

Coming to his feet, London met his commanding officer's dark gaze. "I have a plan."

ACKNOWLEDGMENTS

My heartfelt thanks to everyone who lent a hand in bringing *Allegiance* to life:

Mom, Cara and Kendra for being the weirdest, most amazing family anyone could wish for.

Everyone at HarlequinTEEN, in particular my editor, Natashya Wilson, for her invaluable making-book-better skills, and Lisa Wray for her continued efforts to connect me with the rest of the human race. Everyone at HQT is an absolute joy and I wouldn't be where I am without you!

My agent Kevan Lyon for her fabulous work and for making me believe in myself.

My foreign-rights agent Taryn Fagerness for conquering the world.

And finally, thanks to anyone who's reading. You have the power to change the world—you've definitely changed mine.

Until next time,
Cayla Kluver

Q: Please tell us a little about yourself and your interests apart from writing.

A: I'm from Wisconsin, where breweries and dairy farming dominate, although my family owns horses rather than cows. I love horseback riding, reading, singing and—if I'm being honest—video games. When I got my hands on "Mass Effect 2," I stayed up for two days straight to play it through.

Aside from those hobbies, I love working with kids, particularly kids who are trying to follow their dreams or are coming out of broken homes. There is so much strength to be found in young people, and it's inspirational. Sometimes all they need is a hand or a word of encouragement in order to take on the whole world, and being able to provide even a small amount of support to people in those situations is a gift.

Q: Legacy ***has a long publication history worldwide. What has the journey been like for you?***

A: *Legacy* has traveled more places than I have—while my book has gone to Japan, South America, Greece, Turkey and all over Europe, I've pretty much stayed in Wisconsin. I think because of that, the reality of how widely *Legacy* is being read hasn't hit me. Intellectually I know that what's been happening is huge, but emotionally I still feel like a small-town girl. This reaction might just be part of who I am though—my mom told me one day that she thought she was having a heart attack, so I nodded, got the keys and suggested we go to the emergency room. I tend to handle important things very understatedly, but scream and cry when Amazon delivers a season of *Law & Order* late.

Q: You have strong insight into how people act under pressure. Who or what inspires you to create the characters in your books?

A: My characters who handle pressure well are definitely inspired by my mom. She's a lawyer and she's always cool-headed and in charge. She's the kind of frustrating person against whom you can never win an argument because she never loses her temper. She's the strongest person I know. On the flip side, my dad is a massive worrywart (sorry, Dad). Together my parents comprise the entire spectrum of human reaction. They're polar opposites, and for the purpose of my writing I can sort of stroll between them for whatever personality I need.

Q: ***Why did you choose to write in a historical fantasy world?***

A: I love history—the different styles of dress and speech, how people lived, the culture. But what I wanted for this series wasn't straight historical fiction. I wanted to create my own kingdoms and conflicts. Mythology and magic, while not highly prevalent in the Legacy Trilogy are still important to the arc of the story, and incorporating these themes into a fantasy novel was a lot more comfortable for me.

Another huge reason I chose a historical fantasy setting was that I wanted the opportunity to construct a major dichotomy between two kingdoms—one dominated by men and one dominated by women. A secondary goal of the series is to illustrate that neither society is ideal—equality is what we should strive for.

Q: ***Your setting and attention to detail are part of what bring Alera's world to life. What kind of research did you do while writing the books?***

A: I did a lot of research online about medieval European history; I also hit the bookstore and collected dozens of history-related books that are now highlighted and dog-eared through and through. Because the series is first and foremost a fantasy, I did my research as I went along. I could pick and choose what aspects I wanted to be a part of Alera's life, which gave me the freedom to create a world I really enjoyed writing about. *Legacy* was like the most exhilarating research paper I've ever written.

Q: ***All right, let's get down to what everyone really wants to know—who would you choose, Steldor or Narian? Or Tadark?!***

A: Steldor has come a long way, but at his heart he's still a chauvinist, and as a modern girl, I couldn't put up with that. Anybody who tries to tell me where I belong will end up with their pride sliced and diced through means of verbal warfare. Aesthetically, I would definitely choose Steldor though. I can't resist big brown eyes and the intensity of dark hair.

As tempting as Tadark is, I would go with Narian. For me, the most attractive thing in the world is a man who legitimately respects women. *That* I can't resist.

Q: ***What advice do you have for aspiring authors?***

A: Write what you want to write. Lately I've been hearing, "I'll write what's selling until I'm established, then I'll write what I want." I don't think it works that way. If what you want to write is also what's selling, power to you. But the beauty of being an author is that you're given the chance to put something in a reader's hands that they didn't know they desired. What you put on paper should always be something you would defend with the passion of an infuriated ninja. Don't let anybody take that away from you. Also, don't give up. Nobody ever got what they wanted by taking no for an answer.

Thank you, Cayla!

A GODDESS TEST NOVEL

"A fresh take on the Greek myths adds sparkle to this romantic fable."
–Cassandra Clare, *New York Times* bestselling author of *The Mortal Instruments*

In a modern retelling of the Persephone myth, Kate Winters's mother is dying and Kate will soon be alone. Then she is offered a deal by Hades, god of the Underworld–pass seven tests and become his wife, and her mother will live and Kate will become immortal. There's one catch–no one who has attempted the Goddess Test has ever survived.

Kate Winters won immortality and will rule the Underworld at Henry's–Hades's–side. But before she can be crowned, the secretive Henry is abducted by the one being powerful enough to kill him–the King of the Titans. And it's up to Kate to get him back.

HTGT2011TR2

THE LEGACY TRILOGY

“I recommend you get this book in your hands as soon as possible.”

—*Teen Trend* magazine on *Legacy*

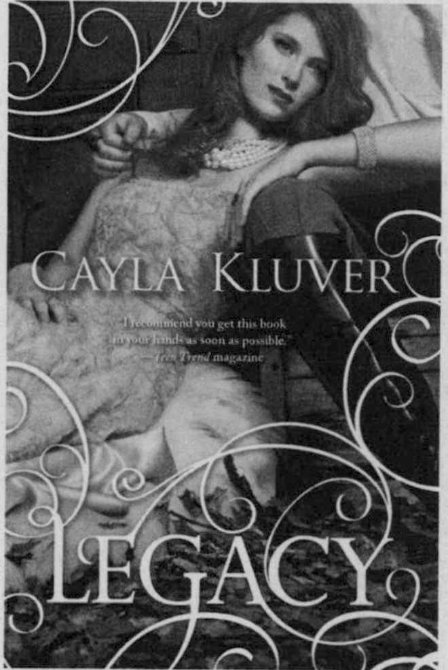

Crown princess Alera of Hytanica has one duty: marry the man who will become king. But Alera's heart is soon captured by a mysterious intruder—a boy hailing from her country's deadliest enemy. With her kingdom on the brink of war, Alera must choose between duty and love.

Bound to a man she cannot love, Queen Alera of Hytanica faces leading her people in dark times. As the enemy Empire of Cokyri attacks, Alera is torn between her duty to her kingdom and the love she still holds for Narian, leader of the Cokyrian armies....

Look for the third installment of this enchanting trilogy, coming November 2012!

HTLEGTR2